PRAISE FOR T

"Daring, sophisticated, and literary... Exactly what good erotica should be." — **Kitty Thomas on *The Siren***

"Kinky, well-written, hot as hell." — **Little Red Reading Hood on *The Red: An Erotic Fantasy***

"Impossible to stop reading." — **Heroes & Heartbreakers on *The Bourbon Thief***

"Stunning... Transcends genres and will leave readers absolutely breathless." — ***RT Book Reviews* on the Original Sinners series**

"I worship at the altar of Tiffany Reisz!" — ***New York Times* bestselling author Lorelei James**

"Sensual, smart, and hilarious." — ***Library Journal* on *One Hot December***

"*The Bourbon Thief* isn't just good, it's exceptional. The story captured my imagination; the characters captured my heart." — **Literati Literature Lovers**

"I loved the Original Sinners series... Her prose is quite beautiful, and she can weave a wonderful tight story." — ***New York Times* and *USA Today* bestseller Jennifer Probst**

MORE ORIGINAL SINNERS

Novels

THE SIREN (#1)

THE ANGEL (#2)

THE PRINCE (#3)

THE MISTRESS (#4)

THE SAINT (#5)

THE KING (#6)

THE VIRGIN (#7)

THE QUEEN (#8)

THE PRIEST (#9)

THE CHATEAU (standalone)

PICTURE PERFECT COWBOY (standalone)

Novellas and Collections

THE CONFESSIONS

THE GIFT (previously published as SEVEN DAY LOAN)

IMMERSED IN PLEASURE

THE LAST GOOD KNIGHT (PARTS I–V)

LITTLE RED RIDING CROP

MICHAEL'S WINGS

MISCHIEF • THE MISTRESS FILES

SOMETHING NICE

SUBMIT TO DESIRE

TIFFANY REISZ

Winter Tales

AN ORIGINAL SINNERS
CHRISTMAS ANTHOLOGY

8TH CIRCLE PRESS • LOUISVILLE, KY

CONTENTS

DECEMBER WINE

THE CHRISTMAS TRUCE

POINSETTIA

THE SCENT OF WINTER

BONUS SHORT STORY: BLOOD & SNOW

DECEMBER WINE

CHAPTER ONE

Author's Note: This story takes place between the end of The Mistress *and the beginning of* The Saint, *the fourth and fifth books in the Original Sinners series.*

Paris, France

THEIR TRAIN ARRIVED in Paris after six. They went immediately to their hotel, *Castille Paris*, but as soon as they were alone in their suite, Nora said, "Let's find some coffee." This idea was met with approval. She put on her red trench coat; he hadn't even taken off his wine-colored overcoat yet. They set out south along the *Rue Cambon*, where they strolled around the gardens. Even in winter, Paris was lovely, romantic, and strange, though there was no snow on the ground and the little city trees were all bare. A mist of rain hung suspended in the gray evening air, creating hazy halos of gold around the street lamps. They barely spoke and Nora heard little more than the sharp sound of the hard heels of her black boots echoing against the sidewalks. They weren't the only people about, but they felt alone together, sheltered by their shared secrets. Nora clung to his arm as they walked and he pulled her even closer, his arm around her back as they neared the café. Anyone who saw them might think they were in love, as they couldn't stop catching each other's eyes and laughing, or smiling, or looking just to look. They did love each other but it wasn't romance that had brought them to Paris together. No, Nora had brought Zach to Paris for a different reason.

But first, they had to talk.

They found the café, a quiet one with a menu only in French, which guaranteed fewer tourists. They took off their coats—Nora had on a gray cashmere turtleneck with dark jeans and boots; Zach, a black pullover that made his blue eyes look even bluer. He spoke easy French to the waitress—he'd lived in Paris a few years in his twenties and visited France often—and after they were served hot and fragrant coffee in tiny white cups, he sat back in his chair and crossed his arms. "Are you ready to talk about it?"

Nora said, "Depends on what 'it' is. Is 'it' Fionn? Then no, because I'll start crying again and won't be able to stop for a week. If 'it' is why we're here, sure."

"I meant Fionn," Zach said. "But if you can't talk about him yet, I understand. We'll table it for now. Just tell me one thing first—are you all right?"

"I am…" She paused to find the right word or words, couldn't find them, did the best she could instead. "…better than all right. You?"

"I can safely say without exaggerating, since Fionn's birth…it's the happiest I've ever been in my life."

"Fatherhood looks very good on you."

He grinned that sexy halfway smile she knew and lusted. The Zach Easton sitting across from her was a far cry from the Zach Easton she'd met three years ago in her office. He'd been depressed, angry, bitter, lost, God, so lost. Now he was hopeful, happy, at peace, found. His wife had found him. His son had found him. And he hadn't even known they'd been looking for him.

"Thank you. Shall I ask how *he* is?"

Nora raised her hands, shrugged. "I don't know. I mean, obviously he was happy when he heard, but the next morning, I woke up and he was gone. He'd left me a note saying he was off to some monastery, who knows where. Probably pouring his heart out to Father Ballard."

"Who?"

"His confessor."

Zach's eyes widened. "Søren has a confessor? That poor man. The confessor, I mean."

"Considering the things Catholic priests are getting in trouble for now, it'll probably be a relief to Father Ballard that all Søren did was father a child with a consenting adult woman. That's practically a mark in a priest's favor, these days."

"True," Zach said. "But I thought we weren't talking about that."

"We aren't. Not yet." She took another sip of her coffee. It gave her a few seconds to recover herself. Christmas night —she was alone with Søren at the Sacred Heart rectory. The phone rang and it was Zach. Calling for Søren. It seemed her Jewish editor had a Christmas gift for her Catholic priest lover. Nora hadn't anticipated anything good coming out of that conversation, especially since she'd known more than just a little flogging and spanking had happened during that wild night between Søren and Zach's wife. Had Grace confessed to it? Was Zach calling Søren out? Was there going to be a duel? She would watch that show with hot-buttered popcorn.

But no. None of the above. Zach had said to Søren, *I realize it's Christmas, but I'm calling to wish you a Happy Father's Day. It's a boy.*

And when Søren heard that, it stunned him into a moment's silence.

Then he'd laughed.

Nora would remember the sound of that laugh all her life. She'd remember it on her deathbed, in those last seconds when her life flashed before her eyes, showing her all the best memories. That would be one of them, that laugh. That sound of purest joy.

"Nora?" Zach said.

"Sorry." She came back to him, back to the present. "Just...needed a moment there."

"Trust me, I understand. I've needed more than a few moments myself." He laughed a little, laughing at himself, at his own private joy that Nora was honored to be able to witness. She was finally starting to understand why Christmas outshone Easter as the most important day on the Christian calendar. The birth of a baby was certainly a worthy cause for a worldwide celebration. Now that Fionn was here, she doubted Christmas would ever feel the same to her again.

For unto us a child is born. For unto us a son is given.

"We'd better talk about something else before we both start crying," she said. "Again." Last night in London, she'd seen Fionn in person for the first time. She'd held him for about ten seconds before bursting into tears. She'd handed Fionn back to Grace and collapsed weeping into Zach's arms. Fionn was the only one in the room *not* weeping by that point.

"How about we discuss the subject of tomorrow?" Zach tilted his head, then pointedly cleared his throat. "We are here in France for *une raison, oui?*" he reminded her.

Nora sat up straight and felt steadier already.

"*Oui,*" she said. "Tomorrow. We meet Nicolas Delacroix and tell him, 'Welcome to the family.'"

Yes. That was why they were in France. Because Kingsley had a son, somewhere in this country, and Nora was going to find him.

BEHIND HIS COFFEE CUP, Zach smiled. Or was it a grimace?

"What?" Nora asked.

"Nothing. What's the plan?"

"I don't have a 'plan,' really. We pick up our rental car tomorrow morning, drive all day, check into our little inn—"

"It's an inn?"

"It's a tiny inn in a tiny village. That's the only reason the detective I hired managed to find the kid."

"How did he find him? How did he even know where to start looking?" Zach asked. This was a good line of conversation, Nora decided. No risk of her bursting into tears so long as they stuck to talking about detective work.

"I knew the name of the village where King's family went on vacation when he was a kid—Mozet. Friends of his father lived there. When King was twenty-two, twenty-three, he was shot. He went there to recuperate. Fond memories, I guess." Nora shrugged, one eyebrow firmly arched. "I gave the detective a photo of King from his twenties. He went to Mozet and showed it around, saying he was looking for a 'Nicolas.' All I knew was his name and that he looked like King."

"And he managed to track him down with only that information? Amazing."

"A miracle," Nora said. "Apparently, it was a seasonal farm worker who talked. No one else would."

"Small villages can be very insular, suspicious of outsiders."

"This farm worker wasn't. He spilled it all. He thought the photo looked a lot like his boss's son. The detective found out the kid's name, date of birth, counted forty weeks backwards and checked the inn sign-in books around that date. Found a K. Boissonneault had stayed there at just the right time to make a baby."

"What else do you know about young *Monsieur* Delacroix?"

"Not much else." Nora shrugged. "His family owns a small vineyard. They make Syrah. Mother was very young when she married the father. From Iran. Father's family has owned the vineyard for generations."

"How's it doing?"

"Not a lot of money but lots of awards. It's very prestigious. King will be very proud."

"Nora, not to be a wet blanket here, but he might not be Kingsley's. Have you considered that?"

Nora slipped her purse off the back of her chair, opened it, and took out two photographs—one of Kingsley at twenty-nine, the other of Nicolas Delacroix at twenty-three.

"What do you think?" she asked, her voice carrying a challenge.

Zach perused the photos carefully. "Handsome lad. And there is a resemblance. If I didn't know who they were, or that the photos were taken years apart, I'd say they were brothers. That being said...people do have doppelgängers. It's not unheard of."

Zach passed the photos back to her. Nora looked at the photo of Nicolas one more time before putting it away. The detective had found it in a French magazine profile of the vineyard. In the photo, young Nicolas posed in front of the stone gates of the vineyard. His white t-shirt was dirty, his jeans dusty, his work boots mud-covered, his smile genuine, his pose awkward. He clearly didn't like being photographed. Thank God he had been, though. He looked like Kingsley Junior in the photo. Identical noses and, according to the detective, it was a nose which looked nothing like his mother's nor his father's. Identical jaw line, too. Strong but graceful. Same forehead. Same ears. The eyes were different, though. King's were dark brown, almost black, like a strong cup of coffee. Nicolas Delacroix had eyes like glazed celadon, like an ancient jade bowl.

"He's King's," she said to the photograph. "I know he is. He has to be."

Zach didn't argue with her, although she could tell he was skeptical. She knew he didn't want her getting her hopes up.

"Does anyone else know?" Zach asked.

She shook her head. "I couldn't do that to Søren or Juliette—make them keep the secret from King until I'd figured it out, one way or the other. And if I told King, and then it *wasn't* his son? God, he might never recover. Nobody knows but you and me."

"You and I."

"You're off-duty, Zach. Shove it."

"Consider it shoved." He lifted his cup in a salute and

drank it down before setting it on the tabletop again. "Any idea what you'll say to the man?"

"Honestly, I don't know. How do you tell someone that the father who raised him his entire life may not be his biological father?"

"No clue," Zach said. "But when you find out, tell me. I may be having that conversation myself in ten years."

Nora reached across the table and took Zach's hand. She squeezed his fingers and he squeezed back. She didn't let go and neither did he.

"Am I doing the wrong thing?"

"Nora. I...I'm biased here. Certainly not the best man to ask."

"You are exactly the best man to ask. You're in the same position Nicolas's father is in, raising a son that isn't..."

"Mine? I told the biological father. Clearly, I'm on the side of full disclosure. Some things shouldn't be secret. And even if they should be, or you want them to be, sometimes they simply can't be."

"Why did you tell us?" *Us*, meaning her and Søren. She let go of his hand, sat back in her chair.

"I asked myself what I would want if it were me, if I had fathered a child I didn't know about. Would I want to know, even if it threw a wrench into the works of my entire life? The answer was 'yes.' Without a doubt."

He picked up his coffee cup, put it down again without drinking. "Hard as it is, and it is hard, I won't lie...for Fionn's sake, we had to tell Søren. And you, of course."

"I suppose it's good to have medical knowledge for both sides of the family tree."

He shrugged. "That, yes, but more than that...I wouldn't want things to get any more complicated than they already are. Better we all get on the same page from the start." This time he did drink his coffee. When he put his cup down, he smiled at her. "And how could I ever look you in the eyes again, knowing the secret I was keeping?"

Get on the same page. A euphemism Nora didn't need translated for her. Zach was afraid of Søren. Of course he was. Who wasn't afraid of Søren? If Zach and Grace had kept Fionn a secret from him, and Søren discovered it anyway...things could have gotten very ugly. Accusations, recriminations, custody fights. Better they all play nice from the beginning, for Fionn's sake.

"You're a good dad," she said. "I had a shitty dad. I would have loved it if someone had come along and said, 'Hey, guess what? You have another dad and he's not shitty.' But if Nicolas has a good father, he might not appreciate having that relationship...I don't know, changed? Challenged?"

"Fionn is my son," Zach said. "If the day comes when he learns that he has a different biological father, he'll still be just as much my son as before he knew. You won't be taking his father away from him, if that's what you're worried about. But there is a very good chance he won't appreciate some strange woman from America inserting herself into his family. Don't be surprised if he wants to shoot the messenger."

"Why do you think I brought you with me?"

"Well, if explaining our own complicated family situation helps, I'm happy to do it."

"I meant you could stand in front of me and take the bullet if he does shoot."

Zach threw his napkin on the table, feigning a French hissy hit.

"*C'est ça*," he said. "I won't be treated like this." He spoke in a mock French accent.

Giggling, Nora reached for him, grabbing his wrist.

"I forgot to tell you something very important," she said.

"There is nothing you can say to me that will change my mind." *Say* was *zey* and *change* was *shhange*.

"Grace said you and I could sleep together this week. If you want."

Zach's right eyebrow shot up like a rocket.

Slowly, he sat back down again. Returning to his impeccably posh English accent, he said, "Shall I get the check, then?"

CHAPTER TWO

THEY RETURNED to the hotel and Nora collapsed, dramatically and seductively, onto the sleek black sofa in their suite. She unzipped her boots and tossed them off, then laid on her side, using her arms as a pillow, facing Zach.

"Really?" he said, settling into the black-and-white striped armchair.

Nora nodded slowly, but didn't smile.

"When did this conversation take place?"

"That night." Playing the vixen, she ran a hand through her wavy black hair and tossed it over her shoulder.

He cocked his head. "You mean 'that night' as in the night my son was conceived while I was on the other side of the planet?"

"After what we went through... Well, you know how it is. Sometimes you need a good stiff drink. Sometimes you need some good stiff kink. I had a bruise the size of a soccer ball on my ribs so I couldn't do it."

"So you volunteered my sweet, darling, gentle, school-teacher wife for the job."

"She'd been there for him at the worst moment of his life. I sent her to him. I guess you could say she earned him."

Søren had told her what Grace had done, how she'd walked with him at dawn, keeping him company on his way to his certain death. But Grace had refused to accept Søren's sacrifice. She'd run back to Kingsley to tell him what Søren had done. To give him one last chance to save them all.

And Kingsley had, thanks to Grace. Together, they'd saved them all.

"It's a blur mostly," Nora lied. She remembered the moment like it was yesterday. "But I do clearly recall saying something along the lines of, 'I'll let you have Søren for a night if I can have Zach for a week.' And thus the unholy deal was struck." She giggled wickedly, the only way she ever giggled.

"Now wait." He furrowed his brow. "How is one night with him equivalent to a week with me? Are you and my wife implying I'm one-seventh of the lover that he is?"

Nora shook her head solemnly. "I drive a very hard bargain. One night with him was enough for her. One night with you wasn't nearly enough for me."

"It wasn't, was it?"

She shook her head again. Zach groaned. His head fell back and he stared at the ceiling.

"What?" Nora sat up on the sofa, tucked her legs under her. "I won't make you do it. I'm only saying we can. I even checked with Grace before we left."

"You did what? When?"

"Before we left, when you were saying goodbye to Fionn. Grace gave us her blessing. Call her. Ask her. Text her. Sext her. I'm not kidding. Your sweet, darling, gentle schoolteacher wife isn't nearly so sweet as you think she is.

Do I need to remind you that she spent a night with Søren? Willingly? Dare I say...happily? As happily as you spent a night with me that time?"

Zach slouched in his chair, looking like the sexiest college professor in the long and storied history of sexy college professors. "Point taken."

"You're the best anal I've ever had, you know."

The slouching immediately ceased. "I am?"

"Absolutely."

"Really?"

"You need this in writing?"

"I wouldn't mind it in writing."

Zach was joking but Nora rose off the sofa anyway. She went to the desk, far too modern for her taste, found the pad of hotel stationery and wrote a quick note on it.

"Nora."

"Hush, I'm writing," she said. "You're my editor. You know how hard it is to get me to sit down and actually put words on paper."

"That's an unfortunate fact."

She finished her note, folded it, slipped it in an envelope and presented it to Zach.

He unfolded it and read aloud, "Dear Zach, You gave me the best ass-fucking I've ever had in my life. And that is saying a lot. Love, Nora (and her ass)."

Zach returned the note to the envelope and tucked it into his jeans pocket. "Well. I'll be saving that for posterity."

Nora waited. She didn't push or prod. This was Zach's decision. She'd already made up her mind to go for it if he was in. Why not? This was going to be a rough week, trying to convince a total stranger to let her upend his entire life. Having something to look forward to every night—sharing a bed with Zach, specifically—would make this trip much more fun. Why not mix in some pleasure with their business?

"You sure about this?" Zach asked, eyes narrowed. "Really sure?"

She looked away from him, past his shoulder, out the hotel window where a cold winter rain was beating softly against the glass. If she opened that window and breathed in the cold clean air, she would smell Søren's skin.

"I love Søren so much it scares me," she said. "Not a day passes when I don't go back into that house, and gunshots are ringing in my ears...but I know I'm going to live through it—because Søren has shoved me into a tiny corner of the room and put his own body between me and the gunfire." She blinked and tears ran down her face. Without a word, Zach stood and came over to her, sat at her side on the sofa. "He's my everything." She turned her head and met Zach's eyes. "Still...sometimes, when you and I are on the phone fighting about something, I have this wicked little thought... well, just like I said. One night wasn't enough."

Zach collapsed back on the couch, groaned, laughed, then groaned again. "I've said it before and I'll say it again— I can't believe I'm doing this," he said.

Nora turned, straddled his lap and put her hands on his shoulders. "I've said it before and I'll say it again." Nora put her mouth to his ear. "I can."

SHE THOUGHT if it would happen, Zach would kiss her, then and there. He didn't. Instead, he wrapped his arms around her back and pulled her into his lap. He held her to him then, just held her. She rested her chin on his strong shoulder and wrapped her arms around his neck.

He was one of those men who always smelled like he'd just stepped out of the shower, like cedar and verbena soap. He had half a day's stubble on his cheek and she pressed her face against it, relishing the gentle friction.

"What are we going to do?" His voice was soft, almost a whisper, a question for her ears only.

"Run away, you and me," she said. "I hear Tuscany is nice. We'll get a crumbling villa with no telephone, change our names, spend all night eating and drinking and all day in bed."

"Sleeping?"

"Not just sleeping..."

"Very tempting." He kissed her finally, but only on top of her temple.

"You want to go to Italy?"

"You're very tempting, but I'd never survive the heat in Tuscany."

"You'd never survive leaving Grace and Fionn," she said. "Any more than I'd survive leaving Søren."

"You're angry."

"I know I should be. It's like I'm too scared to be angry. I thought I knew what the rest of my life looked like." Nora pulled back, met Zach's eyes. "I thought I had it all planned out. King and Juliette are moving to New Orleans to raise Céleste. Søren's teaching at Loyola. I bought a house there. We're starting a new life in a new city and it was supposed to be our new normal. Søren won't be in charge of a church anymore. My house and King's house are on the same block. We were all going to be this nice little family. Finally."

She laughed at her own naiveté, that she really thought it would be that easy.

Now, anything could happen and everything was up in the air. Would Søren tell his superiors in the Jesuit order he'd fathered a child? Would he be defrocked for it? Would he leave the priesthood and move to London? Would he press for joint custody? Would Søren insist he and Nora get married, for the child's sake? Would she leave him if he tried? She had before.

"Now there's Fionn," she said with a shuddering breath, "and I have no idea what the future looks like anymore except there's this baby boy in it." She smiled. "And maybe another not-so-baby boy."

Nicolas and his strange celadon eyes flashed into her mind again. She caught herself sneaking looks at his picture a dozen, two dozen times a day. She'd already convinced herself he was Kingsley's son...so why couldn't she stop looking at him?

"Søren and I were talking in bed last week, about what happened to me in that house. The 'ordeal'..."

The ordeal—that was what they called it, their euphemistic shorthand for the time when Kingsley's supposedly long-dead sister returned with a vengeance, determined to punish both Kingsley and Søren for deceiving her about their relationship. Months of taunting culminated in Nora's kidnapping. Easier to give it a name, to file it away under O for *ordeal*.

"So much good came out of the ordeal," Nora said. "Kingsley and Søren finally figured their mess out. Wes and I...well, that was long overdue. I figured out who I belonged to, now and forever. Søren, if you were wondering."

Zach smiled. "Wasn't wondering."

"And Kingsley and I had some issues, too. We finally worked those out. But even with all that...it didn't quite feel like the ordeal was worth the terror and the nightmares and the therapy bills. Then I held Fionn and suddenly...

suddenly, it was all worth it. At least for me. Do you know what I mean?"

Zach ran his hand through her hair, captured a curl, tickled her chin with it. "I know what you mean."

She believed him. He'd been through an ordeal of his own. She'd watched him with Fionn, rocking him to sleep, and when he'd caught her watching he'd smiled and said to her, "Thank you."

Nora hadn't needed to ask him why he was thanking her. She'd sent Grace to Søren that night. She'd set the wheels in motion. Nora had whispered, "You're welcome."

"Juliette says King's still having nightmares about it."

"The ordeal?" Zach asked.

Nora nodded. "I can't help but think this will make it all okay again. If I can find him, and he is King's son...then all of it, the whole ordeal...it will finally go away. For all of us."

At the café, Zach had been skeptical, reasoned, trying to temper her out-of-this-world expectations. Now he said exactly what she needed to hear:

"We'll find him."

Nora kissed him. She had no expectations for how he would respond. No hopes or dreams. She wasn't trying to seduce him anymore, either. He'd simply said a kind thing to her, what she needed him to say, and she'd kissed him to thank him. Lips on lips, soft and warm. He returned the kiss, as softly as she'd given it. A kiss that didn't say everything was fine, but rather a kiss that said everything, some-day, would be.

The kiss ended. The room was quiet. Nora looked at Zach and Zach looked back at Nora.

"Say something," she said when she couldn't stand the silence anymore. The silence and the suspense.

Zach kissed her again, soft and warm and deep. She

opened her mouth and let him slip his tongue between her lips, touched his tongue with hers in reply.

Zach broke the kiss and laid his head back on the sofa. "I'd forgotten what a good kisser you are," he said.

She kissed him again, so he wouldn't forget it.

The kiss was soft and warm and deep *and* wet this time. A kiss that couldn't be taken back. A kiss that had big plans for the night. A kiss that meant business.

Nora's body warmed and she became aware of her cashmere turtleneck sweater prickling against her hot skin. She pulled the sweater off and tossed it onto the floor. Zach ran his hands up and down her back, over and over, and before she knew it, her head was on his shoulder again.

"If I told you I needed this, would you believe me?" she asked. "Or would you think it was a line?"

"I need it, too."

"I'm thinking too much, about too much." Søren. Fionn. Kingsley. His son. This trip. This quest. The future. The past. "Can you get me out of my head?"

He stroked her hair, kissed it, and whispered, "Let's find out."

CHAPTER THREE

GENTLY HE PUSHED her up and off of him. She stood and he stood. He kissed her and she kissed back. He went to the bedroom. She followed.

The hotel was modern, chic, the suite black and white and *très élégant*. Zach switched on a light hidden inside a silver sconce next to the large bed. Nora turned off the overhead light. *Parfait.* He sat on the side of the bed and she stood in front of him. He kissed her again, between her breasts, on the rounded tops of them, his hands roaming all over her stomach and back, shoulders and arms. She could only take so much enjoyment of her own before she had to give some of it back in return. Grasping his sweater with both hands, she tugged it up and off in one smooth motion. Then she pushed him on his back, climbed onto the bed and straddled his stomach. With her palms pressed to either side of his head, she dipped her lips to his mouth and kissed hard, harder, hardest...

With no warning, Zach grabbed her by the hips, rolled her onto her back, and rolled himself on top of her.

He pointed down at her face and said, "Behave."

"Oh, goody. Zach's in a toppy mood tonight."

She rubbed her fingers together like a mad scientist brewing a potion.

"I'm on holiday," he said. "The reason we go on holiday is so we can do things we can't do at home."

"You're going to tie me up and fuck my ass, aren't you?"

"The tying up is optional."

"Says who?"

He kissed her to shut her up. Nora didn't mind. Not when he pulled the strap of her bra off her shoulder, tugged down the lace cup, and kissed her right nipple. Kissed it and licked it and ran the tip of his tongue around it. She arched her back and he took the hint, pulling the nipple into his hot wet mouth and sucking deep and long. While he worked on her breasts, she licked and bit his shoulders. If he'd forgotten how good of a kisser she was, she'd forgotten how delectably bitable his shoulders were. Under her teeth and tongue, she felt him flinch, heard him gasp. She ran her hand up his arm, feeling the strength of his biceps, the curve of his shoulder-blade, the long line of his back to his hips. So much warm male skin. He'd been nothing but a voice on the phone, an invisible, playful email correspondent for the past two years. She'd forgotten he was a body, too. A body that pressed her hard into the bed, a body that rubbed its hips up against her hips, a body that pushed its erection insistently against her wet aching crotch through their clothes.

She had to touch him, had to feel him in her hand. She reached down, wiggling and wriggling to get enough room to find the button of his jeans, the zipper, the soft cotton of the boxer briefs she remembered he favored, and then...him. She slipped her hands into his pants and wrapped her fingers around his cock and stroked up and down, down and up, taking as much pleasure in feeling him as he took in being felt. He tilted his head back, eyes closed, and Nora smiled at his male delight in this, the simplest of erotic pleasures. The tip of him was wet, and dripped on her fingers.

"Been awhile?" she whispered into his ear.

"Ever had a newborn at home?"

"So that's a yes."

"If I don't get inside you soon, there's a very good chance I'll come in your hand."

"That would be such a waste."

Zach pushed up and rolled off her. He peeled her leggings off, then her black lace panties, which he was wicked enough to sniff before tossing over his shoulder. She laughed and he slid off the bed to remove his jeans. Then she wasn't laughing. He was naked, and so hard that his cock was red. He crawled back onto her, kneed her thighs apart and settled between them, putting his full weight onto her. She lifted her hips and opened her legs wider. His cock slid between the wet lips of her vulva and nudged at her entrance.

"I think we forgot the foreplay," Zach said. His hips pulsed into hers, and with each pulse he moved a little more into her; just a little, one centimeter at a time.

"We'll do foreplay after."

"Fore, short for 'before.'"

"When you're planning on fucking my ass, fucking my pussy *is* the foreplay."

They moved together, just moved, pushing up, pressing in, not trying to make anything happen, simply enjoying the slide and slip of his hardness over her wetness. With the slightest lift of her hips, Nora took him deep inside her. Her vagina opened, and she drew him in even further, grinning as Zach groaned into her ear.

Nora sighed. "I love foreplay."

After that, there was no more talking. No quipping. No pretending this was two friends playfully misbehaving. They were fucking and they were taking it fucking seriously.

Zach shifted up, pulled her legs around his lower back, spread his knees and went at her with slow, hard thrusts. It felt too good. Nora could barely give back the pleasure he was giving her. Her head lay on the bed, her eyes closed as he dropped long kisses into the hollow of her throat. He kissed a path to her ear. "You have lube, I suppose?" he whispered.

"In my bag with the handcuffs and rope. Want me to get it?"

"You brought your toy bag?"

"Never leave home without it."

Zach pulled out of her, sat up. "Stay," he said.

Oh, she did love it when he was in a toppy mood.

———

SHE DIDN'T QUITE "STAY" as ordered. She pulled the covers on the bed down, revealing the lush white sheets and sinking into them. When he returned, he had her black silk scarves in one hand, the lube in the other. He set them down on the bed, then turned to leave again.

"Now where are you going?"

"I need backup," he shouted over his shoulder as he disappeared through the door.

"I..." she began, to herself, and then continued, loud enough for him to hear, "...I don't know what that means."

Zach returned again, carrying her vibrator.

"Oh, that's what that means," she said.

"That's what that means," Zach said as he crawled

across the bed to her. Heaven was a warm hard male body on a cold soft winter night, and Nora was in heaven as he settled on top of her again. She took him in hand and guided him inside her, craving the connection. He held himself up over her on his elbows, gazing down, his hand in her hair.

She smiled tenderly at him. "Hey there."

"You know," he said, "I really was reconciled to us being friends, only friends." He stroked her cheek. "Least, I thought so."

"We'll go back to being friends next week. Until then..." She moved her hips up and into him, squeezing her inner muscles around him, making his eyes flutter.

"Nora..." His voice was almost a growl.

"Sorry. That's a lie, but still, sorry."

Zach pulled out of her, which she thought was very bad form. "Turn over," he said, a polite request. She politely acquiesced, rolling onto her stomach. Zach took her wrists in his hands and one by one tied them to the bedpost. He tapped her left hip. "Up, up," he said, sliding a pillow under her lower stomach when she lifted her hips for him.

"You're being very scientific about this," she said.

"Thorough." He flipped open the cap on the lube. "Simply being thorough. I do have a reputation to live up to, after all."

Thorough indeed. Nora lay on her stomach, relaxing into the pillow as Zach worked his wet fingers into her. He took his time, enjoying her. She knew he was enjoying her because he told her so, quietly, between kisses on the back of her naked shoulder and neck. As always, the prep work was uncomfortable at first, parts of her being touched that weren't usually given much attention. Tense, tight, toes clenched...then eventually, thanks to Zach's patience, his willingness to be "thorough," she relaxed, melting like hot candle wax.

"Ready?" Zach whispered into her ear.

"I've been ready for this for months, years..."

He laughed. "You always know the right thing to say."

He moved up on her, over her, straddling her. She moved her thighs wider to make it easier for him to enter her. Although he'd joked about being seconds away from coming, he didn't rush this part, not at all. He went slowly, carefully, not pushing into her so much as letting her accept him. It hurt at first, it always did, but as she inhaled and exhaled deeper and deeper, the discomfort faded, turned to fullness.

She felt his hot breath close to her ear. "All right?"

"Good," she said.

"Promise?"

"Promise."

His entire body lay flush against hers, prone on the bed. His legs tangled with her legs, his chest warmed her back, his breathing tickled her neck as his hands stroked her arms all the way up to her bound wrists. And this was what made him so good at it. Anal sex with King was all about domination—it was a game and he was going to win it, until they switched and she took her turn and won. With Søren, it was about pain. He was a sadist. The more it hurt, the more he liked it. But with Zach...it was just another way to make love. A more complicated way, maybe, but more intimate, too. He cared about her pleasure, and actively avoided giving her pain. Nothing turned her on quite like Søren's sadism, but Zach's cock in her ass was making a strong play for second place.

"Don't stop," she said.

"Wasn't planning to."

"Ever, I meant."

He dug his hand into her hair, lifted it off her neck, bit behind her ear. She was open now, taking him easily inside her. Still, he didn't push or prod or pump. He just slid in and out of her, his cock slick and her body slicker. This was what she needed, to get out of her brain and into her body. The only thoughts in her mind were *more...deeper... more...again.*

Maybe she said "more" out loud, because Zach reached for the vibrator. Nora gave her consent without words by spreading her legs wider, bowing her back so he could move his hand under her. The soft buzzing sounds came first and then she felt the touch of the tip on her clitoris. She shuddered in pleasure as Zach teased her. Then he wasn't teasing anymore as he found the entrance of her vagina and pushed the humming vibrator into her.

Nora lifted her head and moaned.

"I hope our neighbors heard that," Zach said.

The whole city might have heard it, but Nora heard nothing except her own ragged breathing. She writhed as much as she could being tied and pinned down. Her inner muscles stretched and tensed, clenched and clutched around the vibrator, around Zach. Even he was breathing hard now, pumping into her. They moved as one body— tightening, coiling, panting, pushing. Far away, Nora heard Zach make a sound that was almost a cry of pain. It was one of the sexiest sounds she'd ever heard a man make. He was coming undone and she was doing it to him. Tied up, impaled, pinned to the bed, she still could own him.

It didn't just feel good. It felt *too* good. Keening sounds came from the back of her throat. She couldn't move but moved anyway, writhing on the bed where Zach had her trapped and speared. Her clitoris throbbed. Her vagina clenched. Her ass was filled. She pulled on the silk scarves hard enough to bruise herself. Not that she felt the pain— she felt nothing but the pulse of the vibrator inside her and the fullness of Zach's cock inside her ass. Again, she lifted her head, cried out, and this time she came, shaking hard, her mouth buried into the pillow in a futile attempt to silence her own unholy moans. She finished first, recovered first, and glanced up in time to see Zach's face in the hotel mirror, his long body cast in shadow as he fucked her mindlessly, his hips grinding into her ass, his eyes closed and lips parted as he gave all of himself into her. She could see the veins on his forearms pop out as he came, his fingers twisting tightly into the sheets, his head down and then up again for one final spurt into her. He filled and filled her and she took it all because she wanted it all, she deserved it all.

And then, after, the inevitable collapse.

She whimpered as he pulled the vibrator out of her still-pulsing vagina and slid his cock out of her ass. He straddled her back, untying her wrists from the bed at a leisurely pace, still breathing heavy.

"You all right?" he asked for the third time.

She liked it, liked that he worried about her, worried about hurting her. As if he could ever hurt her. As if anyone or anything could ever hurt her again. But that was the afterglow talking. Or was it?

"Now I know," she said, still panting, "why ex-lovers say, 'We'll always have Paris.' "

CHAPTER FOUR

THE SOUTH OF FRANCE

MOZET WAS a full day's drive from Paris. Nora took the first shift behind the wheel and Zach the second. The sun had set around five, but Nora still watched the darkened landscape roll by from the passenger window, trying and failing not to think about Nicolas Delacroix and what she was about to do to his life. Was this really the right thing? Find this young man and tell him everything he thought about himself and his family was a lie? Reveal a woman's deeply personal secret—that she'd had an affair—to her son, without her permission? She could destroy a marriage, destroy a family, destroy the way Nicolas Delacroix saw himself. What choice did she have, though? This boy was a secret she couldn't keep. Not from Kingsley. She would think about it every time they were in the same room together: that Kingsley had a son he didn't know about, would never know about, all because of her silence. She'd kept the secret for over a year and it weighed on her like the proverbial stone around her neck. How many times this past year had Søren asked her what was on her mind because she was being quiet, far too quiet? How many times had Kingsley demanded to know if something had happened during the "ordeal" that she wasn't telling them? How much longer could she go on lying to the two most important men in her life?

She almost hoped Zach was right. Maybe Nicolas wasn't King's son after all.

But there was only one way to be certain.

"This should be it," Zach said as he slowed the car. "Can you read the sign?"

Nora rolled down her window to clear off the rain. *VILLAGE MOZET*, it read, black paint on a white board. Under it, another sign read *L'Un Des Plus Beaux Villages De France.*

"One of the most beautiful villages in France," she translated. Her heart clenched. Suddenly, it was all real. The fantasy was becoming a reality. Excitement turned to fear.

"This is it."

The road into town was lined on either side by houses and shops that couldn't have looked much different than they had when they were constructed three or four hundred years ago. The tallest buildings were only three stories high. Nearly every house and shop was built in the timbered style, each a different color of the rainbow. A blue pub. A pink café. A yellow boulangerie. The shop windows were all decorated for Christmas.

"This is the prettiest little town I've ever seen in my life," Nora said. "Add some snow and you'd have a medieval French Christmas card."

"Very quaint," Zach said. "I've been to the South of France dozens of times and never heard of it."

"The detective said it's not much of a tourist town. He warned me almost no one would speak English here, even if they know it." It's why she'd brought Zach along. One reason, anyway. Her French was decent, but Zach was fluent and could pass for French if need be. If Nicolas Delacroix started asking complicated questions, she'd need someone fluent to make sure she wasn't making things worse.

"I think that's our hotel. The only hotel in town." She checked the directions she'd printed out and pointed to a large white home with black timbers crisscrossing the exterior. "*Les Florets.*"

They turned off onto a cobblestone side street and parked in the lot. There was only one other car.

They wandered into the small lobby. They were well past late check-in, but, if the parking situation was any indication, their room would still be available. She paced the parquet floor, inspecting the potted flowers decorating the lobby while Zach checked them in. *Les Florets* was aptly named: even in late December, the hotel was alive with jasmine and begonias and desert roses and—

"We've been upgraded," Zach said, returning to her with a slight grin on his handsome face. "Honeymoon suite."

"Did you flirt with the old lady at the desk to get it?" Nora asked, taking a key from him.

"I told her you were a famous author here to research your next book."

"So you lied."

"It worked."

They carried their luggage up the two flights of stairs. They'd been offered a bellhop, but Nora hadn't wanted to wake the poor boy up. He was on the red sofa in the lobby, a copy of yesterday's *Le Monde* over his face.

The honeymoon suite wasn't large—only a sitting room, bathroom, and bedroom of average size—but it was beautifully decorated. The bedroom's carved wood four-poster bed, rosé-colored damask wallpaper, and heavy black rotary-dial phone made Nora feel as if she'd stepped back into the 1930s.

"Nice," she said, nodding her approval. "We'll have very good sex in this room."

Zach dropped his bag onto the luggage rack. "Does the decor improve performance?"

"You get a room this nice, it makes you want to have good sex in it. Gorgeous old bed. Fancy wallpaper. Beautiful view. No television. They *designed* this room for fucking. Hate to let the decorators down, you know."

"Tomorrow. Tonight we sleep, and in the morning we find this kid."

"Or we could just stay inside tomorrow and fuck all day."

He took her face in his hands and kissed her on the lips. "Not a chance, darling." Then he slapped her on the ass—hard. "Supper, then bed. You like following orders. Those are my orders. Come on."

Nora stared in shock as Zach waltzed out the door. "See if I ever let you ass-fuck me again," she called after him.

AFTER A LATE SUPPER, they went to bed. No sex, because Zach was a cruel, evil man, immune to her begging and pouting. He refused to touch her again until she'd gone through with her mission.

So it was no surprise that Nora was out of bed first thing the next morning, mapping their route to the Delacroix vineyard on her phone. Fifteen miles from the village. That's all. A fifteen-mile drive on a winding two-lane road. So close that the reality of what she was about to do finally hit her.

She couldn't go through with this...which was why she had to do it sooner rather than later. Even if Zach hadn't been withholding himself from her, he had the right idea: work first, then play.

Zach took the wheel again today. Her nerves were so frayed, she couldn't drive; in fact, she'd skipped breakfast, a rarity for her.

It had been dark when they'd arrived yesterday. Now she saw the countryside in the cold light of morning. The sea was south of the village, the vineyard north in the rocky hills. They snaked their way up the winding road, through the dense pines.

Eventually the scenery changed. The pine trees gave way to fenced-in pastures and fields, and then grape vines and arbors—acres and acres' worth.

The landscape matched the photographs in the magazine article the detective had given her. The wooden fences soon turned to stacked-stone fences. The fields, previously barren aside from trellises and arbors, began to fill with wooden sheds, barns, outbuildings, houses big and small, all surrounded by trees and sleeping winter gardens.

They reached the turn-off to the vineyard. Nora read the simple sign on the open gates: *Vignoble Delacroix*.

Past the open gate was a narrow lane, all gravel and rutted from the wheels of farm machinery. She saw a small orange tractor parked to the side of an old wooden shed.

"It really is a farm," she said.

"What did you think it was?"

"You just don't think of vineyards as farms."

"They're grape farms."

"I'm trying to picture Kingsley on a tractor. Whatever happened to the apple not falling far from the tree?"

"Says the erotica-writing dominatrix whose mother is a nun."

Nora glared pointedly at him.

They entered through the gate, pressing slowly on down the lane, but the ride was choppy.

"Bit muddy," Zach said. "Might be easier on foot."

Nora agreed. She'd prepared for walking today, dressing in her black knee-high leather boots and leggings, which she'd paired with a red sweater and her red trench coat. Zach had on jeans and hiking boots, and a leather coat over his heather gray pullover.

They abandoned their car in a small gravel lot and headed down the winding lane, which was bordered on both sides by white fences. On their right, a few black and white cows roamed and drowsed in their pastures. On their left, the vines stretched into the distance. They were brown, still, sleeping. No grapes in sight, of course—not during this time of year. A listless wind blew through it all.

Still—the sun lurking behind the clouds turned the sky a palette of pale pastel colors, and Nora knew she was seeing what Monet must have seen when he'd painted his winter scenes in pink and yellow and blue. And though it was winter, she smelled spring in the air, swept in on a sea breeze. There was life here, lurking behind the trees and inside the vines and under the ground and over the clouds. Life, biding its time, hiding, waiting...

"It's just so beautiful."

"You look smitten," Zach said. "Never imagined you sighing over a farm. Not even a grape farm."

She smiled, laughed to herself, at herself. Nora was anything but a country girl. Yet as they walked along the lane, Nora felt the strangest sensation. It was almost as if she was supposed to be here. But of course she was. She *was* supposed to be here—finding King his son. That wasn't quite it, though. She didn't generally give much credence to premonitions, but now she tingled all over with the inexplicable sensation of coming home again. Like when she visited the house her grandmother used to live in, and, even though a stranger lived there, Nora somehow still felt like it was her home.

Nora reached for Zach's hand, took it, held it, practically clung to it. She had to, otherwise she might have hopped the fence and ran through the fields as if she owned them. The stress was getting to her, making her lose it a little. Or maybe it was knowing Kingsley must have walked this very same lane twenty-five years ago. Possibly when he was a child, too, coming here with his parents to visit friends on their long holiday. That didn't quite explain it to her satisfaction, however. This place was from Kingsley's past. Why did it feel like a part of *hers*?

They stopped at a crossroads. An old-fashioned fingerpost-style sign pointed left and right, as the lane split in two. It listed the various buildings on the grounds—wine shop, tasting room, event barn, cuverie.

She looked to Zach. "*Cuverie?*"

"It's where they store the wine vats," he translated. "I suppose we want the tasting room."

The turned right. The lane sloped uphill and at the crest stood a small timber-frame barn, converted into what looked like a restaurant. Troublingly, the parking lot was empty. The website for the vineyard didn't say anything about it being closed in December. It listed the daily tour schedule as usual. Then again, it hadn't been updated since early November. She'd placed a few calls, all of which had gone to voicemail. She began to experience a sinking feeling in the pit of her stomach, and it wasn't hunger...

As they neared the barn that housed the tasting room, they saw one of the big double doors standing slightly ajar. The lights were on inside. Her heart skipped a beat.

Even if the vineyard was closed to the public, somebody was here. She would use Zach's lie, she decided—that she was an author writing a book set at a vineyard in this region, and she would love to meet young Monsieur Delacroix, if he would be so kind. She would, of course, bat her eyelashes a little. She also wasn't above bribery.

They paused as they reached the double doors. Nora heard voices through the crack. One female, one male. Both young, by the sound of their voices. The woman asked a question in rapid French, to which the man responded, *"Non, pas aujourd'hui."*

No, not today.

Another question, and then, *"Dans l'ancienne grange."*

In the old barn.

The woman pressed him again about something, her French too fast for Nora. *"Je vais bien, ne t'en fais pas,"* the young man said.

I'm fine. Don't worry.

"Shall we?" Zach whispered. "I'll do the talking."

She took a breath and nodded. Zach squeezed her hand and pulled her inside.

The young man was gone. Nora noticed immediately, because she'd scanned the room for him at once. The barn's ceilings were high, with exposed beams. The back wall was lined with a bar featuring a massive wine rack. Behind the bar stood an open door. The man whose voice she'd heard was back there in that little room, Nora knew. She stared at the door, willing him to come out, to show himself.

The woman was on a ladder, dusting the blades of a large ceiling fan. She noticed them, lowered her dust rag, and smiled. "*Bonjour?*"

Zach replied in his fluent French: "Hello there. How are you?"

"Very well, thank you." Pretty girl, about twenty-two or three, with braided brown hair.

"Is the tasting room open?"

"Only for cleaning," she said and smiled more broadly. "We're getting ready for a wedding on New Year's Eve."

Zach apologized for barging in, and the young woman went on talking, pleasantly, but Nora wasn't listening anymore.

A silver tabby sat on the bar, doing that odd little cat thing where it licked its paw and then ran the wet paw over its ear to clean it. It stopped its bath when Nora reached it, looking at her with bright golden eyes. Nora held out a finger and the cat tilted its head magnanimously, allowing her to pet it.

The girl called out, "Nico? Guests."

And then Nico—Nicolas Delacroix—finally appeared.

CHAPTER FIVE

HE STEPPED through the open door behind the bar, and Nora's knees nearly buckled. It was King. The nose. The broad shoulders and trim waist. The way he stood. The way he lifted his chin. His mouth. The lips. The jaw. Then Nora blinked and Kingsley was gone and another man stood in his place. One who was wholly himself, unique, who she would never mistake for Kingsley ever again, not even in the dark.

It was rude to stare, but Nora was rude and so she stared...and stared and stared.

His hair was shaggier than in the photograph. He was a little thinner, too, which made him look even younger than in the picture. With summer long gone, his skin was paler, though still far darker than hers. He had a black and gray checkered flannel shirt tied around his waist. His t-shirt had sweat stains, and he held a small drill in his right hand. A drill? Never in her life had she seen Kingsley holding a drill. Wait. Yes, she had, but at the time he hadn't been using it for the purpose God intended.

The young man worked hard. Too hard, she could tell.

She wanted to cook him a huge meal, though she didn't do that sort of thing. And she wanted to hold him. She wanted to bring him home with her and welcome him into the family.

"I didn't hear you," he said to the woman on the ladder. "What did you say?"

"Nico, visitors," the young woman said. *Nico.* That was his name. Not Nicolas, but Nico.

He saw Zach first, nodded his head in greeting, said, "*Bonjour.*" Then he saw her standing with the cat, her hand still resting on its back.

"*Bonjour,*" he said to her.

"We saw the gate open," Zach was saying, the same spiel he'd given the girl. "But you seem to be closed."

Nico didn't look at him when he answered, saying, "We're open." No, when he said that, he was looking at Nora.

The girl on the ladder sighed, and it was a sigh that wanted to be a laugh.

"Are you? Thank you," Zach went on. "I came from England. She's American, but—"

"American," he said with some awe. Nora didn't expect that from a Frenchman. "Where are you from?"

He'd shifted immediately into English, very good English.

"New York," she said.

"Ah. I lived in California for a year. Napa."

"Did you? I hear it's nice there," she said, not knowing what she was saying. Or why she said it. Or why he was looking only at her, why she kept petting the cat as if her life depended on it. The cat didn't seem to mind, at least.

He held out his hand. Nora hesitated before putting her hand in his. She made the handshake quick, but not so quick she didn't feel how calloused his hands were. A farmer's hands.

"Nico Delacroix," he said.

"Nora."

"Nora." He nodded like he approved. "What brings you here to Mozet, Nora?" His questions were polite, the sort of questions the proprietor of any tourist establishment might ask the tourists. Except he'd said her name twice, like he was trying to memorize it. "I hope it's our wine."

Nora couldn't bring herself to lie to his face. She thought she could, and had planned to lie to him, to get to know him a little before telling him the truth. Face to face with him now, though, seeing him live in the flesh, she couldn't. But she couldn't tell him the truth, either.

"I've never had it," she said. "Is it as good as they say?"

"Better," he said, smiling. The smile transformed him. The boy became a man with that smile. "You want to try Rosanella?"

"Very much, thank you." She felt stupid talking like this, all her confidence gone, her nerves rattled to the bone.

Zach wandered over to her side. She grabbed his hand and held it tight. She didn't want Nico to see how much it was shaking.

Nico. Nico. Nico. She played his name in her head like a new favorite song. That's exactly who he was. He was a Nico, not a Nicolas. And she was a Nora, not an Eleanor. Except to Søren, and only Søren. So he must be a Nicolas to someone. His mother, probably. Maybe his father. Or a lover? Surely a young man this beautiful, King's *son*, after all, had a lover. Maybe several.

"Come on, Pinot," he said to the cat. "You know you can't be up here." He plucked the cat off the bar, scratched his head so he would know he wasn't really in trouble, and set him on the ground. "Sorry. He thinks he owns the place."

"Pinot?" Nora asked as Nico picked up a damp bar towel and wiped the counter down. "I thought you only had Syrah here?"

His eyes clouded over but the cloud passed quickly. "My father named him. Named all our cats Pinot, Chardonnay, something like that." His French accent was light but lovely. She adored hearing him speak. "Tourists would come and make a joke. Only Syrah on the wine list and they'd ask for a Pinot, ask for a Burgundy. He would say he had Pinot in the back. He'd come out holding the cat and drop it in their laps. 'You want a Pinot? Here's your Pinot,' he'd say."

He *would* say... The article about the vineyard had come out last spring. In it, his father was still at the helm of the vineyard. Had he retired, leaving Nico in charge, or... had he passed? Either would have gone a long way to explain the tiredness, the weight loss, the clouds in Nico's eyes.

He seemed to suddenly notice Zach existed. "Hello," he said politely. "Nico. I'm the vintner." He held out his hand to Zach and they shook.

"Zachary Easton. A pleasure."

"You two married?" Nico asked. "On your honeymoon?"

"No," Zach said quickly. "She's a writer. I'm her editor. We're on a sort of research trip together."

"Ah." Nico nodded, smiled again with more interest than before. "A writer. What do you write? I read when I can. Maybe I read something you wrote."

"You're not old enough to read what I write."

His eyebrow shot straight up. He laughed and shook his finger at her. "You're funny."

Zach reached into his coat pocket and pulled out his phone to check the time. "Ah, I have a conference call soon. Do you mind?" he asked her. "I'll just be a minute."

"Take your time," Nora said.

He didn't need to make a phone call, she knew. No one worked in publishing in December. This was his way of giving her a chance to be alone with Nico, to tell him.

"I'll walk her back when we're finished," Nico said.

"Thanks," Zach said. "Good man. I'm off. Don't drink too much." He shook Nico's hand again and told the girl on the ladder goodbye as he walked out.

When he was gone, Nico addressed the girl on the ladder and said, "It's good. You can finish. Thanks."

The young woman came down the ladder, threw her dust rag over her shoulder and sauntered out with a lilting, "*Au revoir...*"

Nora glanced back at Nico, who was looking at her expectantly. Now they were alone.

"PRETTY GIRL," Nora said. "She work here?"

"My cousin," Nico said, rolling his eyes. "Thinks she owns the place, too."

"Who runs things now?"

"Me," he said. "My father left it all to me."

Left it all to him? He hadn't retired; he'd passed away. Oh God.

"Did that...happen recently?" She tried to keep her voice even, kind, politely curious. "I read about this place in a magazine not that long ago. They interviewed your father."

"November," he said, not looking at her, just wiping the same spot on the counter again and again with the bar towel. "Heart attack in the fields. Found him under the vines." He smiled a pained smile. "It's how he said he wanted to go. On his land, with his vines. Working."

"I'm sorry," she said. Hot tears pricked her eyes. Could her timing be any worse?

He turned and plucked a photograph off the wall that hung over a line of wine bottles.

"This is him," he said. He showed her a photograph of himself and a much older man standing side by side under an arched grape arbor. One of those pale men who never tanned, just turned pink as wild salmon. He had a large Roman nose, nothing like Nico's. An enormous man, even taller than Søren, and broader, too. Nora would have guessed he was in his early 70s in the photograph, though ages were impossible to guess with people who worked outdoors. He and Nico couldn't have looked more different if they'd tried. And Nora could easily imagine the boredom of a young wife, married to a much older man, a farmer, too, falling for Kingsley—young, handsome, wounded—in a week.

"He looks so happy," she said. "He must have lived for this place."

"He lived for me," Nico said. Nora stared at him, waited. "He told me that so many times. Frost, fire, bad year, no money, whatever...he'd say to me, 'You're alive. I'm alive. Your mother's alive. What else is there?' " He blinked and Nora saw his eyes were red. "I thought he'd live forever." He seemed to suddenly catch himself. The smile he gave her was sheepish. "I'm sorry. I don't know why I'm saying all this to you. Still feels like his place, not mine."

"Sometimes it's easier to talk to a stranger."

"Why is that? You didn't even know my father."

"That's why, probably." She rested her elbow on the bar, her head on her hand. "Everyone here knew him, right? And loved him, too."

"He was worshipped here. We've had people working here for forty years."

"So they loved him, and they're grieving, too. But none of them are his son, so none of them are grieving as much as you are. Maybe you resent that a little, that they don't miss him as much as you do. Maybe you resent having to go on, because now you're in charge. But I didn't know him, so you don't resent me for not covering myself in ashes and sackcloth."

He laughed softly, so softly it was more of a breathy smile than a laugh.

"You're smart." He tapped his temple. He took a big breath. "It's not fair of me to expect them to miss him as much as I do. Why would they? I'll stop talking about him now. You came here for wine, not my life story."

Keep talking, she wanted to say. She had a thousand questions and she needed answers.

Are you all right?

Are you eating enough?

Aren't you too young to be running a business this big on your own?

Have you been sleeping?

Is anyone helping you?

Is anyone taking care of you?

Does anyone love you like you should be loved?

Nico took the framed photograph, turned and hung it

on the wall again. "If I get enough wine in you, maybe you'll tell me about your books."

Nora watched as Nico straightened the picture, then adjusted it again until it was straight. He turned around.

"You want to see our list?" he asked.

At once Nora knew she couldn't do this. Not now. Not to him. On the verge of a panic attack, she said, "I need to go."

His head cocked, his brow furrowed. "Go? Now? You don't want wine?"

"I'm sorry. I...I need to get back. I'm very sorry," she said. She reached for her scarf she'd laid on the bar. "This was a mistake."

"What was a mistake? Hey." He reached across the bar and touched her arm lightly. "What's wrong?"

She met his eyes—another mistake. Those celadon eyes of his were imploring her to stay, to speak, to explain herself. In a moment of weakness, he'd confided in her and here she was, leaving him so abruptly. She'd hurt him. His hand on her hand was light, but she felt as if her arm was nailed to the bar.

"I can't tell you," she said.

"Can't tell me what?"

"Why I'm here. The real reason I'm here. I can't tell you. I thought I could, but I can't. And I can't lie to you either."

"Lie to me? About what? You don't know me." He took his hand away from hers, as if she was scaring him. God, she was ruining this. Kingsley would never forgive her.

Nora rubbed her forehead, sighed.

"Nora?"

The way he said her name, like he knew her...

"I came here because I do know you," she said. "In a

way. Maybe. Ah, this is impossible. I wanted to talk to you about something kind of personal, but I have no idea how to do it."

He smiled. "You're mysterious, you know. It's a little crazy."

"I really am very sorry," she said.

"Don't say you're sorry. Say the truth."

She glanced around. She heard more voices outside the barn. Other workers. His cousin. They were trying to get the place ready for a wedding. Anyone could walk in while they were talking.

"This isn't the right place. Can we talk later?"

"Where are you staying?"

"*Les Florets*. Do you know it?"

"I know it. I can be there at eight."

"Perfect. I'll try to pull myself together by then."

"Eight then. Come on. I'll walk you back."

"You don't have to."

"I said I would." He untied the flannel shirt from around his hips like it was a done deal. As if *I said I would* meant the same thing as *I will*. It didn't, for most people. "We don't have to talk when we walk, if you don't want."

Nora was shocked to find that she did want him to walk her back. So she said, "All right." Then she said, "Thank you." And finally, as they were walking out of the barn and down toward the open gates, with Pinot the cat half-heartedly following them, she said, "You."

"Me?" he said. "What about me?"

"You asked me earlier what brings me to Mozet. The answer is 'you.'"

CHAPTER SIX

ON THEIR WALK back to the parking lot, Nora was both surprised and impressed that Nico hadn't said anything for a full two minutes.

"No questions?" she said.

"Too many questions."

"You can ask. I won't answer if it means having to lie to you."

"Are you with the bank?"

Nora had to laugh. Did she look like a banker? "What bank?"

He shrugged and the shrug was so like Kingsley that she shivered. "We had an investor," he said. "He pulled out when my father died. He doesn't think I can run the place on my own, says I'm too young. So I'm trying to get a loan. If everyone paid their bills on time, I could cover payroll without a loan. But even restaurants with Michelin stars are bad at paying their bills. If we can make it to spring, we'll be okay but...you know. It's just business."

"I'm not from the bank. I'd give you the loan if I could,

though. And I promise, I always settle my bar tab by the end of the night."

He laughed. "I believe that."

"I know someone who might be able to help you," she said as they walked. "A friend of mine. He used to come to Mozet when he was a boy. And in his twenties, too—decades ago. Before you were born."

"Your English friend?"

"Not Zach," she said. "Have you ever heard the name 'Kingsley Boissonneault'?"

He frowned. "Never. Why would he help us?"

She didn't answer.

"You're being mysterious again," Nico said. "It's not as funny as it was before."

"I know. This is so hard."

"*Difficile?*" he teased.

"*Très difficile.*"

She wanted to scream, cry, grab him by the shoulders and shake him, shrieking *You are Kingsley's son!* That would have been seriously impetuous. Even for Nora.

"You don't seem like the kind of woman who would let something *très difficile* stop her." He grinned at her, eyes gleaming. He was letting her see a glimpse of the Nico he'd been before his father had died—playful, self-possessed, a little wicked. Then, like someone blew out a candle, the light went out of his eyes again and there was nothing to be seen but grief incarnate. But she had seen the light in his eyes now and wanted to shield that flame, to keep it safe, to stoke the embers that would allow it to keep burning.

"I can't lie to you. But I can't tell you the truth. So all I can do is...say nothing. First time for everything."

"Please talk to me," he said. "Tell me *some*thing."

She knew that she owed him something, some sort of

explanation, even if she wasn't able to give him a full answer, not yet. "Nico, what would you say if I told you that I knew something about you—something that you might not want to know?"

"How do you know that I don't want to know it?"

"I don't *know*, but I would predict...you don't want to know this."

"And I would say, you don't know me well enough to predict what I would or would not want to know."

"But how could I know, without telling you?"

"Do you want to tell me?"

"Not really. But I have to."

"Why is that?"

She paused for a moment, took one soft breath. "Loyalty, I suppose."

"Loyalty?" he repeated. "You're loyal to someone, and that's why you're here?"

"Yes."

"Loyalty is good, if the person deserves it. Does this person deserve your loyalty?"

"He saved my life. A few different times, in a few different ways. And even if he hadn't, I'd still be here."

"He's someone special to you?"

"Very."

"I see."

"Not like that."

"*Non?*"

"Well, maybe a little like that. We're not a couple. We're too...weird for that."

He laughed again, a real laugh with no irony in it. "Too weird. You *are* weird, aren't you?"

She loved the way he said "weird," somehow adding an extra syllable into it. *We-ah-ard.*

"You have no idea, Nico."

"Are you here trying to save his life? Let me guess. He and I have the same blood type, and he wants my kidney?"

"He doesn't want your kidney, I promise."

"So it's my liver, then."

Nora laughed. "His liver is fine. Probably. I hope."

"Good. I need my liver. I'm using it."

She shook her head. "The French and their livers."

"You have to take care of your liver, you know. My father always told me that—take care of your liver and your liver will take care of you."

"How do you take care of your liver?"

"He never told me that part. I should have asked." He looked out across the acres of his vineyard. Was he looking toward where his father died? "Now it's too late."

And that, Nora wanted to say to him, *is why I can't tell you why I'm here. Because your father is dead and you are grieving him so hard that I can feel your pain, like you're the epicenter of an earthquake and the world is shaking under my feet from the power of your grief. You will hate me when I tell you what I came here to tell you. You will hate me, and I don't want you to hate me. You're King's son. I couldn't stand it if you hated me.*

"Tell me something else, then," Nico said.

"What do you want to know?"

"Anything you can tell me. Tell me about your books. Tell me about New York. Tell me about your editor. You two seem...close. He's wearing a wedding ring."

So he'd noticed that.

"I write adult novels," she said. "*Very* adult novels. Some are even in French. New York is exactly like you think it is, and nothing like you think it is. And Zach's married." She paused. "I'm not."

"Yet you travel alone with him?"

"Like you said, we're close."

"And his wife doesn't mind?"

"She doesn't, believe it or not. And he wouldn't leave her for me, not in a million years. And I wouldn't leave my someone for him, either."

"So you do have someone?"

She nodded slowly. "I have someone."

"And he's not jealous that you're here with another someone."

"Jealousy isn't our thing. Our relationship is sort of... open. I'm sure you understand. You French are very nonchalant about that sort of thing."

"Meanwhile, Americans aren't nonchalant about anything. Except how you dress."

"Not fair," Nora said, laughing. "I don't wear my pajamas out in public. Not very often, anyway."

They reached the main lane and she saw Zach standing by the car, maybe fifty yards or so away.

"I'll let you get to work," she said. "I know you're busy."

"So?" There was that shrug again, with a little toss of the hand that was so French, so Kingsley Edge, it gave Nora vertigo. "What is it?"

He must have noticed her expression.

"Nothing. You remind me of someone I know, it's... You gave me *déjà vu* there for a second."

"Who is it?"

"The other friend I mentioned," she said. "The French one. Take it as a compliment—he's one of the five most handsome men in the world."

"Ah, *Monsieur*...Boissonneault, was it?"

He didn't look particularly flattered at being compared to another man, even favorably. In fact, he looked apprehensive, like he wanted to say something but couldn't quite bring himself to say it. She hoped he would screw up the courage to just ask, demand an answer, force it out of her right now and get it over with. But he didn't. Maybe he sensed what she wanted to tell him and wasn't ready to hear it yet.

"See you at eight?" she said.

"Of course. Eight."

They exchanged numbers and said their goodbyes. She almost went in for a hug, but caught herself—this wasn't King.

Nora watched him walk away, watched until he transformed more fully into Kingsley again at a distance—his height, his build, the set of his shoulders, the confident stride.

Nora returned to the car and Zach wrapped up his pretend phone call. "I don't see any bullet holes," he said. "He didn't shoot the messenger?"

"The messenger chickened out."

"Nora."

"I know. I know. But there were people around. I couldn't tell him and have him fall apart in front of his employees. He's coming to the hotel tonight. I'll tell him then."

"It's not like you to be this...careful with people." A cruel comment, but too true for Nora to argue.

"His father died last month. Last month, Zach."

Zach winced, looking genuinely pained.

"Exactly. And he's a wreck over it. I don't blame him. His father was your dream father. Nico showed me a picture of them together. He almost started crying."

"Did you tell him anything? Or just ask him to supper?"

"I said I needed to talk to him about something important. So he knows something's up. What do I do?"

"Let's get back to the hotel. We'll figure it out there."

"I have a better idea," she said. "Take me to the sea."

"You want to swim in December?"

"No," she said. "I want to drown in December."

ZACH, for some reason, refused to drown her in the sea, and called her melodramatic for suggesting it. When they returned to the hotel, she said she was going to drown herself in the bathtub instead. He told her he would miss her when she was gone.

The man had no respect for her feelings at all.

Nora ran her bath, filling the large claw-foot tub with the hottest water she could stand.

She stripped naked and sank into the steaming bath. When she resurfaced, Zach was in the doorway, one eyebrow arched, looking amused, bemused, and annoyed all at once. His default expression around her.

"You were going to let me drown?" she asked.

"No sex in the afterlife. I knew you'd rally."

Nora sighed, grabbed the nearest towel, wiped her face. "Are you going to watch me take a bath like a creep or are you getting in?"

"Room for two?"

She lifted her wet legs out of the tub to display to Zach how much room there was.

"Haven't taken a bath without a baby in my arms in the last three months," he said. "Sounds luxurious."

Nora laid back in the water and watched with pleasure as Zach stripped. He stepped into the water and sat down.

He looked so inviting wet and naked, that she had no choice but to glide over to his side and lay back on his chest.

"That's a very cute image, you taking a bath with Fionn."

"Technically, *he's* taking a bath with *me*. I'm in charge of the bath. I just let him join me."

"He likes it?"

"Loves it. Loves being splashed. Loves to float. Loves pissing three feet straight up in the air." Zach mimed a water spout.

"Three feet?"

"The joys of baby boys."

Nora giggled. Zach wrapped his arms around her. "Did you know? From the beginning, who his father was?"

"I knew there was a chance. Grace told me right away. Before she even knew she was pregnant, she told me. And when he was born, I couldn't see any of me in him."

"Were you angry?"

He exhaled, hard enough she moved like a wave on his chest. "Hard to explain what I felt. We were already talking about using donor sperm at that point, or adopting. We'd even met with an adoption counselor. The doctors were all so convinced the problem was with Grace, because she'd had the ectopic pregnancy years before. They thought it was scar tissue or some other kind of damage. Took months before they even bothered testing me."

"What was it? Sorry. That's a personal question."

"We're naked in a bath together. Under such circumstances, personal questions are allowed. To answer your question, I have an ulcer. Had one for years. Named it Nora." She splashed him for that. "Been on drugs for it for years. Turns out, one of the side effects of the drugs is infertility."

"It killed off your swim team?"

"Precisely." Zach ran his wet hands up and down her arms. "I'm not getting any younger. And Grace was so desperate to have a baby... You know, I just read an article in *The Guardian* about British women getting donor sperm from Danish men. Apparently one of Denmark's more unusual exports."

"Grace went straight to the source."

"Skipped the middleman. Very efficient." He laughed a little, then stopped. "If you had seen her suffering..." And there he stopped, as if to collect himself. "She tried so hard not to let me see how it was killing her, not being able to get pregnant. But I'd hear her through the bathroom door, sobbing as softly as she could. I'd find the towels later, with her face imprinted on them from where she tried to muffle her crying. To not be able to help your wife when she's in that sort of agony... It got so bad that I started to understand why some women kidnap other mother's babies."

"So you weren't mad when she told you it might not be yours?"

He sighed again. "If I was...and I'm not saying I was, but *if* I was, if there were any hard feelings at all, they evaporated the second the nurse put Fionn in my arms. And I knew then that I had been given a gift I could never hope to repay. So I finally have one reason to like that priest of yours. But just the one. That, and he let me have you this week. Two reasons, I suppose."

Nora laughed softly.

Zach ran warm hands full of hot water over her arms. "What are you going to do tonight?"

"I have no idea," she said. "You tell me."

"You have to make this decision yourself. But I will say one thing—you aren't telling him who his 'real father' is. He has a real father. *Had*, before the man died and broke his son's heart. You need to understand that you aren't doing the boy any favors. You're telling him his mother had an affair with another man. You're telling him his parents kept a secret from him his entire life. You're forcing him to make choices he never should have had to make. Don't lie to yourself or him—you're doing this for Kingsley, and for yourself, not for Nico. The very least you can do for him when you blow his family apart is to be honest about your motives."

His words hit her harder than Søren's whip ever had, but just like the lash of a whip, she took it without complaint. "Thank you, sir. May I have another?"

Zach's chest rumbled with his laugh. "You asked my advice. You didn't ask me to cheer you up."

"Fine. Now cheer me up."

He tugged her wrist, turning her to face him. They were both wet and slick. She turned and pressed her breasts against his chest, her mouth against his mouth. As they kissed more and more deeply, his hands found her hips and he rocked her against his cock. The water sloshed in the tub and onto the floor.

Zach didn't waste time, bless him. He reached out of the tub and into her make-up bag for the lube. He also picked up a towel.

"What's the towel for?" she asked.

He laid it over the rim of the tub. "You," he said. He didn't say anything else or give any orders. He just moved her into place, her stomach on the pillow of the towel, her hands on the floor. Her hips were out of the water, with Zach behind her. She closed her eyes and let the heat of the water seep deep into her skin as his fingers sank deeply into her body. One finger. Two. A little lube, then more, more. Then it was nothing at all but him pressing his tip against her hole and waiting for her to push backward, eagerly taking him inside her. No shoving. No rushing. Slow, easy thrusts. The water barely splashed as he worked his way deeper into her. She lowered her head, chin to her chest, as he tunneled in, carefully, his hands on her shoulders and back, calming her, caressing her.

In the bathroom door mirror, Nora could see Zach's head leaning back, his throat bared as he worked himself into her. She watched the tight pulses of his hips. That's all that moved. No other part of his body but his hips—an obscene sight. And then, to make it even better, if that was possible, he bent over, resting his chest flush against her back, wrapping his hand around her thigh to find her clitoris with his fingertip. He'd barely touched that sensitive aching knot before Nora flinched with pleasure.

"Good?" he asked.

"Please do that again."

He did. He stroked her while fucking her. Slow strokes. Slow fucking. Zach's fingers slipped into her, and his fingertips found the hollow just inside her. He rubbed it, kneading that tender spot in concentric circles that set Nora moaning. All the while, he kept up his slow steady thrusts, the long deep pumps into her.

"Come on my hand," Zach said softly. "Let me feel it." He worked her hard with his fingers, rubbing in widening spirals that opened her up to him and made her tense at the same time. All sensation in her body was concentrated in her hips, her stomach. The tension grew unbearable. She bore it anyway, holding off, breathing shallow breaths to make it last, but she couldn't make it last long, not when Zach pushed a third finger inside of her vagina, opening it, spreading it. Faster he worked her with his hand until she was out of her mind. His fingers went deep at the same time his cock did and she couldn't hold back any longer. Her head dropped down and her back bowed; she thrust her hips into his hand as she came, the orgasm ripping through her hard enough that she splashed half a gallon of water onto the floor.

She was finished, done for.

Zach wasn't. He took her by the waist with both hands and pulled her onto him, burying himself fully in her and coming with a ragged gasp that reverberated in her ears like a bell.

He eased out of her and sunk back into the water. Nora was so hot from the sex, she turned on the cold water and splashed her face with it.

"Hit me," Zach said. She tossed cold water on his face and chest. "Thank you."

Nora giggled mindlessly. After all, how could she giggle any other way after Zach had just fucked her brains out? But slowly, rational thought did return to her.

"Wait," she said. "Didn't you say you weren't going to fuck me again until I accomplished my mission?"

"I did, didn't I?"

"And didn't you just fuck me, with my mission still unaccomplished?"

"Yes, but I have a good excuse."

"And that is?"

"I wanted to."

"Very good excuse."

"But now I *really* won't fuck you again until your mission is accomplished."

"Unless you want to. Right?"

"Right."

She knew she and Zach were friends for a reason.

CHAPTER SEVEN

NORA WAS SIPPING coffee in the hotel dining room when Nico arrived a fifteen minutes 'til eight. He furrowed his brow when he saw that she wasn't alone—Zach was sitting with her.

"I'm early," he said to her. He turned to Zach and, with infinite politeness, said, "Sorry to interrupt."

"No need. Just finishing my dinner," Zach said. He tossed his napkin on the table. "Back up to the room to get some work done. She hasn't eaten yet."

"We were talking about work," Nora said, putting her cup down and waving the waiter over for more coffee. "So I'm *thrilled* you're early."

"See you later," Zach said. He rose, leaned over the small round table and kissed her cheek. "Nico. Have a good evening." They shook hands. "I'll be upstairs if you need me."

Zach left them alone and the waiter, who was also the hotel's bellhop—he'd roused himself from the couch for the evening shift—cleared the table of everything but coffee, put down new silverware, and brought over a menu.

"You look different," Nora said. She sat back in her chair and nodded approvingly. "Haircut."

He ran his fingers through his hair. "I needed one."

"Looks nice," she said. Understatement. He looked incredibly handsome with his hair tamed to short waves. He'd cleaned up for dinner—no work boots or dirty jeans. His shoes were suede and his jeans freshly laundered. The gray scarf and leather jacket were a nice touch.

"Your hair is...nice, too," he said, repaying her compliment with all the suaveness of a man in his twenties. He sat down. "You haven't eaten?"

"Not yet. I was waiting on you. I'm starving," she said with relish, and truth. After her bath—and sex—with Zach, she'd fallen into a deep sleep. When she'd woken, it was almost evening. Too late for lunch. Too early for dinner. "Ever eaten here? What's good?"

"I always get the *boeuf bourguignon*," he said.

Nora smiled to herself.

"What?" He asked.

"Nothing. The friend you remind me of...he loves *boeuf bourguignon*. Are you a coffee snob, too?"

"I don't know if I'm a *snob*," he said, wrinkling his nose a bit. "But, you know, I wouldn't drink Starbucks if you threatened me with the guillotine."

"Don't say that. I have a guillotine."

He narrowed his eyes at her.

"Just a little one," she said.

"You're not joking."

"It really is a very little one. It's for threatening men."

"You like to threaten men?" He didn't sound horrified, more intrigued and amused, like he couldn't imagine ever finding her threatening.

"I'm a dominatrix. Do you know what that is?" If she

was going to tell him about Kingsley—*everything* about Kingsley; the good, the bad, and the kinky—she might as well start slow. If he couldn't handle her being a dominatrix, he'd never be able to handle Kingsley being... well...Kingsley.

"You said you were a writer."

Interesting. He seemed more wounded that she had possibly lied to him than that she beat up men for money.

"I do both. It's not easy to pay the bills from writing alone. I needed a side gig."

He nodded, as if that made perfect sense.

"Really? No follow-up questions? No who, what, when, where, why the hell are you a dominatrix?"

"What's so wrong with being a dominatrix that you would have to answer all those questions? It's not illegal in America, is it?"

"No, not really." Now it was her turn to narrow her eyes at him. "You are a very interesting young man. *Très intéressant.*"

He made a face like she'd just said something *très stupide.* "What? No. I'm nobody."

"You're what...twenty-four? You run your own vineyard."

He snorted the purest French snort, and the eyeroll he gave her should have been on the French flag. "Not by choice. If I had my choice, I'd be working for my father still."

"You don't bat an eyelash when I tell you I'm a sex worker."

"You're a beautiful woman. I think it's a good job for you," he said as he glanced over the menu again. The way he'd said it, it was like he was talking to a tall man and said, *You're seven feet tall, of course you play basketball.* He didn't seem to be pretending, either—pretending to be okay with who and what she was.

The waiter appeared before Nora could say anything in response. She ordered the Niçoise salad. Nico ordered only soup and coffee.

"Just soup?" Nora asked after the waiter had left. "What happened to *boeuf bourguignon*?"

"Not hungry."

"You need to eat something more than soup."

He glared at her.

Nora winced. "Sorry. Really. I'm not... I don't think I've ever said 'you need to eat more' to anyone in my life before. I'm not *motherly*. At all."

"I bring it out in you?" His tone implied he would not appreciate any further mothering.

"It's not that. It's...I feel protective of you. I don't know you, but I..."

Her voice trailed off as she noticed Nico glancing away. His fingers toyed with his tiny coffee cup. "Nico?" she asked.

He smiled. "Makes me feel very...I don't know, strange when you say that."

"That I feel protective of you?"

He nodded.

"I don't mean to make you feel strange."

"It's a good type of strange. I don't know. I wish there was a word for that." He smiled at her, drank his coffee. Abruptly he put his cup down and said, "You have to tell me why you're here." He leaned in closer, reached his hand, still warm from the coffee cup, across the table and touched her hand. "Please."

She looked at his fingertips resting on top of her hand.

He seemed to realize he'd gone too far, took his hand away. She could still feel the heat of it on her skin.

"Just promise me one thing, Nico."

"Anything."

"Please don't hate me for what I'm about to tell you."

———

HE STARED at her with a look of worry in his green-glass eyes. She waited for him to make his promise, but he didn't. She appreciated that he was wise enough not to make promises he couldn't keep.

"Why would I hate you?" he asked.

Instead of answering, Nora took a deep breath. She pulled her bag off the back of her chair. She'd hoped this could wait until after dinner. But it wasn't fair to Nico to make him sit there and stew in his fear and uncertainty over what she had to tell him.

"Before I tell you, let me say again... I am sorry, Nico."

He turned his head, smiled nervously. "You're scaring me now."

"It's not bad news. I'm not the Angel of Death or anything. I just know something that I can't, in good conscience, keep secret from you or the other person involved."

"I can't tell you to ignore your conscience. Go on then. Tell it to me."

"It's a long story," she began as she pulled a file of photographs from her bag. "And I won't go into the whole thing right now. But the short version is...someone came here on a trip and saw you, and when they saw you..."

"What? What did they see?" His voice was soft, scared. She hated herself for doing this to him.

Nora took another breath, opened the folder and took out the first photograph—the one of Kingsley when he was nineteen, the one where the resemblance between he and Nico was the most obvious. She moved the coffee pot and set the photograph on the table between them.

"Kingsley Boissonneault," she said. "The man who saved my life. The reason I'm here."

Nico leaned over the table again to get a better look. He could have picked it up but didn't. Maybe he saw it right away. Maybe that's why he didn't want to touch it.

"Who is he? A long-lost cousin of mine or something?" Nico asked.

"You see the family resemblance?"

He shrugged that Kingsley shrug again. "I guess. I mean, we do look alike."

"He was a few years younger than you when that picture was taken. Here's one from when he was twenty-nine." She showed him another picture of Kingsley. He was in profile in this picture, taken for the society page of a New York magazine. "Turn sideways."

Nico slowly turned his head. Nora held up the photograph by Nico's profile. "Your noses are twins."

"All right, so who is he?" Nico asked. "Don't tell me I have a brother out there." He laughed nervously, as if he knew what was coming and could make it go away by joking about it.

But it wouldn't go away.

"Kingsley came here to Mozet twenty-five years ago. He was in *La Légion*. He'd been shot and he came here to recuperate. In May, twenty-five years ago. He was here for one week...thirty-eight weeks before you were born."

Nico said nothing. He just stared at the two photographs on the table.

"You shrug like him," she said. "Just like him. You have identical noses. Same jawline. Same build. You both love *boeuf bourguignon* and you are both coffee snobs. When you walked away from me today, you looked just like him from—"

"Stop," he said.

Nora stopped.

She'd never heard a silence so deep as the silence of a young man's heart breaking over a cup of coffee. The silence was so heavy, she couldn't bear it longer than a minute.

"You and your father looked nothing alike," she said softly. "There's no way you didn't notice that you looked nothing like him, like his side of the family. The doctor who delivered you would have noticed it. The private detective I hired found you because he showed around a picture of Kingsley, asking if anyone had seen that man. Someone thought he was *you*. That's not a coincidence."

That silence again. The longest, coldest silence.

Then, Nico spoke.

"My mother went into labor early with me. Too early," he said. "It had snowed that day, thirty-six centimeters. A record. It almost never snows here. We have no plows. My father—my *real* father—couldn't get the car out of the garage, and the ambulance couldn't get to the house. He *carried* her, half a kilometer down the driveway to meet the ambulance on the road. He hadn't stepped in a Catholic Church since he was a little boy, but he prayed that day. He prayed out loud to Saint Nicolas. My mother said she'd never heard him pray out loud before. She didn't even know he prayed at all. He prayed to Saint Nicolas because he said that was the only saint he remembered. The doctors helped her, saved me... I was born six weeks later, healthy, because of him. *That* was my father. This man..." He picked up the photographs only to toss them carelessly aside. "He's nothing to me. Nothing. *Rien.*"

And that was it. Nico walked out of the dining room just as their food came out of the kitchen.

By 8:14 P.M. she was back in her suite. Zach looked up, surprised, as she walked into the room.

"Well?" he asked.

"That," she said, "could have gone better."

CHAPTER EIGHT

THEY WENT to bed early that night. Zach read a novel and she lay on his chest thinking, thinking...doing too much thinking, until he closed his book and set it on the nightstand.

"You can't be surprised," he said. At her request, they hadn't talked about Nico and his reaction.

"No, I'm not surprised."

"You have to give the man some time."

"I thought he'd have questions. You'd think he'd want to know *something* about Kingsley."

"He will. Eventually."

Nora snuggled closer, trying to absorb as much of Zach's warmth as she could. She'd felt cold all evening like she was getting ill. It was the guilt weighing on her.

"He doesn't even know he has a baby sister yet."

"You blew his world apart tonight. You did it to me, once. Eventually I thanked you for it. He will, too. Someday."

"From your lips to God's ears," she said and kissed

Zach's lips. She rolled onto her side and he rolled against her, holding her until she fell asleep.

She woke abruptly at the jarring blast of a telephone. A real telephone. The kind with wires and a bell that ripped both her and Zach from their dreams. Nora fumbled for the black handset on the bedside table.

"Hello?" Her voice sounded confused and groggy, even to her own ears.

Heavy breathing. Then: "It's me."

"Nico..." She lay back on her pillow, hand on her forehead. According to the glowing numbers on the clock by the hotel phone, it was three in the morning. "Are you all right?"

"No."

"Where are you?"

"*Le Chien Noir*. It's across the street."

She'd seen the building from the hotel window. It was a bar. Not that she could judge him. That's how she might have handled the news as well.

"Stay there," she said. "I'll be right over."

He hung up and Nora put the phone back on its cradle.

"Nico?" Zach said.

"He's at a bar across the street."

"Ah, getting plastered—the final stage of grief."

"I thought that was acceptance."

"You accept the loss. Then you get drunk."

"I'm going to run over and talk to him, make sure he's okay."

"You want me to come—"

"It's fine. Go back to sleep." She started to get out of bed, but Zach grabbed her arm gently. With the curtains slightly parted, she could see the outline of him in the dark, the outline of the worry on his face.

"Be careful. You represent the man who may try to replace his father. He might lash out, try to hurt you, in order to hurt him."

"He won't hurt me."

"You don't know that. You don't know him."

She kissed Zach on the lips. "I know him."

Nora dressed quickly. She threw her hair into a loose knot at the nape of her neck. The cold barely touched her as she ran from the hotel to *Le Chien Noir* two doors down. She found Nico alone behind the bar, pouring a glass of wine for himself.

Nico saw her at the door, lifted his glass in a mocking toast.

"Nico? Are you all right?" she asked, approaching him cautiously. The bar was empty but for the two of them.

He shrugged, lazily, drunkenly. "I've been better." He smiled at her. Bad sign. He shouldn't be smiling.

"You own this place, too? A vineyard and a bar?"

"A friend owns it. She gave me a key."

"She? Girlfriend?"

"*Non.* Just a friend. Like your friend. Zach."

"I'm having sex with my friend Zach."

Nico's eyes widened. She wasn't sure why she'd said that so bluntly, so coldly, but her instincts were telling her to put some distance between them.

"Okay," he said. "Maybe not like your friend." He picked up the wine bottle and pulled the cork out again, poured more into his glass, filling it to the brim.

"You want something?" he asked. "What's your poison? Isn't that what they say in America?"

"Only in movies. And no, nothing for me," she said. One of them needed to stay in their right mind.

"Your loss." He tipped the glass back and took a long,

deep drink. His hand was unsteady, and a few red drops of wine sloshed out when he went to set it back down.

"Maybe you should call it a night. As it is, you look like you're headed for one hell of a hangover."

"You forget that I'm a vintner. I know all the secrets." He leaned close to her and whispered, "If I stay drunk forever, I'll never get a hangover."

"Or you could let me drive you home. How about we do that?"

He surprised her by crossing his arms on the bar top and dropping his head down onto it. It was the posture of a man who had given up. Nora couldn't stop herself from reaching out, putting her hand on his head, running her fingers through his hair. He had the softest hair she'd ever felt in her life.

"That feels good," he said. "Never stop."

Nora laughed softly. "Your accent gets thicker when you're drinking."

"I speak perfect English," he said.

"*Yez, pair-feect Englissss.*"

He raised his head, stared at her. She put her hands back in her lap, then decided she had better sit on them before she started playing with his hair again.

"I wish you weren't so beautiful," he said.

It was Nora's turn to shrug. "You and me both, buddy."

He laughed. She wanted him laughing. No man laughed with his friends in a bar and then walked away and threw himself off a cliff. She hoped.

"Why do you wish I wasn't so beautiful?"

"I want to hate you," he said. "It's very hard to hate a beautiful woman, especially one who knows exactly how to scratch your head."

"Even when she ruined your life?"

He made a sound, almost like a laugh. Almost. Not quite. "If my father dying didn't ruin my life..."

He didn't finish the thought, didn't have to. Nico picked up his glass of wine, looked into it like he was trying to scry his future, then set it down again without drinking any.

"I called my mother."

Nora wanted to ask what she had said, decided silence was a better tactic.

"I said, 'Do you know a man named Kingsley Boissonneault?' That's what I asked. And after, she was quiet for a long, long, *long* time. Then she said...uh, she said, 'I'll come tomorrow. We'll talk about it.' " He picked up his glass and this time he did drink from it. He put it down, looked at Nora. "So I guess that's that. He's my...ah." He couldn't even say it. "I remember once...I think I was six? My parents were fighting, the only way they ever fought." Nico lowered his voice. "Very quietly. All in whispers. Kids, they don't listen so much when parents scream, but they listen real good when parents start to whisper in another room."

Nora knew that was true.

"I was coming down the stairs. I heard them whispering. I sat there on the bottom step outside the kitchen and listened. My mother, she said, 'He's old enough to know. If he finds out, and we haven't told him, he'll hate us.' And my father, he said..."

Nico blinked. His eyes were red but there were no tears.

"He said that he wouldn't let anyone come and take his son away from him," Nico said. "I had, uh...I forget the English word. *Des cauchemars.* Bad dreams? Scary dreams?"

"Nightmares," Nora said.

"That's it. I had nightmares for a year after that of a man busting into the house and taking me from my father."

"Oh, Nico," Nora said softly. "Your parents must have known you were having nightmares, didn't they?"

"I said I was dreaming that a monster came to get me." He took a long breath. "My father would stay with me until I fell asleep again. He would tell me over and over again, 'No one is going to take you away from me. No one in *tout le monde.*'" All the world.

Nora opened her mouth to apologize again, knew it would be wasted words.

"Maybe," he said, "I think I always knew? I didn't want to know. And now I know."

SO THERE IT WAS. Nora took the first full breath she'd taken since finding out herself. She hadn't even realized how tense the not-knowing had made her until now. And now that she knew for certain, her entire body went limp. She put her head down onto the bar and this time, Nico stroked *her* hair. She hoped he was doing it to mock her for doing it to him earlier. That was the only good reason he should touch her like that right now. Just in case that wasn't the reason, Nora lifted her head, sat up, sat back.

"Do you want to know about him?" Nora asked. "You must have questions."

"No. No questions."

"None? Don't you want to know if you have siblings or what he does for a living or where he lives or what he's like?"

"Nothing. Don't tell me anything."

"Nico—"

"You said at the hotel you hadn't told him about me, either. Will you tell him now?"

"I have to."

"You don't."

"I was supposed to go to jail when I was fifteen. He kept me out. You can't imagine what kind of a debt I owe him."

"You don't owe him *me*." He pointed at himself.

"No, but I owe him the truth." This was not a conversation they should be having while Nico was drunk.

"Let me take you home," she said. "Please? We can talk about this tomorrow."

"My mother is coming tomorrow. To talk to me about... all this." He ran his hand through his hair, tried to tug on it and couldn't. "I forgot I cut my hair." He laughed again.

"You're shit-faced. I mean, *merde*-faced. I'm taking you home, right now. My car or yours?"

"My car is a stick. And it's not so easy to drive."

"I can drive a stick. I can drive anything."

He dug his hand into his jeans pocket and pulled out his keys. He held them out and she reached for them, but he closed his hand around them at the last second.

"Nico."

"Are you in love with him?"

"What? Who? Zach?"

"Not him. *Him*. Kingsley Boissonneault." He didn't say the name so much as sneer it. Poor Nico was nowhere near the "acceptance" stage of grief.

Nora's first instinct was to simply say no, of course she wasn't. That was a fact. She'd never been in love with Kingsley. Lust, yes. Who wouldn't be? But this question was loaded, dangerous.

"Why do you ask?"

"I don't know. You won't tell me?"

"*You* won't tell *me* why you're asking."

"I told you, I don't know why I'm asking. Maybe it's the

only reason I can think of that you would do this to me. Because you are in love with him."

"Are you a virgin?" Nora asked.

Nico was shocked into laughing. "What? No."

"Straight? Gay?"

"Only women, *s'il vous plaît*."

"So you've had sex with women. Sex with women can lead to pregnancy. If you had a child out there you didn't know about...wouldn't you want to know?"

"Of course. But—"

"If you had a friend who knew about this child of yours, and she didn't tell you, she kept that child a secret from you for years, would you be angry at her when you found out? Would you feel betrayed? Would you ever be able to forgive her for keeping your child a secret from you? Especially if you'd saved this woman's life?"

Nora watched as Nico momentarily sobered, as her questions stuck into him like sharp arrows. Slowly he opened his hands, gave her his keys.

"Take me home, please," he said. "*Merci.*"

CHAPTER NINE

NICO DROVE AN ANTIQUATED RANGE ROVER. And it was a stick shift and it was tricky—which made driving it *so* much fun.

"You're good," Nico said from the passenger seat as she shifted gears with the ease of a seasoned race car driver.

"I've had a little practice," she said. The Range Rover was so old, Nico had rigged up a CD player with wires running into the radio/tape deck. She heard the sound of a guitar, lonesome and haunting, playing softly through the speakers and although it was familiar, she couldn't place it. "What are we listening to?"

" 'Coming Back to Life,' Pink Floyd," Nico said.

Briefly, Nora tuned into the lyrics, heard an aching male voice asking, *Where were you* over and over.

Maybe Nico had been thinking of Kingsley while listening to this song. Where was King when Nico was hurt? When he was helpless? Where was King when Nico was growing up? He had no idea that he even had an adult son, much less one who was suffering right now.

"It's beautiful," Nora said. "I wouldn't have figured you for a Pink Floyd fan. They're not very French. And you're way too young. They were around before I was born."

"Ah, had a girlfriend in California. She turned me into a fan."

"Was she older than you?"

"A little," he said. "When do you leave?"

"Tomorrow. Back to Paris, then to London to drop off Zach, then home to New York."

"Have you seen the sea yet?"

"This isn't a sight-seeing trip," she said as she came to a fork in the road.

"Go south," he said. "Left."

"Home is north. Remember?"

"I want you to see the sea."

"It's freezing out."

"It's worth it. Please?"

She would have said no but for the *please*. She heard the woundedness in his words, the vulnerability. He was a child now, again, a scared little boy sitting at the bottom of the stairs, hearing his parents fight in whispers and being afraid for a year after that some strange man was going to come and steal him away from the only father he knew, the only father he wanted.

She turned left.

Nico stared out the window as she drove. He rubbed at his eyes as if battling tears. She reached over and put her hand on his, squeezed it.

"Don't say you're sorry again," he said softly. "If you were really sorry, you wouldn't have come here."

"I'm not sorry for coming here. I'm only sorry for hurting you so much."

"I'm not sorry," he said.

"What do you mean?"

"I don't know." He turned his head, looked at her as she drove, looked at her like...like he shouldn't be looking at her. She blamed the wine. "But I'm not sorry."

She remembered Zach's words about Nico hurting her to hurt King. She let go of his hand.

They said nothing else until Nico had to give her directions to the little beach. A private beach, he said, owned by a friend of his father's. Most of the waterfront in this area was either private land or protected parkland. That's why they had so few tourists, why Mozet was so insular and small.

As they neared the sea, which was more of a bay than the sea itself, the clouds thinned and parted. When Nora parked the car on a rocky little lot by a wooden fence, the moon was out high and clear, surrounded by a hazy winter aura.

They got out of the car and Nico led the way. The crisp night air seemed to sober him. He walked on almost-steady feet to the wooden stairway that led down the small cliff to the pebble beach below. He didn't go all the way down, only to the first landing. Nora joined him at the railing, leaning forward to study the moon on the water, their elbows resting on the top rail, nearly touching.

She heard the water lapping gently against the beach, the thrum of a not-too-far-away boat passing, the cry of a seabird who didn't mind the cold. The moon was full and so bright that she could see the beginning of the five o'clock shadow on Nico's cheeks.

"You're right. This was worth the trip," she said. The air was warmer here by the water.

"We came here in the summertime. Every Sunday. My mother's day off from being a mother—she'd spend it in Marseille, and my father would bring me here."

"So it was just you two, alone?"

"And some friends. My friends loved my father. Everybody loved my father." Nico lowered his head, chin to his chest. "Ah...*merde*."

Nora picked up the end of her scarf and used it, playfully, to wipe the tears from his face. "Maybe you should keep this," she said, draping it around his neck.

"I will keep it." He looped it twice around his neck. "*Merci*."

"*De rien*," she said and smiled. A heavy silence weighed the air down around them. Quickly, Nora turned away, pretended to stare out at the water again.

"I bet it's even more beautiful here in summer."

"It is. My father loved summer. Hated winter. He felt it too much, in his joints. And this part of winter he hated the most, when the nights are so long and the days so short. He, uh...there's this saying. Do you know? '*Au milieu de l'hiver, j'apprenais elfin qu'il y avast en moi un été invincible.*'"

She'd thought his lightly-accented English was lovely. It was nothing compared to hearing him speak French.

"*In the midst of winter*," she translated, "*I found there was within me an invincible summer*. Camus."

"Very good," he said.

"It's on t-shirts and bookmarks in America."

He smiled. "My father said that quote was about wine. He thought everything was about wine. He said wine was invented for the last days of December, because that's when you needed summer the most. And wine was 'summer in a bottle.' I made a joke, uh...four or five years ago, said we should sell December Wine, wines made to be drunk only in winter. Wines that tasted like an 'invincible summer.' So he planted some new type of grape, a sweeter variety. He was going to call it '*Été Invincible.*' It's still in the barrels in the cuverie, aging. We were supposed to taste it together this week. The first of our December Wine."

"You should drink it. Make a toast to him. And then pour a little for him, in his memory."

"Maybe I will. I think I need it. If I have a summer inside me, it's not the invincible kind. It's gone."

Nora didn't know what to say in the presence of a grief so deep. Instead of saying anything, she took off her gloves and took his cold hand into hers and chafed it until it warmed.

"You can have some of my summer," she said. "Until you find your own again."

She felt his eyes on her as she warmed both of his hands in her own.

"Better?" she asked. He nodded. "Good. I'll take you home."

Back in his Rover, they didn't speak. She remembered the way to the vineyard from her trip there earlier in the day. When they reached the main gates, he told her to stop there. He would walk the rest of the way.

"Are you sure? If you tell me where your house is, I can drive you to the door."

"Better if you don't."

"It's pretty cold, Nico." She was hovering again, being protective again.

"It's fine. It's better if I just...I just go now."

Nora stared at him, studied him. He said so little but every word seemed weighted down with meaning. But what was the meaning? They were both speaking English but it still seemed like he was trying to tell her something she simply couldn't hear.

"Goodnight, then. I'll leave your car at *Le Chien Noir*."

"I won't see you again before you leave."

"No. You said your mother is going to be here tomorrow. I think you should talk to her before we talk again."

He took that well, didn't argue. He put his hand on the door latch to open it, but didn't. "You're going to tell him about me?"

Nora exhaled heavily. "I have to."

"Even if I ask you not to, you will do it anyway?"

Nora sighed. She grabbed her handbag and dug out a large sealed envelope. "Will you take this? Please? You don't have to open it now, or ever. But it's got his address in it, some pictures. You have a sister," Nora said. "There's a photograph of her and her mother. My contact information is in there, too, if you have any questions, and you're not ready to talk to him."

"I'll never be ready for that."

"I will tell him your father just died, and you aren't ready to talk or meet or anything. I can do that. But I can't promise he won't contact you anyway. If you only knew—"

"What?" Nico looked at her. The 'what' wasn't a challenge but a real question, the first one he'd asked about Kingsley. If only he knew *what*?

"The second he finds out about you, he will love you with all his heart," she said. "You will have a guardian angel who will swoop in at the first word of your first prayer to him. When you need five Euros, he'll give you five thousand. When you need to talk to him on the phone, he'll fly over to talk face to face. If you're in the mood to hear a violin concerto, he'll rent out Carnegie Hall and hire a symphony orchestra to play your favorite pieces for you. If you want a snack, he'll serve you a feast. And if anyone ever so much as hurts a single hair on your head, he will bring down the hammer of God on them so hard your enemies will never so much as breathe in your presence again. If you had any idea... Nico, if you knew how shitty fathers could be—trust me, I know all about shitty fathers—you would realize you won the father lottery. Twice. If you knew how lucky you are to be the son of my King...you'd already be on a plane to New York. You would have been on it yesterday." She shook her head. "I would kill to have had either of your fathers."

Nico took a heavy breath.

"Tell him whatever you want. You will anyway."

With that, he got out of the car and walked away. No goodbye. At least he took the envelope with him.

This time when he walked away, she didn't see Kingsley in him. She saw only Nico and she knew she would never see Kingsley when she looked at him again.

SHE DROVE BACK to the hotel, thinking the whole time about Søren. She wanted to talk to him so badly, if only to hear his voice. But even if she knew where he was, knew how to reach him, she knew she wouldn't last one minute without telling him about Nico. Instead, she simply pictured him in her mind. If he'd gone to Father Ballard, he'd be wearing his cassock. And knowing what little she knew about Father Ballard, Søren was probably on his knees right now in some medieval-looking chapel, saying a few thousand Hail Marys, a few thousand Our Fathers. He'd say them, maybe, smiling the whole time behind his prayer-clasped hands while thinking about Fionn.

His son. Søren had a son.

And so did Kingsley.

It had to mean something, didn't it? That this was happening for all of them at once? A son for King. A son for Søren. But what about Nora?

Silly thought. Stupid thought. She didn't want children. She had everything and everyone she needed in her life, didn't she? Of course she did. No one was missing. Nothing was missing. She had everything.

Except she sort of wished, just a little, only a little, that Nico was still in the car with her. But only so they could talk some more, so she could convince him of what he would be missing without Kingsley in his life. No other reason.

The person she really needed to talk to was Søren. That's why she was feeling an emptiness inside her, a space needing to be filled. Surely that was the only reason.

"I miss you, my priest." She whispered those words to the night sky and prayed God would carry her words to Søren's heart, wherever he was.

When she got back to the hotel, it was four in the morning. In the dark, she stripped down to her underwear and got back into bed with Zach's warm body. He stirred and pulled her to him.

"Well?" he said, only half-awake.

"He doesn't want me to tell Kingsley about him."

"What will you do?"

"Tell Kingsley about him."

Zach didn't say anything but she sensed he wanted to.

"Does that make me a terrible person?" she asked.

Zach chuckled, kissed the top of her head. "No. Of all the things that make you a terrible person, that's not one of them."

Playfully, or not-so-playfully, she swatted his leg.

"You're between a rock and a hard place," he said. "Neither choice is a good one. And whatever you do, I know you'll do it with your heart in the right place."

She wanted to believe him, prayed Nico would understand one day, but she wasn't sure he would.

"I never told you this before," Nora said. "I was pregnant once."

He sat up in bed, and even in the dark she could see the shock in his eyes, the surprise on his face.

"It was King's," she said. "Søren was off getting his Ph.D. His second Ph.D."

"What happened? I suppose I can guess."

"It was early enough I could take the pills. So that's what I did. It was the right thing for me, and I don't regret it. The thing is...the thing that's always stayed with me, is knowing how much Kingsley wanted kids. Not with me, but still... Anyway, he didn't try to talk me into keeping it. He let me decide. And I can't tell you how grateful I am to this day for that. It was probably one of the harder things he ever did in his life. I can't help but think that maybe I was the one God picked to find out about Nico so I could, you know...make it up to him. Give him a son after all."

Zach took her hand, lifted it, and kissed it. "You are an unusual woman, Nora Sutherlin."

"You just figuring that out now?"

"I've had my suspicions." He lay back down again, pulled her to him.

"Let's leave tomorrow morning," she said. "One more night in Paris. One more day. Before I have to give you back."

"All right. One more night. Wonder what we'll find to do."

Nora kissed the center of his chest before laying her head on that kiss. "I have a few ideas."

Zach had a few ideas of his own. He rolled her onto her back, and told her exactly what they were.

He always had such good ideas.

CHAPTER TEN

PARIS, FRANCE

THE RETURN to Paris was long and uneventful. Melancholy winter sky. Desultory drizzle. Sporadic conversation. They made it to Paris in time for either a very late lunch or a very early supper. As Zach was studying the wine list, he smiled.

"They serve two vintages from *Le Vignoble Delacroix* here," he said. "Something called *Rosanella* and another called *Libellule*. Shall we order a glass? We never did try his wine."

"No, thanks," Nora said. "You can order it if you like. It's a little too early for wine."

A lie. It was never too early for wine in Nora's opinion. She wanted to try Nico's wine, but not here, with Zach. With Nico, next time she saw him.

If she saw him again.

They left the restaurant and walked back to their hotel. With New Year's Eve a day away, Paris was bustling with tourists. Nora clung to Zach's hand so they wouldn't be jostled apart by the crowds. They'd be parting ways again soon, tomorrow, and Nora knew this wasn't only their last night together on this little quest of theirs, but their very last night together. Forever. Zach had a child now, a family to think of. For him, this was one last fling, a final settling of accounts, putting old feelings to bed for good, tucking them in, and letting them sleep forever.

It was for her, too, wasn't it? One last little fling before she moved to New Orleans and her life settled down again? No more crazy love affairs. No more flings. No more wild nights with ex-Navy Seals, male escorts, and pretty boys from Kentucky. No more men—other than Søren, of course. No more trouble. She was done with all that nonsense.

Right?

They were in the same hotel as before, but in a different room. This one was wrapped in red and white decor like a candy cane. Nora pulled back the covers on the bed and discovered that even the sheets were red.

"Ah, it's my color," she said, collapsing onto her back.

Zach loomed over the bed, arms crossed over his chest.

"You're looking at me like you're thinking about fucking me," she said. "Or am I projecting?"

"I was thinking, 'If she's going to lay on the bed, she really should take her shoes off.' "

"If I take my shoes off, will you fuck me again?"

"Probably. Probably even if you don't."

"Are you going to fuck my ass? Again? For the..." Nora paused to count on her fingers. "For the fifth time this week?"

"I had something else in mind, if you're open to suggestions."

Nora lifted her legs and spread them wide. "I'm open."

With a laugh, Zach kicked his shoes off, then crawled

onto the bed, holding himself over her. "You said I gave you the best anal of your life, yes?"

"I did," Nora said, nodding. "I not only said it, I put it in writing. For posterity."

"Did I ever tell you that no woman in the whole wide world has ever sucked my cock as well as you have?"

"You did mention it, yes."

"I'm mentioning it again."

"Should I get the whiskey?"

"No. Let's do this one mostly sober."

"Handcuffs?"

He smiled and shook his head. He stroked her cheek with the back of his fingers. "I'd like to be able to touch you this time."

It always happened so fast with them, the way they could go from joking and flirting, everything light as air, to falling all over each other. It was Zach's fault, really—the way he would say something out of the blue that made her remember why she still thought about him a little too much sometimes.

She wasn't fooling herself, though. She didn't have any ambition to steal him from Grace and run away with him. More like she knew that in another world, another place and time, they could have been very, very good together.

Funny thing was, she thought the same thing about Søren and Grace. Not that she would ever tell either of them that.

"Would you be so kind," Nora said, "to lay on your back and get comfortable?"

Zach was so kind. He did lay on his back, but only after giving her a kiss, a long and deep one that felt a little too much like goodbye for her taste. Not that she mentioned anything. It wasn't time to say goodbye yet. Tomorrow. Until then...

Nora straddled Zach at his waist. She leaned over and played as if she'd kiss him, but when Zach lifted his head to meet her lips, she pulled back.

He narrowed his ice-blue eyes at her. "Nora."

"Just reminding you who's really in charge here."

"Well, *Mistress* Nora...what are you orders? I'll do whatever you command of me." Simple words but heady when mixed with a posh English accent.

"I order you to lie there and enjoy every second while I suck your cock until you come in my mouth and I swallow it."

"Demanding minx. If you insist. Mistress."

She kissed him this time, rewarding him for addressing her as "Mistress" without any sarcasm. It didn't take much to get on Nora's good side—all she ever wanted was a little abject devotion and total erotic surrender. The simple things in life.

Zach's erotic surrender took the form of lying on the pillow, hands clasped behind his head. The very picture of male satisfaction and contentment. Nora lifted the bottom of his long-sleeve t-shirt to unveil his lovely hard stomach. She scored his skin with her fingernails, delighting in watching the sculpted muscles twitch as she gave him pleasure spiked with pain. Scratching...rubbing...caressing...kissing... She bent to kiss and lick his stomach, going lower with every lick, every kiss, until she reached the waistband of his jeans.

"I really ought to tease you some more, make you wait for it," she said, "but that means I'd have to wait for it, and I hate waiting for it."

"We wouldn't want that, Mistress."

"You keep calling me 'Mistress' and I might not let you go home again."

"I know one or two people who might object to that," he said. But then added, because he was in a mood, "Mistress."

Nora shook her head and unzipped his jeans. She grabbed the waistband and tugged them down below his hips. Cock wasn't enough for her. She had to have hips, too. Especially Zach's absolutely delectable, delicious, bitable hips. So bitable she bit them, one by one, digging her teeth into the skin, making sure she nipped the bone a little, too.

"Such a strange sensation," he said, exhaling hard. "I can't tell if I like it or not. All I know is I'm glad you did it."

"Then I'll do it again."

And she did. Then she swirled her tongue over each of his lovely stark hip bones. She did adore those male divots where the hip met the stomach. She kissed a path across his lower abdomen. His cock was red and hard, straining, eagerly awaiting her mouth. She took it in her hand as she was licking his stomach, and stroked it slowly, happy to see his eyes flutter and close, his chin lift, his lips part. She stroked him more until she was certain he was completely lost in the pleasure of being touched, and only when he started breathing harder did she suddenly, without warning, bring her mouth down onto him. He inhaled so sharply she laughed with his cock in her mouth—which made him breathe even harder.

Zach's face was usually composed into a mask of detached amusement, but not now. Now he was a lost man, losing himself more and more the longer and harder she sucked on him. But she needed to concentrate, so she tore her gaze from his face and went to work.

God bless him, Zach was an easy man to please. Nothing fancy, nothing difficult. No sticking her finger up his ass while her other hand played with his balls, all while she was sucking his cock, not like some men she could name, but wouldn't (Kingsley).

All she had to do with Zach was suck and lick, then suck harder and lick harder, move her mouth up and down him, down and up him, over and over and over again until he came. If he thought she was particularly adept at it, that was because he was rewarding her points for enthusiasm. She loved his cock—the shape of it, the girth that fit her mouth so well. Sucking it was a pleasure, so much so that she was almost sad to hear him nearing climax. His breaths grew ragged and he grunted softly, giving low little moans— sounds sweeter than any music. His hands reached down, sought her shoulders... He found her hair and ran his fingers through it, found her cheek and stroked it, cupped the back of her neck and held it. She took the hint and went as deep as she could, taking him fully into her mouth until he nudged the back of her throat. She wrapped her fingers around the base of his erection, worked it and sucked him at the same time.

When Zach came, it was more of an explosion than orgasm. His shoulders came all the way off the bed and he spurted hard, deep into her throat, his hand holding her neck forcefully, not hard enough to bruise but close. Nora drank him in, the thick salty fluid, swallowing every drop. She only stopped swallowing when he collapsed onto his back, playing dead.

She wiped her mouth with the back of her hand, while Zach watched her through hooded eyes.

"You're going to miss me, aren't you?" she asked him.

He reached up, grabbed her sweater, tugged it off.

"I already do," he said.

AFTER THEY MADE LOVE, Nora took a shower. When she turned off the water, she heard Zach's voice in the hotel's sitting room. He was laughing at something, laughing hard.

"Zach? You all right?" she called out.

He didn't answer. She put on the hotel bathrobe and went to find him. He lay on the sitting room sofa, phone to his ear. When he saw her, he waved her over. Nora sat on the sofa and rested her head by his chest.

"You have to hear this," he whispered. He hit the button for speakerphone.

Nora listened. Then she heard something like the peep of a bird. Then a second later, another one.

"He has the hiccups," Zach said. "First hiccups."

Hic. Nora laughed in delighted surprise.

"Fionn," Nora said to the phone. "Hold your breath and count to ten."

"That never works," Zach said. "Grace will have to pull his earlobes."

"I have to pull his what?" Grace asked, her lilting Welsh accent filling the room.

"It works," Zach said. "Pull his earlobes."

"They're tiny. I'll pull them off. Wait. He's stopped."

"You scared them out of him by talking about pulling off his earlobes," Nora said.

"I cured Zachary's hiccups once by telling him someone named Jon-Franz-something-or-other called looking for him, but I'd forgotten to get his number." Grace giggled.

"You're lucky I didn't throw you in the Thames for that."

Grace said, "I can swim." A pause, then, "Shall I ask

how the trip is going, or would that make me a glutton for punishment?"

"Not great," Nora said. "I know Zach told you about our 'mission.' "

"Sounds like it didn't go as planned."

Nora gave Grace the lowdown on Nico, how he reacted to the news, the drunken phone call, asking her not to tell Kingsley about him. She left out the part where Nico, drunk and suffering, had said something about her being too beautiful. That was private, between her and Nico. Plus, she knew it was, as he had said, the wine talking. The wine and the grief. And probably the anger, too. Zach had said he might try to take his anger at Kingsley out on her. What better way to insult Kingsley than by sleeping with one of his lovers? Sons had been getting revenge on their fathers by seducing their stepmothers since time immemorial. Freud had been onto something.

Good thing it had been Nora on this mission. If Nico had tried that with Juliette, she would have run him over with the Range Rover, backed up, and done it again.

"I can't say I'm too surprised," Grace said. "Wonder if we'll be going through this again in ten or fifteen years."

"Hope not," Nora said. "Once is enough for me."

"I better get this little lad off to bed," Grace said. "You two behave. Or not. The Lord knows I have no right to tell anyone to behave."

Nora left Zach alone to give his love and goodbyes to Grace and Fionn. She went back into the bedroom. When Zach came in, she looked up from the bed.

"Kingsley never got to hear Nico hiccup," she said. "Or see him take his first steps. Hear his first word. Teach him to swim. Take a bath with him and get pissed on in the face."

And more. There was more she thought about but

couldn't say out loud. In the lamplight, she looked up at him, stricken. He pulled her head to his shoulder.

She sobbed, hard, deep, and long. She'd thought she'd run out of tears after the first time she'd held Fionn, but those were only the first waves as the hurricane built. And here came the storm.

"You can say it," Zach whispered against her hair. "It won't hurt me."

"Søren didn't get to hear his hiccups. Søren won't see his first steps and won't hear his first words. He won't teach him to swim or how to play piano." Her voice broke on "piano" and after that she couldn't talk anymore, her lungs were heaving too hard. Zach rubbed her back, kissed her head and let her cry for a few minutes.

"You're going to make yourself ill if you keep crying this hard. Please don't vomit in the five-star hotel," Zach teased.

She laughed and it hurt almost as much to laugh as it had to cry. Slowly she sat up and swiped hard at her face.

"Stupid man. Not you," she said to Zach's look. "Søren. Has he not figured out yet that I *know* him? That I know he will be in pain every day because of this."

"Because he can't have Fionn?"

Nora nodded. "And when he hurts, I hurt. But I wouldn't change it for all the money in the world. Why? It doesn't make sense. It doesn't make any sense. Maybe I'm the stupid one"

Miserable and exhausted, Nora lay her head on Zach's lap as he stroked her hair. "What am I going to do? About Nico? And King? And Fionn and Søren and you and Grace and us and the...the world? Any ideas?"

Zach laughed, still stroking her hair. "I have one."

"What is it? I'll take it."

"If we hurried, we could make the very last train from

Paris to London. We could be home by midnight. You could spend a little time with Fionn."

"Will *he* tell me what I should do?"

"If he takes after Søren, he probably *will* tell you what to do."

As soon as Zach suggested it, that they could go to London right then, Nora knew that was exactly what she needed—to hold Søren's son in her arms again.

Nora dressed while Zach took a quick shower. They packed quickly because they'd barely unpacked at all. When they dropped their key off at the desk, Nora said, "Sorry. We only needed it for an hour."

CHAPTER ELEVEN

LONDON, ENGLAND

THEY MADE it to Zach's house three minutes after midnight. He and his family lived in a two-story townhome on a street in London with not one but two antiquarian bookshops. This, she surmised, was not a coincidence.

"You did warn your wife you were bringing the woman whose ass you've been hitting all week back to your house tonight, didn't you?" Nora asked, noticing the house was completely dark.

"Sent her a text," Zach said, fumbling with his keys on the steps. "She didn't reply, which means she's already asleep."

"I'd hate to wake her up."

"I wouldn't," Zach said, grinning. "She's been alone with a baby for days. She'll weep with joy just to hear full sentences again."

In the entryway, he hung up their coats and switched on the light in the front room. Baby toys on the coffee table. Baby books on the floor.

"Home sweet home," Zach said. He kept his voice low as they went through the house and up the stairs. He peered into a half-open doorway. "Dead to the world," he whispered to Nora.

"Fionn?"

"Grace."

He took her one more door down, to Fionn's nursery. A lamp in the shape of a yellow hot air balloon sat on the dresser, filling the room with tender light and heavy shadows. Zach went straight to the crib, leaned over and whispered, "There's my boy. Come here, lad." Nora watched, her chest tight and her stomach in knots, as Zach carefully lifted Fionn and wrapped a striped blue and white blanket loosely around him.

Nora didn't even realize she was moving her feet until she was there, by Zach, her hand resting lightly on the back of Fionn's tiny blond head. His hair was like pure silk, spun from pale gold. Her eyes filled with tears as Zach dropped kisses on his son's sleeping forehead. Fionn's head was turned to Zach's chest so Nora couldn't see his face.

"Feel better yet?" he asked.

"Getting there."

"Here. Take him. When you have a sleeping baby in your arms, all's right with the world."

"I don't know about—"

Gently, but with the confidence of a natural father, Zach passed Fionn to Nora. She winced as Fionn's slight weight—Nora's handbag weighed more the child—settled into her arms. Zach made it look so easy, like a holding a baby was as simple as snuggling a stuffed animal. But Fionn wriggled in her arms and his weight was uneven and his head seemed too big for his fragile little neck and—

"You better take him back—"

"Relax. It's fine," Zach said. "Sit in the rocking chair. That'll make it easier."

"What if I drop him?"

"We have carpeting."

"Zach."

"Babies bounce. And you won't drop him. Sit."

He pointed at the white rocking chair. Normally she was a fairly graceful woman but she suddenly found she didn't know how to hold something and sit down at the same time.

"Zach. Help."

She stared at him, pleading with her eyes.

"Fine." He took Fionn back but only so Nora could sit. Then he wrapped the blanket more tightly around Fionn, swaddling him, and returned him to her arms.

"Better now?" he asked.

Nora stared down at Fionn's sleeping face. She whispered, "Better."

"You two talk," he said. "I'm going to go and kiss my wife awake."

"What? No. You can't leave me alone with him."

Zach looked at her with suspicion. "Why not?"

"I don't know what I'm doing."

"No one does."

"What if he gets hungry? Has he been fed and...I don't know, watered?"

"Watered? He's a baby, not a houseplant."

"What part of 'I don't know what I'm doing' did you not understand?"

"You're doing fine." He bent over and kissed her on the head, then kissed Fionn. "I'll be back soon."

Fionn blinked, yawned, and for a split second his blue eyes opened before closing again.

"Not too soon," Nora said.

"I knew this was what you needed."

She pushed her foot on the floor to set the rocker rocking. "This is what I needed."

He smiled, started to leave. She stopped him at the door by whispering his name. He turned.

"Thank you," she said. "For all your help."

"My pleasure. Literally." He wagged his eyebrows. Then he looked over his shoulder. "Whew. Still asleep."

Nora laughed silently, hoping the movement of her chest wouldn't wake Fionn again. Fionn. Zach's son. Søren's son.

"What will we do when it's his turn?" she asked. "When he figures it out. What do we do then?"

Zach shrugged. "We'll play it by ear."

"Yeah, but whose ear?"

He nodded toward Fionn. "His."

Zach left and Nora was alone with the baby in her arms.

She kept the rocker in motion and soon Fionn's small weight felt so natural in her arms that she knew when she put him down again, she'd feel like she was missing something.

"You won the father lottery twice, too," she said to the sleeping blond boy. "You don't even know it yet. But you'll find out. You've met Zach, but you haven't met Søren yet. I think you'll like him. He's...unusual. He's very serious a lot of the time, but don't you be intimidated by him. It might be a very long time before you get to meet him. His situation is a little bit complicated." She paused. "That's an understatement. You're English, so you'll learn all about understatement. Your father—your other father, I mean—he's actually not supposed to have children." She winced. Fionn had opened his eyes again at the sound of her voice. He almost seemed to be listening. "Søren sort of broke a big rule bringing you into the world. But rules like that were made to be broken, weren't they? So don't feel bad or anything if you don't get to meet him for a while. It doesn't mean he doesn't love you. I can tell you this for a fact, little man— right now, wherever he is, whatever he's doing...he loves you. He loves you so much. In fact, he loves you so much that if you decide someday that you don't want him in your life at all, he'll honor that. Your happiness matters more to him than his own, that's how much he..." She kissed his head, smelled his hair—lavender—and patted his bottom through the blanket. "That's how much he loves you. And how much I love you."

She cradled Fionn closer to her chest so that his head lay in the crook of her neck. That's where he fell back asleep, listening to the sound of her heart beating, and soon the only two sounds in the room were his tiny even breaths and the slight squeak of the rocker treads on the floor.

Zach came back an hour later and took Fionn from her arms to put him back in his crib. "Stay the night?" he asked.

She knew that would be pushing it. "I booked a hotel."

He walked her to the door. Her cab was waiting at the curb.

"Thanks for a great week," she said.

"Let's do it again sometime."

"I better not kiss you goodbye."

"Better not." He leaned against the doorframe, arms crossed over his chest.

"Well," she said. "Happy New Year."

"Happy New Year."

She didn't kiss him, but she did hug him, and he hugged her close to him, a little longer than he probably should have. Nora pulled away and started to go.

"Sent you a little something in your email," Zach said. "Check it later. Cab's waiting."

Nora could only blow him one last kiss and walk away.

As the driver wove through the streets of Mayfair, Nora looked at her phone. She had one email from Zach, with the subject line "For you and Søren."

She was certain it was photos of Fionn...but she was wrong. It was a sound file. She opened it and held the phone to her ear.

Fionn...hiccupping.

Two hot tears ran down Nora's cheeks. She closed the email and made the call she needed to make before she changed her mind.

Nico answered after the second ring.

"I'm sorry to call so late," she said. "I, uh...didn't want to wait."

"I was awake. Are you okay? Are you crying?"

"I am, but for unrelated reasons."

"I don't want you to cry."

"I'll stop, I promise." She'd ruined Nico's young life and here he was, more worried about her than his own problems. "Listen, I called to tell you...if you don't want me to, I won't say anything to Kingsley about you. I'll keep you a secret."

"You will?"

"Yes." She nodded, even though she was on the phone and he couldn't see her.

"Why?"

"I realized something tonight. Whether you like it or not, Kingsley is your biological father. And whether he knows it or not, you're his son. And I know if Kingsley knew about you, he would tell me to do what *you* wanted, not what he wants. To do what's best for *you*, not what's best for him. So if you don't want him to know about you, then... that's okay. If King ever finds out about you, finds out I knew, I'll tell him I was just doing what was best for you, and he'll understand."

"I thought you were loyal to him."

"He would want me to be loyal to you."

Silence. A long silence.

"You don't have to decide anything now," she said. "I just wanted to tell you that. So...*au revoir*."

"*Au revoir*," he said. "For now."

He hung up and Nora stared at the phone for a long, long time.

WHEN SHE RETURNED to the States, Nora went straight to her house in Westport. She used their upcoming move to New Orleans as an excuse not to go into the city. She had to pack, of course. Packing her books alone would take a solid month, she'd told Juliette, who Nora could tell was only pretending to buy her excuses. Nora even skipped Kingsley's annual New Year's Eve party. Thank God Søren was still at whatever monastery he'd run off to. She missed him so much she had chest pains when she thought of him, but in a way she was grateful Søren wasn't around right now. The weight of the secret she held was so heavy, she didn't know if she was going to be strong enough to carry it alone. If he asked her what was wrong, if he asked her one more time why she'd gone to France...she might tell him. And she had promised Nico she wouldn't.

Then the mail came, the day after New Year's. Airmail from France. Overnighted.

Nora sat on the floor of her office amid the towers of

boxes. With shaking hands, she opened the envelope. The letter was written in cramped but neat handwriting.

> *Nora,*
> *Call me, please.*
> *Nico*

Her entire body shook as she fumbled to find her phone and called Nico's number. She didn't even bother checking if it was the middle of the night in France. He answered after two rings.

"You didn't have to send a letter," she said. "You could have called."

"I like letters. When you get a letter, you have something you can hold and keep."

"Nico," she said. Just that. Just his name. A plea and a warning, but what she was pleading for and what she was warning him about, she couldn't say. It was happening again, that feeling they were having two different conversations, that he was trying to tell her something she couldn't—or wouldn't—hear yet.

"So...I called like you asked," she said, trying to sound as professional as possible. Detached, professional, neutral. "What did you want to tell me?"

A long pause followed and Nora held her breath.

"I'm not ready to talk to him," he said. "But...you can tell him about me."

And just like that, the weight was gone. Her chest eased and she took the deepest breath she'd ever taken in her life.

"All right," she said. "Thank you."

"There is a caveat," he said.

"What's the caveat?"

"I'm not ready to talk to him. If he needs to tell me

something, he tells it to you, and you tell it to me. If I need to tell him something, I tell it to you, and you tell it to him. I don't want to hear his voice at all. Not yet. Only yours."

"You're the devil," Nora said.

Nico laughed his quiet laugh. "Why do you say that?"

Oh, he knew why she said that. He knew exactly why... Suddenly Nora was fifteen years old again, sitting in a police station in handcuffs and Søren was sitting across from her, demanding she obey him for all eternity. And if that's what he wanted from her, she would give it to him... with one caveat.

But now she was on the other side of the table, in Søren's seat, and this twenty-four-year-old French kid had somehow managed to manipulate her from the other side of the ocean. Her opinion of Nico, already high, shot through the roof. If she'd ever doubted he was Kingsley's son before, she would never doubt it again.

"This isn't a good idea," she said.

"It's the only way I'll do it."

Nora almost applauded the man. She'd never been so decisively cornered before. And he knew it. Nico Delacroix was thoroughly, if quietly, ruthless.

"Fine. But I'm only agreeing to this because I know you're going to love King—eventually."

"So you say." He sounded skeptical.

"I should go. I'll call you later and tell you what Kingsley said."

"No, write it to me."

"What?"

"Write me letters."

"Letters?"

"I told you...with letters you have something to hold and to keep. Write a letter to me. Tell me my sister's name."

"I can tell you her name right now."

"Write it to me."

Nora winced, almost growled. In a flash, a sudden urge came over her and she could see herself ordering Nico onto his stomach on the floor so she could put her booted foot on the back of his neck. Immediately she pushed that mental image out of her brain and forbade it to ever return.

"Fine. I'll write you." She sighed heavily. "I should go."

"I'll look for your letters."

"Right," she said. Before this conversation got any more complicated, Nora said, "Nico, thank you for this. Thank you for not hating me."

"Nora, I don't hate anyone. But if I did, it would never be you."

She closed her eyes, shook her head. Ruthless, manipulative, and a mindfucker. He was already one of them.

There was no safe reply to what he had just said, except "*Au revoir.*"

"I drank the December wine," he said before she could hang up.

"You did? How was it?"

"I'll tell you in a letter."

Then he hung up.

"Son of a..." She didn't let herself finish that statement. Son of a King, that's what he was.

And now she had permission to tell the man himself about Nico. She threw her coat on and drove to Kingsley and Juliette's Riverside Drive townhouse.

She entered through the side door without knocking. She heard voices upstairs and went through the living room, toward the stairs. The tree was still up, and she paused to look it up and down. It was hard to believe this was their last Christmas in New York. By this time next year, they'd all be celebrating the holidays New Orleans-style. Considering it was eleven degrees outside, Nora could not wait.

"Ahem?"

Nora froze. Søren was coming down the main staircase, dressed in his favorite off-duty uniform of jeans and long-sleeved black t-shirt. She dropped her bag, met him on the third step, and kissed him—not an easy task, because of his height. She broke their kiss to lead him all the way downstairs, where they resumed on level ground.

And while they kissed, this thought ran through her head: *No matter what happens next, I will never love anyone as much as I love you.*

But where had that come from? And what did it mean, *No matter what happens next?* What could possibly happen next? She pushed the thought aside and broke the kiss. "Hello, Sir. How was the monastery?"

His hands were on her face. He kissed her again. "Hello, Little One. The monastery was what I needed. When did you make it back?"

"Yesterday. I'm sorry I didn't call. I have a good reason, I promise."

"Ready to tell me yet?"

"Soon. Very soon."

"When you're ready, I—"

She interrupted him, which she rarely did. She couldn't help herself. "I held him, Søren. I held your son."

He sat down on the steps. Right then. Right there. Just sat on the third step and she stood in front of him, waiting as he breathed once through his hands, and then again once more. And finally, he pulled himself together to look up at her.

"You did?" he asked.

"He's perfect."

"He is?"

"Of course he is." She blinked and tears ran down her face. "Here. Zach sent this for you." She picked up her bag off the floor, pulled out her phone, turned up the volume and hit PLAY on the file she'd saved.

"Fionn had the hiccups. Grace recorded it."

The sound of a little baby boy hiccupping miserably filled the hall. They both listened, staring at her phone, saying nothing. But Søren had her hand in his and he squeezed, tight, with every hiccup. The sound file came to an end a minute later.

"What are we going to do?" Nora whispered.

Søren had the answer. He always had the answer.

"Play it again," he said. So she played it again.

As they listened, Nora found herself staring at the antique porcelain Nativity scene displayed on a small marble-top Louis XIV console table. She saw Mary bending over her son; Joseph, standing guard over his wife and son; the animals, the shepherds coming to pay their homage; even the three kings. But where was God, the Father, in the Nativity scene? The Creator, who had given his only son to a scared and humble teenaged girl, and her even more terrified husband? Where was He in the Nativity scene? Up in heaven with His angels, holding a phone in His hand and listening to a recording of Jesus's first hiccups? *Do you hear that?* He'd ask Raphael and Gabriel. *That's my son,* He'd say, beaming with such pride that the night would turn to morning.

That's how Juliette, Kingsley, and Céleste, fast asleep on her papa's shoulder, found them five minutes later; Søren sitting on their stairs with Nora next to him, cradling her phone in her hands as they replayed the tiny yips again and again.

"What's going on?" Juliette asked.

Nora let Søren tell them. "My son had the hiccups."

"Poor baby," Juliette said, tutting a mother's tut.

When the next yip came out of Nora's phone, Kingsley put his hand on Søren's shoulder and Søren put his hand over Kingsley's. The four of them—Céleste was still asleep—listened to the recording, over and over. Then Nora stopped it by putting her phone away.

"You saw him?" Kingsley asked her.

"I saw him. I held him."

Next to her, Søren was silent, and what he was thinking she couldn't begin to guess.

"You want another?" Juliette playfully elbowed Kingsley. "Try for a boy this time?"

Kingsley grinned at her. "Let's try right now."

This was Nora's chance. She took it.

"You don't have to try," she said.

Kingsley looked at her. Juliette looked at her. Søren looked at her.

She reached into her handbag and took out the photograph of Nico, the one from the magazine where he stood in front of the gates of the vineyard, smiling. She held it out to Kingsley. Juliette, somehow sensing something momentous was happening, collected Céleste into her arms as Kingsley took the picture from Nora's hand.

"What's this?" Kingsley asked. He stared at the photograph and Nora saw his eyes narrow. Juliette peered over Kingsley's shoulder and softly gasped.

"His name is Nico," Nora said. "Nicolas Delacroix. Happy Father's Day, King. It's a boy."

FIN

THE CHRISTMAS TRUCE

I. NORA'S CHRISTMAS TRUCE

Author's Note: This story takes place three Christmases before the first Original Sinners novel, The Siren, *during Nora and Søren's five-year estrangement.*

Now playing: "River" by Joni Mitchell

"KING, I NEED YOUR FINGER," Nora said.

Kingsley rose from her overstuffed gray suede armchair and sauntered—as Kingsley did—across the living room floor, his wine glass in his right hand.

"Only one?" he asked as he sat down on the floor next to her. "I thought three was your finger preference?"

"This is my finger preference," she said, showing him one finger in particular.

He raised his hands, surrendering the battle of innuendo. Good. Nora was too tired to play it tonight anyway.

"Where?" he asked.

"Right there," she said, nodding toward the package she was wrapping. "Put your finger on the twine so I can tie a bow here. Consider it an order."

"You don't have to order me to help you wrap my Christmas gifts."

Nora bumped her shoulder into his. "It's more fun for me if I pretend it's an order."

He laughed drunkenly although he was only on glass of wine number two. Then again, Nora had very large wine glasses.

With the help of Kingsley's finger, she tied the bow on the box.

"Who is this one for?" Nora asked as she picked up the package tags.

"What was it?"

"The Canon? The big fancy camera?"

"Simone," Kingsley said.

Nora's eyes widened. "That's a two-thousand-dollar camera, King. Have you been fucking her lately without telling me?"

"She's been you-know-who's personal whipping girl for months now. He left bruises big as your hand on her back two weeks ago. I caught her in my drawing room taking pictures of them."

"To show the cops?"

"She's making a scrapbook of her favorite bruises. That's why I bought the camera with the tripod and timer. The girl deserves hazard pay."

"I never got hazard pay," Nora said under her breath.

She finished writing out the tag—*To Simone, Thank you for your service. Love, Mr. King*—and tied it to the gift.

"You're frowning," Kingsley said. Nora heard a touch of mockery in his tone.

"Am not."

"Green is a Christmas color."

"I am not jealous," she said and meant it.

Kingsley scoffed. "I am."

"Slut," she said. Kingsley rolled onto his back on her floor and balanced his wine glass—still half full—on his stomach. If he spilled red wine all over her new rug, she would flog him within an inch of his life. As sexy as he looked lying there in his jeans, fitted black pullover, and bare feet, she might flog him within an inch of his life anyway. The best part—well, one of many good parts—of being Kingsley's domme was getting to see him like this—relaxed, off-duty, dressed casually. He'd had to go out into the "vanilla world" today finishing his Christmas shopping and had come to her straight after, bags in hand, begging her to save him from the hellish task of wrapping his own gifts. She could never resist a pouty Frenchman. Who could?

She plucked the wine glass off his stomach and took a long deep drink of it before putting it down again. *On a coaster*, because she, unlike Kingsley, was not a savage. She'd recently moved into her new house, and she wasn't about to let Kingsley break or stain anything when she'd finally gotten everything exactly the way she wanted it.

"Is it the wine or do you look sexier than usual tonight?" Kingsley asked.

"Both." She had her new black silk pajamas on and even she had to admit, they did look damn good on her. Her cleavage was looking, in King's words, *magnifique*.

"I thought so. Shall we fuck?" he asked. "If yes, I want to be on top. I'm in a toppy mood."

Nora glared at him. "And they say the French are the romantic race."

"With Juliette, I am a romantic. With you," he said, grinning his devil-may-care grin that made the underwear of every woman in the tristate area evaporate on sight, "I am an unrepentant whore. You got the better deal, *Maîtresse*. Any man can be romantic. Only an elite few of us have mastered the art of true whoredom."

"Did you ask me to wrap your gifts just so I'd let you into my house and my vagina?"

"It might have occurred to me. But you are much better at wrapping presents than I. Than I? Than me? Fuck, I hate English. I'm shit at wrapping gifts. That is what I'm saying. Women are better. In general. At all things always and forever."

"Yes, that day they take us out of class and you boys thought we were learning about tits and periods? They were actually teaching us how to wrap presents."

Kingsley narrowed his eyes and nodded. "Ah...I always suspected."

Nora stood up. She had to twist and stretch her back after spending two hours on the floor wrapping Kingsley's gifts to the 8th Circle crew.

"*Merci*," he said, still on his back.

"For what?" she asked.

"Wrapping my gifts for me. Thank you."

"That's what friends are for," she said.

"But we aren't friends," Kingsley said. "You're my *Maîtresse*."

"This is true," she said. Calling her and Kingsley *friends* would be like calling Bonnie and Clyde *a cute couple*.

"Which has me wondering why you asked me to do it. Calliope usually does this stuff for you, right? Did she quit? Oh, God, did you fuck Calliope and make her quit?"

"Calliope still works for me and adores me and no, I didn't fuck her. She's too young. I don't fuck women under the age of twenty-five anymore."

Nora raised her eyebrow at him.

"Admittedly, it's a rule made to be broken," he said. "However...you are too suspicious. I wanted to see your new house now that you are moved in."

"You did?" Nora did not buy this excuse for one second, but she enjoyed watching Kingsley lie. "I thought you hated my house."

"Not true. I hate that you live in *your* house instead of in *my* house. The house itself is fine. It's nice. It's..."

"What?"

"It's quite...Christmas...y?"

"It is Christmas Eve. It's supposed to be Christmassy. Do you think I overdid the decorating?" Nora asked, glancing at her eight-foot-tall Christmas tree. Real, not artificial.

"No, no," he said, shaking his head. "Not at all. Only...I have to ask, when exactly did you schedule the gangbang with all the Macy's Santa Clauses? I want to be here to film it. You know, for the children."

Nora yanked a stuffed reindeer ornament off her tree and lobbed it at Kingsley.

"My house does not look like a Santa Claus gangbang," she said sternly, and if Nora ever thought saying "Santa Claus gangbang" with a straight face would be easy, she quickly revised that assessment.

"It's a little much." Kingsley sat up cross-legged and ran a hand through his hair. "That is all I'm saying."

"Why? Because I live alone? Just because I'm single, and I don't have living relatives within a ten-hour driving radius doesn't mean I don't get to do a little Christmas decorating."

"A *little* decorating? You have two trees, *Maîtresse.* Two. You have a candle in every single window. You have been playing Christmas music non-stop since I arrived. You have even hung red curtains."

"Red is my color."

"They have snowflakes on them. Big ones. And you have Christmas coasters, towels, lights on the front of the house, lights on the back of the house. You even have one of those stupid Christmas villages set up in your kitchen."

"They're cookie jars. I like cookies. Everyone likes cookies."

"Is that eggnog in the refrigerator or did Santa come—"

"Stop it, asshole," she said, laughing. She grabbed another reindeer off the tree, looked at it, then realized having multiple reindeer ornaments on her tree was not helping her case any. "We do not talk about Santa's semen on Christmas Eve."

"Did you buy that big black snow globe just because it matches your hair?" he asked, pointing at the snow globe on her side table.

Nora put the reindeer back onto her tree before collapsing into the big gray armchair. She picked up the snow globe with the white-frosted Christmas tree inside it, smiled at it, and put it back down again carefully.

"Søren's mother sent it to me. She must not know we're not together anymore. I guess he hasn't told her yet."

Kingsley got up and sat on the coffee table directly across from her. She put her feet in his lap, and, without having to be ordered, he began to gently rub them like the good man-slut he was. He might have a point about her overdoing the Christmas decorating. Next to the mantel clock stood a nutcracker, the traditional Victorian kind, not the sort she kept in her toy bag upstairs. The house did look nice though. Even Martha Stewart would have approved of the final product.

"When I was a little boy," Kingsley said, caressing the dips and divots around her ankles with his thumb, a touch more comforting than erotic, "I think I was eight... *Maman*, she decided we had to have the best Christmas ever. Big tree. Three times as many presents as the year before. Lights. Candles. Christmas concerts. Walks in the park when it snowed. Christmas cookies every single day. A few years later I told my sister that was my favorite Christmas we ever had. She laughed at me. It was *not* a nice laugh. She said I was a stupid little boy because that year, she said, was the year our father confessed he'd gotten drunk at a business lunch and kissed his secretary. Infidelity is more accepted in France than in America but my mother, she was *very* American. She didn't take it well. She almost left *Papa* over it. And she was going to take us with her back to Maine to live with my grandparents. It could have been our last Christmas with our father in France. And I had no idea. But...I am not eight years old anymore."

Nora blinked back tears. Kingsley lifted her leg to his lips and gently pressed a kiss onto the top of her foot.

"You're right," Nora said. "We should fuck. Right now. But I'll be on top. You just lay there and stay hard."

"You can tell me," he said. "I tell you when I'm miserable."

"You're French. Even when you're *miserable* you're still sexy," she said, saying "miserable" in an exaggerated French accent, as the word should be said. "Miserable doesn't look nearly as good on the Germans."

She wiped another tear from her eye. When did she turn into such a sap? She'd listened to Joni Mitchell's song "River" on repeat all yesterday and today while decorating. The broken-hearted woman's Christmas anthem.

"It's not fair, you know," Nora said, as Kingsley continued to press soft kisses onto the top of her foot and her ankle. His dark wavy hair fell over his eyes and he paused in his worshiping only to tuck that wayward strand behind his ear. "No man should be as sexy as you and as good in bed *and* smart. I shouldn't be sad and wet. It's a weird combination is what I'm saying."

"Now you know how it feels to be French," he said. "I could go down on you while you cry. I don't mind. Wouldn't be the first time."

"I'm never letting Juliette leave you alone again at Christmas," she said. "Babysitting your cock while she's visiting her mother is exhausting. I better get a good present."

"I've been trying to give you your gift all night," he said, his eyes glinting.

"A sub giving his mistress an orgasm is not a gift. A sub should give his mistress orgasms every day that ends in Y."

"Ah, very true," he said. "But perhaps I wrapped a forty-thousand-dollar diamond tennis bracelet around my cock?"

"Did you?" she asked, suddenly feeling very Christmassy.

"I did, but for Jules. That was her Christmas gift."

"That's a big gift," Nora said.

"I had to do something big. That fucking asshole Brad Wolfe sent her diamond earrings from Tiffany's just to piss me off," Kingsley said.

"Clearly it worked."

"Of course it worked," Kingsley said. "But I made her wear the earrings while I flogged her and fucked her. Then I called him and told him all about it."

"It was your bright idea to fall in love with the most beautiful woman in the world. These things will happen."

"Don't blame the victim," Kingsley said. "It's a good thing I'm rich. Keeping up with all of Juliette's suitors is expensive." While his tone was annoyed, his eyes were shining with pleasure. Spoiling Juliette was his new favorite hobby.

"Did you get Søren anything for Christmas?" she asked.

"Socks," Kingsley said.

"You got a sadist...*socks*?"

"When you spend forty grand on your lover at Christmas, someone else is going to get socks. I bought you some, too."

Kingsley dug into a shopping bag from Saks and tossed her a small red box. Nora opened it and found red-and-white candy-cane striped socks nestled in tissue paper.

"These are very cute," she said. "I hope you got Søren the same kind."

"Plain black boring socks," Kingsley said. "Not that I'll even see him until New Year's, if then."

"When did you last talk to him?" she asked.

"Two months ago? Almost?"

"Two months?" Nora said, stunned. She thought Kingsley and Søren talked all the time.

"It was right after my birthday," Kingsley said. "He was at the club to meet Simone. I nodded at him when I saw them leaving for his dungeon. That was it. How long has it been since you've seen him?"

"Three months. He called me, said he needed me. I

dropped everything like I always do and went over. It was a good night until your name came up," she said.

"*Moi?*"

"*Toi*," she said.

"Now you have to tell me the whole story if I'm in it."

Nora rubbed her forehead. "He beat me and it was lovely. He fucked me and it was lovely. We were in his bed and it was lovely. I said something about how sometimes—not often, for the record—I miss being the one on the receiving end of the flogging. Søren said he was surprised I didn't let you top me anymore. I said I was your domme now, and we didn't switch very often. He asked me if I fucked you."

"Which you do," Kingsley said.

"Which he knows," Nora said. "But I said that was between your asshole and my strap-on. And he said something like, 'You know, he's only using you to hurt me.' "

"Not at all true," Kingsley said. "I'm using you for pain and sex. *And* to hurt him."

"Which we *all* know," Nora said. "But instead of saying that to him, I said...something not nice."

"What did you say...?" Kingsley asked, his lips twitching into a smile though his tone was scolding.

"I said, 'At least I know how to fuck King without putting him in the hospital for three days after I'm done with him.' "

Kingsley blinked, slowly, twice.

"I know," she said. "That was bad."

"Do you have a death wish?" Kingsley asked. "You really said that to him?"

"Yeah," she said with a regretful sigh. "And it is true. I do know how to fuck your ass really well."

"You're the goddess of sodomy, but that is not the issue,"

Kingsley said. "You threw my past with him in his face. That's my job."

"He pissed me off," Nora said, raising her hands in exasperation. "First of all, it's none of his business what you and I do in private together. Second, it's none of his business why I top you and you let me. And third..."

"Yes...?"

"He pissed me off!" Nora groaned and then laid her head on the soft squishy chair arm. "After that, I just...I stormed out. That was the last time we talked-slash-fought." She smiled apologetically at him. "I'm sorry. I shouldn't have brought up your past with him. That's between you and him, not me."

Nora still regretted that fight and her closing argument. It had been a low blow, especially since Kingsley's first time with Søren was his most precious memory, not the sort of thing she ought to be wielding as a weapon. If not for Søren's sake, then Kingsley's.

"It's very sweet, you defending me," Kingsley said. He bent and kissed her on the forehead. "And it's even sweeter, you picking me over him."

"Oh, but I'm not." She wagged her finger at him. "I'm picking *me* over him."

"Do you regret it yet?" Kingsley asked.

"Sometimes. Occasionally. Except..."

"What?"

"When I'm beating you," she said and gave him her own devil-may-care grin, the one that made male submissives all over the world hard as bricks.

"Good thing I'm here then. And good thing you are. We can pretend we don't wish we were with him tonight."

"I don't," she said. He raised his eyebrow at her. She was a very good liar, but Kingsley was even better at seeing through her lies. She picked up a pile of Christmas cards from off the side table. The pile wasn't very thick. A card from her bank. A card from her doctor's office. An exquisite *Joyeux Noël* card from Juliette, which Kingsley likely signed under duress. And one other card.

She handed it to Kingsley.

"What's this?" he asked.

"What's it look like?"

"A boring Christmas card with a church on the front," he said. "What is it?"

"A boring Christmas card with a church on the front." She smiled. "It's the annual Sacred Heart Christmas card. I got it in the mail a week ago. I am embarrassed by how excited I got when I saw it was from 'Rev. Marcus Stearns, SJ.' I knew it was the church's Christmas card. I knew I got it because I've always been on the mailing list. I just thought...I thought maybe he'd write a special message in the card for me. I was shaking when I opened the envelope. I had to sit down." She waved her hand in front of her chest, miming how her heart fluttered.

Kingsley opened the card.

"Just a signature," he said. "His and his secretary's."

"Right. Just a signature. And the same boring card a thousand other people got this year. Including his bishop, the mayor of Wakefield, and Pope Benedict."

"I would have been hurt, too," Kingsley said.

"My throat's been hurting ever since I got this card in the mail. But it's not a cold. I've been trying not to cry for a week. Hard on the throat."

"Elle..." Kingsley said, his tone pitying.

"I did all this decorating for him," she said. "I have this recurring fantasy that one evening I'll be in my office writing, I'll hear a knock on the door, and he'll be there.

And I wanted the house to be beautiful so he'd see it and..."

"He'd realize what a stubborn ass he's being? He'd magically have a change of heart about you going pro? About you and me?"

"Now that you say it out loud, it does sound incredibly stupid." She laughed at herself. "I guess I just keep hoping he'll miss me so much he'll come around on the idea. I can't go back to him if he's going to take that away from me," Nora said.

Søren wanted her back and would take her back in a heartbeat...but only if she gave up this whole new wild world Kingsley had given her. Her world or Søren? Søren or her world? Should have been an easy choice, especially since for her entire adult life, Søren had been her world. But it wasn't easy.

"He may never change his mind," Kingsley said. "You know that, yes?"

"I know," she said. "But I keep hoping..."

"*Moi aussi.*" He raised his glass to her in salute. She returned the salute and started to drink her wine, but found she'd lost her taste for it when it came to her lips. She set the glass down on the side table, still full. Kingsley took the card from her lap, the one from Sacred Heart. He opened it, flipped it over and around as if looking for a secret message.

"Maybe he wrote something in invisible ink," Kingsley said, holding it up to the lamplight.

"Nope," she said. "It's just a card with all the Christmas mass times. Guess when Midnight Mass starts."

"Midnight, I would assume."

"11:30, actually," Nora said. "They're having Christmas music for a half hour first. So...right about now," Nora paused and glanced at the clock, "Søren is in his bedroom at the rectory putting on his clerical shirt and collar. Socks and shoes. Mirror check. Gotta make sure the perfect blond hair is perfect, which it is, of course."

"Of course," Kingsley said.

"Then he's—right this second—striding down the steps, probably adjusting his cuffs as he goes. Jacket on in the kitchen. Short walk from the rectory to the church, so he might skip his overcoat. Then again, it's freezing and it snowed last night so maybe he's putting it on. Lights off. Out the door. Straight to the church. Soon as he walks in, Diane will be there in her red Christmas dress with her gold tree broach on. She'll let him know everything is running smoothly. He'll go to the adoration chapel and pray. The rosary first, then whatever novena he's working on. He'll pray for all the sick people in his congregation, he'll pray for the dying, he'll pray for the dead. He always says a long prayer to St. Dymphna at Christmas. She's the patron of mentally ill and depressed people who always get screwed over at the holidays. Then he'll pray a simple Christmas prayer for his congregation.

> *God of love, Father of all,*
> *The darkness that covered the earth*
> *Has given way to the bright dawn of your*
>   *Word made flesh.*
> *Make us a people of this light.*
> *Make us faithful to your Word,*
> *That we may bring your life to the waiting*
>   *world.*
> *Grant this through Christ our Lord,*
> *Amen.*

"And that's it for the chapel," Nora continued. "At

11:15, he'll check with Diane again, give her her Christmas bonus, and she'll cry and hug him and tell him he's too generous. He'll make a joke about skimming it all from the collection plate. She'll kiss his cheek and wish him a merry Christmas. Then he'll go to the sacristy where the deacon's already there waiting. They'll help each other put on their vestments. And in the background, Søren will hear the choir begin to sing Christmas music. He'll enter into the sanctuary right after midnight. Old Testament reading. New Testament reading. Gospel reading. Then a homily to make even the Grinch weep and call his mama. And the good Father Stearns will end mass wishing everyone a merry Christmas, and then it'll officially be Christmas because he said so."

Kingsley said nothing, only looked at her long and hard.

"I was there at the rectory a lot of Christmas Eves. We would...we would make love under the tree at his house. Take a quick shower together. He'd leave to go to Midnight Mass, and I'd wait and sneak in late so people wouldn't see that I was coming from the rectory. I know his routine."

She knew his routine. She knew his secrets. She knew his needs and wants and desires. And for years she could have sworn she'd known his heart. But she wasn't sure she knew his heart anymore. Three months since their fight. You could forget anything in three months. Maybe in three months, he'd forgotten he loved her. She knew he hadn't. Of course he hadn't.

But what if he had?

"I forget sometimes you weren't just his lover," Kingsley said. "In so many ways, you were his wife."

"I was never his wife," she said. "Wives get the boring moments. I only got the highlights and the holidays. No mornings, just nights. I can count on two hands how many times we sat at his kitchen table and had morning coffee."

She wiped another tear and Kingsley put his head on her knee.

"I didn't want to be alone," he said.

"Tonight?"

"I understand why Juliette visits her mother on Christmas. We're the opposite of you and him. She gets me all the boring times. We have coffee together every morning. She has nights *and* days with me. Her mother needs the special times. The holidays. But I miss her. She's become so important to me so fast that I forget most of the time how much I love him because I'm so busy loving her. Then as soon as she's gone..."

"You remember," Nora said.

"I remember," Kingsley said, "too many things I want to forget."

"So, you pouted at me to wrap your Christmas gifts just so you'd have an excuse to come over?"

"*Pathétique, non?*" he asked.

"If I could have one thing for Christmas, it would be to have coffee with him tomorrow morning. Just coffee in his kitchen. How *pathétique* is that?"

"Your Christmas wish is more likely to come true than mine," he said.

"What's yours?"

"I want to swallow Søren's come again," Kingsley said.

Nora narrowed her eyes at him, her lips slightly parted. A rare moment when Nora Sutherlin was rendered speechless.

"For old times' sake, I mean," he said.

"This is why I keep you around," Nora said. She grabbed his earlobe, tugged it hard the way she knew he liked. "You make me laugh and gross me out when I need it most."

"That is what I'm here for," he said. "That and to be beaten and fucked."

Nora grinned into her wine glass, took a small sip when she wanted to guzzle the whole thing down.

"I don't know why I'm taking this so hard," she said. "It's not like this is our first bad Christmas. Our first Christmas...that was probably the worst. Spent all Christmas Eve crying in bed."

"What happened?" Kingsley asked.

"You don't remember? That was when I was sixteen," she said. "I broke all his rules in one night. I went and saw my father—rule broken. I didn't water the stick I was supposed to water. Another rule broken."

"You showed up at my house without being invited, fooled around with...who was it?"

"Lachlan," she said with relish. She'd always liked that guy. "He called me Bite-Size. Then he bit me."

"Ah, that bastard Aussie who stole my girlfriend," Kingsley said, nose wrinkling in disgust.

"That was the first night I ever laid eyes on you," Nora said. "God, you were so arrogant. I can still see you standing there wagging your finger at me. 'Tsk, tsk, no children allowed.'"

"What was I supposed to do? Give you a glass of Pinot and take you to bed with me? I admit I considered it."

"It would have been much more fun than getting yelled at and dumped."

"That's what happened after? He yelled at you?"

"He doesn't really yell, you know. Until you push him."

"Oh, I know. I've pushed him."

"Søren took me home in your Rolls. On the way there,

he made it very clear he and I had gotten too close too soon, and I was way too young to be part of his life. After that, it was the silent treatment for almost a full year. Except for a couple times I got desperate and snuck over to see him. Christmas was the first time I caved."

"What happened?" Kingsley asked.

"You really want to know?" she asked. "This was... what? Thirteen years ago. It's all stupid maudlin teenaged goo."

"I love your stupid maudlin teenaged goo. All your goo really."

Nora was glad Kingsley was here to keep her from getting too maudlin.

"Come be my foot warmer," she said, "and I'll tell you the story."

Kingsley obeyed without a word of protest. He set his wine glass down and laid at her feet. Nora slipped her cold toes under his shirt and onto his warm stomach. Ah...bliss.

"My dad had just gotten sentenced the day before," Nora said. "Christmas Eve *Eve*. Talk about sadism, sentencing a guy the day before Christmas Eve."

"Hard day," Kingsley said.

Nora slowly nodded. "Hard winter."

She hadn't been Nora Sutherlin then—just plain Elle Schreiber—though maybe if she had been, her teenaged self would have handled it better, hearing from her mother that her father would be spending the next fifteen years on Rikers. She was sixteen and that meant he wouldn't be out until she was thirty-one. Thirty-one seemed a thousand years away to her. She could only imagine how long it seemed to her dad.

And even worse, Søren had stopped talking to her. He'd cut her off, cut her out. No more visits to his office, standing in the doorway and only putting a toe over the threshold because of "Father Stearns' Rules" about not letting anyone under the age of seventeen into his office unattended by an adult. So she'd stand there in the doorway, with her toes on—but not crossing!—the threshold as she pelted him with questions. It should have annoyed him—it would have annoyed any normal priest—but it never did, because Father S was not a normal priest. But all that was over. No more getting help with her math homework. No more hot cocoa. No more intimate conversations that left her shaking and shivering and smiling for days after.

It was all her fault, though, and she knew it. She'd screwed up, and had no one to blame but herself. She'd knowingly disobeyed his express orders and gone to see her worthless father, which ended in her half-frozen and wandering the streets of the city. Maybe if she could prove to Søren how sorry she was, he'd lift the ban on them being friends? Maybe if she could fix things with the right words or the right Christmas gift? Maybe if he knew how much she loved him, his heart would melt and he'd let her back in?

Worth a shot anyway.

Her mother had decided to work at the hotel on Christmas Eve night for the overtime and the holiday pay. There she was, all alone at midnight, wide-awake and miserable. She couldn't possibly get any more miserable, could she? Might as well go to church.

Elle got dressed and put her hair into a loose braid, wrapped up in her coat and boots and scarf and walked over to Sacred Heart. She was late. She wanted to be late so she could be alone with Søren after everyone left. While everyone milled around, hugging and kissing and saying 'Merry Christmas' to everyone they knew, Elle snuck up the side stairs and sat in the front pew of the choir loft. Finally, the church cleared out and she was all alone.

Leaning forward, she peeked over the balcony and watched. She waited for ten minutes, then fifteen. After twenty minutes, she thought she'd made a mistake. Maybe he'd gone straight to the rectory. But the small weight in her pocket reminded her of the reason she came, so she made herself wait a few more minutes.

Finally, she heard footsteps echoing off the hardwood floors. Søren strode to the front of the church, turned around, and paused. His dark gray eyes scanned the sanctuary, and she bit her bottom lip to stop a smile, her first smile in weeks. He was looking for her. She knew it in her soul. Part of her wanted to call out and wave to him, but she stayed silent and kept watching. Usually it was his eyes on her watching her even when she didn't know it. For some reason, and from the very moment they'd met, they had some sort of secret understanding between them. She'd tried explaining it to her friend Jordan late one night when Elle had slept over at her house.

"Elle...he's a priest. You can't be in love with a priest."

"It's not like that. Not totally. I don't know, Jordan. I think I belong to him. I think I'm *supposed* to belong to him."

"That doesn't make any sense," Jordan said, throwing the covers over her head and sinking down into the pillows. "You're crazy. People can't belong to other people. They can only belong to God."

But Elle knew there was a way to belong to someone, a way that wasn't like slavery but more like Jordan said, like the way Christians belonged to Jesus. Or the way people in arranged marriages belonged to each other even years before they'd met?

Elle hadn't tried to explain it to Jordan. Either you got it or you didn't, and Jordan didn't.

Søren went to the piano and began to play "O Holy Night." When she was certain they were alone in the sanctuary, Elle crept down the stairs and walked toward the front of the church. Søren didn't pause in his playing, but he moved slightly to the side to make room for her on the piano bench. She sat down, her back to the piano.

Closing her eyes, Elle leaned against his shoulder as the last haunting strains of her favorite Christmas song rang out for a melodic eternity before quietly dying.

"It's a pretty song," she said, sitting up straight. "But it's no 'You're a Mean One, Mr. Grinch.' "

Søren said nothing. Not a word. His fingers continued to tickle the keys and, though the sounds were lovely, it was no song she recognized, just beautiful noise.

"I got an A on my European History exam," Elle told him. "Got my report card two days ago. I'm keeping my grades up, but English and History were my only A's."

She waited, hoping and praying for a response, a congratulations, something.

More silence.

"We learned about something cool on the last day of school," she continued. "Mr. Stone taught us about the Christmas Truce of 1914. You ever heard of it?"

Søren didn't nod or smile but only continued softly playing.

"Well, it was a World War I thing," she said. "There were these French and British soldiers on one side of no man's land in their trenches, and there were these German soldiers on the other side of no man's land in their trenches. And then somebody...who knows who? He decided there ought to be a day off fighting the war. I mean, it was Christmas, right? Who fights a war on Christmas Day? So somebody went up and over into no man's land. And then somebody on the other side did the same. And somebody brought out a soccer ball and the war turned into one long soccer game. Mr. Stone showed us this famous picture of the soldiers who were killing each other the day before and would kill each other the day after, talking and lighting each other's cigarettes. One French soldier even gave a German soldier a haircut. I mean, if they can declare a truce on Christmas Day I thought, maybe you and I could?"

Søren's fingers stilled on the keys.

Elle smiled as Søren closed the fallboard. Leaning back, she rested her elbows on the fallboard.

Søren raised his hand and tucked a snowy strand of hair behind her ear. She quivered at the touch of his hand and the fingers that lingered meaningfully on her cheek and her ear.

"I'm glad you came to church," he said, his voice so soft she thought at first he was speaking to himself.

"I'm here."

"I was worried you wouldn't come. Whatever happens with us...our difficulties should never come between you and God."

Their *difficulties*? What a nice way to phrase it.

"God's not really talking to me either these days, so don't worry about that," she said.

Søren tilted his head to the side and gazed at her with sympathy. "How's your mother?"

Elle shook her head.

"Not doing well?" he asked.

She shrugged. "Is she ever? Dad got sentenced yesterday. Nice of them to do it just before Christmas, right? Mom's a wreck. She was coherent enough today to say she'd give me money to go buy new clothes for Christmas. Clothes...yay," Elle said entirely without enthusiasm. She didn't want new clothes for Christmas. Or money. What she wanted she knew her family couldn't give her anymore. Only Søren could give her the things she needed. If he would, please, someday, she prayed.

"I'm so sorry, Little One." Søren crossed his perfect hands in his lap. "I wish I could make that better for you."

She found it surprisingly easy to smile for him. "You make everything better for me. Except when you make it worse."

"It's Christmas. You aren't allowed to tell me you hate me today," he said, turning his body more toward her. "Truce, remember?"

"Right," she said. "Truce."

Elle laughed a little, then rolled forward, and collapsed against his chest. The tears came out in near-silent waves as Søren held her with his chin on top of her head. As she cried he whispered to her, something in Danish, his native language. She would have given anything to know what he said to her then. But really it didn't matter, the words themselves comforted her, the words and the man who spoke them.

She wasn't even sure why she was crying. She'd known for months her father was getting sentenced in December. Life was better without him anyway. And for years now her mom had been slowly losing it. She'd wanted to be a nun as a girl and had instead fallen for Elle's dad and abandoned her convent dreams. Now she had a convict for an ex-husband and a daughter with a criminal record. Proof, her mother thought, that marrying and having a child had been against God's will. Great for Elle's self-esteem, right? But none of that was news. All the bad stuff had been bad for a long time. For some reason Christmas made it really hard to ignore the bad stuff like she could the rest of the year.

Slowly the tears dried up. She pulled back and swiped at her face. Søren took a black silk handkerchief out of his pocket and gave it to her.

"Is it a sin to get snot on a priest's cassock? If so, I am a big fat sinner."

"My cassock is in my closet and safe from all harm. And any sins you commit against my jacket are merely venial."

"Well, that's good to know. Do you really have a cassock?" she asked, trying to imagine Søren wearing a cassock. She'd only seen those weird ankle-length robe things on the pope on TV and occasionally on a priest visiting from the mission field.

"I do," Søren said, nodding his regal head. "All Jesuits do."

"How come you never wear it?"

Søren paused and considered her question. He was the only adult she knew who did that, who took her questions seriously enough to think about them before answering.

"I suppose I find it too distinctive. It's far better for a parish priest to blend in with his congregation."

Elle snorted, and Søren's eyes widened slightly at her reaction. "You? Blend in with us? Have you seen you? You're like eight feet tall and gorgeous. You don't blend in with anybody. You wouldn't even blend in with other eight-foot-tall gorgeous priests."

Søren pursed his lips at her. "Eleanor, haven't we had this conversation?"

She exhaled noisily. "Yeah, I know, I'm not supposed to tell you that you're gorgeous because you're a priest and that's inappropriate, and I stopped listening after that because I was imagining what you looked like in jeans. You probably don't even own a pair of jeans. You probably sleep in your vestments."

"I do own a pair of jeans, and I sleep in a bed."

Elle pictured him in his bed. She shouldn't have done that. Because what did he sleep in? Really? She couldn't imagine him as a boxer shorts and t-shirt kind of guy like her dad. And he was definitely not the sort to wear old man pajamas.

Naked. He slept naked. She knew it. She'd bet her life on it.

"Wait, what kind of bed?" she asked.

"We shouldn't be having this conversation," he said, turning his head, no longer looking at or even near her face. "This is what got us into this mess in the first place."

"I know. I'm sorry. I just really miss you," she said.

"It's been far too quiet in the doorway of my office without you," he said. "I do have something for you. That's why I'm glad you came."

"Something? A gift?"

"A very small gift." He reached into the pocket of his jacket and pulled out a tiny purple velvet drawstring bag. She took it from him and with shaking hands, opened it.

"It's a saint medal," she said, staring at the silver coin on the end of the silver chain.

"St. Louise," he said. "Her feast day is March 15th."

"My birthday."

Elle put the necklace on and felt the cool metal of the medallion against her skin and near her heart, right where she wanted Søren.

"Thank you," she said. It was a nice gift, a safe gift, a very Catholic gift. The sort of gift a priest could give to a member of his parish without raising eyebrows. Her gift, however, would raise eyebrows. Specifically, his.

Still, she'd come all this way in the cold and the dark.

"I have a little gift for you, too," she said.

"You should not be buying me gifts. Ever."

"It's just a stupid thing, okay? And I didn't buy it. I already had it so take it, please, and don't laugh at me. Then I'll leave."

She dug the tiny wrapped package out of her coat pocket and dropped it onto the fallboard of the piano. He picked it up and carefully—as if it were a bomb— unwrapped the tissue paper.

"I had a whole set of them as a kid," she said. "Bears and sheep and tigers and stuff. Dozens of these little plastic animals. I had to dig through like a million boxes to find that one."

"A stag?" Søren asked, staring at the small antlered deer in his hand.

She shook her head. "It's a hart. Which is also a stag. But I'm calling it a hart. That's the traditional name for it, I guess. A male red deer. I like puns. It's a visual pun," she said, flushing a little. It had seemed like such a good idea at the time, but now as soon as she'd given it to him and explained it, she realized how truly stupid the whole idea was. A plastic toy deer? That's what she gave the smartest, handsomest, weirdest man in the world for Christmas? This man she loved with every cell in her body?

"*As the hart panteth after the water brooks,*" Søren said, "*so panteth my soul after thee...*"

Oh. So maybe the hart had been a good idea after all.

Søren still stared at the toy.

"Was that a Psalm?" she asked.

"Psalm 42, verse one," he said, his eyes looking deep into hers. Something glinted in those dark gray depths, deep as the ocean and just as mysterious...

Elle reached out and stood the stag upright on the center of his palm. The little hart's proud head and dark eyes stared straight at Søren.

"So, there it is," Elle said. "I give you my *heart*."

Slowly Søren closed his fingers around the tiny hart and pressed his fisted hand to his chest. "Thank you, Little One," he said, his voice hardly a whisper.

Elle merely leaned against his shoulder once more.

"Merry Christmas, Søren."

She heard him take another deep breath through his nose as if he preparing to say something important, maybe even forgive her and end their separation.

But no.

All he said was, "Merry Christmas, Eleanor."

She got up, put on her coat and started to leave. At the sanctuary door, she stopped and turned around.

"It's too bad it isn't Christmas every day," she said. "Then nobody would have to go back to fighting stupid wars."

Søren said nothing, merely turned away, still holding her hart in his hand.

Nora blinked and two hot tears rolled down her cheeks. She wiped them away before Kingsley saw them. Nora lifted her feet off his stomach, and he sat up, still at her feet but with his chin on her knee.

"Strawberries," Kingsley said.

"What? You want strawberries or is that your new safe word?"

"Your hair," he said. "It smelled like strawberries that night. When Søren breathed in right before he wished you merry Christmas, he was smelling your hair. He told me the next day he was ashamed of himself for how weak he was at that moment, that he sniffed your hair while you weren't looking. I remember him telling me your hair smelled like strawberries."

"That was my shampoo. Suave, strawberry-scented. Only ninety-nine cents a bottle. He told you about that night?"

"He told me he saw you after mass and talked to you, and that he was having a very hard time with the separation from you," Kingsley said. "He said you looked so beautiful he couldn't stop himself from smelling your hair."

Nora laughed. Better to laugh than to cry. "That whole year we were 'separated' or whatever...I thought he hated me. Or worse, that he'd forgotten about me. I'd rather him hate me than forget me."

Kingsley shook his head. "Forget you? Sometimes he'd show up at my house at two or three in the morning, and I wouldn't even have to ask why he was there. I'd hear his Ducati in the alley. I'd get up, let him in, and find him whatever pretty masochist was lying around the house for him to 'vent' his frustrations on. All because of you."

"Are you serious?" she asked. "He never told me that."

"He wouldn't want you to know how weak you made him feel."

"But I want to know," she said.

"Did you know he thought about kidnapping you?"

"What?" Nora was agog.

"I asked him once what he would have done if I hadn't been able to keep you from going to jail after you stole all those cars. He said he would have taken you to live with his mother in Denmark. I've smuggled people out of and into various countries before without getting caught. Lucky for you, it didn't come to that."

"Lucky for his mother," Nora said.

"But that bad year you two weren't talking, he admitted

to me under the influence of a very potent Cabernet that he wished he had packed you off to Denmark."

"He probably thought his mother would take better care of me than my own mother did." And he was likely right about that.

"He thought he wouldn't be so tempted to beat you and fuck you if you were living an ocean away from him and under his mother's roof. That's what he was thinking."

"God," she said.

"I could tell you *many* stories about that year," Kingsley said. "The time I chained his ankle to my bed is a very good one. It was either that or he was going to murder a boy at your church he overheard talking about your tits in glowing terms."

"I feel like I should tell you I'm sorry," Nora said, wincing.

"Don't. It was a terrible year for him. For me?" He pointed at himself. "I was having the time of my life."

"I had no idea he was feeling so much during that year. He always acted like he had it all under control, meanwhile I was the one falling apart."

Kingsley blew a little disgusted *pfft*.

"Pfft?" Nora repeated.

"Pfft. Grown men who have their shit together don't go around sniffing the hair of teenaged girls," he said. "He'd probably sniff your hair again if he got near you."

"Fuck, I'd sniff his hair right now if I could," she said. "I love the way he smells."

"Frost on pine trees," Kingsley said.

"Fireplace smoke in the distance."

"New-fallen snow."

"The way peppermint hits your nose," she said, then laughed at herself. "We're insane."

"All his fault," Kingsley said. "We were normal until him."

"Damn straight we were. Both of us, little angels."

Kingsley laughed.

"What?" she asked.

"I just noticed something on the card," he said.

Nora leaned over and watched as he flipped the Sacred Heart card over and pointed out a tiny red deer with antlers under the name of the printing company of the card.

"It's the card logo," she said. "Christmas card companies sometimes have reindeer for logos."

Kingsley licked the tip of his finger and ran it over the deer and the card company name. The ink of the company's name didn't smear. The ink of the deer did.

"He drew a 'hart' on your card, *Maîtresse*."

"God damn," she said, the knot in her throat now the size of a golf ball. "He did."

Nora met Kingsley's eyes, and he smiled at her, proud as a little boy who'd solved a riddle that stumped the grown-ups in his life.

"King, what if he's not giving me the silent treatment," Nora said. "What if he thinks I'm giving *him* the silent treatment? I've been waiting for him to talk to me. Maybe he's been waiting for me to talk to him."

Once upon a time, thirteen years ago, she had given Søren her "hart" for Christmas. He'd given her his heart, too, this Christmas, and hidden it on her card. He hadn't forgotten her at all. He hadn't forgotten her, and he still loved her. And that's when it happened, that's when Christmas came to her house. It wasn't in the tree and it wasn't in the kitchen and it wasn't on the mantel and it wasn't hanging in strands off the eaves or even knocking at her door. It was in that tiny hart on her card. If she'd blinked she would have missed Christmas. Good thing Kingsley had better eyes than she did.

She touched the little hart, its little hand-drawn antlers. *As the hart panteth after the water brooks...*

Nora slapped her thighs and stood up. "Come on, Captain. We're going over the wall."

"What? Where?"

She waved the card in front of his face.

"To Sacred Heart?" Kingsley asked.

"I have to see him. I have to," she said. "And if we leave now, we'll get there in time for the homily."

"Then go," he said.

"Come with me, please?"

Nora could tell Kingsley was tempted but didn't want to be a third wheel. No matter how many times she told him Søren cared about him as much as he cared about her, Kingsley never could or would let himself believe it.

"Ah, I should go home," he said. "The dogs miss me when I'm gone at night."

Nora narrowed her eyes at him. Pathetic excuse.

"I bet you one-thousand dollars I can guess the first two words out of Søren's mouth when he goes up to give his homily," she said.

"One-thousand dollars?" Kingsley asked.

"Cash," she said.

"No bet. It's 'Merry Christmas,' isn't it?"

"Nope."

"Then there's no way you can know. He gives a different Christmas homily every single year, doesn't he?"

"He does. But I can still guess the first two words he'll say. You believe me?"

"No."

"One-thousand dollars says I can." She scratched him

under the chin like a cat. Then he grabbed her finger and held it tight. She knew she had him then. The chance to prove her wrong *always* got him.

"All right," he said. "I'll take that bet. You better bring the money."

"I got the money," she said. They shook hands on the bet. "Let's go to church."

II. KINGSLEY'S CHRISTMAS TRUCE

Now playing: "All I Ever Get For Christmas is Blue" by
Over the Rhine

IT WAS twenty degrees and falling when they left Nora's
house. Kingsley cinched his scarf tighter around his neck as
he got into her car.

"I better win that money," was all he said as she took the
highway to Wakefield.

"Kiss it goodbye, King," she said and turned up the heat
and the radio. A velvet-throated jazz singer crooned "All I
Ever Get For Christmas Is Blue" at him, and he was
tempted to call the golden-voiced singer and offer to cheer
her up a little in his own particular way.

"You know, we could be fucking right now," Kingsley
said. "Church versus fucking, and we picked church?"

"Well, too late. We're here," she said as she pulled in
across the street from the brightly-lit church. Even in the
car, Kingsley could hear the music pouring through the

doors, which were decorated with massive green and red-ribboned wreaths. "Shall we?"

Kingsley took a fortifying breath. "Once more unto the breach."

They walked into the church. Kingsley and Nora stood at the open sanctuary doors, toes touching but not crossing the threshold. The congregation finished singing and everyone sat. An air of expectation filled the room to the rafters. Breaths were held. Babies shushed. All eyes looked ahead.

Søren came to the pulpit.

Kingsley so rarely saw Søren in his vestments that it took his breath away to see his former lover wearing a snow-white chasuble and a silver and gold-embroidered stole. With his blond hair shining in the candlelight—and perfectly in place as always—he glowed like an angel. Which, Kingsley thought, perfectly demonstrated how deceptive appearances can be.

Nora leaned in, put her mouth to Kingsley's ear, and whispered two words:

"Lights, please?"

Søren began to speak from the pulpit. "Lights, please?" he said.

The congregation roared with laughter.

"Dammit," Kingsley sighed.

"Why does that always work for Linus?" Søren said, playfully peering up at the balcony as if searching for his missing spotlight. "Not once has it ever worked for me."

Kingsley pulled out his wallet and counted ten Benjamin Franklins, which Nora merrily pocketed in her coat.

"Merry Christmas," Søren said.

"Merry Christmas, Father," the congregation responded in unison. Nora was grinning, basking in her victory.

"It's wonderful to see so many of you here," he said. "And so many faces I haven't seen since Easter."

The church rippled with chuckles and groans. Clergy humor.

"I see Regina tapping her wristwatch to warn me to make this quick," Søren said. "I'm allowed twenty minutes, Regina. What was that?"

Søren leaned forward to listen to someone speaking from the front row.

"Ten? I only have *ten* minutes?" Søren sounded aghast. "But this is my moment, Regina. Why are you trying to kill my moment?"

The entire congregation laughed again. Kingsley felt it as much as heard it—the laughter of five-hundred people in a confined space could register on the Richter scale.

"Who is this man?" Kingsley whispered to Nora. "They adore him."

"Kingsley Edge, meet Father Marcus Stearns."

"Oh, I can have thirty on Easter?" Søren said, still negotiating with an elderly woman in the front pew. "That's fair. Thank you, Regina. May I begin now? I can? Good. Start your stopwatch."

How could it be that this gentle, playful charming Father Stearns was also Søren, the boy who'd taught Kingsley the meaning of the word *pain*?

"Yes, I know it's late," Søren said. "And we all want to get home to our families or friends or, if you're me, to bed. Some of us don't get to take Christmas Day off." He pointed at himself, playing the martyr.

Kingsley grinned as two young women in front of him looked at each other and wagged their eyebrows. Undoubtedly they were imagining their priest in bed. Welcome to the club, ladies.

"I hear there is a War on Christmas. In fact, I hear it every year, but I have yet to see armed men using Christmas trees for target practice in the park. Very disappointing to find nothing but families with children walking around enjoying the lights and ornaments and not a grenade to be seen. Perhaps there is a War on Christmas, as in there are wars going on, and they don't stop for Christmas Day. The war in Iraq, Darfur, Somalia...I could go on. And other wars, too. The eternal war between good and evil. The cold-shoulder war between left and right in this country. The wars in our own lives and hearts. The war against our addictions, our illnesses, our rivals, ourselves." He paused. "It may come as a shock to you that I have a habit of antagonizing those who are closest to me..."

Another ripple of knowing laughter spread through the church. They loved their priest, that was clear, but they also had his number.

"And once, a long time ago, I was in a cold war with someone I loved. This someone had the kindness to remind me of the Christmas Truce of 1914, when all through the trenches, peace broke out between the French, British, and German soldiers who just the day before had been shooting at each other. We see the photographs reprinted in newspapers—soldiers lighting each other's cigarettes, playing soccer, talking. The Christmas Truce also allowed each side to safely recover fallen comrades. The friend who reminded me of the 1914 truce said something that's always stayed with me. 'Too bad it isn't Christmas every day. Then nobody would ever have to fight stupid wars.'"

Kingsley appreciated the sentiment but knew it was wishful thinking. Even as the truce broke out in patches along the fronts in World War I, it didn't break out every-where. The fighting went on. And by 1915, when the war had grown even more brutal and bitter, there were no more spontaneous truces, even on Christmas Day.

And yet...here he was, a former captain in the French Foreign Legion, holding the hand of his Mistress, the great-granddaughter of one of Kaiser Wilhelm's *Rittmeisters*. In 1915, an act of treason. Tonight, merely, as Nora said, a day ending in Y. Perhaps there was hope for mankind. A little, anyway.

"The more I think about the Christmas Truce of 1914, the more baffled I am by it," Søren continued. "How did it happen? I've counseled people who haven't seen close blood relatives in years because of a fight over politics or religion—a war merely of words—at some long-ago Thanks-giving dinner. But these men in the trenches had been killing each other—literally shooting at each other for months—when the truce broke out. How did it happen? Why? I may have a theory. Winter is cold, and nowhere is winter colder than a trench in Europe. The soldiers were as cold as they'd ever been and ever would be. But Christmas is warm. It's hot cider and candles and the Yule log burning and too many people packed into a church."

More soft laughter.

"The soldiers were blocks of ice by the time Christmas came around. And we know what happens when you drop ice into a hot drink? The ice cracks. This phenomenon is known as 'differential expansion.' The inner core of the ice cube stays cold and solid, but the outside of it that comes in contact with the heat, expands. And just like that, it cracks apart. Christmas came to those ice-cold soldiers, poured over them, and they cracked wide open. Maybe that's why Christmas hurts so many of us. We feel that fissure, that broken place where Christmas has cracked us apart. I think that's why at Christmas we feel so much of the cold, dark things inside us coming out—the anger at another year gone already, so much time wasted with so little to show for it, the loneliness of wanting to spend Christmas with someone who doesn't want to spend Christmas with you. Or worse, the feeling we've simply been forgotten."

Out of the corner of his eye, Kingsley saw Nora surreptitiously wipe a tear away.

"But..." Søren said, "perhaps there's some good that comes out of that crack Christmas knocks in our hearts. It makes a place where the good things can slip inside, the bright, warm things. The candlelight. The music. Old friends dropping by unannounced. And more...love? Hope? Forgiveness? It makes sense that Christmas makes us want to forgive each other, if only for a day. For Christmas, you see, is ultimately an act of forgiveness. In the beginning, God gave us all a gift—the world. And the world was pristine and beautiful and pure, and we broke it five minutes after he gave it to us. We were children in a China shop, and we broke the world without realizing we were breaking ourselves along with it. And yet instead of striking us all off His Christmas shopping list for eternity—as I would have done—God gave us *another* gift. In fact, God gave us the most precious thing in the universe to Him—His newborn son. And that gift, the gift of His child, couldn't be broken. Although we tried, didn't we? We did try."

Søren glanced meaningfully at the large crucifix on the wall.

"However..." he continued, smiling with priestly beneficence. "There is good news. God gave us His Son in an act of extravagant forgiveness. And we did try to break Him, and it looked like we had succeeded for a few days. Oh, but we didn't break Him. Because Jesus is love and love, real love, can be dropped and kicked and knocked around, whipped and beaten and nailed to a cross. And yet it lives. True love lives and it lives forever. So as I wish you all a merry Christmas, I also wish our Lord a happy birthday, for He is reborn every year in our hearts. And that is the meaning of Emmanuel—*God is with us*. Christmas is with us as is the forgiveness it carries in its open hands."

The homily ended, and Nora tugged Kingsley's hand, pulling him out of the sanctuary and into the narthex.

"Are you all right?" Nora asked.

"Me?"

"You were squeezing my hand so hard I thought you'd break it."

"I was?" Kingsley asked. "Sorry."

"He got to you, didn't he?" she asked, smiling with sympathy.

"A little," Kingsley confessed.

"Happens to the best of us."

The music had started up again in the sanctuary.

"Do you want to leave?" she asked. "Or do you want to go to his house and wait for him?"

"Just for a few minutes," Kingsley said. "I can give him his socks."

"All right. Follow me," she said.

She led him out the front doors of the church and around the side. In the winter's moonlight, they walked down the path that led from the side of the church to the thick copse of trees that shielded Søren's small house from prying eyes. Nora walked right up to the door and turned the knob. Locked. She pulled her key ring out of her coat pocket.

"This never happened," she said and unlocked the door

with her own personal key.

The door opened into Søren's kitchen. Nora switched on the light and Kingsley saw an old-fashioned cookie tin on the table.

"Oh my God, Claire," Nora said as she opened the lid of the cookie tin. "I love that girl. She always sends Søren two dozen of the best frosted sugar cookies every Christmas."

"You're eating his cookies?" Kingsley asked. "He didn't say you could have any."

"If you've sucked a man's cock, you get to eat his cookies. In perpetuity. That's the law." Nora unbuttoned Kingsley's coat for him and pushed it off his shoulders.

"Is it?" he asked, shrugging out of the coat.

"It is."

"In that case," Kingsley said, "give me one."

Nora laughed and popped a cookie in his mouth. It melted on his tongue like butter, which made sense, as it was approximately 78% butter.

She hung his coat up and led him into the living room where he and Søren had gotten tipsy—well, drunk—so many times over the years. Kingsley treasured those nights, the nights Søren's walls came down a little. Those drunken nights they spent talking until dawn. Sometimes Søren would lie on his back in front of the fireplace and let Kingsley lay his head on his stomach like old times. Sometimes Søren would even run his hands through Kingsley's hair and tug it, but that wouldn't happen tonight.

Nora plugged in the Christmas tree, and Kingsley had to blink through the sudden dazzle of the lights.

"Looks like I'm not the only one hosting a Santa Claus gangbang," Nora said. She switched on the electric candles in the window. Even the fireplace mantel was decorated with candles—real ones, and she lit them one by one by one until the entire room glowed. On top of the grand piano sat Søren's advent wreath. Nora lit all four candles inside the wreath while Kingsley started a small fire in the grate. He found a beautiful scarlet poinsettia on the floor by the wood pile.

Bambi, the attached card read. The rest of the inscription was in Italian: *I stole this off the altar of the Jesuit motherhouse. Love, Magdalena.*

Bambi?

"Hey," Nora said, flipping through a thick stack of cards she'd taken out of a basket. "I found the secret to getting a lot of Christmas cards. Join the clergy. There must be two-hundred cards here."

"Not worth it," Kingsley said. "I can buy my own cards."

"Look, it's us," she said, holding up a *Peanuts*-themed Christmas card. On the front was the blond pianist Schroeder, the black-haired muckraker Lucy, and Snoopy.

"I'm the fucking dog?" Kingsley asked.

"You've humped your fair share of legs."

"Speaking of, how did you know he would make that *Peanuts* joke?" Kingsley asked.

"I dared him a long time ago to say that when he got up to give his Christmas homily," she said, still flipping through the cards. "I didn't think he'd do it, but he did. Every few years he does it to get a good laugh."

"How did you know he would do it tonight?" he asked.

"I didn't know for sure," she said. "But that bet got you to come with me, didn't it?"

"If you'd lost the bet, I would have taken you for a thousand dollars."

"Worth it to get you here," she said. "I stuffed your

grand in the church's poor box. I'll let you take the tax deduction." She winked at him.

Nora put the cards back in the basket and the second she turned around Kingsley took her by the waist, pulled her against him, and kissed her deeply. He tasted the sugar in her mouth, the warm butter of the cookies. He could spend all night kissing and tasting this woman who put a thousand dollars on the line just so he'd go to church with her.

"Ahem?"

They broke apart like two teenagers caught making out by a dad with a shotgun. Søren stood in the doorway between the kitchen and his living room, arms crossed over his chest with a look of amused annoyance stamped on his face.

"Sorry. Mistletoe drill," Nora said. "Gotta be ready. Mistletoe can strike at any moment. You walk very softly, by the way."

"I saw lights on in my house that were not on when I left. I thought I might have a very stupid thief in the house. Or...*two* stupid thieves."

Søren looked at them and they looked at him. Kingsley wasn't sure what to say or do or how to explain their presence. Thank God for Nora.

"Merry Christmas, Søren," she said and walked over to him. He held out his arms immediately, without reservation or hesitation. Kingsley watched as she rested her head against Søren's chest, and he rested his chin on her head.

"Did you see your hart on your card?" he asked.

"Kingsley saw it. I missed it. It made me happy."

"Diane thought I'd lost my mind. I kept drawing tiny harts on the draft of my Christmas homily."

"I heard it," she said softly. "Your homily. I was in the

back."

"Did you like it?" Søren asked.

"You stole my line."

"Borrowed."

"I *borrowed* two of your Christmas cookies."

"Then we're even," he said and kissed the top of her head.

Kingsley watched, amazed. All was forgiven, just like that. Neither of them apologized. No "I'm sorry." No "You're forgiven." They simply held each other.

Nora slowly disentangled herself from Søren's embrace, but she kept his hand in hers.

"Hope it's okay I dragged King over here with me," she said.

"Merry Christmas," Søren said.

"*Joyeux Noël*," Kingsley said.

"I'm going to open some wine," Nora said. She left them alone together.

"She did drag me here," Kingsley said. "If you want to be alone with her, I can take the car and go. I don't want to ruin your Christmas with her."

Søren said nothing. Kingsley got the message.

"I'll leave your gift under the tree," Kingsley said. "You can open it whenever you want. Or toss it in the fireplace." He took the small gift of elegantly wrapped socks off the mantel and placed it under the tree. When Kingsley stood up again, Søren was there.

Søren grabbed Kingsley by the back of the neck and hauled him into his arms. Kingsley was too shocked at first to even react. Standing there, Kingsley had one fleeting thought—if this rough embrace was all he got for Christmas, it would be enough. It would be more than enough.

It would be an extravagance.

Kingsley buried his head against Søren's shoulder as Søren whispered in his ear.

"The only way you could ruin my Christmas is by leaving now," Søren said, his words tender but his tone steel-tipped. "Burn the tree down, burn the house down, I don't care. But don't leave."

Kingsley breathed in the scent of Søren. That night he smelled of fresh fallen snow, as always, but something more. In his clothes was the scent of the church's incense. One thing Kingsley did recall from his Catholic school days—that the prayers of God's people rose before His altar in the form of incense. That meant Søren smelled like a prayer.

"I won't," Kingsley said, his eyes suddenly hot and hurting. "I might eat all your cookies though."

Søren abruptly released him and pointed to the door. "Get out."

Kingsley laughed so hard he had to sit down. He collapsed into the armchair and kicked off his shoes like it was just another drinking night at Søren's.

"You bastard," Kingsley said as Nora brought in three glasses of red wine, which took a great deal of careful balancing on her part. "I may burn your house down before the night is over."

"Ah...insults and threats of arson," Nora said, grinning. "Now it really feels like Christmas."

Nora passed out the wine and sat on the arm of the sofa. Søren stood by the fireplace and pulled his white collar out of his shirt and undid the top button. An unconscious gesture, but Kingsley couldn't quite stop staring at Søren's bare throat.

"Dare I ask what brings you two to my humble abode tonight?" Søren said.

"It's Christmas," Nora said. "We thought we'd stop by,

see if you wanted to hang out? Drink wine? Watch *Rudolph*?"

"Fuck?" Kingsley said.

Nora glared at him. "Hush, Kingsley, or Momma will take all your Christmas presents back to the store."

She shot Søren a look of apology. "You'll have to excuse my man-whore," she said. "He's gone thirty-six whole hours without getting laid. You know how it is: submissives—can't live with them, can't hang them from your dungeon ceiling and exsanguinate them."

"It's not a bad suggestion, actually," Søren said.

"Exsanguinating Kingsley?" Nora asked. "That's more of a Valentine's Day thing."

"No," Søren said. "Fucking."

Kingsley made the mistake of attempting to swallow his wine while Søren was announcing his agreement with the fucking idea. It got caught in his throat and nearly came out of his nose before he managed to swallow it.

"Did you expect me to say no?" Søren said. "It's been *considerably* longer than thirty-six hours for me."

As Kingsley was recovering from nearly choking to death on a full-bodied Pinot Noir, Nora walked to Søren, placed her hands on his chest, and rose on her tiptoes to kiss him.

"Just when I think I have you all figured out," she said after the kiss, "you agree to a threesome on Christmas. Or a twosome if Kingsley dies."

"I won't die," Kingsley said. "I think. Can I have some water?"

Nora fetched him a glass of water, which he drained and returned to her hand.

"*Merci, Maîtresse.*"

"You're welcome. Don't die," she said. "I might be

needing your cock later."

"Are we sure he was serious?" Kingsley asked, moving his head to look past Nora to where Søren still stood at the fireplace, wearing an infuriatingly enigmatic expression on his face.

"I don't know if he was serious," Nora said. "But I am. I'll be upstairs waiting in bed, either to fuck or sleep."

She swished upstairs as only Nora could and would swish in the home of a Jesuit priest at 1:16 in the morning.

Once they were alone, Søren looked at him, one eyebrow slightly cocked. Kingsley sat back in the armchair and tried to look casual.

"It was your idea," Søren said.

"I was joking, Friar Fuck."

"If you're not interested," Søren said, "we'll sleep. Eleanor makes an excellent pillow."

Kingsley was up and on his feet approximately one light second later. "No, I'm interested. Only...you caught me a little off-guard."

"It isn't as if we haven't done this together before," Søren reminded him.

"We haven't been with each other in a long time. That's all," Kingsley said. "You and her...all the time. But the three of us? Not since before that year."

Yes, that year. Kingsley thought of it as "that year" or *that year*. Always in quotes or italics as if it were something fictional or foreign. *That year* he and Nora disappeared, left New York, left Søren, left each other and came back very different people than they had been before "that year."

"You certain you want me there?" Kingsley asked.

"Eleanor's quite fond of you for reasons that escape me."

"I didn't ask if she wanted me there. She always wants

me there," Kingsley said, unable to resist any opportunity of poking Søren in his ego a little. "Do you?"

Søren turned and faced the fireplace, and with the tip of his black shoe, toed the poinsettia back into place by the wood pile.

"Who the hell is Bambi?" Kingsley asked, recalling the note on the poinsettia.

"Me," Søren said. "Short for 'bambino' since I was a 'baby' Jesuit when we met."

"Magda called you Bambi? And you let her?"

"She saved my sanity more than once," Søren said. "I'm not sure I would have survived seminary without her."

"You know, if someone just like you..." Kingsley said, "if *you* from the past, age nineteen, age twenty, came to me tomorrow in need, I would say to you, 'I know who can help you—Mistress Nora.' "

"You're trying to make a point," Søren said. "Don't."

Søren sipped his wine, stared deep into the glass.

"Magdalena never sent me a poinsettia," Kingsley said.

"She and I have history," Søren said. "Like you and I. And not all of it is bad."

"None of our history was bad," Kingsley said. "Not until the end, anyway."

"Eleanor disagrees."

"She's sorry for bringing that up," Kingsley said. "She told me tonight she was sorry."

"Did she?"

Kingsley nodded. "Are you?"

"Sorry? For what?" He sounded insulted by the very idea he could be sorry for anything.

"Saying I'm only with her to hurt you? That isn't fair to either of us."

"Aren't you?"

"As a matter of fact—"

"For a man so *easy*, you are being incredibly difficult," Søren said. "You've never required an engraved invitation to come to bed with us before."

Kingsley tapped his foot over that for a few seconds. "*C'est vrai. Mais*...it is Christmas. You want me at your threesome? Ask nicely. Gift-wrap it a little for me. Decorate it."

Søren plucked an ornament off the tree and hung it on Kingsley's shirt collar, pressing the silver hook into his flesh.

"Son of a bitch!" Kingsley said, prying the ornament—a tiny snowflake with a nasty hook—from his person. He rubbed his collarbone and a dab of blood stained his finger. "Why did you do that?"

"Because *that* is how I decorate," Søren said.

"Stop flirting when I'm playing hard to get." Kingsley hung the ornament back on the tree, bloodied hook and all. "I'm a little rattled. I saw you in your vestments. Now I'm supposed to see you fucking?"

"I still can't believe you went to mass on Christmas Eve."

"I didn't. I peeked in, that's all. You were...different. Like a whole different person. It was bizarre."

"Bizarre? It's been my job for fourteen years."

"You fucked me half to death on the floor of a forest. I'm allowed to find it bizarre when you're standing at a pulpit talking about Jesus, wearing all white and shining like a fucking angel."

Søren dropped his chin to his chest. If Kingsley had to guess, he would guess Søren was counting to himself to calm down. Probably to one hundred.

One-hundred thousand, that was.

"Fine," Søren said, sighing. "You win. Yes."

"Yes? Yes, what?" Kingsley asked.

"Yes, I want you in bed with us. Now. Tonight. And yes, I want it to be like it used to be, though I know that's an impossible wish. For one night, please, as a gift to me, let's pretend *that year* never happened. So there it is, gift-wrapped. We can either stand here and keep fighting or go upstairs and pretend there's not a war on for an hour or so. Your choice. Whatever you decide, please don't blame me later when you regret it."

Kingsley opened a button on Søren's black clerical shirt while he simply stood there, letting him do it.

"You talked me into it, Father Stearns," Kingsley said. "And I won't blame you when I regret it. Because I won't regret it."

Kingsley kissed Søren on his bare throat in the hollow under the Adam's apple.

"I am the same man in my vestments as out of them," Søren said. "Whether I want to be or not."

Kingsley kissed Søren's throat again.

"You think we should go upstairs now?" Kingsley asked. "Our lady probably fell asleep waiting on us to make up our cocks."

"Our lady is probably at the top of the stairs eavesdropping on us," Søren said.

"Am not!" Nora yelled down.

"She is in so much trouble," Søren said slowly, smiling. Kingsley's blood temperature shot up a good five degrees at the sight of that smile alone. There was nothing in the world sexier than the smile of a dominant about to destroy a submissive's good mood.

They walked upstairs and went straight to the bedroom where they found Nora lounging on the bed, feet propped against the headboard and naked but for a pair of red and white candy-cane striped knee socks. Kingsley put an arm around Søren's shoulder as they stared admiringly.

"About time, gentlemen. I was going to start without you," Nora said. It was perfect, the whole scene utterly *parfait*. Nora looked delectable in her cheeky Christmas socks, lying on her back in invitation. Søren had hung Christmas lights around his bedroom window and the room filled with their soft white glow. If Kingsley could freeze a moment and frame it, this one would hang on the wall over his bed so he could stare at it every time he fucked.

"If Mrs. Claus looks anything like her," Kingsley said to Søren, "it would explain why there are so many songs about Santa coming at Christmas."

Nora chose that moment to spread her knees apart and lift her hips in a languorous seductive stretch.

"It really is the most wonderful time of the year," Søren said. He turned his head and glared at Kingsley. "Why are you still standing there? Can't you tell she's a little chilly?"

"I'll warm her up for you," Kingsley said, slapping his hands together and rubbing them. As he walked to the bed he turned on his heel and made sure he had Søren's eyes on him when he stripped out of his shirt. He dropped it and crawled onto the bed with Nora. He took her by the hips and dragged her to him.

"Hello, Mr. King," she said. "Do you like my socks?"

"They'll look very good on my back," Kingsley said, dipping his head to kiss the soft smooth flesh of her stomach. Nora slid her hands up his arms to his shoulders. He found her mouth and kissed it.

The kiss was hot and wet and deep and went straight to his head and to his cock simultaneously. He kneed Nora's thighs wide so he could nestle between them. He pushed his erection against her, and she murmured a soft sound of pleasure into his mouth. She reached between them and—still kissing Kingsley—managed to unbuckle his belt, undo his zipper, and take his cock into her soft, smooth hands. She rubbed the shaft, teased the tip. Fluid leaked out and she caught it on her fingers and massaged him with the wetness...without once breaking the kiss. Nothing might have broken the kiss except for her sadism. She wrapped her full hand around him and stroked upward, pulling slow and hard. As he started to moan, she bit into his bottom lip. The pleasure coupled with the pain was so intense he almost ejaculated onto her stomach.

"Fuck..." he groaned, then laughed at his own reaction. Nora grinned wickedly up at him.

Søren stood at the side of the bed watching them, which made everything better and worse. He leaned casually against the bedpost but there was nothing casual about the hungry look in his eyes.

"She's not very well-behaved," Søren said. "We'll have to do something about that."

Nora opened her mouth to object, but Kingsley slapped his hand over her lips to silence her. She groaned against his palm. He'd warned her he wanted to top tonight. If she needed reminding, he'd remind her.

Søren had opened the large steamer trunk he kept at the end of the bed, the "linen" trunk which hid all his toys of torture. He pulled out rope cuffs and a rattan cane. Kingsley almost objected to the cane. He was no angel himself, but a cane could do a world of damage. When Nora saw it, however, she smiled. She kissed her way from Kingsley's lips to his ear.

"It's all right," she whispered. "It can be a black *and* blue Christmas."

"Children," Søren said. "Do we have something to share

with the class?"

"Nothing," Kingsley said.

"We were discussing the condom situation," Nora said, lying smoothly.

"And what is the condom situation?" Søren asked.

"I have condoms," Kingsley said. "That's the situation. Also...throw me those." He pointed at the rope cuffs in Søren's hand. Søren tossed them to Kingsley, who caught them in the air and then, quick as a flash, he had Nora's wrists bound to the bar of the headboard.

He looked at her underneath him. Naked, her body smooth and pale enough that the white Christmas lights strung around the bedroom window shimmered on her skin, in her eyes. Her breasts rose and fell with her quick breaths, and her nipples, reddish pink, were already hard, hard and irresistible. Kingsley wrapped his hand under and around her left breast and lifted it roughly, sucked the nipple deeply. He was keenly aware of Søren watching his every move. He met Søren's gaze while suckling her breast. It was nothing but eye contact. Intense, heated, unbroken eye contact. He took Nora's right breast in his hand and fondled her nipple. Curious just how closely Søren was watching, Kingsley pinched her nipple hard enough to make her flinch. Søren inhaled sharply, if quietly, at Nora's flinching. Kingsley would have laughed if he didn't have Nora's beautiful nipple in his mouth.

"Kingsley," Søren said in a deceptively calm tone. "I think you've forgotten something."

"What's that?" Kingsley asked, sitting up on his knees and still groping Nora.

"You're still dressed."

Kingsley left her on the bed while he slipped off to finish undressing. He stood in front of Søren and took his jeans off. The socks too. He was a firm believer only women could pull off the "naked except for socks" look successfully. Nora was proof of that. Søren only blinked once during the proceedings.

"I've seen it before," Søren reminded him as he tapped the rattan cane against his calf.

"Seen it," Kingsley said. "Touched it, sucked it, jacked it off while fucking me too many times to count..."

"Hey, me too," Nora said from the bed.

"Is your pussy wet enough to take my cock yet?" Kingsley demanded.

"It's—"

"Doesn't matter," he said. "It's going in anyway."

Søren smiled his approval. Nora spent most of her twenties getting threatened with their cocks.

Kingsley climbed onto the bed again, knelt between her thighs as he rolled on the condom. With his fingers, he pushed open her inner lips of her vulva and gazed down at the glimmering wet red flesh. Nora lifted her hips in invitation. Kingsley put the tip of his cock inside the entrance of her pussy.

"With your permission?" Kingsley said to Søren.

"Granted and encouraged," Søren said.

With that, Kingsley thrust his cock into Nora who took every inch. Kingsley grunted with pleasure as he was enveloped by her hot vagina.

"Christ," he muttered as she clenched around him.

"Tried to tell you I was wet enough for your cock, Mr. King," she said in a taunting tone.

"You keep talking, and I'll gag you with my socks," Kingsley said. "Or my cock. Whichever."

"I have a better idea," Søren said. He crawled onto the bed and bent over to kiss Nora. It was a deep, long kiss and

Kingsley watched as their tongues touched and mated. All the while, Søren still held the cane in his hand. The longer Søren went without using it on either of them, the more Kingsley became aware of it. Kingsley continued ramming his cock into Nora, but he kept his eyes on the cane. He took her breasts in his hands, held them and squeezed them as he fucked her...but he kept his eyes on the cane. He rubbed his thumbs over her hard nipples, teasing them until she moaned into Søren's mouth...

But he kept his eyes on the cane.

"What are you planning to do with that?" Kingsley finally asked, his voice strained as he pumped into Nora.

Søren broke the kiss and turned his head.

"Help you," Søren said.

"Help me?" Kingsley smiled. "How?"

Søren sat up and snapped the cane. He flicked it quickly enough Kingsley heard it slicing the air with a brisk hiss and flinched out of instinct. But Søren didn't strike either of them with it. He brought it down gently on the small of Kingsley's back.

"Like this," Søren said. He used the cane to prod Kingsley to thrust into Nora again. But slower this time, at Søren's pace, not Kingsley's. Kingsley pulled out when Søren lifted the cane an inch off his body and only thrust into Nora's pussy again when Søren and the cane indicated he could. As he was forced to slow his thrusts, he made each one count more. Nora lifted her hips to take him as he slid into her wet hole all the way to her cervix and withdrew slowly, knowing that Søren was watching his cock enter and leave her and enter her again. Nora's head fell back in her ecstasy and Kingsley nearly died from having his every movement controlled by the feather-light touch of the cane on his back.

It shouldn't have felt as erotic as it did. Just a cane tip against his hip telling him exactly when and how hard to fuck. But it worked some kind of magic on Kingsley. He felt used, like he was nothing but an object, a toy, and he was being wielded by Søren for Nora's pleasure.

And he fucking loved it, Søren controlling his every move, his every breath, his cock, his orgasms, his come.

"She's enjoying this too much," Søren said as he looked down at Nora. "She's not allowed to come yet."

"Have you told her that?" Kingsley asked. Nora was breathing so hard and so rapidly, he doubted she could hear a word they said. He was close to coming, too, and he could barely speak. His hips were tight and his cock straining and still the cane pushed lightly against his body, mastering his every move.

"We should probably stop before she comes," Søren said.

"What about me? Can I come?" Kingsley asked, and he didn't care what Søren said. Asking him for permission to come was more arousing than any old orgasm.

"I suppose," Søren said.

Søren flicked the cane again, flicked it hard, brutally hard. Flicked it out and brought it down against the back of Kingsley's thigh.

The pain was sudden, burning, blinding. He thought Søren had split his thigh open to the bone.

Kingsley cried out in pain. Every nerve in his body fired at once. His back arched and he lost total control of himself. He thrust into Nora and came, the orgasm obliterating all self-awareness, all self-restraint.

As he slowly returned to his senses, he was vaguely cognizant of the sound of arrogant laughter. "You think that's funny," Kingsley said as he pulled out of Nora and rolled onto his back.

"If you were any more of a whore," Søren said, "you would be..."

"Me?" Nora asked. She was grinning broadly, the proverbial pussy who ate the canary. Kingsley was the canary.

"Exactly," Søren said and bent to kiss her on the lips again.

"You two are going to kill me," she said.

"And that," Søren said, "is why the French call 'orgasm' the little death."

"Fuck the little death," Kingsley said. "That was almost a big death. Warn a man next time before you're going to force him to come his brains out of his cock."

"My name is all the warning you should need," Søren said.

"He has a point there, Mr. King," Nora said, stretching and sighing.

"Eleanor?" Søren said.

"Yes, sir?"

He touched his finger to her lips to quiet her. "Hush. Men are speaking."

Nora's mouth fell open in shock. She obeyed and remained silent, but her eyes spoke volumes and all those volumes had MURDER written on the front cover.

"She's going to kill you for that later, *mon ami*," Kingsley said.

"Perhaps," Søren said. "But there's nothing she can do about it now."

Kingsley rested a few seconds before he had the strength to roll up and dispose of the condom.

"Now what?" Kingsley asked. The welt on his thigh

burned like Greek fire. He was already half-hard again.

Søren gazed down at Nora and smiled. He spoke Kingsley's three favorite French words.

"*C'est a moi.*"

"Your turn," Kingsley said.

Søren stood and undressed quickly while Kingsley stretched out alongside Nora, touching her vagina, caressing it, opening it while she panted. Now naked, Søren crawled over to them, and Kingsley started to pull his hand away from her body.

"Stay there," Søren ordered. Kingsley raised his eyebrow at Søren but did as instructed. He kept one finger inside Nora as Søren moved on top of her, and remained inside her as Søren entered her with a long thrust. Nora took it all. She groaned, and Kingsley couldn't quite tell if it was from pleasure or pain. She spread her legs so wide Kingsley draped one over his hip. She breathed hard through her lips. It couldn't have been easy to take so much of both of them into her. She had before, but she was tight tonight from her near-brush with orgasm. She didn't complain, though, because the pleasure outweighed the pain or because she knew her pain gave Søren so much pleasure.

Kingsley could hardly breathe as he moved his finger in and out of her in time with Søren's slow thrusts. Touching her and Søren at once was bliss. The long slide of Søren's wet cock over his finger, the back of his hand...the slick heat of Nora's pussy...the sounds of three lovers moving together, their breaths mingling... Kingsley was hard enough he could have come again with a word. The head of his penis pressed against Søren's thigh, rock hard with tension, and when Søren moved in Nora, his thigh stroked Kingsley with sweeter friction than a hand. Nora's eyes were closed in concentration, the sure sign she was close to climax. Yet Søren didn't increase the pace of his thrusts. He lingered over her, fucking her like he had all winter to warm himself inside her. Kingsley was in no rush either. When Søren pulled out to the tip, Kingsley pulled out as well, and as Søren entered her again, Kingsley stroked him. Søren looked at Kingsley, met his eyes, and said nothing as he thrust into Nora's body and into Kingsley's hand at the same time. When Søren's eyelashes fluttered and his eyes rolled back, Kingsley felt a sense of triumph that was better than anything anyone had ever given him for Christmas.

The moment passed and Søren was in control of himself again. He pushed deep into Nora, who lifted her head and her hips at the same time.

"Either kill me or let me come," she begged. "Please, sir?"

"Which shall it be?" Søren asked Kingsley.

"Better let her come," Kingsley said. "It is Christmas."

"Then you should do the honors," Søren said.

As Søren moved in her, faster now, Kingsley stroked Nora's swollen clitoris. The hard little knot throbbed against his fingertips. She lifted her hips in quick pants and pulled hard against the rope cuffs. The bed shifted and rocked as Søren fucked her and Kingsley fingered her. Her exquisite full breasts rose and fell with her breaths. Kingsley caught her nipple between his lips and sucked it while she writhed and squirmed and dug her heels into the sheets, her fingers clinging to the headboard. Søren went at her hard, pounding her mercilessly while Kingsley edged her closer and closer to release. When she was there, and he knew it because of the high arch of her back, he pushed two fingers into her vagina, and crooked them, digging into the deep hollow of her g-spot.

Nora didn't orgasm. She exploded. Her pussy contracted so hard around Kingsley's fingers it hurt. She shuddered under Søren, shuddered around his cock and even he, master of self-control in such moments, gasped quietly and dug his hand roughly into the soft flesh of her hip.

Now spent, Nora collapsed back onto the bed.

"Jesus Christmas," she sighed between rasping gasps. "I think you fucked my spine. Can you put iodine on a pussy? My vagina's going to be in traction for a week."

"Are these compliments?" Søren asked, smiling down at her. He stroked her forehead gently, tenderly brushing the damp hair off her face.

"It's a fact," she said. Kingsley smiled blissfully as he lay on his side next to her, lightly fondling her breasts for no other reason than it pleased him to do so, and she was in no position to object.

"I suppose I should finish so we can sleep," Søren said.

"Sleep is overrated." Kingsley could do this all night with them.

"Do you know what isn't overrated?" Nora asked. "Cocksucking."

"Underrated, in fact," Kingsley said.

"Are you hinting at something, Eleanor?" Søren asked.

"You might have broken my pussy," she said. "So if you want to come inside me, I'm thinking my mouth might be the best bet. If it pleases you, sir."

She looked at Kingsley and grinned, her eyes alight with erotic mischief.

"I'll allow it," Søren said. "Though I think you're offering so I'll untie you from the bed. If you attempt to murder me for telling you to hush earlier, I'll make you sleep on the floor without a blanket, and if you think I won't do it, ask Kingsley how many times I've punished him that way."

"Seven," Kingsley said. "Not that I kept count."

He'd kept count.

"I have no ulterior motives, I swear," Nora said, a sure sign she was lying.

Søren quickly loosened the rope cuffs so Nora could free her hands. She sat up slowly and stretched as Søren lay back, his head propped on a pillow. Nora slid on top of him, kissed him on his mouth, a deep kiss that Søren returned with teeth and tongue and passion. Nora broke the kiss first but only to kiss his neck and then his broad chest, his hard stomach, his sides and his hips. She lingered long over the hips, and Kingsley knew she was engaging in both foreplay and torture. A true switch, she could please and tease all at once.

Søren, however, was a *true* dominant, and all it took was a pointed clearing of his throat to communicate to her that further delay would be against her best interests. Nora got the hint. She went up on her hands and knees between his thighs and took his cock into her mouth. Kingsley watched as she sucked him slowly and deeply into her throat before pulling out to the tip which she lavished with long licks of her tongue. But Kingsley wasn't content to merely watch. He was hard from touching Søren so intimately and needed to come again. He knelt behind Nora, who was too engrossed in her task to even notice him slipping on a condom. But when he rose up on his knees behind her, took her by the hips, and started to enter her...she noticed.

She grunted—all she could do with her mouth full—but she didn't stop sucking. Her vagina had seemingly recovered from its brush with death. It was hot and slick and welcoming as Kingsley pushed inside her, impaling her pussy as Søren impaled her mouth. Kingsley didn't know which of them would come first—him or Søren—but smart money was on Kingsley. Really, no matter who came first, they were all winners here. And was there any better view in the world than this—Søren on his back, his cock in Nora's mouth, his hands tight around her neck, and Kingsley's cock inside her pussy? He pumped into her in short, fast thrusts as she sucked Søren. Kingsley might have lasted longer if he hadn't made the mistake of looking at Søren. Nora gave masterful blow jobs—Kingsley knew this from experience—and even Søren could be unmanned by them. His head fell back on the pillow, his long throat exposed, his eyes closed, and his fingers digging into the nape of Nora's neck with such force she was sure to have blue bruises by morning. Søren spread his legs wide and lifted his hips, fucking Nora's mouth. The whole scene was so utterly obscene Kingsley couldn't stand it. He let go, rutting into Nora's dripping wet hole and came with a low cry. He heard a gasp, a low throaty gasp, and he saw Søren lift his hips once more and Kingsley knew he was coming into Nora's mouth. Kingsley sat back on his knees as Søren collapsed onto his back.

Nora rose up, turned her head, and grabbed Kingsley hard to kiss him. It was a sudden kiss, unexpected, and when she opened her mouth against his, he nearly came again. She hadn't swallowed Søren's semen. She'd held it in her mouth and now passed it to him with a kiss. Kingsley took her face in his hands and kissed her harder than he ever had before. He licked every drop of come out of her mouth and swallowed it with a hunger for the taste of Søren he didn't know he still had in him.

And when he'd taken every drop of come from her, she pulled back and licked her lips.

Then she winked at him.

"Merry Christmas, King."

And from the bed, Søren said, "Do I want to know what that was about?"

Both Kingsley and Nora agreed he probably did not.

A few minutes later, after water was drunk and lights turned out, the three of them lay in Søren's bed, warm and cozy under his thick winter quilt.

Nora lay stretched on top of Søren, her head in the center of his chest, eyes closed and seemingly sound asleep.

"How does she do that?" Kingsley asked, lying on his side next to Søren. "She falls asleep just like that."

"You'd crash hard, too, if you'd just taken two cocks in you at the same time," Nora murmured sleepily.

"Shh..." Søren said, stroking her back. "Sleep, Little One."

"Is it all right if we stay?" Kingsley said.

"I wouldn't have turned out the lights if it wasn't," Søren said. "And even if it wasn't, she's out already."

"Are we sure she's asleep this time?" Kingsley asked.

Søren took a strand of her hair in his fingers, and tickled her nose with it. She slept on. As Nora was on Søren's chest, Kingsley took his usual place on Søren's stomach. That lasted all of about one minute before Søren sighed heavily.

"This is profoundly uncomfortable," Søren said.

"For you, maybe," Nora said. "I'm nice and toasty."

"I am a person, not a heating pad. Eleanor, get off of me, please. You too, Kingsley."

"I'd rather get off *for* you," she said.

Søren rewarded that cheek with a hard slap to her ass. Nora giggled and rolled onto her side.

"Kids," Kingsley said. "Can never get them to sleep when they know Santa is coming."

Søren stretched out on his back. Even in the darkness, Kingsley could see him close his eyes and ready himself for sleep. Kingsley would sleep, too, eventually, but not yet. He wanted to enjoy this moment in Søren's bed with his new mistress and his old master.

"Kingsley," Søren said softly.

"*Oui?*"

"I *do* want to know what that was about."

Kingsley grinned. "The snowballing?"

"Yes. That."

"So, ah...earlier tonight I was at *Chez Maîtresse,* and I might have—and this was a joke, I promise—I might have said that all I wanted for Christmas was to swallow your come. For old times' sake."

"Hmm..." Søren paused to digest this information. "I'm glad Eleanor was the intermediary on delivering that particular gift and not Santa Claus."

"What? You've never had your cock sucked by a man in a red suit with a white beard?"

"As a matter of fact, I have not."

"You and I lived very different lives in the late eighties, *mon ami.*"

"Thank God."

Søren rolled onto his side, facing Nora. He adjusted his pillow and moved the quilt up higher. The sky had cleared —no more snow tonight—and the moon shone its light in through Søren's bedroom window. Kingsley rolled to face Søren's back and, before he could stop himself, he kissed Søren between the shoulder blades. He put his hand on Søren's hip, and when Søren didn't object, Kingsley gently touched him.

"It's still there, I promise," Søren said.

"I thought she might have sucked it off."

"I tried," Nora said.

"Eleanor," Søren said, "sleep or death? You decide."

She quickly feigned snoring.

Although he was soft, Kingsley still liked feeling Søren's cock in his hand. He held it until Søren grabbed him around the wrist with so much force Kingsley winced. If Søren gripped him any tighter, he might break a bone in the wrist.

Ah, like old times.

"Sorry," Kingsley said and started to pull his hand away. But Søren didn't let him. Instead, he pulled Kingsley closer until he lay flush against Søren's back. He put his nose to the back of Søren's neck and fell asleep breathing the scent of snow and prayers.

Kingsley woke at dawn and found Nora asleep still, basking in the pale watery light of Christmas morning, looking almost angelic but for the black and blue bruise on her neck, a gift from Søren's fingers. Kingsley felt the mattress shift slightly, and he rolled over to find Søren sitting on the edge of the bed, dressed in his black trousers and t-shirt. He was freshly showered and shaved, the blond hair looking perfect as always. He was putting on his socks. New black socks.

"Nice socks," Kingsley said.

"Santa left them for me under the tree," Søren said.

"I couldn't decide between getting you socks or getting you underwear, and then I remembered I don't approve of underwear."

"The socks are perfect," Søren said. "Thank you."

Kingsley glanced at the bedside clock. Six a.m.

"Ah, do we need to go?" Kingsley asked.

"Not yet," Søren said. "And you don't have to sneak out. My brother-in-law and his girlfriend are allowed to visit me on Christmas morning. It's hardly a scandal."

"If you don't want a scandal, wipe that smile off your face or everyone will figure out you got laid last night."

"I'll tell them it's Christmas cheer," Søren said.

Kingsley slowly stretched out. He was sore from last night's sex, his favorite sort of pain. He glanced over at Nora, seemingly sound asleep.

"Dead to the world," Søren said.

"You sure?" Kingsley asked.

"Let's find out." Søren whistled softly. "Eleanor? Pancakes?"

Nothing.

"We wore her out," Kingsley said.

"We're good at that." Søren started to stand and Kingsley stopped him, reaching out to put a hand on Søren's arm.

"What is it?"

"Can I tell you something before she wakes up?" Kingsley asked. "It's a confession."

Søren's eyebrow went up half an inch. "Go on."

"I did something stupid yesterday," Kingsley said in French. He waited for the inevitable joke, Søren saying something like "Shocking" or "Only yesterday?".

But there was no joke. Søren simply nodded for Kingsley to continue.

"When I was Christmas shopping," Kingsley said, "I went into a toy store. I saw this little soccer ball, a small one for toddlers. I picked it up and a woman asked me how old my son was. I told her he was one-and-a-half."

Kingsley's eyes burned. If he and Nora hadn't...if they had decided to...if they had gone ahead with...yes, he or she would be about a year and a half old now. And he never thought about that. *Almost* never, but yesterday in the toy store, he had thought about it for the first time in months, thought about how he'd failed her, how he'd failed himself. Right after he'd gone to Nora's house with a made-up excuse to be with her.

He waited for Søren to absolve him or mock him or order him to lay there and think about why Kingsley tortured himself like this sometimes. Søren did none of these things. Instead, he ran his fingers through Kingsley's hair once, twice, and on the third time through, he tugged Kingsley's hair, hard. Hard enough, in fact, to take the pain away.

"When does Juliette come back?" Søren asked, his fingers still deep in Kingsley's hair.

"Tomorrow." Kingsley smiled when he said it. Thinking of Juliette's return always made him smile.

"You'll feel better when she's back."

True. Kingsley only got like this these days when Juliette was gone. Next year, he'd tie her to the bed to keep her from leaving him on Christmas again. She wouldn't complain.

He sat up and Kingsley lightly punched Søren in the upper arm. "You're a good priest."

"Don't tell anyone that," Søren said with a wink.

Kingsley stretched out his back.

"Can you get her up and dressed?" Søren said, nodding toward Nora, still lost in dreamland.

"I can do that," Kingsley said.

"I'll see you downstairs."

Søren started to leave when Kingsley glanced at Nora, still sleeping. "Hey," he said to Søren in a half-whisper. "Will you make coffee?"

Søren gave him a puzzled look. "Coffee it is."

Once Søren was gone, Kingsley rolled over and lightly touched Nora's shoulder. She wore the tiniest smile on her lips. What did dominatrixes dream about, he wondered. Later he would make her show him.

"Wake up, *Maîtresse.* Time for sadists to rise and shine," he said.

"Five more minutes, Big Poppa," she said in a pouting little girl's voice.

"Oh, no, no, no," he said. "Don't get me hard on Christmas morning."

She grinned, her eyes still closed.

"Elle, get dressed and go downstairs," Kingsley said. "I got you a present."

Her eyes flew open. "Present? What is it?"

"You'll have to go down to see it."

She slowly dragged herself out of bed and pulled on her clothes.

"Better be good," she said as she walked to the door.

"Oh, it's good," Kingsley said. "Santa King delivered exactly what you wanted."

Kingsley lingered in Søren's shower for a good ten minutes. He wanted to let Nora have a couple cups of coffee with Søren before he joined them. He toweled off and dressed in yesterday's clothes, made the bed as best he could, and went down to the kitchen.

He entered to find Nora refilling Søren's coffee cup, bustling and beaming like a new bride the morning after a very successful wedding night.

"Morning, King," she said, still grinning. "Your coffee's getting cold."

She'd poured a cup for him, too—in a Sacred Heart Catholic Church mug, of course—and for some reason that touched him so much he had trouble taking his first swallow.

"What's on your schedule today?" Nora asked Søren as she sat in the chair next to Kingsley's.

"Mass at seven and ten. Then Claire is coming to pick me up, and I'm staying with her in the Hamptons for three days," he said.

"You'll miss our Christmas party," Kingsley said. "Glad I brought you your gift."

"Yours is up there," Søren said, nodding at the refrigerator.

Kingsley picked up the small package wrapped in brown paper and white twine.

"Should I open it now?" Kingsley asked.

"Later," Søren said. "I have to get to church. Some of us have to work on Christmas."

"We should get going, too," Nora said, looking at Kingsley. "Take me to your place and put breakfast in me, please."

"I'll put something in you," Kingsley said.

She started to stand but Søren grabbed her and dragged her into his lap. "Merry Christmas, Little One," he said, rocking her in his arms.

"Merry Christmas," she said. They kissed, a quick gentle kiss, all tenderness, no passion. It was too early for that, and they were spent and tired from the night before. Kingsley pulled on his coat and soon they were at the door, ready to leave.

"See you soon?" Nora asked.

"Soon," Søren said. He kissed her forehead. Kingsley held out his hand for Søren to shake. When Søren took it, Kingsley leaned in and kissed Søren right on the lips.

"Mistletoe drill," Kingsley said. Then he pulled back and walked out of the house before Søren could kiss him or kill him in return.

Nora put her arm through his as they walked away from the rectory toward her car still parked down the block. She had a strange look on her face.

"You okay?" Kingsley asked her.

She pulled a framed photograph out of her handbag—a picture of her and Søren in his mother's home in Copenhagen. Søren's two Danish nieces sat on their laps, smiling. Anyone who didn't know otherwise would assume Nora and Søren were married and these were their two beautiful daughters, blondes like their father.

"My Christmas present," she said.

"A private family photo," Kingsley said. "A very sadistic Christmas gift."

"A punch in the stomach would have hurt less." She cradled the photo in her hands like a Fabergé egg. "What did he give you?"

Kingsley took the small wrapped bundle out of his pocket and tore off the paper as they crunched through the hard-packed snow.

"Very fitting," Kingsley said. "I gave him socks. He gave me insoles."

They were the high-tech gel insoles that runners put inside their shoes. Søren went through a dozen pairs of them a year. A gift as meaningless as socks.

"You don't get it?" Nora asked. "It's a pun. Like when I gave him the little hart, the deer toy? I gave him my heart for Christmas. Søren gave you his soul."

"You're overthinking it," Kingsley said.

"Søren wouldn't give you insoles just to give you insoles. You hate jogging."

"He wouldn't give me his 'soul' either. That belongs to God," he said.

"Supposedly so does his body."

"*Touché,*" Kingsley said, though he wasn't convinced at all there was a double meaning to the gift, no matter what Nora said. Juliette had certainly warned Søren he was getting nothing but socks for Christmas from Kingsley, and so Søren had returned the gift in kind. Which was fine. What else did Kingsley want or need after falling asleep with his chest pressed to Søren's back, his arm around him last night? Nothing. Not even Søren's soul.

Or his insoles.

As they reached the car, Nora started to open the driver's-side door. Kingsley stopped her for one more coffee-flavored kiss.

"Mistletoe drill?" she asked when the kiss ended.

Kingsley looked around them. The bright morning sun had turned the snowy streets into glittering diamonds. The trees were all tipped in white like they'd been frosted with sugar. With or without Søren's soul in his pocket, it was the most beautiful Christmas morning he'd ever seen.

"No," he said. "Just...merry Christmas, *Maîtresse.*"

"It was a good night, wasn't it?" she asked as they drove away.

"More fun than a Santa Claus gangbang," Kingsley said. "I almost forgot why we fight with him all the time."

"Me, too," she said. "But don't worry, any minute now he'll remind us."

They drove on a while in silence before Nora broke it with a child's wish.

"Too bad it can't be Christmas every day."

Now playing: "*Happy Xmas (War is Over)*" *by John Lennon*

POINSETTIA

POINSETTIA

Author's Note: This story takes place when Søren was twenty years old and in seminary.

ROME, ITALY

MAGDALENA SAT in the window of her parlor smoking a cigarette and balancing her antique walnut writing lap desk on her thigh. She wasn't writing, although she should have been. The letters had been piling up for weeks—invitations, assignations, a letter or two from an old friend... Tonight would be a perfect night to catch up on correspondence as she was alone and the house was closed up. Alone on purpose, of course. The notorious and exalted Signora Magdalena did not sleep alone except by choice.

And it had been her choice, she reminded herself. She could have had company if she'd wanted it. Magdalena had told her girls the same lie she told them every Christmas season: *I don't keep Christmas and never have. Run along home. I want to do nothing but sleep for the next two days. If I see you at the house before the twenty-sixth, you're fired.* Then she'd slip them two million lira each as a holiday bonus and shoo them off. She'd told Giovanni and Alessandro, her two most devoted paramours, they must leave her alone because she was tiring of them. A tiny untruth as she liked them both, but when one slept with masochists, one must be cruel as a rule. Kindness was always the exception.

Lies, lies, all lies. The truth was, Magdalena missed celebrating Christmas. But she was a madam—a notorious madam at that, if one believed the ribald verses scrawled on the sides of buildings—and a madam had to remain aloof, tough, an object of fear and respect. If her girls—loyal to a fault—knew she spent Christmas alone just so they could be with whatever friends or families they had left, they might stay with her out of pity. Or, God forbid, beg her to join them at their grandfather's or grandmother's or mother's house. No. Magdalena couldn't allow that to happen. Better to simply sleep for two days, eat dinner alone on Christmas Eve, and catch up on all the correspondence she'd been putting off since September. But this part wasn't a lie—if any one of her girls showed up between now and the twenty-sixth, Magdalena would fire her.

It certainly sounded like someone was getting fired tonight.

Or, in the case of an intruder, murdered.

Magdalena quietly laid her writing desk aside and crushed out her cigarette in the ebony ashtray. Taking the fireplace poker in hand, she crept down the dark hall from the parlor to the sunken kitchen where she'd heard the creaking of the floorboards under what she assumed were human feet. The house was old—three centuries old—and it creaked like an old man getting out of bed in the morning.

While on the outside the house appeared to be nothing but a crumbling old villa—yellow plaster, peeling green wood shutters, chipped marble door frames—inside she'd remodeled it to resemble the love child of a palazzo and a bordello. But for all the work she'd had done on the house inside, Magdalena never fixed her creaking floors. She considered them a security system. No one could take a step in this house without her hearing it. And whoever was in the house was taking a lot of steps in her kitchen.

Their last steps.

Magdalena kept to the left side of the staircase as that was the quiet side. Her heart raced more from excitement than fear. Perhaps it wasn't excitement. Considering her trade, perhaps it was blood lust.

The lights were off in the kitchen, but there was a soft glow coming from inside the open refrigerator. Somebody was rummaging through it, blocked from her view by the fridge door. Breathing deeply to calm herself, she raised the fireplace poker over her head and stepped into the sunken kitchen—

"You have an entire rack of lamb in here," came a voice from inside the refrigerator. "I didn't think you ate mutton."

Magdalena groaned and lowered her poker. "I don't, but Antonia is teaching herself to cook. And what are you doing here?" she demanded. "It's past your bedtime."

"Eating."

"Do they not feed you at the Gregorianum?"

"What they feed us should not be called 'food.' What it should be called is a word that should not be used in polite company."

"Good thing you're in my company then."

Her intruder closed the refrigerator door as Magdalena flipped on the kitchen lights. He had a bowl of her leftover penne alla primavera from last night in his hand, a bunch of pale green grapes hanging from between his fingers, and her last annurche apple clutched between his teeth.

"Now I remember why I didn't want children. You boys eat your mothers out of house and home," she said, shaking her head.

He sat down on the bench at her rough wood kitchen table, took a loud bite out of the apple, swallowed, and set it next to his bowl. Half the apple was already gone. He'd bitten all the way to the core.

"Are you a boy or a wolf?" she asked.

"Do you have a fork?"

"Would you prefer a shovel?" She crossed her arms over her chest. She hadn't been expecting company so she wore only her favorite black slip and black silk robe. Hardly attire for mixed company. Not that her "guest" seemed interested in her attire at all. He had eyes only for her food.

"A fork will do."

With a sigh, Magdalena opened a drawer, took out a fork and held it out to him. He reached across the table to take it from her, and she pulled it back at the last second.

"Tease," he said.

"Say 'please.' "

"Why are you so mean to me?"

"Someone has to be."

"I don't deserve it." Marcus gave her an innocent look. She didn't buy it for one second.

She smiled at him and softly whispered, "We both know you deserve it."

Wisely, he chose not to argue.

"Please," he said.

"Good, Bambi." She gave him the fork.

He glared at her. Such a glare, it would have scared anyone on the planet, anyone but her.

"You're cute when you're murderous," she said.

"Why must you insist on calling me Bambi?" he asked.

Magdalena leaned across the table and pinched his cheek. "Because you're my little baby priest, Bambino. And you won't let me call you Marcus, so Bambi it is."

"You are the most evil woman I've ever had the pleasure of knowing."

"So far."

"Don't do that."

"You're going love this girl. She's more vicious than I am," Magdalena said with her best evil grin, the one she reserved just for her baby priest.

" 'She' does not exist."

"Oh, she exists. She's going to ruin you and you're going to thank her for it." She clapped her hands in fiendish glee. "I can't wait for you to meet her."

"If you are right, I'll eat my collar. But as you didn't know it was me in your kitchen tonight, forgive me if I don't buy stock in your psychic abilities."

She shrugged. "They come and go."

"Will Antonia mind—"

"If you touch her lamb, she'll break your arm. You know she will and you know I'm speaking literally. She's put men in the hospital for less."

"I knew I liked her for a reason."

"Eat your pasta. I'll open the wine. Oh no, I forgot. You're not old enough to drink."

"I am."

"Not in America."

"We're in Rome. We do as the Romans do, remember?"

"The Romans crucified Christians. Good thing I have a cross with your name on it."

There was that glare again. She made it her personal mission in life to make this young man glare at her as much as humanly possible.

"Open the wine," he said. Then he added, "Please. I did turn twenty-three days ago."

"Did you? Aww...my little Bambi is growing up." Magdalena pretended to wipe a tear from her eyes. She placed a glass of Brunello in front of him on the table and kissed the top of his golden blond head. "I'll get my special books from my room. I think it's time you learned about the birds and the bees."

"You're ruining my appetite, Magda."

"Don't be embarrassed. Sex is a very beautiful act between a woman and a man's wallet."

He pushed the bowl of penne away. But not out of disgust with her. He'd already finished eating it.

"My God, you were hungry."

"I'm a growing boy, remember."

"I know you are. Go and stand in the doorway."

He gave her the sort of stare that could flatten a weaker woman than she. "Do I have to?"

She raised her chin.

"Fine." Marcus walked to the kitchen doorway and stood with his back to the frame. From a drawer, Magdalena pulled out a pencil and a ruler. She placed the ruler on top of Marcus's head and made a mark on the doorframe.

"Well?"

"You've only grown half a centimeter in the last two months," she said. "For a grand total of 193-and-a-half centimeters, which is probably where you'll stay."

"That half centimeter makes me half a centimeter taller

than my father. He'll be thrilled I'm taller than he is. And by 'thrilled' I mean he'll hate me more than ever." He grinned as he said this, but it wasn't a happy sort of grin. More a grin *and* a grimace.

"I'll keep feeding you, then, if only to spite your father. No one enjoys torturing bad parents more than I do. Have you heard from him recently?"

"He sent me a letter calling me an ingrate, a degenerate, and a disgrace to the family name. Oh, and he told me I had to get married or he's cutting me off."

"And what did you tell him?"

"I reminded him that I'm under a vow of poverty so I have, in effect, cut myself off. Also, I told him that considering he's a rapist who preyed on young women and children, I was quite pleased to know I disgraced his name. I wrote this in his Christmas card."

"Happy Christmas indeed. You've earned this."

She handed him his wine glass. It looked small in his hands. He had massive hands, large as Michelangelo's *David* and as well-sculpted.

"Thank you. And thank you for second dinner."

"If you keep eating like this, I'm going to start charging you," she said, pointing the wine bottle at him before uncorking it again.

"Vow of poverty."

"I accept several forms of currency," she reminded him.

"Vow of chastity."

"There are no free meals in this house," she said.

"I brought you a gift. Does that count as payment?"

"A gift?"

"Two gifts, actually," he said. "One is there." He pointed at the kitchen counter. "The other is coming later."

Magdalena turned to find a potted poinsettia on her counter, blooming hugely with bright red leaves.

"How lovely," she said, smiling and stroking one graceful leaf. "My mother always called these Christmas Stars. Where did you get it?"

"I took it from the Motherhouse. A wealthy patron sent a hundred. They won't miss one."

"Took it from where in the Motherhouse?" she asked, narrowing her eyes at Marcus, who didn't meet her eyes.

"I might have taken it from the chapel altar."

"You stole the poinsettia off the altar in the chapel at the Jesuit Motherhouse to give to the madam of a brothel?"

"I'm simply relocating it."

"Knowing you, I'm surprised you didn't eat it. Come to the parlor, Bambi. This will look darling on my side table."

She picked up the bright red poinsettia in one hand and her wine glass in the other, and started toward the downstairs parlor.

"You never ask, do you?" He followed her with his wine glass in his right hand, the wine bottle in the left. "You only give orders."

"You think I'm controlling?"

"Commanding," he said. "People want to obey you. Not me, of course. But I like studying you to see how you do it."

"People want to obey anyone. If you act like you're in charge, people will follow your orders simply out of relief that someone else is leading the way. It's easier to follow than to lead. Leading takes courage, which is why so few people want to do it."

"I want to lead."

"You want to be a dictator."

"I don't deny it," he said as they entered the parlor. He switched on the crystal table lamp and she set her poinsettia next to it. "If you know you're better at leading than others, why not take charge?"

"People like leaders," she said. "They do not like tyrants."

"I can be a benevolent dictator, can't I?" He set his wine glass down on the end table and went to work on her fireplace.

"You're already a dictator. Now let's work on the benevolent part."

"I am benevolent," he said. "I brought you a poinsettia."

"Yes, and I'm highly suspicious of the gesture."

"I was attempting to be kind."

"Is this Father Ballard's doing again?"

"It might be," he said, crouching in front of the gray marble fireplace. He lit the tinder under the log and carefully coaxed a fire into life. She watched him as he worked, intent and calm and capable. She always left the men's work to the men in the house. Only thing they were good for, in her opinion. That and the money they spent here.

"What was his assignment for you this week?"

"He told me to give someone a Christmas gift, someone Christ would give a gift to. He said if I act like a human being, I might eventually turn into one."

"Fake it until you make it? I believe that's what you Americans say."

"I told Father Ballard to keep his expectations low. He said they couldn't possibly get any lower where I was concerned."

Magdalena laughed as she sat on the love seat and tucked her feet under her robe. "I wish I could meet your confessor. Father Ballard sounds like my sort of man."

"He's trying to teach me to have Christ-like compassion for my fellow man."

"How is that proceeding?"

Marcus stared into the fire. "I loathe my fellow man."

"Carving you into a human being is proving to be one of the labors of Hercules. But we'll get there, Father Ballard and I. And when I'm done sculpting you, I'll put you on my mantel."

"Is that what this is? Sculpting?"

"You are a work in progress, my dear. I just need to sand down a few more rough edges. Then you'll be perfect."

"I have no rough edges."

"You scare Bianca."

"Then Bianca is a coward."

"Bianca is a sadist and her father's a capo in the Sicilian mafia. And yet you terrify her."

"Why do I terrify Bianca?" He lit a match and let it burn all the way down to his fingertips. He didn't blow it out, even as it singed him. All the while, he watched dispassionately like an alien performing a procedure to study human reactions to pain. When the match finally burned out, he flicked it into the quietly roaring fire.

"I can't imagine," she said.

He stood up and faced the fireplace, testing the heat and adjusting the damper. As usual, he was clad in all black tonight—black trousers, black clerical shirt, black jacket. No white collar. He rarely wore the collar in her presence. She almost wished he would—the hollow of his throat was an object of preoccupation for her. She'd already promised herself she wouldn't sleep with him...although she did love to flirt with him. He really wasn't her type despite his undeniable appeal. He needed to put on a few pounds to flesh out his tall frame. He had a trim waist and hips and broader shoulders than a priest would ever need. And she did love a blond. Blond men were so rare in Rome. He had a lock of hair that would fall over his right eye after he'd exerted himself with Caterina, the one girl in the house brave enough or stupid enough to play with him in his darker moods. Magdalena tried to convince herself she let Marcus into her home and her life because she found him attractive. She did, but that wasn't why. Usually male sadists repelled her. It wasn't personal. Like repelled like—she and Marcus were two north ends of a magnet. But while Marcus was a sadist, he was still nothing more than boy. He wasn't competition, nor was he a threat. He submitted to her not as a slave to a Mistress, but as a student to a teacher. Better he learn from her than on his own. An untrained boy of his strength and intensity with that level of sadism could kill someone by accident.

"Where's your fireplace poker?" he asked as he crouched in front of the fire again, apparently not satisfied with its output.

"In the kitchen. I was going to use it to knock you unconscious before I knew it was you."

"You gave me a key to your house. Don't be surprised if I use it."

"I gave you the key so you could feed Moussolini when I was gone on my trips, not so you could raid my refrigerator."

"You didn't specify I could only use the key for feeding your cat. And I refuse to call him by that name." He took his usual seat in the large red and gold armchair with the gilt legs. A chair fit for a king. Probably because it had once belonged to King Charles Emmanuel IV of Sardinia.

"Moussolini doesn't care what you call him as long as you feed him," she said, lifting her small drowsing black and white tuxedo cat out of his basket at the end of the love seat. The cat immediately spied the poinsettia and hopped on the sofa arm. With his one white mitten, Moussilini batted at a red leaf. "Isn't that right, sweet Mous-Mous?" She tickled his chin whiskers.

"Don't let him eat that," Marcus said. "I heard they can poison pets."

"Holly berries," she said. "Those are poisonous. Poinsettias aren't. He'd have to eat dozens of leaves to get sick from a poinsettia."

Still, Magdalena plucked the cat from the chair arm and scratched his ears. It was an activity Moussi usually enjoyed, except her naughty tyke suddenly noticed his favorite human was in the room. The cat leapt lightly off her lap, trotted across the Persian rug, and jumped into Marcus's lap.

"Go away," he said to the cat.

"It's Christmas Eve. You have to be nice on Christmas Eve. If you can't have compassion for your fellow man, surely you can have compassion for a cat."

"He's shedding on my trousers."

"It's what cats do. And you know you love him."

"I sympathize with him, that's all," Marcus said as he stroked the cat between the ears. "He's named after someone terrible. I'm named after someone terrible. He has to put up with you. I have to put with you. We share many sorrows, don't we, Mus?"

"Mus?"

"Danish for 'mouse.' "

"You speak Danish. Your first language?"

He cocked his eyebrow at her. "I also speak Swedish and Norwegian and French and Latin and German and Italian and—"

"I only want to know where you're from. Why don't

you tell me more about your childhood?" she asked. "Why all the secrets?"

"You know enough of my secrets."

"Never enough," she said, grinning. "I want *all* of your secrets."

"Ask Mus. I told him my secrets in August when you were in Greece, and he and I had the house to ourselves."

"He's a cat. You can't get a straight answer out of a cat. I've tried."

"You know perfectly well you could find out anything you want to know about me. You have your ways," he said.

Magdalena leaned forward and rested her chin on her hand. "But I don't want to *know* your secrets," she said. "I want you to *tell* me your secrets. The secrets aren't the prize. You giving up your secrets to me—*that* is the prize."

"You know about Kingsley," he said.

"He's only one of your secrets."

"He's the only secret that matters."

She smiled at him. "You want to believe that," she said. "But you don't, and neither do I."

He leaned back in the chair and stroked Moussi from the tips of his ears to the end of his tail. Moussi stretched and preened and purred under the attention.

"My pussy loves you," she said.

"Mus, are you old enough to be living in this den of iniquity?" he asked the cat.

"Moussi is two years old, which is twenty-five in cat years, which is still older than you are, Bambi."

"Do you hear what she calls me?" he said, looking down at the cat. "Why do we put up with her?"

"Because I give you both exactly what you need to stay alive—food for him, willing victims for you."

"She makes a good point, Mus." Marcus scratched Moussi under the chin and if a cat could smile, this one did. "I wish I could argue with her, but she'd take my willing victims away."

"No willing victims tonight, I'm afraid. All the kids are home for the holidays."

"You're the only madam I know who refers to the women in her employ as 'the kids.' It's somewhat unnerving."

"I am the *only* madam you know. Also, I like unnerving people. It's what I do for a living. Unnerving, undressing, unmanning..."

"I've noticed."

"Did you come here for release tonight? If so, we can call Caterina. She's home with her lover, and he lives close by."

"I came because it's Christmas. And to eat your food. But mostly because it's Christmas."

"You knew I'd be alone?"

"I knew I'd be alone."

She narrowed her eyes at him. "Don't play me," she said. She didn't like it when Marcus voluntarily showed any vulnerability. She didn't trust it. It was a game and she was the Game Master around here, not him.

"I like playing people," he said. "It's what I do."

"You won't make me feel sorry for you. I refuse to feel sorry for you."

"Then why did you take me in?"

"Because you're beautiful and rare, and I like looking at beautiful, rare things. As you see..." She waved her hand around the room, at the eighteenth-century Seymour card table, at the van Dyck painting hanging over the fireplace, at the priceless Qianlong jade bowls on the end table. "And this of course." She stroked one bright red poinsettia leaf.

"My only Christmas decoration. I tell the kids I don't keep Christmas so they'll leave me alone in the house for two days."

"Do you want me to leave you alone?"

"No. I want you to stay," she said. "Although I don't know why I do. You're wholly unlikeable."

"You did say I was pretty."

"No, I said you were beautiful. And I do have a Christmas gift for you, so it's good you came by."

"You do? Why?" Not *what*. He didn't ask what the gift was. He asked *why*. He didn't trust her any more than she trusted him.

"I don't know," she said. "You mentioned something you wanted a while ago, and I decided to get it for you. Of course you'll wish I hadn't given it to you when I do give it to you. *If* I give it to you. What do you think I should do, Moussi?"

Moussi only answered with his roaring, rumbling purr. That whoring slut of a cat had rolled onto his back and offered Marcus the soft underbelly for scratching, which Moussi never did with her. She was taking all his Christmas sardines back to the store.

"I've received very few Christmas gifts in my life," Marcus said as he buried his fingers deep into Moussi's fur. "I went to school in England and spent holidays with fairly distant relatives. Distant in every sense of the word. I was nothing but a boarder. My mother gave me a Christmas gift last year, and I didn't know how to thank her."

"What did your mother give you?"

"A lovely handcrafted straight razor that had belonged to my grandfather."

"Your mother gave you a straight razor. How appropriate. Considering."

"I only use it for shaving."

"You're old enough to shave now?"

Marcus looked at her. That look again. She did love that look.

"What about you?" he asked. "What was Christmas like for you as a child?"

"No gifts for me either," she said. "Christmas was nothing but going to mass. *Mamma* would take me to church with her on Christmas Eve and Christmas Day if she wasn't working. My father was Roma and they weren't married. *Mamma* was an outcast from her own family. She had to move us to another town to escape the scandal and our poverty was extreme. We had no money for gifts, no money for large holiday meals—only the Church."

"Your family had an excuse—poverty," he said. "Mine didn't. Except for a poverty of the soul, perhaps. I worry sometimes I inherited their poverty."

Magdalena sat on the arm of his chair and tucked a strand of golden blond hair behind his ear. "Bambi, darling, I'm going to tell you something and you must believe that it's true."

"Yes?" he asked.

"You did."

He looked at her for a very long time before laughing. A year and a half ago he wouldn't have handled such a bare-faced insult so well.

"You are a magnificent bitch." He made it sound like a compliment, and she took it as such.

"It's true," she said. "You had to have your own confessor tell you to bring me a Christmas gift because otherwise it wouldn't occur to you to give something to the woman who took you in. Would it? Sounds like poverty of the soul to me."

"You only took me in because you find me attractive."

"No, I took you in for the same reason I took in Mous-solini—I needed help keeping the vermin out. A baby priest is as good as a bodyguard."

He leaned his head back on the chair and stared flatly at her. "I brought you a Christmas plant. Couldn't you pretend to be nice to me for one minute?"

"I can be nice to you for..." She glanced at the grandfather clock on the opposite wall. "Fifteen seconds. Starting now. Bambi, I do find you very attractive despite the fact that you are cold and distant and self-absorbed, thoughtless, a snob, utterly entitled and—"

"Your fifteen seconds is almost up."

"There is a spark of something inside you that's as beautiful as the outside. Since I can see that spark, I feel it's my duty to blow on it and start a wildfire."

Magdalena leaned forward, pressed her lips together and blew, aiming for the hollow of his throat. He closed his eyes and leaned his head back, baring his throat to her. She wanted to bite it, hard, sink her teeth into him and make him bleed. She'd had more than one lover accuse her of being a vampire and perhaps she was. But she had no desire to drink blood. No, she wanted to drink pain and Marcus... her Marcus, his pain was the finest of vintages. Old pain, well-ripened, seasoned with sex and betrayal and sadism— her favorite flavors.

"I should have asked for your body for Christmas," she said.

"It's not going to happen," he said.

"Why not?" She pouted at him. He hated pouting.

"I have a very good reason," he said. "And it's not the reason you think it is."

"That you're a coward who is terrified of his own sexuality?"

"No. Nor am I terrified by yours."

Magdalena's blood cooled a few degrees.

"What do you mean?" she asked too innocently, too casually. "My sexuality?"

She sat on the arm of his chair and leaned across his lap, Moussi in-between them.

"You are the most beautiful woman in Rome. This is saying something," Marcus said.

"You really think so?" She batted her eyelashes to make him laugh. He didn't laugh.

"You have the thickest, most luxurious black hair I've ever seen. It's a starless night in your eyes. Your breasts are magnificent and your hips are everything a man who loves women could hope and dream of. You have long shapely legs. You dress like a fashion plate. You smell like an orchard in June—everything delicious and ripe for the plucking. And you're tall. I love how tall you are. And you have exquisite warm olive skin like Kingsley's and to say there's anything like you that's like him is the highest compliment I can give anyone. There is nothing undesirable about you. That is all I will say on the subject."

Magdalena exhaled heavily. "I see you know my little secret," she said. "May I ask how you know?"

"You were right—my mother is Danish. I visit her in Copenhagen when I can. Copenhagen is both a large city and a small town. When I came by in August to feed Mus and bring in your mail, I saw you had received two letters from a surgeon in Copenhagen. A legendary surgeon. There's only one reason people outside of Denmark go to Denmark for surgery, only one reason they go to this partic-ular surgeon."

She nodded slowly. "I see."

"You know I don't care, yes? I need you to know that."

"You're being considerate of my feelings. How...unlike you."

"If you're going to think ill of me—"

"Which I do."

"I want you to think ill of me for the right reasons, not because I care you weren't born female."

"I was born female. But there were...*are* some 'abnormalities' present, as the doctors called them. These 'abnormalities' have caused complications in my life. This particular abnormality is something some men find horrifying and other men with a particular fetish find irresistible. Then again, you're not most men, are you?"

"Are you having surgery? I realize this is not any of my concern."

"But you're still asking."

"You ask me rude personal questions all the time."

He had a point but she hardly wished to concede that.

"My mother raised me as a boy until puberty started and it became obvious that a boy wasn't what God had intended me to be despite the presence of what looked like a very male organ on my person. As I developed as a girl, I started dressing like one, acting like one. The priest at our church called me 'demon seed,' 'unnatural,' an 'abomination.' You don't forget something like that. You don't forget being called demonic. It stays with a person like a brand or a burn. You carry it with you, in you." She touched her chest over her heart where the anger still burned.

"That's why you left the Church?"

The first night Marcus had come to her house she'd almost refused him. He wasn't the first priest to seek release in her home, but he was the first she'd let in—if only because he wasn't a priest quite yet, and she thought perhaps she could save him from that path. When he'd asked her about her hostility toward the Catholic Church, she'd told him only that her priest had hurt her family, that she could not forgive the Church. If God wanted her back, he could send the Church to her. For she would never return to it.

"I didn't leave the Church," she said. "The Church left me. It rejected me, cast me out. I do not go where I am not wanted."

"You are perfect as you are," he said. "You are not demon seed."

"A priest said I was."

"Yes, a dried-up evil old priest who lusted for the little boy he thought you were and despised you for failing his sick pedophilic fantasies."

"Tell me how you really feel, Bambi."

"I would never tell you what to do with your body. But—"

"That's not true at all," Magdalena said. "You once told me exactly what I could do to my body. I believe the statement started with 'go' and ended with 'yourself,' with a third word in-between that was most unbecoming a priest-in-training."

"That was a figurative statement I said only after you had a police officer arrest you in front of me—for murdering a client. It wasn't until he had you in his car that you revealed it was all a joke. At my expense."

"That was a fun evening, wasn't it? I love jokes."

"You don't need surgery. You need psychoanalysis."

Magdalena laughed and laughed. Nothing made her happier than driving Marcus mad. And it wasn't easy to do, which is why it was so rewarding when she succeeded.

"If I had psychoanalysis and started behaving myself,

then would you want to sleep with me, Bambi?" She tossed her hair over her shoulder, placed her finger on her lip in a perfect pout, feigning innocence.

"Oh, God no." He sounded utterly disgusted by the very idea of her behaving herself. "Sleeping with you would be enjoyable for an hour or two. Torturing you by not sleeping with you? That will never cease to be fun for me."

"What if I let you hurt me like you hurt Caterina?" Torturing beautiful men was her absolute favorite hobby. She could do this all day. And usually she did.

"I couldn't hurt you with a chainsaw and a Kalashnikov."

"That's true enough," she said. "But you and I both know that's not it. You're terrified of falling in love again, aren't you?"

"You would be too if you were me."

"Eventually you will have to let go of your fears for Kingsley. He's an adult."

"He is if he's still alive. Both his parents are dead, his sister is dead. And he has a bad habit of engaging in incredibly reckless behavior even under the best of circumstances."

"He did sleep with you."

"My point exactly."

His jaw was set like a granite statue and he wouldn't meet her eyes. She and Marcus taunted and teased each other constantly and the insults were never-ending, but when the subject of his former lover Kingsley came up, Marcus did not play.

"I haven't seen him since he left school, and he still drives me to distraction. He'd be so proud of himself if he knew I worried every day he was dead." He looked up at the ceiling and shook his head. "Kingsley."

The name sounded like a plea.

Or a prayer.

"Love is a curse," Magdalena said. "Love is a burden. A beautiful curse. A beautiful burden."

"I'd cut out my own heart if I could," Marcus said.

"I'd cut out your own heart if I could, too."

"Oh, you're too kind."

Magdalena caressed his cheek. He had the most marvelous cheekbones. A ship's navigator could use them as a sextant to align ships and stars. "Listen to me—whatever happened in the past is past. That's why it's called the past. In time you will love someone again and you won't have to be afraid."

"Her?" he asked.

"Her."

"When you talk about the future as if you know it, you sound deranged."

"My father was the king of the gypsies—*Mamma* told me that. I have his gifts."

"Your mother lied to you. There is no such person as 'the king of the gypsies.' And you know even better than I do you aren't supposed to call them that. Your father may have been Roma, but he couldn't do magic and neither can you."

"Ha," she said. "I can't do magic...says the boy in training to turn wine into blood."

"I said you can't do magic. I didn't say I couldn't do it."

"Someday you'll see I'm right. Someday you'll know." She bent to kiss his forehead.

"You may do that again."

"You like having your forehead kissed?" she asked, running her fingertips through his hair.

"I like being able to see into your gown." He touched his forehead again over his left eye. "Right there. Best angle."

She kissed him where he asked her to because it gave her the chance to smell the fireplace smoke in his hair, a warm, earthy scent. Very male and mouthwatering. Well worth the price of flashing him her breasts.

"I have no plans on having any surgery," she said. "Although I thank you for your entirely unsolicited advice. I visited the good Danish surgeon because he's writing a paper on the particular condition I have, which is now believed to be caused by a hormonal abnormality in the womb as opposed to the work of the devil."

"Good," he said. "Surgery carries risk. I wouldn't want to lose you."

"Because you like me so much?"

"I don't like you at all. But, as you said, you provide me with food and willing victims. Therefore my continued ability to function is in your hands."

He smiled at her, the sort of smile that dared her to slap him. And she considered it. Then again, she was a sadist. She wanted to slap nearly every man on earth. She refrained. For now.

"I should never have brought a baby priest home." Shaking her head, she walked to the fireplace to warm herself. "I'm always bringing home strays. At least Moussilini pulls his weight around here. Haven't seen a mouse in six months."

"You want to put me to work for my keep? I will work."

"Can you work?"

"I can reach items on high shelves."

"I have a much better idea. Up." She crooked her finger at him.

He pointed at his lap. "Mus is asleep."

"He'll forgive you for waking him. You're his favorite."

With a sigh, Marcus plucked the sleeping Moussi off his lap. The cat went limp in his hands as Marcus carried him over to his basket and laid him gently inside.

"Stay," Marcus said to the cat.

"That is a cat, not a dog. He doesn't respond to commands."

Together they watched as Moussi turned in a circle in his basket, turned in a circle again, and then laid down.

"How do you do that?" Magdalena asked.

"I have no idea," he said with a shrug, a surprisingly adolescent gesture from Marcus. Then again, he had been a teenager until three days ago.

"Let's see how well you respond to commands. Come up to my bedroom."

He cocked that eyebrow again and she wondered if he'd practiced that in the mirror.

"Not for sex," she said. "Your gift is up there. Also I need a guinea pig to test a new toy."

He looked at her, not moving, not blinking.

"If your eyebrow gets any higher, it will end up on the back of your neck," she said.

"What toy is it?"

"It's nothing invasive, I promise," she said as she strode from the room. "I test the butt plugs and vibrators on myself. Come, come."

She patted her thigh as if calling a dog to her.

Magdalena half-expected he wouldn't follow her. She half-expected he would simply leave as she walked away. It's what she would have done in his shoes as it was the most sadistic thing. Someone offers you a gift, but says you must earn it? Walk away. Reject the gift, reject the giver. Nothing hurt more than having a gift rejected. To his credit and to her pleasure, he followed her up the main stairway to her bedroom.

"You keep your bedroom door locked?" Marcus asked as she unlocked the door with a key she wore tied to her wrist with a red cord.

"I value my privacy. You will, too, whenever you have privacy again."

"I doubt I will. Jesuits tend to live in community. Makes it harder to have a private life."

"Which is what you have me for. Tell me 'Thank you, Magda.' "

He exhaled. "Thank you, Magda."

"Good Bambi."

She opened the door to her bedroom and switched on the Tiffany lamp at her bedside.

Marcus remained standing inside the door.

"Do you like it?" she asked, as she sat on her bed. "My bedroom?"

"It isn't what I expected."

"What did you expect?"

"Something less...girlish."

"This room isn't girlish. It's feminine. Like me." She stretched out on her side and the robe parted to reveal a long bare leg. The room was entirely white but for the deep blue tile floors. White padded headboard and footboard on the bed, delicate white table and chairs, white and gilt dresser, white and gilt chandelier glowing with the softest gold light.

"I assumed there would be whips on the wall, chains on the bed, and for some reason I pictured swords crossed over the fireplace."

"I think you're describing your dream bedroom."

"My dream bedroom wouldn't have crossed swords over the fireplace. Crossed scalpels, however..."

He glanced over his shoulder at her with a look on his face to curl a girl's toes.

"Now I know what to give you for Christmas next year," she said.

"Obsidian blades, preferably."

"You should take your shirt off," Magdalena said as she casually twirled the cord of her black robe. "It would please me."

"I'm not taking any clothes off until you tell me what you're doing to me."

"I'm not telling you what I'm doing to you until you take your shirt off. And if you don't take your shirt off, you won't get your Christmas gift."

"A gift you already said I would regret taking from you."

"Yes."

"It's a miracle of God when two sadists alone in a room together manage to agree on anything, isn't it?" he asked.

"Less theological musing, more stripping."

"I may not want this Christmas gift after all."

"I know you aren't modest, Bambi. I've seen you naked."

"That was a different situation. I was trying to prove a point."

Magdalena laughed her lowest, most throaty laugh, the one she used when seducing rich men into handing over their wallets. Last summer her lover Alessandro had taken her, the girls, and Marcus out on his boat for a lazy day in the sun. Antonia, Bianca, and Caterina colluded together the night before the trip, deciding to tease and torment Marcus as much as possible on their trip. A pretty nineteen-year-old Jesuit? Magdalena's new pet? How could they resist? Once they'd cast anchor a few kilometers offshore in the deep blue waters of the Mar Tirreno, the three girls set up their *chaises longues* and stripped off their bikini tops and started teasing him—*Marco, come put oil on my back... Marco, come put oil on my front... Marco, come tell us all about Jesus...* They'd all stared at him, daring him to refuse, daring him to do it. They were all at least five years his senior, all three beautiful, sadistic, and *very* well-trained prostitutes. And her girls were absolutely certain they were scandalizing him with their naked breasts and their incessant flirting. In response to their requests, he'd simply replied, "in a moment," before stripping off every last stitch of clothing, folding it neatly, and then diving off the side of the boat into the water. Five minutes later, now wet as well as naked, he'd climbed up the ladder, wrapped a towel around his waist, and dutifully applied the tanning oil to the backs of each of Magdalena's suddenly subdued employees. Her girls had stripped half-naked. He'd stripped *completely* naked, and in doing so he'd put their shamelessness to shame. No longer was he "Marco" or "Magda's Pet." After that day he was "*Signore*."

"Still waiting," Magdalena said. "And you're still wearing your shirt."

"Can you at least give me a hint why you want me to take my shirt off?" he asked. "I've seen what you can do with a branding iron. I don't want to have to explain a phallic-shaped third-degree burn to the school nurse."

"I have no intention of branding you. Not tonight."

"Will this involve bleeding?"

"Anything could involve bleeding when you and I are involved."

He still didn't make any sort of move to undress. With a sigh Magdalena left the comfort of her big soft bed and walked over to him.

"Here. I'll help."

First she slid his jacket off him and hung it on the corner of her dressing screen. Then she unbuttoned the top button of his shirt and waited for him to say something. He didn't.

"It's not like you to be shy," she said. "You know you have a fabulous body, if a bit too thin for my tastes."

"My reticence is neither cowardliness nor shyness. I'm feeling vulnerable tonight, and I would prefer it if you didn't take advantage of me in my current state."

Magdalena laughed in his face. Loudly.

"You don't believe me?" he asked.

"No."

He clasped his hands behind his back. "I wouldn't either."

Magdalena unbuttoned the rest of his shirt buttons. "Are you really feeling vulnerable tonight or are you playing me again?"

She and Marcus had yet to have a conversation where one of them didn't attempt to fuck with the other's mind. She'd gone as far as telling him she was dying of cancer to see how he'd react. He'd gone as far as telling her he'd fallen in love with her and was leaving the Jesuits to be with her. She'd almost believed him and had laughed so hard when he'd revealed himself that she'd almost wept. If he told her he was feeling vulnerable, two motives were possible—he *was* feeling vulnerable, or he wanted to play with her mind. The first was possible but unlikely. The second was a near certainty.

"As you are continuing to undress me," he said, "it's clear my answer to that question is irrelevant."

"It's not irrelevant. I simply care about my desire to see you shirtless more than I care about your desire to remain shirted."

He exhaled heavily as she pulled his shirt out of his waistband. She let the tails fall as she took his hands one by one in hers and unbuttoned his cuffs.

But she didn't take his shirt off, not yet. She placed her hands flat on his chest. "Your heart is racing. I make you nervous."

"You make me very nervous."

"Are you nervous or are you aroused?"

"You could tell if I were aroused."

She glanced down. Pity. "Nervous, then. Are you worried I'm going to hurt you?"

"I would be a hypocrite if I were. I hurt Caterina frequently."

"Caterina is a masochist. You are not a masochist."

"I'm here, aren't I?"

"Cheeky." She stroked his chest from his collarbones down to his waist and up again. She didn't linger in any one particular place. She merely wanted to familiarize herself with his body, his skin. The day on the boat she'd only watched him undress, watched him walk naked to the side of the boat. She hadn't touched.

Now she wanted to touch.

"I suppose I must have some masochistic tendencies in me to join the Jesuits."

"Why did you?" she asked as she pushed his shirt off his shoulders and slid it down his arms. He had warm skin, smooth as only the skin of a young man of twenty can be.

"I felt called to join. I can't explain it."

"Do you wish you hadn't been called?" she asked as she held out his shirt in front of him and then pointedly dropped it on the floor.

"Not often, but sometimes."

"Tell me when."

She ran her hands up and down his arms. He had marvelous arms—beautiful, firm biceps, well-defined even in repose. Lovely veins from his hands to his elbows. She could see his pulse throbbing in his right wrist. The urge to bite that throbbing vein was nearly overwhelming.

"When I'm sitting in class and being taught things I already know by a priest who likely wouldn't recognize Jesus if Jesus were to walk up to him and slap him in the face with a wooden sign reading 'Hello, I'm your Lord and Savior' in three languages."

"When else?" she asked, circling him, not taking her hand off his body for one second. She stood behind him and caressed his back with her fingertips. His flesh bristled at her touch but he didn't move away.

"When I remember I have a baby sister I barely know," he said. "I would like to be in her life, but she's in New York and I'm here. Her mother sent me a Christmas card and Claire signed her own name in purple crayon."

Magdalena could hear the smile in his voice, the wonder that children grew so fast, the sorrow that Claire was growing up so far away from him.

"Flawless..." she sighed as she tickled his back with her fingertips, starting at the top of his shoulders and scoring his skin gently all the way to his hips. "Not a welt. Not a bruise. Not even a freckle. You are a pure blank canvas of flesh."

"Tempting, isn't it?"

"If you let me I would whip you until your back was broken open to the sinew, open to the bone." She was aroused just thinking of it.

"Have you ever whipped anyone that hard?"

"Yes," she said.

He whistled, impressed.

"Jealous?" she asked.

"I covet your sadism," he said. "And your willing victims."

"He was my slave and he was dying. He asked me to fulfill all his masochistic fantasies before he grew too ill and weak to enjoy them. I hastened his death but gave meaning to his life. His words."

"Your cruelty was an act of mercy."

"It always should be. Remember that."

"Yes, Magda."

He said it like a teenage boy might say "Yes, Mother." She nearly got her whip out then and there. Instead she untied the silk cord of her robe and drew his wrists together behind his back.

"Magda—"

"Hush. This is part of your training. You bind Caterina's hands when you beat her. You should know how it feels."

"I know how it feels."

That raised her eyebrow, but it didn't stop her from wrapping the black cord around his wrists and tying it off. "Who dared to bind your wrists before me?"

"You do not want to know the answer."

He'd hinted at some trauma in his childhood, something to do with his sister Elizabeth, something that caused them to write letters to each other once a month but avoid being in each other's company whenever possible.

"I am inclined to agree with you. Simpler question: do you like it?"

"No."

"Do you dislike it?"

"I'm annoyed by it."

"By it or by me?"

"Both in equal measure."

"Does it hurt?"

"No, but I can imagine my fingers would start to go numb if I stayed in this position for longer than a half hour."

"See? This is why I do these things to you. You must learn empathy. You need to understand what your slave or submissive will feel."

"Lesson learned."

"Did you do this to Kingsley?"

"Tie him up? Of course."

"I mean, did you tie him up and interrogate him?"

"Often," Marcus said. "I liked making him tell me secrets he didn't want to tell me."

"What secrets?"

"He told them to me, not you."

"You're discreet. Like a good lover. Are you a good lover?"

"I've had worse."

"You're deflecting because you don't want to answer and the answers you do give me you give begrudgingly. You are a terrible submissive, Bambi."

"I'm not a submissive."

"That certainly explains why you're so very wretched at it. Now answer the question. Are you a good lover?"

"I admit I'm not certain how to answer. Pray tell, Magda—how would I know?"

"You would know if you weren't. If your lover didn't respond to you, if your lover didn't come back begging for more..."

"Then I was apparently a very good lover. Kingsley was quite enthusiastic, very good at begging. And rather shameless about it."

"What did he beg for?"

"More. Always for more."

"More what? More sex? More pain?"

"Yes and yes. More everything." He paused as if letting himself remember something. "More affection mostly. I'm... not as affectionate as I should be. As I should *have been*," he corrected.

"What stops you from showing affection?"

"I..." He sighed, a surprisingly defeated sound, unusual from someone so defiant. "I don't know."

"Because you aren't very good at it?"

"I haven't had much practice in my life. I was close with my older sister Elizabeth until we were separated by my father. I kept to myself after that, as much as I could. Until Kingsley. But even after that, when I met my baby sister the first time, I didn't hold her. Kingsley did, but I couldn't."

"How did you feel when you saw him holding your baby sister?"

"I felt...jealous."

"Jealous? Of a child?"

"Jealous because he was better at something than I was. Something that came so easily to him was impossible for me. I wasn't accustomed to being bested at anything."

"You have thousands of strengths. If you didn't have a few failings, you'd be even more insufferable than you already are."

"He was a natural with her. I'd never seen anything like it. He was born to be a father."

"Ah. There we go. Now I see all. You were jealous because you saw he was not only good with children, but he wanted children. And you two can't have children together. You were jealous because you discovered he wanted something you couldn't give him. That's why you felt jealous when you saw him with your sister."

"I don't want to talk about Claire and Kingsley."

"Fine. We'll discuss only Kingsley. How often did you fuck him?"

"Magda."

"Answer me."

"These questions are unduly personal."

"You're tied up in my bedroom. Did you expect a quiz on Roman architecture?"

He exhaled. "At first we only met once a week for three weeks. He was impatient for more time with me, and I let him believe I was doing him the greatest of favors by allowing him more time with me."

"But you wanted more too."

"I did. Not that he needed to know that."

"So how often then?"

"We would sneak out to the hermitage three nights a week. Then four. Then five. Then nearly every night, every chance we could."

"How many nights?"

"Fifty-seven."

"You counted."

"I remember them all."

"From anyone else I would consider that romantic hyperbole. Not from you. You aren't the sort to exaggerate."

"And I have a very good memory where my body is concerned."

"And your heart."

"And my heart."

She drew a cross on his back with her fingernail—one line down from the nape of his neck to the small of his back, one line across from shoulder blade to shoulder blade. Then she pressed her lips to the spot where the two lines intersected. He shivered.

"You like being kissed?" Magdalena asked.

"You caught me off-guard."

"You're never off-guard," she said, scoffing. "You like being kissed? Yes? No? Answer me, Bambi."

"Who doesn't?"

"You never kiss Caterina."

"Kissing is for lovers," Marcus said. "We're friends only."

"You flog her, cane her, cut her, burn her, and ejaculate on her back when you're finished."

"This is why I have so few friends."

"Do you like kissing?"

"I remember liking it."

She kissed his right shoulder blade. "Does kissing arouse you?"

"No. But neither does petting Mus, eating your pasta, or looking at the stars, but I enjoy them all the same."

"Most men find kissing arousing." She bit the center of his back—not hard enough to break the skin but hard enough to leave teeth marks in his flesh.

"As you said earlier, I'm not most men."

"And me touching you doesn't arouse you."

"No. But again, I enjoy it."

"You enjoy being touched?" She licked the center of his back over the bite mark she'd left behind

"Not usually. I can count on three fingers the people I would enjoy touching me."

"Me."

Behind his back Marcus extended one finger.

"Kingsley," she said.

Marcus extended a second finger.

"Who's number three?" she asked.

"I don't know," he said. "According to you, I haven't met her yet."

"I'm honored to be in such exalted company. Your two soul mates..." She slipped her hands into his trousers pockets to squeeze his hips. "And me."

"Magda—"

"Oh, what have we here? A love note?" She pulled a folded sheet of paper out of his right pocket.

"Hardly," he said. "It's homework. You may put it back in my pocket now."

"Not yet. *Mamma* has to check your homework before she lets you turn it in. What was the assignment?"

"We had to write a few hundred words from the first person point-of-view of a character in the Nativity scene."

"You Jesuits are turning into such...such hippies. I remember when Jesuits were terrifying."

"That's hardly something to aspire to."

"Speak for yourself."

She unfolded the paper and smoothed it in her hands. Marcus had lovely handwriting, very strong script, masculine. Not surprisingly, he pushed down so hard with his pen so that the page bore not only his words on the front but the raised indentations from the words on the back.

"It's a silly assignment, but it's due right after the Christmas holidays. So again, I need that back. Please."

"Patience, patience. I hope you wrote in the point of view of Mary's ass."

"Melchior of Persia, one of the three Magi. And it's really not worth—"

"The more you protest, the more I want to read it," she said in her most teasing tone. "And of course you'd choose to play the part of one of the three Wise Men, wouldn't you?"

"Yes, well, considering I'm tied up in your bedroom, I'm now questioning that decision. Wise man I am clearly not."

She glared at him over the top of his homework assignment. "Quiet," she said. "I'm reading."

With an exaggerated throat clear, Magdalena began to read aloud. Marcus looked upward as if beseeching the heavens for deliverance from her. Let him pray all he wanted. She wasn't going anywhere.

The king was behind them now as was the star they had followed to find him.

"Good first line, Bambi."
"You're the worst person on earth."
"Flattery will get you everywhere."

Their steps were heavy and slow, the steps of tired men who'd walked far to attend a birth and found themselves instead at a funeral.

Magdalena stopped reading and glanced at Marcus. He didn't meet her eyes. This wasn't quite the story she'd expected. More curious than ever, she read on.

Behind them arose the cry of a child—a hungry child longing for his mother's breast. Balthazar winced as if it were his own son who wept thusly and he powerless to comfort the boy. I felt as he felt but kept my feelings off my face.

"His death is on his forehead," Balthazar said. "And he only a child."

"I saw it too," said Gaspar who looked at me as if hoping I would contradict them.

"As did I," I said, unwilling to lie though I was tempted to comfort my companions. I hoped the child's mother could not see his death as we could. Even in his laugh, in his bright

dark eyes I saw the shadow of his suffering, black wings on a white dove—the angel of death hovering near. All men suffer and all men die, but to see such a brutal death in the eyes and on the forehead of a small blameless boy is to know that the price of knowledge is far greater than gold.

Balthazar stopped in his tracks as if the child's cry had ensnared him.

"Is it wrong to look back?" Gaspar asked.

We faced East toward home, and the child king we left behind us in the West. Our steps coming to him had been light and quick. To leave him was to step with naked feet onto shattered glass.

"You can look back," I told him. He did and so did Balthazar, but I kept my eyes toward home. If I looked back I feared I would stay, never to see home again. And yet, strangely, though I knew home was East in Pārsa, my heart pulled me West to the child as if he was where my true home lay.

"What do we do now?" Gaspar asked. While Balthazar and I sought answers to questions, it was Gaspar who sought the questions themselves, a different form of wisdom though no less needful. "How do we go on?"

"One step. Then another," I said. "As always."

"How do we serve the king so far from him?" Gaspar asked.

"It seems wrong to leave him," Balthazar said. "Yet wrong to stay."

"He came to us first with his birth," I said. "Then we came to him. We return home and wait for him to come to us again."

The child's cry had ceased at last, and I imagined him in his mother's arms, a mere child holding a child. The king would be well cared for by young Mary and her older *husband, Joseph. Wisdom taught us to love a child and fear a king, but it was the child I feared and the king I loved.*

"How do we love the king from afar?" Gaspar asked as if he'd read my mind. Perhaps he had. "How do we keep our faith?"

"We wait." I took a step forward and away from the king, another step onto shards. They went so deep into my foot I felt the pain in my throat. "The love is in the waiting."

"The love is in the waiting," Gaspar said after me.

Balthazar nodded his noble head. "Yes, the love is in the waiting." They turned East again. We walked on.

By our clocks and calendars and charts, it has been one thousand eighty-nine years since that night we put our backs to the star.

I am still waiting for my king.

Magdalena's hands shook as she slowly and neatly refolded Marcus's homework assignment and slipped it back into his pocket.

"I hope you receive a good grade," she said softly.

"I always do."

"Thank goodness they don't grade on personality."

Marcus's eyes flashed as if the insult had struck home instead of glancing off as her insults usually did. "But—"

"Interrogation over," she said.

Magdalena quickly untied his hands. She shouldn't have read his homework assignment and she regretted it. She'd read love letters less personal and intimate than those few hundred words in the voice of a man who loved a king and had to walk away from him. "You're boring me now."

"But you said you had a new toy to try out."

"I do. But I don't need you shirtless to test it."

"Then why did you make me take my shirt off?"

"To see if you would."

He grabbed his shirt off her screen and pulled it on in a manner both irritable and perfunctory. If she had to characterize his expression, she would have used the word "petulant."

"Forcing me to remove clothing to earn a Christmas gift is not how normal people celebrate Christmas," he said.

"How would you know?"

"I was trying to have a nice Christmas with you, Magda."

"Why? You're not nice. Neither am I."

"Should I leave? Let me rephrase that: I should leave."

He buttoned his shirt on his way to the door. She put herself between him and it and raised her hand, daring him to take another step forward. He didn't.

"You do not have permission to leave," she said.

"You call me a coward, but it's you who shrinks back in horror when you see you me as human being for one single second. If you don't want to know what's in my heart, you should stop cutting it open."

"It wasn't horror, Bambi. It was boredom. And you do not have permission to leave," she repeated. They had these contests of wills all too often. If she didn't win, he would lose. This boy had to learn to lose or he would be more dangerous than he already was. For his sake and the sake of anyone he would ever pastor, ever befriend, or ever love, he had to learn to lose well.

"I didn't ask permission."

"You didn't ask permission to come into my house tonight. You will not leave until you have been given permission."

"Then give it to me fast or I'll leave without it."

"You are acting like a child. No, not a child—a brat. We

have made too much progress for you to regress into the pouting, beastly little boy you were when we met. You asked me to help you become a 'good sadist.' Your words, not mine. You want to know how to be a good sadist, brat? Don't make your kink somebody's else's problem, and as they say in your country...don't dish it out if you can't take it."

For what seemed like an uncomfortable eternity, Marcus said nothing. He said nothing and he didn't look at her. He looked past her at the wall. *Give in, Marcus*, she willed silently. *You won't break if you bend a little. You don't have to win every fight. Giving in is a form of giving and Christmas is a time for giving. Give me your surrender. Give me your submission. I'll reward it a thousand times over, I swear.*

But she could say none of that aloud. He had to surrender freely or it would be a worthless gesture.

"I'll stay," he said. "Until you tell me I can go."

"I want you to stay. I do."

"I want my Christmas present," he said.

That made her smile. He sounded so young when he said it. "You do? Why is that?"

"You know me...intimately. Few people do. I would like to know what someone who knows me thinks I would like for Christmas."

Magdalena touched his face and straightened his collar. "Good boy. But first, we still haven't tested out my new toy."

"What is this new toy you're determined to have me test?" he asked with an exasperated sigh.

"This." She stepped aside and pulled back the room divider separating the main bedroom from a large alcove. A piano sat under the arched ceiling. A baby grand that her latest conquest—a former *assessore* in Venice or something of the sort—had given her last week. Marcus's eyes widened slightly at the sight of the piano. She loved it when she managed to impress this usually inscrutable young man.

"Is that a Broadwood?" he asked.

"It is. A 1929. Giovanni gave it to me because I told him I'd never see him again."

"Why would did you say that?"

"I thought I could get a piano out of him. I was right."

"Do you play?"

"I do," she said.

He furrowed his brow at her. "Why have you never told me?"

"Because you never asked. Someday you'll learn people other than yourself exist. Maybe you'll even like those people."

"I doubt it. May I?"

"I insist." Magdalena waved her hand at the piano bench.

"St. Ignatius had a Broadwood. My school, not the founder of the Jesuits. I have no idea what sort of piano St. Ignatius had."

"You're happy," she said, lightly stroking his cheek. "You only tell jokes when you're happy."

"I...I have happy memories of playing the Broadwood at my school. I was playing it when Kingsley saw me the first time, when I saw him. He didn't know I saw him. He still doesn't know." He took a seat at the bench and rolled up his sleeves. She'd forgotten just how attractive a man's forearms could be when they were sinewy and strong, and a pair of large sculpted and terribly talented hands were attached to them.

"What should I play?" he asked.

"I have a piece if you don't mind sight-reading."

"I don't mind."

She opened the window seat in the piano alcove where she stored the sheet music and pulled out a very special folder. She didn't hand the music to Marcus but placed it on the music rack herself. Then she sat at his side.

"A bit of the Red Priest to be played by my Golden Priest." She ran her hand over Marcus's golden-blond hair. He looked up at her. "You like Vivaldi?"

"I haven't played '*il Prete Rosso* since starting seminary. But 'Winter' is fitting for the season."

"Yes, very fitting," she said with a tight smile. "I'll forgive you if you falter. Vivaldi is trickier than he looks."

"I won't falter. It hasn't been that long."

"Of course. The piano's been tuned. Play when you're ready."

She watched his eyes as he scanned the front page of the sheet music, re-learning the opening bars of the concerto with his eyes before playing. She hoped he wouldn't turn the pages to look over the entire piece right away—that would spoil the surprise. But he had the arrogance of both youth and talent, as she'd counted on, and thus started playing at once.

He played slowly, more slowly than the movement called for, and yet the pace didn't drag so much as it meandered gently around the room, calling to mind a walk in the snow, a morning walk on morning snow. She wondered if he thought of Maine as he played. He'd told her about his school days at St. Ignatius and the solace he'd found there in the forest with the Jesuits. He'd told her how much he liked the priests at the school, one especially who'd gone out of his way to help him and protect him from his father. He'd said he'd found Maine beautiful, especially its brutal and bitter winters that made one grateful for the smallest of things—a roaring fire in the library fireplace, the gift of a hand-knitted afghan and scarf sent from his sister Elizabeth, a hot cup of Lapsang Souchong tea in the mornings. And Kingsley. He had been grateful for Kingsley, Marcus had said. Kingsley who stole the covers and kicked in his sleep and swore most violently when attempting to start a fire in their little hermitage's fireplace while Marcus watched over his shoulder, mocking Kingsley's failures and trying not to laugh out loud at his French lover's cursing. On the coldest nights, Marcus refused to touch Kingsley until the room was warm enough for them to take their clothes off, a refusal which made building the fire an emergency proposition for the ever-eager Kingsley. She could easily picture Marcus's young lover, sixteen years old, in the first blush of his male beauty, long dark hair falling over his even darker eyes, narrowed in concentration, his fingers working feverishly with tinder and matches, his exhalation of relief as the fire finally took hold of the wood, and, of course, the kiss that would follow. The kiss of victory when Marcus rewarded Kingsley for his efforts...and then, soon after that kiss, Magdalena could imagine the first red flickers of firelight dancing over Kingsley's naked olive skin as Marcus beat him with his belt or a cane. Yes, Magdalena could see it all as Marcus played the concerto. His steel-gray eyes were soft now, not steely at all, and only half open as he played like a man half-asleep and daydreaming. His lips were slightly parted as if in preparation for a kiss. She'd never seen him look this young, this peaceful, this unguarded and gentle. They did say music soothed the savage beast. She almost hated to destroy this lovely moment of peace with him.

But she did it anyway.

Marcus reached the end of that page's music and he nodded to her. Magdalena turned the page.

Immediately Marcus's fingers faltered on the keys, a terrible atonal noise, and then all the sound ceased.

Marcus reached out with both hands and lifted the photograph.

"How?" he asked. It was all he asked.

"Six months ago you said, and I quote, 'I would give anything to know if Kingsley is alive. That's all I want to know. I don't need to know how he is, where he lives, what he's doing, and I don't want to know. But if I knew he was alive, I could sleep better at night. I could be at peace.' Do you remember saying that to me?"

"Yes." His voice sounded hollow as a reed.

She rested her chin on his shoulder, smiled and pointed. "You see the marquee there? It says *Monstre Sacré*? That's a student film and it played in that theater for only two days as part of a competition. And that was ten days ago. So, as of ten days ago, your Kingsley was alive and well. That is him, isn't it?"

She looked at the eight-by-ten photograph in Marcus's hands, the photograph she had placed between the pages of sheet music for him to find. A young man in a long coat was walking toward the camera, a scarf tied carelessly around his neck. A tall young man with sharp and elegant features, short dark hair with a touch of wave in it, and eyes like a cat's—enigmatic, watching, careful, predatory. Luckily for the photographer, a telephoto lens could see farther than those eyes.

Slowly Marcus nodded and in a low voice, a voice she could barely hear, he whispered, "Yes, it's him."

"He's more handsome than you are. You have good taste in boys, Bambi."

"He's not handsome. He's beautiful."

Abruptly, Marcus stood up and walked away from her,

the photograph in his hand, his eyes on the page. She turned on the bench, wanting to watch his every move, his every expression. He paced the floor of her bedroom, back and forth in front of the fireplace, stalking across the tile like a caged leopard gone mad from captivity and therefore all the more dangerous.

"How did you find him?" he asked, not looking at her, only at the photograph.

"I hired someone. I knew your boy's name and the *arrondissement* he grew up in. It took all six months—he's not an easy one to find."

Marcus sat on the end of her bed but stood up again as if he'd sat on a spring. "His hair is short. I've never seen it short. Why would he cut his hair?"

"I don't know. Maybe he had to cut if off for his work."

"What does he do?"

"I don't know."

"Where does he live? Is he in Paris now? Is he in school? He's intelligent. He should be in university."

"I don't know where he lives. I didn't ask."

He turned to face her. "Why not?" he demanded.

"Because I didn't want to know. If I knew, I'd be tempted to tell you. And you said that all you wanted to know was if he was alive. So that's what I'm giving you for Christmas—proof of life. His life. He lives. I can't answer any other questions about him."

"But you could have found out for me?"

"Yes."

"And you didn't? Why? To torture me?"

"Of course."

"Do you hate me?"

"Oh...poor Bambi." She shook her head, tsk-tsked him. "I know it hurts. Every boy who falls in love the first time thinks he invented the concept. I've been in love too. I know what torture it is. But I'm not merely torturing you—although I am. I wanted to teach you a lesson. If you're going to make wishes, you should learn to ask for what you want, not what you think you should want. You wanted to know if he was alive. That's all. So that's what I gave you."

She crossed her legs and rested her elbow on her knee, her chin in her hand. She smiled and wondered if he would strike her. It wouldn't surprise her if he did. That smile she wore had caused more than one man in the past to attempt to slap it off her face. Those men failed, of course, and one of them lost use of that slapping hand for his trouble.

In two long strides, Marcus traversed the floor from fireplace to piano bench, stopping unnervingly close to her. She braced herself.

He bent over and kissed her lightly on the lips. So lightly it was like being kissed by a bird's wing. Her lips tingled as if they'd been tickled.

"Thank you for my Christmas gift, Magda."

"You're quite welcome, Bambi." She patted the piano bench and he sat next to her again, the photograph still clutched in his hands.

"Can I keep this?" he asked.

"It is yours, but let's keep it here at the house. For your own sake, dear." She patted his knee and he allowed it, his grief for his long-lost lover making him a child again. He leaned his head on her shoulder and she kissed the top of his head. "Don't you think it should stay with me?"

He inhaled deeply and nodded.

"But you can visit it anytime," she said. "You can keep my house key."

He nodded again and sat up straight as if suddenly remembering he was a grown man and should act like it.

Poor lamb. From the tension in his jaw, she could tell he wanted to weep, but his pride wouldn't allow it.

"He's smoking," he said. "He shouldn't smoke."

Magdalena noticed for the first time that the young man in the photograph, Marcus's Kingsley, held a cigarette between two fingers of his right hand. A Gauloise by the looks of it—the soldier's breakfast. She'd lied to Marcus. Nothing new there, of course. She lied to him all the time. Two years ago, Kingsley Théophile Boissonneault had joined the French Foreign Legion, which is why he'd been so difficult to track down (*La Legion* were often deployed). It was why he'd cut his hair; it was why she didn't tell Marcus what Kingsley did for a living. Learning Kingsley had joined the French Army would hardly give Marcus the peace he sought.

"Of course he smokes," she said. "He's French. And besides, I smoke. When have you ever complained?"

"You're not Kingsley."

"So I can give myself lung cancer, but he can't."

"I would never have given him permission to start smoking. I would have refused to kiss him. That would have made him quit."

"Ah...young love. Ordering your lover to change to suit you. It's cute when you're a teenager. Not nearly as much as you get older. But what would you know of that? You'll never fall in love again, will you?"

"No, I won't."

Magdalena smiled to herself, but didn't tease him. She'd done enough of that tonight.

"You're right, he really is a beautiful young man," she said, looking at the photograph. "Wonderful bone structure. A good Greek nose. And those lips... I would have bitten that bottom lip until it looked like a bee had stung it."

"I did bite his lips. Not hard. I couldn't leave marks where others would see them. Or I tried not to. I failed a few times."

"On purpose?"

"No. I don't think so."

"But you aren't sure?"

He shook his head.

"Well..." she said. "I've had many a client 'accidentally on purpose' wear a lipstick-stained shirt collar home to his wife in the subconscious hope of getting caught cheating."

"It wasn't that. All the students at school were afraid of me," he said. "I admit I cultivated that fear. I didn't enjoy it but it was for the best I kept myself apart from them. For their sake and mine. But with Kingsley...he loved me. I wanted everyone to know someone could love me. And that I could love. I don't think they would have believed it even if Kingsley shouted it from the rooftops. They'd already made their minds up about me. Only Kingsley saw me as I am, not as I wanted to be seen."

"That must have driven you mad—being infiltrated, having all your defenses breached."

"I wanted to strangle him for pursuing me, not for the usual reasons I'd place my hands around someone's neck. Although..." He stopped and smiled as if remembering something dark and something beautiful. "I swear I did everything I could to discourage him. I almost broke his wrist the first time he kissed me. He kissed me without asking first, and I pushed him off me and onto the bed, held him down by his wrists. I heard one pop. It..."

"It aroused him."

"It did. I could see it in his eyes. He almost came from it. I knew I'd found someone like me. The one."

"There's more than one."

"There's only one Kingsley."

"There's more than one masochist in the world. Trust me. I have most of them in my Rolodex."

"I know there are. I know..."

He lowered his head for a moment as if praying.

"You will see him again," Magdalena said.

"Is this another prophecy of yours? You know, in the book of Deuteronomy, we're instructed to put false prophets to death."

"Not a prophecy. I simply know you'll see him again. Somewhere, someday..."

"I want to believe that. And yet, I don't want to."

"The love is in the waiting," she reminded him. "Come, finish playing my song for me."

"If I can."

"Why couldn't you?"

Marcus held up his hands in front of him. They were shaking. She knew how he felt. All too well.

"Let's have more wine," she said. "That's what we both need."

She stood up and paused at a sound she hadn't expected to hear—a knock on the door.

"Who on earth..."

"It's your Christmas gift," Marcus said. "Your other Christmas gift. I'll play for you later."

He stood up and headed for the door. She didn't follow.

"What did you give me?" she asked, her eyes narrowed.

"Something you will probably hate."

"You make me curious."

"Can you trust me long enough to at least see if you want your gift?"

"No, but I suppose I have to."

He held out his hand, which surprised her. He didn't

seem the handholding sort of man. She reached out but he pulled his hand back at the last second.

"You bastard," she said.

"Vengeance is mine, sayeth the Jesuit. Now come with me or you'll never get your gift."

She raised her hands in surrender. "Very well. But if this isn't the best gift I've ever been given, I'm banishing you from the house until after New Year's Day."

"That's six days away."

"New Year's Day of 2015."

For all her consternation, she *was* rather curious, so she followed him from her bedroom and down the steps to the parlor.

"I'll get the door," Marcus said. "You stay here."

"You're telling me what to do in my own house?"

"Yes."

He left her alone in the parlor. To say she was irritated would be an understatement. It was a good thing Marcus was such a pretty boy or she wouldn't allow him such liberties. She really should stop spoiling him. In fact, if this gift disappointed her, she would likely insist he submit to her in a much more meaningful way if he wanted to keep coming to her house, eating her food, and playing with Caterina. She'd make him her footstool. She'd make him cook for her. She'd make him bathe her and shave her legs for her. With his straight razor.

Marcus walked back into the parlor and much to her surprise, he had a man with him. A man of about forty years of age, salt and pepper hair, wearing a cassock.

"You brought me a priest for Christmas?" she asked, glaring at Marcus.

"Magdalena, I'm pleased to introduce you to Father

Stuart Ballard, my confessor. Stuart, this is Magda, my other confessor."

She smiled. "I'm also a prostitute and the madam of a brothel, Father Ballard. Are you sure you should be here?"

"My God, your English is flawless," Father Ballard said, grinning broadly, a kindly grin, fatherly almost. "You even speak with an English accent. Bit of Yorkshire in there. How on earth did you come by that?"

"When I was sixteen, my pimp sold me to the Shadow Chancellor of the Exchequer. I learned English from him. And piano. He was quite proper when he wasn't buggering underage prostitutes."

Father Ballard seemed to digest this information. "Tory, I imagine."

"However did you guess?"

"Thatcher's been buggering the whole country."

"Stuart," Marcus said, his tone that of a son embarrassed by his father. "Politics is hardly an appropriate topic of conversation at Christmas. Or buggery."

"You're getting stuffy in your old age, lad," Father Ballard said. "Christmas is nothing but politics. King Herod murdered Jewish toddlers because he didn't want to lose his throne to the newborn king. If murdering Jewish people for power isn't politics, I don't know what is."

"You must be quite a treat at Christmas parties," Marcus said.

"I don't go to Christmas parties, Marcus. Too many young people at them who have no concept of history."

"He's allowed to call you Marcus and I'm not?" she asked, glaring at Marcus but pointing at Father Ballard.

"He is *not* allowed to call me Marcus," Marcus said. "He does it anyway."

"I'll just put my things over here on this table. You two talk. But talk loudly. I've missed hearing my native tongue."

"Bambi, a moment please."

"She calls you Bambi?" Father Ballard said, half-laughing. "No wonder you let me call you Marcus."

"Marcus and I will be back momentarily. Forgive me. *Marcus?*" She grabbed Marcus's ear, pinched it, and dragged him by it to the corner of the room.

"That was more painful than I imagined it would be," he said after she released his ear. "I'll try that on Caterina. I promised her I'd break her on New Year's Eve."

"Why is your priest in my house? And why is he putting napkins on my end table?"

"That's a corporal and a purificator. He's preparing to celebrate mass."

"Mass? In my house?"

"Months ago you said, and I quote, 'I will never step foot in a Catholic Church again after what my priest did to my family. If God wants me, He can send the Church to me.' Since I'm not a priest yet, I can't say mass, therefore I asked Stuart to come celebrate Christmas Midnight Mass at your home."

"Your priest is here to say mass for me?"

"Yes."

"Just me?"

"And the choirs of angels. Myself as well. I haven't taken Communion yet today."

"Mass. At my home. For Christmas. Said by a Jesuit priest."

"If you'll allow him to. He will leave if you ask."

She put her hand to her forehead and turned her back to him.

"Magda?"

"Do you have any idea how much the Catholic Church has hurt me?"

"Yes, sorry about that."

"Yes, so sorry," Father Ballard called out from the other side of the room. He looked genuinely sheepish as he gave her a little wave.

"Sorry?" She spun back around. "I was called 'demon seed' by my priest when I was a thirteen-year-old child for doing nothing more than being a girl. My priest told my mother I needed an exorcism to save my soul. I had to run away from home to save myself and you know who took me in? A pimp. And he was kinder to me than the fucking priest was, and you say 'Sorry'?"

"We're *very* sorry?" Marcus said.

"May I speak with you a moment, Ma'am?" Father Ballard asked. "Please?"

"At least this one has something akin to manners," she said. She crossed the room to where Father Ballard had set up his makeshift altar, Moussi at his feet watching him curiously.

"Yes?" she said to Father Ballard. "You may speak."

He clasped his hands in front of him and bowed his head a moment. When he lifted his head again, all trace of mirth, of amusement, was gone.

"Marcus has told me a little about you. Knowing what I know, I suppose I should have this conversation in a more penitent position."

"Yes, you should."

"Very well." He slowly dropped to his knees.

"Stuart?" Marcus said.

"I have this, my boy. But thank you for your concern." Father Ballard looked up at her from his kneeling position on the floor. "My dear lady, please allow me to apologize on behalf of my Church for the insults inflicted upon you and the damage done to you and your family. We clergy are far too human. And sometimes we are so human as to seem inhuman. There is no excuse for what your priest did and said to you as a child. None. And I will offer no excuse. God will punish that priest. I have long believed that when a child is harmed by an adult, that person stays a child in God's eyes." Father Ballard's eyes glanced a moment in Marcus's direction. "You are loved as a child, cosseted as a child, forgiven as a child, forgiven *everything* unconditionally because no good parent can stay angry at a small child for long. The Lord teaches us that the last shall be first. In your priest's eyes you were last and lowly. In God's eyes you will be first and honored."

"I like the sound of that."

"Also, Marcus tells me you've taken him in and helped him come to terms with his many, *many* varied and sundry perversions—"

"I only have the one," Marcus said.

Father Ballard ignored him. "Any woman who could put up with that," he said, pointing at Marcus, "and treat him with even the smallest modicum of compassion—"

"Actually, she's very mean to me."

"Shut up, Marcus. Your betters are speaking," Father Ballard said. Marcus stopped talking but his eyes communicated a great deal of information.

"I like you," Magdalena said to Father Ballard. "I wish I didn't."

"You aren't the first to say that to me. As I was saying, any woman who treats that piece of work over there with a modicum of compassion is already a saint in my eyes. God knows he'd try the patience of Job—and the patience of Stuart." He pointed at himself. "As for your former priest...I don't know why he called you what he called you. It doesn't matter in the least to me. Nothing you were or are or did or have done or are doing merited such cruelty. No child merits cruelty. Your very life is a miracle and to call your life and the mystery of your creation 'demonic' is a sin God will punish."

The priest held out his hands, palms up, and she took them in hers, thinking he wanted help off the floor.

But he didn't. He simply held her hands in his. They were large, warm hands, gentle but with calluses on the tips of his fingers. She liked that.

"Dear lady," Father Ballard continued, "I will not ask you to come back to the Church, because the Church does not deserve you. But I would ask you to allow me to say mass in your home and serve you Communion. It would be my honor."

"Your honor? To offer Communion to the madam of a brothel? To a woman who unrepentantly whores herself?"

"There are four women in Christ's lineage—his great-grandmothers, so to speak. Tamar, who played prostitute to seduce her father-in-law; Rahab the Harlot, who gave aid and shelter to Joshua's spies; Ruth, who seduced Boaz; and Bathsheba who committed adultery with King David. Christ called the clergy hypocrites, but he dined with prostitutes. He would have liked you more than me. Even more, Christ would have loved you more than he loved me. I know this. It hurts me and humbles me to say it but it is true—you're closer to God in your brothel than I am in my church. Jesus had a great fondness for women named Magdalena, after all."

She sighed.

Heavily.

"You're good at begging," she said.

"I'm a Jesuit. They teach us to beg. Usually for money from rich patrons, but the lessons apply anywhere."

"Tell me why you have calluses on your hands. Seems suspicious for a priest."

His eyebrow quirked in confusion. "I play guitar. Electric. He hasn't told you that?"

"He has not."

"I force him to play with me."

"What do make him play?"

"Two weeks ago we did a duet of Pink Floyd's 'Shine On You Crazy Diamond.' If I can find the sheet music for The Who's 'Tommy,' we'll tackle that next."

"Surely you're joking."

"He's not," Marcus said. "He makes me play gaudy rock music with him in exchange for him allowing me to play what I want on the school piano. It's neither my style, nor my forte."

"He's far too modest," Father Ballard said. "The boy could tour with Clapton, I swear. Although Slow Hand has nothing on me."

She wanted to smile but didn't. Instead she waved her hand imperiously, like a queen. "You may stand."

Father Ballard came to his feet with more humility than grace, pausing first to pat Moussi on his head.

"You'll allow me the honor?" he asked Magdalena. "And it would be my honor, truly."

"I..." she began and paused. She took a steadying breath, rested her hand on her chest. "I confess I do miss Midnight Mass. My mother always took me every Christmas until I ran away. She would like this."

"But would you like it?" Father Ballard asked. "I will walk out the door right now if you don't want me here."

"I would like you to stay. I suppose you should hear my confession and absolve me before I take Communion."

"Dear Lady, the Church sinned against you far more than you sinned against the Church. We need your absolution. You don't need ours."

She swallowed hard and turned to Marcus, who came to stand at her side. "No wonder you're turning into a human being," she said to her Bambi. "He's good for you."

Marcus bent to kiss her cheek. "You're good for me."

All was forgiven.

"It's midnight," Father Ballard said. "Shall we begin?"

"Yes, we shall." She glanced over her shoulder and crooked her finger at Marcus. He walked to her and stood at her side.

"English or Italian?" Father Ballard asked her.

"I'm older than I look," she said. "Could you say it in Latin? Please?"

"*Dóminus vobíscum*," Father Ballard said.

"*Et cum spíritu tuo*," she replied, the words coming back to her instantly like the lyrics of an old favorite song she hadn't heard in years but had never forgotten.

Father Ballard took a gold chalice from his bag and set it on the table.

"This is a good gift," Magdalena said to Marcus.

"I am truly sorry that my Church hurt you."

"I don't mind being hurt. I don't. Pain is my life. But your Church...it did more than hurt me. It damaged me."

"It did."

"I can't forgive it."

"No, I don't imagine you can. I won't ask you to."

"But..." she began. "But while it's hurt me, it's helped you. I see that. I can give it that much credit."

"I promise you this—when I am a priest I will protect the children like you and like me. I won't harm them."

She nodded, believing his promise.

Father Ballard had slipped into his purple chasuble and stole. He took her poinsettia off her side table and placed it on his altar.

"So that's why you brought me the poinsettia from your chapel," she said.

"I didn't steal it," Marcus said. "I merely relocated it—one altar to another."

"You're much like a poinsettia, Bambi. You really are."

He furrowed his brow at her. "How so?"

"Because everyone has this erroneous idea that you're poisonous. And you're not. You're not at all."

Before Marcus could reply, Father Ballard began the mass.

Outside the window behind Father Ballard, snow began to fall. A little bit of snow, just a flake or two. Magdalena felt a warmth in her chest, joy blooming bright and red as a Christmas Star. Marcus had given Christmas back to her.

Maybe he was one of the Magi after all.

Not that she would ever tell him that.

She much preferred being mean to him.

THE SCENT OF WINTER

ONE

UNHOLY ORDERS

Author's Note: This story takes place between The King *and* The Virgin, *the sixth and seventh books in the series.*

NEW YORK CITY

WHAT WAS the point of cold weather without any snow?

Not that Kingsley minded the lack of snow in New Orleans during winter. There was something to be said for sitting on his back balcony in December and drinking wine with Juliette after putting Céleste to bed. But now that he'd been back in New York for two days, he found himself wishing for snow with the same fervor and longing he'd wished for it as a child, when a rare heavy snowfall meant *Maman* might let him stay home from school. From the window in Griffin's dining room, Kingsley studied the sky and found it empty of snow clouds. The sun hung down from the ceiling of the overcast horizon like a sad, low-watt light bulb.

Winter in New York was a disappointment. The sooner he got back to New Orleans the better. Ah, well, it was a business trip anyway. Not in town for pleasure. Pleasure was back in New Orleans. Nothing in New York these days but paperwork.

"I promise Mick's not dead," Griffin said, interrupting Kingsley's melancholy reverie. Griffin brought two cups of coffee over to the dining room table where they'd been working. Kingsley had offered to sell his old townhouse to Griffin at below market value to use as a base of operations, but Griffin hadn't wanted to leave the apartment he'd shared with Michael for almost four years. He liked the privacy of it, which Kingsley could appreciate. In the old days, people were always tramping in and out of Kingsley's townhouse on Riverside Drive for a dinner party or a music recital, an auction or an orgy.

"Sick?" Kingsley hadn't seen Michael all morning. And not once yesterday either.

"Worn out from finals. He always sleeps for about three straight days when the semester's over. But he'll be up eventually."

"Let him sleep. He's earned it," Kingsley said, taking the coffee cup Griffin offered. "What are your Christmas plans?"

"The whole family's at the ski lodge again this year. Mick's mom is coming, too."

Kingsley raised his eyebrow. "This is the same mother who is now dating your oldest half-brother?"

"Yeah." Griffin winced as he scratched his fingers through his dark brown hair, which was still a little wild from sleep. "If she and Aiden get married, I'll be Mick's step-uncle. That's weird, right? It feels weird."

Kingsley shrugged. "*La Maîtresse* will probably write a book about it, knowing her."

Griffin rolled his eyes, threw his feet up on the table, and sat back in the chair.

"She would, wouldn't she?"

Kingsley examined the last of Griffin's books, leisurely sipping his coffee.

"Well?" Griffin asked. He was nervous, which Kingsley found endearing. Even if Griffin was the new King of the Underground, he still wanted to impress the old King of the Underground. "What's the verdict?"

"I don't see anything of concern. But where are the other books?"

Griffin's eyes narrowed. "What do you mean?"

"Jules and I kept two sets of books. The ones the IRS saw, and the ones the IRS didn't."

"King, my father is the former chairman of the New York Stock Exchange."

"Then if anyone knows how to game the system, it's you."

Griffin laughed. "No second set of books. I'm keeping the clubs on the up and up. The only nefarious behavior going on around here is on *my* sheets, not the spreadsheets."

"It won't be nefarious for long. I hear congratulations are in order." Kingsley closed the pages of the spiral-bound financial report and tossed it aside.

"Save the date," Griffin said. "Mick's going to make an honest man out of me."

"First, he already has. Second, the date is not saved. The entire week is. Nora's house has been taken over with wedding planning books, and Juliette is already shopping for dresses for her and Céleste. Jules is unusually excited the wedding will be in Scotland, and I'm not sure I want to know why..."

"Scottish castle. Who wouldn't be excited?" Griffin drained his coffee in a gulp. "I still can't believe this time last year, I thought I'd lost Mick for good and now we're planning a wedding." Griffin gazed out the large picture window in his high-rise Manhattan apartment and smiled a little dreamily to himself. He was a man in love—and even better, a man contented. It was good to see. Kingsley, too, was a man in love. He wouldn't say no to a little more contentment, however.

"The course of true love never did run smooth," Kingsley said. "No one knows that better than I. Than me? Ah, I still hate English. Than *moi*."

"Speaking of true love..." Griffin said, grinning that old playboy grin of his. "How's the big guy? It's his birthday tomorrow, right? The big 5-1? You two partying together? Picnic in the park? Pairs figure skating? Karaoke night?"

Kingsley took off his glasses and cleaned them with the white silk handkerchief he'd taken from his pocket. He wanted to laugh but didn't quite have it in him today. Spending two straight days pouring over financial records did not do wonders for his sense of humor.

"I doubt I will even see him."

"He's that busy?" Griffin asked. "I thought since the semester was over, he'd have nothing to do but grade finals."

Kingsley shrugged dismissively. "New Orleans is a very Catholic city. Advent is a hectic time at the parish."

"Too bad," Griffin said and frowned, though Kingsley could see he was trying very hard not to smile.

Kingsley tucked his glasses and the handkerchief into his pocket. "Never fall in love with a priest," he said. "God will always be his first priority. If you're lucky, you'll be second."

"Not a big worry of mine. Mick's an ex-altar boy, but the only orders he takes are from me."

"Unholy orders are far more fun than Holy Orders."

"Trouble in paradise?" Griffin asked.

Kingsley shrugged. "I turned fifty last month. I think I'm finally starting to feel it."

"If it makes you feel any better, you don't look a day over forty. You're sexier now than you were when I met you. I'd fuck you in a New York minute. If I wasn't engaged, I mean." Griffin glanced over his shoulder. "Hope Mick didn't hear that. Nah. Doesn't matter. He'd fuck you too. Well, he wouldn't fuck you since he's a bottom. But you get what I mean."

"I do. You paint quite the picture."

"Don't sweat the numbers, King. Sting's in his mid-sixties."

"Now that does make me feel better." Kingsley stood up. He'd seen everything he needed to see. "You've done very well. I'm impressed with your work."

"You are?" Griffin looked like a boy about to burst with happiness but trying very hard to remember he was a grown man.

"You're an excellent CEO," Kingsley said. "Even if you don't quite look the part."

As it was only eleven in the morning, Griffin was dressed in pajama pants and a faded blue t-shirt that read WANT TO WATCH PORN ON MY FLAT SCREEN MIRROR?

"Sorry," Griffin said. "We keep it casual around the house. You're lucky I have pants on."

"Yes, we know how offended I am at the sight of naked men."

"Speaking of looking the part...I see you've given up the Lord Byron duds. I kind of miss 'em. Don't get me wrong, you look damn good. Like one of those sexy Greek tycoons on those romance novels Mom's always reading. But it's kind of an adjustment seeing you look...what's the word?"

"Vanilla?" Kingsley said.

Griffin raised his hands in innocent surrender. "Hey, you said it. Not me."

Kingsley had indeed made a wardrobe change, though he still kept all his breeches, military coats, Edwardian suits, and riding boots in the closet at home and wore them on special occasions. But these days, people were more likely to find him wearing something like what he had on today: an Armani business suit, double-breasted, black, with a white shirt under and a slim black tie.

"I'm keeping a low profile these days," Kingsley said. "And I'm a father now. I'm not quite ready to explain fetish-wear to my daughter. That's what her *Tante Elle* is for."

"Don't worry. When I'm at the clubs, I look the part. You set a high bar. I want to make sure I clear it."

"I have no doubt you do."

"Any suggestions for The Kingdom? It's your baby."

Kingsley shrugged. "I'd watch your overhead at the California location. Opening clubs is the easy part. It's like falling in love. Keeping them running is the real work. I wouldn't expand operations out west until you've turned a profit there two years in a row."

"Good advice. Anything else?"

"Nothing else. I put my realm into the right hands. *Merci. Merci beaucoup.*"

"*De rien, mon ami,*" Griffin said as they shook hands. "I love the work. I feel like I've found my calling."

Kingsley picked up his coat off the back of a chair and pulled it on. Winter had hit New York hard this week. The temperature was barely scraping the bottom of thirty.

"Leaving already?" Griffin asked. "You could reschedule your flight. Tonight's Bisexual Appreciation Night at the club."

"Isn't every night Bisexual Appreciation Night?" Kingsley asked.

"Yes, but tonight we're having punch and pie."

"Tempting. But I must get home. My girls miss me almost as much as I miss them."

"I know. Just had to ask. Let me walk you out."

They strode down the long hall toward the front door of Griffin's penthouse apartment and passed a darkly sensual abstract painting that looked to Kingsley like a red mouth kissing a black bruise. Kingsley almost inquired who the painter was so he could buy one for his home in New Orleans when he saw the artist's name scrawled at the bottom—Michael Dimir.

Griffin stopped at the door to the master bedroom and cracked it open.

"Just a sec. I want to make sure he's still breathing," Griffin said with a wink.

Michael lay on his stomach across Griffin's large platform bed, the sheets pulled up to his waist but no higher. Red welts decorated Michael's pale back diagonally from shoulder to hip. The boy had been transformed into a human candy cane.

"Mick?" Griffin whispered. "You awake?"

Michael raised his head, blinked, and pushed a lock of black hair off his face.

"I'm sort of awake, sir."

"Say hi to King," Griffin ordered.

Michael gave a quick, tired wave. "Hello, Mr. Edge."

"*Joyeux Nöel*, Michael," Kingsley said.

"Merry Christmas to you, too."

Then Michael dropped face first back down onto the bed and Griffin shut the door.

Kingsley looked at Griffin and blinked pointedly at him. "Exquisite welts."

Griffin wore a devilish smile. "He woke up about eight o'clock last night for a couple hours and said he was finally rested up. I must have fuckered him out again."

"The phrase is 'tuckered out,' *non*?"

"Pretty sure it's fuckered out. And if it's not, it is now."

Kingsley kept his mouth shut as the elevator took them from Griffin's penthouse to the main lobby. The welts on Michael's back had sent a jolt of intense longing through Kingsley's body. A longing far too much like envy...envy left him grappling with guilt. He had Juliette, whom he loved and adored and lusted after with every bone in his body. He had his daughter who had kicked in and crawled through every closed door in his heart. He had Nico, who was everything a father could want in a son and more. He had friends like Nora and Griffin, who were a second family to him. He had a beautiful home, a beautiful life, meaningful work...

But.

There was no denying his essential nature. He'd once told a client of Nora's that fetishes were the pet you feed or the beast that eats you. It had been almost three months since he'd fed that chained beast of his. Coming to New York had tested Kingsley's willpower. He knew the phone numbers of every good Dominatrix in the city by heart, and his fingers itched to dial one of them.

He might have succumbed if it was merely pain and submission he desired. But it wasn't. Not even pain and submission *and* pleasure. He simply wanted his priest as soon as possible. Now, preferably. But as he wasn't going to get his priest until Nora left for France in January, Kingsley hadn't even bothered putting him on his Christmas list.

"Can your doorman fetch me a taxi?" Kingsley said.

"Already taken care of," Griffin said, pointing at the doorman, who nodded and picked up the lobby phone. As they waited, Kingsley pulled on his gloves and adjusted his scarf.

"King," Griffin said, pushing his hands deep into his coat pockets. "I wanted to ask you something."

"Ask," Kingsley said.

"It's about the wedding. I was hoping, you know... Would you maybe be my best man?"

Kingsley's surprise must have shown on his face, because Griffin started talking again before he could answer.

"It would mean a lot if you were up there next to me," Griffin went on hurriedly. "My whole life changed for the better that day I woke up in your strip club with your boots on my chest."

"Griffin, I'm honored. Truly. But you have brothers."

"That's the thing. I love my brothers. I can't pick just one without hurting the others. Even if I could, I'd still want you. You saved my life. You did, don't deny it. I know it and you know it and Mick knows it and my brothers know it. You got me into rehab. You helped me find something better than drugs to make me feel like I mattered. There'd be no Griff and Mick without you, because there'd be no Griff. So please say yes. Nora's going to be Mick's 'best mistress' and Søren's already agreed to perform the wedding."

"In that case." Kingsley smiled at Griffin and embraced him. "Of course I will be your best man. It would be my honor."

"Thank you," Griffin said, on the verge of tears. "Seriously. Thank you."

"Stop. You're the new King of the Underground. You can't be this soft in public."

Griffin chuckled before composing his handsome face into a mask of cold hard fury. "I am very scary and dangerous," he said. "Can't you tell?"

"That would be more believable if you weren't wearing Queen Elsa fuzzy slippers."

Griffin looked down at his feet. "They're very warm."

Kingsley glared at him.

"Okay, so they're not as intimidating as Hessian boots. But how did you know what they were anyway?" Griffin demanded. "Secret Disney fetish?"

"I have a two-year-old daughter. What's your excuse?"

"Killer fashion sense," Griffin said. "Car's here."

As soon as they walked out the double glass doors, a sleek black town car pulled forward.

"Very nice," Kingsley said.

"Even a king in exile is still a king." Griffin stepped forward to open the rear door for him.

"It was good to see you again," Kingsley said. "Come down and visit."

"I will. Hey, I'm supposed to give this to you."

Griffin handed Kingsley a crisp white envelope.

"What's this?" Kingsley asked.

Griffin smiled. "Don't be mad. I'm just following orders."

"Orders? Whose orders?" Kingsley demanded.

"Um...let's call them...*un*-holy orders."

And with that, Griffin slammed the car door shut. Outside the car window, Griffin grinned and waved good-bye. Kingsley had a very suspicious feeling that he'd just been kidnapped.

The car pulled into traffic and Kingsley leaned forward to address the driver. "You're not taking me to the airport, are you?"

"No, Mr. Edge."

"I don't suppose you could tell me where we *are* going, then?"

He guessed Juliette had arranged to meet him some-where for a night in the city alone together. She'd talked about it, if Nora were willing to watch Céleste. But what about Griffin's crack about *un*-holy orders?

"I'm supposed to tell you that everything you need to know is in the card."

With his heart in his throat, Kingsley ripped the envelope open and removed the card from within. At first glance it appeared to be nothing more than a standard-issue Christmas card, the sort one received from banks or doctor's offices. A generic forest snow scene, the sky streaked with falling stars.

Except...the forest in the photograph seemed eerily familiar.

Kingsley opened the card, and something fell out of it and into his lap.

A silver cross on a silver chain. The chain was broken, split near the clasp and tarnished with age.

He knew that cross.

He knew that chain.

One dark night long, long ago, he'd torn it from the neck of the boy he'd loved more than life itself. And that hadn't been a cliché that night. He'd loved that boy so much he would have traded his very life for one night with him. That night he nearly had.

Kingsley wrapped his fist around the cross and chain and pressed it to his heart. He knew where he was being taken. He knew because he'd flipped the card over to read the caption on the back. The forest seemed familiar because he'd been in one just like it before.

"Get comfortable, Mr. Edge," was all the driver said. "It's going to be a long drive."

They merged onto I-95 going north.

North to Maine.

"Driver?" Kingsley said.

"Yes, sir?"

"If they give you a ticket for speeding, I'll pay it."

The driver glanced back at him in the review mirror and smiled. Message received. "Yes, sir," he said, putting his foot on the gas.

They drove in silence a few minutes. Kingsley was about to roll the partition up between them so he could make a phone call in privacy when the driver asked him a question.

"So what's in Maine anyway?"

Kingsley could have said "my Christmas gift" if he wanted to be twee. He could have said "visiting a friend" if he wanted to lie. He could have said "rough trade" if he wanted to be obnoxious (and accurate).

But he would tell the truth, though it was a bittersweet truth. Then again, the true meaning of Christmas was bittersweet. A child born to save us? Yes, but also a child born to die.

Kingsley answered the driver.

"Unfinished business."

TWO
CAPTURE THE KING

AS SOON AS the car cleared the city, Kingsley took his phone from his coat pocket and called Juliette.

"*Bonjour, mon roi*," she said.

"You're in on this, aren't you, you wicked girl?" He spoke in French to her so the driver wouldn't understand their conversation if he felt like eavesdropping.

"I had no part in the planning," she said. "But I did give a certain tall blond someone my permission to have you...*relocated*."

"Relocated? I've been kidnapped." Albeit very politely kidnapped. Someone had even left him a picnic basket full of fresh fruit, nuts, cheese, and white wine in the backseat.

"You're so happy you're about to explode, aren't you?" Juliette giggled like a school girl. "I can tell."

"I am very happy, yes." *Très heureux, oui.*

"You need this. You haven't been yourself for too long. I know when it's time for you to go away and be someone else for a few days. And it's past time. You'll come home in a much better mood," she said, her voice still flush with barely suppressed laughter.

"This isn't good for my ego, you sitting there laughing at me while I'm being abducted. You could at least pretend you'll miss me."

"You'll only be gone three days and two nights. And we'll be too busy to miss you. I'm taking Céleste to visit her grandmother for a few days—with your permission, of course. We'll be home in time for *réveillon*."

"You'll be safe?" he asked.

"Nora is coming with us, if that makes you feel better."

"Much better," he said. Nora could watch Céleste while Juliette tended to her mother. "Yes, you have my permission. Give *la Maîtresse* my thanks. She takes good care of both my children."

"In very different ways," Juliette said.

"Don't remind me," he said.

"I love you, *mon roi*. And I will miss you. So will your daughter."

"Tell her I love her and give her a thousand kisses for me."

"Always."

"And a thousand and one kisses for her beautiful, naughty mother."

"*Parfait*," Juliette said. "I'll tell her and kiss her. But you tell your priest something for me."

"What is that?" Kingsley asked.

"Tell him to send you back in one piece, *s'il vous plait*."

Kingsley laughed. "You know the priest. No promises."

"Two pieces then," Juliette said. "One for him and one for me."

They said their goodbyes, and Kingsley hung up.

He'd stayed up most of last night reading through the clubs' account books. He should sleep if he could, as he had a long night ahead of him. The car was spacious and the interior comfortable, the temperature warm and the ride smooth. The driver rolled down the partition an inch.

"Would you like me to put on some Christmas music, Mr. Edge?"

"If you like," Kingsley said. "But nothing modern. If I hear even one bar of 'Wonderful Christmastime,' I'll be forced to violently commandeer the vehicle."

"Christmas classics it is, Mr. Edge."

He rolled the partition up, and Kingsley leaned back in the seat and closed his eyes.

The quiet strains of violins and cellos filtered through the speakers.

In the bleak midwinter...

It sounded like a recording from the Vienna Boys' Choir.

It sounded like a memory.

St. Ignatius.

It must have been a Saturday or a Sunday, as he didn't recall having classes that day. What he remembered was the loneliness. The worst kind of loneliness. The loneliness of being in love with someone he couldn't have.

Kingsley had been so happy to see his sister Marie-Laure when she'd come to the school for a surprise visit. Oh, and how happy had all the other boys been at the sight of her French beauty. But his pleasure in her presence faded shortly after her arrival. She'd quickly become as obsessed with Søren as he was, and Kingsley's only comfort was that although Søren had treated her with unfailing politeness, it was clear he did so only for Kingsley's sake, not hers. Yet she monopolized their time and it became nearly impossible to be alone with him. He and Søren had snuck off campus the week before together in a Rolls Royce and spent the best afternoon of his life in the back of it.

Almost a week had passed since then. Søren hadn't touched him in all that time. He would have gone a week without eating before he'd willingly go a week without Søren. When Kingsley saw Søren and Marie-Laure sitting alone at a table in the dining room, he turned his back on them and walked to his dorm room where he put on his coat, his winter boots and scarf, and set out into the snowy woods in the hopes of letting the bitter cold soothe his burning blood.

The only thing even remotely like submitting to Søren was a walk in a snow-filled, freezing dark wood. There was the cold of his heart, the terror of the darkness, the exertion of trudging in a foot of snow, and the beauty like no other. If he could not have Søren, this was the next best thing.

As he walked, he thought angry terrible things. Marie-Laure didn't even like Søren. She was playing a game with him. She wanted to win his heart like she'd won every other boy's heart in the school. Søren was aloof, showed no sexual interest in her. That's why she was so obsessed with him. And how dare she not love him like he deserved to be loved? She only wanted to conquer and discard him. He almost told Søren to confess to her that he was madly in love with her. Knowing her, she'd pat his cheek and tell him how flattered she was, but she simply didn't feel the same.

As Kingsley trudged deeper into the forest, he realized he had no idea where he was. Above him the tree cover was so thick he could barely see the moon. He tried to orient himself, to find his footprints in the snow in the dark. Six years from that night he'd be alone in the Carpathian Mountains with a sniper rifle strapped to his back, stalking through a forest ten times as thick and dangerous, hunting down a rogue KGB agent. But that night he was still a boy and the boy was lost and scared in the cold dark woods.

And it had started to snow again.

"*Merde*," he breathed as the snow filled up his footprints. Shit. He hadn't told anyone he was going for a walk. No one would notice he was missing until lights out. And even then, the boys in his dorm room were used to him sneaking out after dark because of his "insomnia."

Kingsley's pretend insomnia might get him killed tonight. His coat was warm, but not warm enough to keep him alive all night if the temperature dropped a few more degrees. Though they were likely all hibernating, Kingsley knew there were bears in the woods. And sometimes criminals would use this forest to cross into Canada. His mind was running away from him with fear. Hypothermia. Criminals. Bears.

Then he heard a twig crack.

He spun around, his heart taking off in his chest like a spooked bird.

"You could have told me this was your plan," Søren said, stepping into the clearing.

Even if he hadn't spoken, Kingsley would have known it was him—despite the darkness, what little moonlight filtered through the trees reflected off Søren's blond hair, giving him the illusion of a halo.

"Plan?" Kingsley asked.

"I assumed you came out here so I would have to come and find you and bring you back? An excuse to be alone together?"

"You're here, aren't you?" Kingsley said, trying not to betray his relief in his face. "You didn't need me to tell you the plan."

"I suppose not." Søren gazed up at the sky through the trees. A light dusting of snow fell gently onto his hair and face. "Not even you are foolish enough to walk off into the woods at night without marking a trail back to the school?"

"I marked a trail," Kingsley said. "It's...over there."

"Over where?" Søren asked, his tone mocking, dismissive.

"Over...you know, the same trail you marked."

"You'll have to show me where you marked the trail on our way back, as I didn't notice any markings at all other than your footprints on the way here. They're gone, by the way. Your footprints. You'll be lucky to find mine."

"I'm going back. Stay out here all night if you want." Kingsley brushed past him. "See if I care."

He made it two steps before he felt a hand viciously hard on the back of his neck.

"Not that way."

"That's where you came from," Kingsley said, meeting Søren's steel eyes, which were a perfect complement to his iron grip on Kingsley's neck.

"No. I came from there." Søren nodded to a space between two other trees. "If you'd gone that way for ten more steps in the dark, you would have fallen to your death off the cliff."

"Maybe I want to fall to my death."

"You're not allowed."

"I'm not allowed?"

"No," Søren said. "You are not allowed. You are not allowed to get lost unless I want to lose you. You aren't allowed to be found, unless it's me doing the finding. And the only way you're allowed to die is if I choose to kill you with my own hands. Your life doesn't belong to you anymore, and if I have to murder you tonight and paint the snow with your blood to make you understand that, I will. You are mine, Kingsley. End of discussion."

At the time, Kingsley was certain he would never understand how words as cruel as those, how vicious and possessive and cold, could warm him like a bonfire and heal his wounds like a magic elixir from a fairy tale. It made no sense, but it was true nonetheless. Kingsley nearly collapsed on his knees into the snow right then from the sheer force of his love and his lust and his adoration of this bitterly cold boy with the snow in his veins.

"Are you going to kill me?"

"Probably," Søren said.

Probably?

Kingsley looked at him. "Do other lovers say the sort of things you say to me?"

"Why wouldn't they?" Søren asked.

"Fear of being sent to prison?"

Søren stared at him.

"Just thinking out loud," Kingsley said. "Sir."

"Come on," Søren said, dragging him by the hair to the path.

They walked in silence and Kingsley could have sworn he'd never seen this part of the woods before.

"This isn't the way back to the school, is it?" Kingsley asked.

"We're making a detour," Søren said.

"Where?"

Søren didn't answer. Kingsley had no choice but to follow him. While Kingsley had attended St. Ignatius for only two semesters, Søren had lived here full-time since he was twelve. Søren was as intimate with the woods around the school as Kingsley was with his own cock. And if someone didn't get intimate with his cock in the next few minutes, he would die from blood loss to his brain since it had all gone to his erection. He was about to tell Søren this when they stepped from the edge of the woods and onto a sheet of glass.

"Jesus," Kingsley said, nearly slipping and falling.

"Steady," Søren said. "We're on ice."

"Thin ice?"

"In Maine in December? It's a foot thick already."

Kingsley had known there was a small pond two miles from the school, but he'd never walked in the direction it was supposed to be. It was on someone's private land anyway, someone who'd warned the school to keep the boys away from it lest they be shot on sight as trespassers.

"We could be shot, you know," Kingsley said as Søren led him toward something across the pond that Kingsley couldn't quite make out yet.

"They only tell us that to keep us from breaking into their fishing shack."

"Then what are we doing here?" Kingsley asked.

"Breaking into their fishing shack."

"You really are going to kill me tonight, aren't you?"

"I'm not ruling anything out."

Kingsley needed to learn to not ask so many questions.

It was easy to break into the ice-fishing hut. All they had to do was open the door. Very few people locked their doors in rural Maine. Certainly not when the nearest town was an hour's drive away and their closest neighbors were Jesuit priests and their students.

Inside the shack, Søren set the lantern on the ice beneath their feet. Under the golden circle, shadows wiggled and danced. Fish.

"Take off your clothes," Søren said as soon as Kingsley had the door shut and latched behind him.

"What?" Kingsley demanded.

"You heard me."

"It's thirty degrees in here." There was almost nothing in the fishing shack but two chairs, a pile of plaid wool blankets, and a half-drunk bottle of Kentucky bourbon. There was certainly no electricity, no space heater, no fireplace. Only bare wood walls and a floor of ice.

Søren remained silent. He was waiting. Kingsley could spend the next half hour coming up with excuses, begging, pleading, and Søren would simply wait and wait until Kingsley did what he was ordered to do. He might as well skip the middle step and get right to the obedience.

"I have never hated anyone like I hate you," Kingsley said, dropping his coat.

"I could have left you to die in the woods tonight."

"I wish you had."

"You're so hard I can see it through your trousers," Søren said.

"That's a gun, not my cock. And it's going to be very happy to see you."

"I like the lies you tell yourself to keep from admitting how much you want this."

"It's not a lie. I don't want *this*. I want *you*. There's a difference. Big difference. *Une grande différence. Vive la différence.*"

"Are you finished?" Søren asked. He tapped his foot on the ice, impatient. "I can wait out any temper tantrum you throw."

"Temper tantrum," Kingsley muttered, pulling his heavy wool sweater off and the t-shirt under it. "I don't want fucking hypothermia, and he calls it a temper tantrum. If he shot me in the leg and I screamed, he'd tell me to stop pouting. If he cut my head off and I bled on him, he'd punish me for making a mess."

"I can hear everything you're saying," Søren said.

"Good. That was the point of me saying it."

Kingsley kicked his shoes off and stood on the back of his coat as he removed his socks. He wasn't cold. He was freezing. His teeth chattered and his body shook. Meanwhile, Søren—at the most infuriatingly leisurely pace— kicked a bedroll open on the ice and dropped half a dozen of the blankets onto it. When Kingsley was completely naked, he stood with his bare toes scrunched up in the folds of his coat, desperate for any warmth, any at all. From the air, from the blankets, from the heart of the young man staring at him. But none seemed forthcoming.

"It really is quite impressive," Søren said, nodding.

"What is?" Kingsley said through his chattering teeth.

"That you can maintain an erection in any weather or atmospheric conditions."

"I'm not turned on. It's frozen solid."

"Are you cold?"

"Cold as the ice in your veins, you bastard."

"Do you want to get under the blankets?"

"Yes."

"You may. As soon as you apologize."

"Apologize? For what?" Kingsley demanded.

"Did you or did you not go walking in the woods without telling anyone where you were going or marking any sort of trail to find your way back?"

"Well...maybe." Kingsley blinked tears from his eyes. He wasn't sad, nor remorseful. He was simply so cold that his eyes were watering uncontrollably. At least the tears were hot.

"If someone were to take something of mine, something valuable, carry it off while I'm at dinner, and lose it in the woods so that I had no hope of ever finding it again, would I not have every right on earth to be angry with that person?"

Kingsley felt that strange warmth again, that warmth that came all over him when Søren said something or did something to show that he truly thought of Kingsley as his own private and personal possession.

"I'm sorry," Kingsley whispered.

Søren put a hand behind his ear, cocked his head to the side. "What was that?"

"I said I'm sorry...sir. I forgot myself. I took something that wasn't mine to take and nearly lost it in the woods. I shouldn't have done that. I don't belong to me. I belong to you."

Søren nodded his approval. "You're forgiven," he said. "Now get in."

Kingsley dove into the pile of wool blankets and lay on his side in the fetal position. Søren stood over him, looking down at him. He didn't seem the least bit cold. Of course he had on his winter boots, wool socks, thick black trousers, a shirt, a sweater, a heavy wool coat and a black and white scarf. But it was more than the clothes. The cold seemed incapable of touching Søren. Or it could touch him but it couldn't harm him. Snow fell onto snow but the snow never complained of the cold. It was the cold.

"Warmer?" Søren asked after Kingsley had lain there a few minutes.

Kingsley nodded, still rolled onto his side with his knees to his chest.

"Lie on your back," Søren said, removing his gloves.

Kingsley did as he was told and found that once he lay flat on the bedroll with the blankets over him, he was quite comfortable again. Almost warm. He could sleep out here all night naked under these blankets and he would be fine. Well, until he had to go out and take a piss. But until then, he would be fine.

Søren removed his coat and laid it atop the blanket pile. He took off no other clothing—much to Kingsley's annoyance—but he did slide in under the blankets and on top of Kingsley, which was heaven. Face to face, eye to eye, hip to hip, Kingsley naked and Søren clothed. And Kingsley discovered something lovely then. He wasn't just comfortable. He wasn't just warm. He was hot.

"Better?" Søren asked.

"Much. Thank you, sir."

"You're welcome." Søren kissed him on the lips, a cold hard kiss that left Kingsley sweating.

With Søren's full weight on him, Kingsley struggled a little to breathe. Søren was even taller now than when Kingsley had first laid eyes on him in January. Taller, stronger, heavier...a boy no more, if Søren had ever been one. Kingsley wasn't stupid. He wasn't naive. He knew about those men who acquired boys his age, collected them, seduced them, and then discarded them when they grew into men and lost all their boyish beauty. Would Søren still want him when Kingsley was twenty, twenty-five, thirty, fifty? When Kingsley had crow's feet and gray hair? Would anyone still want him then? Would he even live that long?

"Will you still love me when I'm fifty years old?" Kingsley asked Søren between kisses.

"No," Søren said, pressing his cool lips to Kingsley's neck.

"No?"

"I don't even love you now," Søren said. "Why would I love you in thirty-three years?"

"Ah, good point." Kingsley smiled at the ceiling of the fishing shack. "Well...will you still want me when I'm fifty? Like this?" Kingsley asked, pushing his hips against Søren's.

"You mean naked and pathetic and willing to do what-ever I tell you to do?"

"Yes," Kingsley said, pressing his erection up and against Søren once again.

"Time will tell," Søren said. "Now hold still."

"Hold still?"

Søren reached down and laid his hand flat onto the ice floor.

His bare hand.

The bare ice.

This wasn't a good sign.

Søren's eyes were locked onto Kingsley's, who lay there trapped underneath Søren's body.

"Søren?" Kingsley whispered.

"Yes?"

"Aren't you going to hurt your hand like that?"

"You said I had ice in my veins," Søren said. "Did you not?"

"I might have implied something like that."

"Then the ice won't hurt me, will it?" Søren asked, his hand still pressed flat and hard to the ice.

"I was only joking."

"Were you?"

"I don't really think you have ice in your veins."

"No?"

"No, sir," Kingsley said. "Only living beings have veins."

"That was a joke, too, wasn't it?" Søren asked.

"A little joke."

"You like to make jokes, don't you?"

"Sometimes. I guess." Kingsley wasn't laughing or smiling anymore.

"I know a joke," Søren said.

"You do?"

He nodded. "It goes like this—what did the French whore say when his cock was grabbed by an ice-cold hand?"

"I—"

The punchline to the joke was, of course, a pained animal howl. It was uncontrollable, erupting from deep inside Kingsley, and there was no stopping the scream on the way out.

"That's right," Søren rasped into Kingsley's ear. "You know this joke."

"Jesus fucking God Christ in heaven you evil son of a bitch..." He swore in English. He swore in French. He swore in what little Latin he'd learned.

"Funny joke, isn't it?" Søren said.

"I hate you. I fucking hate you so much..." Kingsley's eyes watered again. His stomach muscles had contracted from the cold so hard he almost ejaculated out of sheer shock to his anatomy.

"Tell me how much you hate me," Søren said. "I like to hear it."

Kingsley might have told him and told him in excruciating detail that involved not only his hatred for Søren, but also for Søren's mother, his father, his grandparents, his cousins, his as-yet unborn progeny and even any pets he might have had in his life or would have someday.

But.

Søren's hand heated up quickly against Kingsley's hot flesh, and now it was an almost-warm hand that stroked his cock under the blankets. A warm hand and growing warmer by the moment. Søren massaged him with long strokes, hard strokes, sensual strokes that brought Kingsley to the very edge of orgasm so quickly he'd forgotten how much pain he'd been in only seconds earlier.

"I have to come," Kingsley panted. The muscles in his thighs quivered with need and his back shook and his hips pulsed and pulsed against Søren's hand, and Kingsley couldn't have stopped if someone had held a gun to his head.

"You're going to come," Søren said, still stroking, stroking... "You're going to come until you're empty. I want you spent. I want you hollow. I want you to have nothing left inside you. No will to live. No will to die. No anger. No fight. No hope. No sorrow. Nothing. You're going to come and come and come until you are a shell of yourself and then maybe, just maybe, I will be able to put up with your company the rest of the evening. I'm certainly not going to spend any time with you until you learn that you're too old for temper tantrums. You understand me?"

"Yes, sir."

Søren stroked him harder, faster, and that coil in Kingsley's groin tightened, tightened like a clock that had been wound too much so that the spring was about to break. Oh, he was about to break. He rocked against Søren's hand, pressing his head against Søren's chest, watching the blankets shifting in the lantern light. Ah, it was bliss. It was heaven. It was ecstasy. His hips rose off the bedroll and he came with a pained whimper. Semen spurted out of him and onto his stomach in a hot wet rush.

"Good." Søren punctuated that word with a kiss on Kingsley's naked shoulder. Then he breathed onto the kiss and Søren's breath was warm, shockingly warm, and Kingsley melted into the floor. It was a miracle the ice didn't steam underneath him. "Now again."

Søren ran his bare hand over the wetness on Kingsley's stomach, then used it as lubricant when he started stroking Kingsley. Søren hadn't been kidding. He really did mean to make Kingsley come again and again and again until he was empty. It hurt at first, being rubbed right after the first orgasm, but soon enough he was rock hard again, pulsing his hips into Søren's hand, coming again with a shudder and a cry.

"One more, I think," Søren said with a kiss to Kingsley's forehead. "It usually takes three with you."

"Three?"

"Three climaxes before you're spent," he said.

"Does it?" Kingsley asked.

"It does. I know your body better than you do," Søren said.

"Because it belongs to you."

"Exactly." Søren smiled as he started massaging Kingsley's cock again for the third time. At first Kingsley was certain it wasn't going to happen. He was already spent. He'd come twice in under ten minutes. A third time so quickly? He was a young man, yes, but still mortal.

"I don't think I can," Kingsley said, wincing as Søren pulled gently on his wet cock.

"You can. I know you can. You can and you will. You don't have a choice."

"I don't?" Kingsley wanted only to sleep now and sleep for ages in Søren's arms. His eyelids were heavy and his body leaden. He was sweating hard from the exertion of two powerful orgasms.

"You don't," Søren said. "You're going to come again because you have to. It's what I want."

"Why?" Kingsley asked. "Why do you want me to come? It's me, not you. You don't get any pleasure out of it. Do you?"

Søren lowered his head and put his lips to Kingsley's ear. "I like the sound you make when you come."

"You do?"

"More than music. Which is why you'll make it for me again, won't you?"

"Yes," Kingsley said, nodding tiredly. "I will for you."

"Right." Søren's hand slipped from Kingsley's cock down to his testicles. He held them lightly and Kingsley shivered with pleasure.

"I don't have any choice."

"No, you don't." Søren stroked the tender skin behind Kingsley's testicles. When Kingsley was about to beg for it, Søren pushed a single wet finger inside him. Kingsley quivered in Søren's arms, in pleasure and in happiness.

"That's good," Kingsley said breathlessly. "I don't want to have a choice. I just want to do what you tell me to do."

"Obedience is its own reward, Kingsley."

Kingsley thought coming so hard half his brain shot out of his cock was a damn good reward, too, but he didn't say that out loud.

Søren pressed his fingertip into that place inside him that ached to be touched, and in that perfect way Søren knew how to touch him. Kingsley's body went tight and taut again. His heels chaffed the blankets as Søren stroked him internally. He was so hot, so aroused, he almost wanted to kick the blankets off. But the one rational cell of his brain that was still functioning warned him he'd regret doing that very quickly. His every breath steamed. The tiny fishing hut felt like a sauna. His body was open and aching. Søren must have felt that openness because he pushed another wet finger into him. Kingsley gasped and moaned, twitching at the tender touches. God, why couldn't he live like this all the time? Naked, a slave to Søren, a toy, a whore to be used at Søren's will as Kingsley served at Søren's pleasure.

Søren kneaded that aching organ inside him and

Kingsley could do nothing but take it. He was lost, insane, writhing in need. He threw his leg over Søren's without asking permission first. Søren didn't object, merely kept pushing and pushing his fingers into that spot—gently but constantly, keeping the pressure firm and right and perfect.

"You're going to come for me again, aren't you?" Søren asked. "From this, you'll come."

Kingsley licked his dry lips. He couldn't talk, only nod.

"Every drop, Kingsley," Søren said. There was a hard edge to his voice. "Don't hold back from me. I'll know, and we'll do this again with you naked on the bare ice."

Kingsley believed the threat. He had no doubt in his mind Søren would make him come while naked on the ice floor if he disobeyed. But he wouldn't. He couldn't. He had no choice but to obey.

The orgasm built slowly and steadily. It was different, coming from the inside of his body than the outside. Deeper. Softer. But more powerful, too, in a way, since only Søren could make him come like this. He writhed so hard against the wool beneath him he could feel his skin abrading. The pain stoked the pleasure. He would come any moment.

"Even if..." Kingsley began. "Even if you don't love me when I'm fifty, I'll still love you."

"Could you be more of a whore?" Søren asked. A rhetorical question, obviously, but Kingsley answered it anyway.

"Probably."

"Prove it."

Kingsley proved it. His back arched as a muscle spasm shot electric pleasure through every nerve in his body. He came with a cry that was more like a shout that went on and on as Søren fucked him—hard—with his fingers. He was impaled, split, and writhing. It wasn't an orgasm so much as a full-body convulsion. The whole valley must have heard his cry of pleasure. He hoped it did. He hoped someone heard. He needed to be heard. Kingsley needed the world to know who he belonged to. If he couldn't shout it from the rooftops, he'd shout it here.

It passed at last, and he lay utterly spent and empty and hollow on Søren's arm, his lover's bicep better than any pillow.

"Now will you behave?" Søren asked him, easing his fingers out of Kingsley's body.

"Define 'behave.' "

Søren only sighed. He tossed the blankets off them and stood up. Kingsley took the opportunity to dress as quickly as he could. He knew he only had a minute or two before he'd start to feel the cold again.

"I'll behave, I promise," Kingsley said. "I want to please you. Always. In every way."

"Don't wander off again and get lost in the woods, and I'll be a very happy man."

Kingsley grinned. "If that's all it takes to make you happy, then you should be a lot happier than you are, *mon ami*."

"I am happy," Søren said.

"You are?"

"Why wouldn't I be?"

Kingsley was happy. He'd just been tortured into orgasming three times. Happy might have been an understatement. They were alone together. The night was so clear and beautiful it could have been a picture off the front of a Christmas card. And they'd just shared a brutal, intimate hour together.

"You like me, don't you?" Kingsley asked.

Søren rolled his eyes. "Come along, Whore. Back to school with you before you wander off again and end up in Canada."

"I might like Canada," Kingsley said.

Søren zipped Kingsley's coat up for him and wrapped his scarf tight around his neck. "Canada might not like you," Søren said. "The people there tend to be decent and polite."

"So nothing like you then," Kingsley said, loosening his scarf so he could breathe. "Too bad. I guess I'll just stay here."

Søren grabbed Kingsley by the back of the hair and set him walking across the ice to the woods.

They walked in silence. It made Kingsley nervous. He'd rather talk, but Søren wouldn't let him. In the silence, he had only his thoughts for company...and they were not good thoughts. If Søren hadn't found him, he might have died out here in the woods tonight. A humbling possibility. And all because he'd let his jealousy get the best of him. It had been juvenile. It had been a temper tantrum. He should be ashamed of himself. And he was.

"Thank you," Kingsley said when they reached the border of the school's property. Søren had darkened the lantern so no one would spot them in the woods. Kingsley felt like a ghost standing there, like everyone was real and corporeal and alive but him and Søren. If only that were true.

"You're welcome," Søren said. He started to step out of the woods and onto the cobblestone path that led back to the dorms when Kingsley reached out and grabbed him by the hand.

"What?" Søren asked.

"I don't want to go back yet. Stay with me. Please?"

Søren looked at him through narrowed eyes. Then he

stepped back into the darkness of the forest, taking Kingsley with him. They made a circuit of the school until they stood in the dense thicket of cedars that backed up to the chapel. Kingsley heard music...singing...

"Choir practice," Søren said.

The school's choir was small—only ten boys—but they were well-trained and had won competitions for their angelic singing. They were singing an old song—"In the Bleak Midwinter." Standing there with his hand in Søren's hand listening to the choir, Kingsley heard the lyrics in a way he never had before. Mary in the stable with the newborn Christ...

> *Angels and archangels may have gathered*
> *   there*
> *Cherubim and seraphim thronged the air*
> *But his mother only in her maiden bliss*
> *Worshiped the beloved with a kiss*

Kingsley wished there were angels here to worship Søren. He deserved it, all of it, the seraphim and the archangels and all the heavenly host. But Kingsley couldn't give that to him. So he kissed him instead.

And lo, a Christmas miracle occurred, and the only miracle Kingsley wished for.

Søren returned the kiss.

The kiss was as heated as the night was cold. It was tender as the night was bitter. It was light as the night was dark. It ended only when the song did—and if Kingsley remembered correctly, the choir had sung it twice.

Søren stepped away from him at last. He turned his back to Kingsley, and started to walk to the school once more. Then he stopped and turned back around.

"I swear on all that is holy, if you ever get lost again..." Søren said, and shook his head.

"You'll kill me?" Kingsley asked.

Søren smiled. "Probably."

"Mr. Edge?"

Kingsley blinked himself awake.

The driver was looking at him through the rolled down partition.

"Yes?" Kingsley said, sitting up again. He'd fallen asleep on the long drive.

The driver pointed out the window.

"We're here."

THREE

TRILLIUM WOODS

FULLY AWAKE, Kingsley glanced out the window at his surroundings.

"Here?" he asked the driver. They were seemingly in the middle of nowhere. The car was parked on the shoulder of a narrow road. To the east, Kingsley saw dense forest; to the west, he saw dense forest. Behind him there was nothing but winding road, a road that wound into even denser forest north.

"There's a path," the driver said. He pointed at a wooden bridge, the sort people erected in their backyards to span a large drainage ditch or to put next to a wishing will. "You're supposed to walk down that path. I'll pick you up at ten in the morning on the twenty-second."

Kingsley opened the door and stepped out onto a snowy road and the second he did, a blast of cold air slapped him right in the face. Kingsley wrapped his coat around him and walked in four inches of snow to the wooden bridge as the driver pulled away.

Kingsley was all alone in the snow in the middle of nowhere and the sun was rapidly setting.

He took out his phone to let Juliette know he'd arrived safely to wherever the hell he was.

No signal.

None.

Sighing, he crossed the footbridge and found a snow-dusted path that lead deep into the woods. He couldn't go back, because there was nowhere to go back to. He had no choice but to walk on.

As he walked, he cursed himself for giving up his boots. While Hessians weren't ideal for snow, they were better than his current footwear.

Thankfully, the trees blocked the wind so that the woods were warmer than the open road. He'd walked about half a mile down the path when he saw light ahead.

It was a strange sort of light. Not sunlight. Not electric light. He walked toward it and found a tall iron lamp casting the light. And not an ordinary streetlight sort of lamp, but a gas lamp. He almost imagined if he turned around he'd see a fawn traipsing through the woods, an umbrella in one hand and brown-paper parcels in the other.

He turned and saw no such creature, but he did see the outline of a house. Not quite a house. That was far too grand a term. A cabin. A small log cabin standing in a clearing. He found it quaint and lovely as he walked toward it. If he had to freeze to death somewhere, it might as well be here.

He knocked on the front door, but no one answered. He lifted the latch and found it unlocked.

"Søren?" he called out, slipping inside. No answer.

Kingsley ran his hand along the wall, seeking out a light switch. Nothing. It was very possible that this cabin had no electricity. He sighed as he walked down the hall and into the living room where a low fire burned in the grate.

Of course Søren would enjoy staying in a cabin in the woods with no electricity. He'd say it was *hygge*. It probably reminded him of his grandfather's fishing village or somewhere equally benighted in rural Denmark.

Well, fuck Denmark.

Kingsley was from Paris, the City of Light. Light required electricity. And so did Kingsley's phone, which was dying.

He went out to the cabin's front porch and held his phone up, searching for a signal. He wanted to text Juliette a quick message: *Get me the hell out of here.*

No signal. And, judging by the lack of telephone poles out here, no landline in the cabin either.

He shoved his phone into his coat pocket with a sigh. Hopeless. It was hopeless. He was trapped, stranded, cut off from the world. And this wasn't good, because Kingsley liked the world. His small corner of it, anyway. He wanted to hear his daughter's voice. He wanted to tell Juliette he'd arrived safely in Maine. He wanted...

From a gap in the trees ahead, Søren emerged, a kerosene lantern and small ax in one hand. He was pulling a sled behind him, atop of which sat a freshly-chopped spruce tree.

Søren had on dark jeans, winter boots and a navy blue peacoat with the collar turned up against the cold. Under the coat, Søren wore an off-white cable knit sweater with a dark scarf wrapped around his neck. His hair was slicked back with melted snow. One stubborn strand fell over his eyes.

Kingsley could not breathe. He tried but his lungs had stopped working momentarily. He would like to have blamed the cold for that, but it was the heat that was the real problem. The old lust rushed through his veins like a runaway train. And the love, too. Always the love.

"Like it?" Søren asked as he came to the porch.

Kingsley could hardly speak at first. He'd had dreams like this before. Good dreams, obviously. Wet dreams, specifically.

Finally, Kingsley managed a couple of words.

"Love it."

"I knew you would," Søren said. He gave Kingsley a quick kiss on the mouth, and glanced around the woods. "It's *hygge,* isn't it? Reminds me of the village my grandfather grew up in."

"I've always wanted to go to rural Denmark," Kingsley said.

"Come in. Let's put the tree up."

Søren hefted the tree off the sled, shook the snow off the branches and carried it past Kingsley into the cabin.

Kingsley promptly forgot his phone ever existed.

Inside the cabin, Søren knelt by the fireplace, building the fire up again.

"Where are we?" Kingsley asked. The logs in the fire sizzled and snapped and the scent of the burning cedar filled the room like incense. By the light of the fire he saw simple wood-carved furniture and homespun rugs and blankets. Rustic, yes, but comfortable, too. *Hygge*.

"Trillium Woods," Søren said. "A thousand acres, privately-owned."

"And...what are we doing here?"

"One of Eleanor's clients lent her the cabin. Lent *us* the cabin. I thought we could use a few days away together before Christmas."

"So you had me kidnapped?"

"I did nothing of the sort," Søren said. "I had you shipped to me."

"You make me sound like luggage."

"Call it a special delivery."

Kingsley chuckled as Søren stood and shucked off his coat, tossing it over the back of a chair. Kingsley looked Søren up and down.

"What is it?" Søren asked.

"You look like the cover model for *Rugged Danish Male Monthly*."

"Is that a real publication?" Søren asked, slicking back that stubborn lock of blond hair—blond *and* silver—so that he was once again the picture of perfection.

"No, but it should be. I'd subscribe."

"You already do." Søren gripped him by the lapels of his coat, yanked him close, and kissed him again, a much harder kiss this time than his earlier greeting. Søren had three levels of kiss, Kingsley had decided.

One: A greeting kiss.

Two: A heating kiss.

Three: A beating kiss.

This was the second type of kiss and it was doing its job. All the lingering coldness Kingsley felt quickly dissipated in the heat of the kiss. Their tongues gently met and Kingsley tasted brandy. Well, that was another good way to stay warm. He preferred the kiss, however. They could drink anytime. They only had two nights for kissing.

As always, it was Søren who pulled back from the kiss first. That was for the best, otherwise their kisses would go on forever.

"You should change," Søren said.

"Into what? I never pack for trips to the city since I keep a second wardrobe at my apartment." He'd gotten rid of the townhouse two years ago, but he'd replaced it with a small if luxurious uptown apartment he could use during his brief visits.

"All taken care of," Søren said. "Bedroom's in there. Suitcase on the bed." He pointed at a closed door. "I'll put up the tree while you change clothes."

"Easier said than done," Kingsley said. "As you have dragged me into the middle of nowhere to a cabin that was built before America was a country—in other words, the good old days—there is no electricity. I refuse to dress in the dark. I only undress in the dark."

Søren sighed.

"I'm simply saying there are cabins that have electricity," Kingsley said. "Even in Maine, I imagine."

"Where's your sense of adventure?"

"It's somewhere far away basking in the cold glow of unflattering florescent lighting."

Søren walked over to the fireplace and picked up a box of long matches. He lit the wick of his kerosene lamp and carried it through the door into the bedroom and set it on the windowsill. By the light of the lantern, Søren lit the two additional lamps on either side of the king-sized bed. Then he lit every candle in the bank of candles on the stone mantel over the wood stove, touching the wicks so swiftly and deftly it seemed the flames came from his fingertips and not the match. The room glowed a flickering yellow and gold. Kingsley saw the headboard of the bed was an elaborately carved forest scene. And the comforter was an old faded crazy quilt and the sheets underneath white and inviting. The room was small enough to be warmed by the wood stove, large enough to swing a flogger. Although rugged, it was also exceedingly lovely.

Kingsley sighed.

"Just when I think I'm out," Kingsley said, "you reel me back in."

Søren mimed reeling in a fish.

"Oh, don't pretend you're a real man," Kingsley said, glaring at him. "I would bet money you've never fished in your life."

"Does putting metal hooks into the mouth of defense-less animals make one a real man?" Søren asked.

"Yes," Kingsley said as he unlocked the suitcase on the bed and found it neatly packed with a new winter wardrobe. Juliette's doing, no doubt.

"I'm a fisher of men, if that counts for anything."

"Ever catch one?"

"I once spent an evening in a fishing shack and caught a very good-sized French whore."

Kingsley smiled. "You know...I was thinking about that very night on the way here," he said. "Getting lost. You finding me. Breaking into the hut. Kissing in the woods. You remember that night?"

"No."

"You mentioned it five seconds ago."

Søren's eyes glinted.

"You're lying, aren't you?" Kingsley asked.

"Probably."

As Søren brushed past him on his way out the door, he yanked hard on Kingsley's hair.

Kingsley instantly melted at the sudden burst of pain.

"Is it time for bed yet?" Kingsley called out after Søren passed into the other room. Kingsley started stripping out of his clothes.

"It's not even seven o'clock."

"Feels later. Probably because you dragged me into the fucking Arctic Circle for some unknown reason."

"I want to brutally beat you and mercilessly fuck you in peace and quiet," Søren said. "How's that for a reason?"

Kingsley froze, his hands on his belt.

He may or may not have whimpered. If he had whimpered, he wouldn't admit to it. Grown men did not whimper.

"That's a good reason," Kingsley said.

"I thought as much," Søren called back.

Kingsley changed into thick dark trousers, wool socks, a heavy cotton t-shirt, and a wool turtleneck sweater. He stuffed his feet into winter boots that laced halfway up his calves.

"Well?" Kingsley asked, displaying himself in the open doorway between the bedroom and the living room. "Do I look like a cover model from *Rugged French Male Monthly*?"

Søren glanced up at him. "You look presentable."

"Are we going somewhere you have to present me?"

"You never know who you'll meet in the woods," Søren said.

"Lions? Tigers?" Kingsley paused, gave Søren a knowing look. "Bears...?"

Søren glared at him from behind the Christmas tree.

"No," Kingsley said. "Not bears. Neither of us has nearly enough body hair for that."

"What are the other options again?" Søren asked.

"Cubs. Otters. Dolphins. Blouses."

"What on earth is a blouse?"

"A feminine top," Kingsley said, tossing one end of his scarf dramatically over his shoulder. He'd learned that one from Griffin.

Søren only glared at him as he steadied the Christmas

tree in the stand. It was almost as tall as he was, but not quite. Søren still had a good four inches on the spruce.

"Very nice. A little naked," Kingsley said. "No decorations?"

"I have lights."

"You have lights? You recall we have no electricity in this cabin. And if you tell me we're going to be old-fashioned and adventurous and put actual candles on the tree, I will see you in New Orleans in a week. If you don't accidentally self-immolate before then."

"Have you never heard of batteries?" Søren asked.

"I have. Juliette and I go through a package of D batteries once a week."

"Box," Søren nodded toward a wooden box on the floor. "Lights."

Kingsley opened the box and found two strings of clear white lights in the box. He pulled them out and unwound them, feeding them foot by foot to Søren as he wrapped them around the tree. It was quite nice—the fireplace bright and warm, the scent of the spruce tree mingling with the burning wood, the quiet pleasure of putting lights on a Christmas tree with the only man Kingsley had ever loved.

Without any fanfare or counting down, Søren switched on the tree lights.

And just like that it was Christmas.

No gifts. No music. No crèche. Only lights. That's all it took. The push of a button. It shouldn't have been that simple, but it was. A little more light where before there was darkness. A little more beauty where before there was emptiness. All the bad things that were there before were still there, but at least there was one more small good thing in the world.

"I forgive you," Kingsley said.

"For what?"

"For dragging me to a cabin with no electricity."

"Our hermitage didn't have electricity," Søren reminded him.

"When you're seventeen, that's romantic. When you're fifty, it's annoying."

"Are you annoyed?" Søren asked, obviously attempting to suppress a smile.

"Not anymore," Kingsley said. "Ignore my moods. It's been a rough few weeks." Kingsley sat down in an armchair covered with a wool striped blanket. "I'm not supposed to be fifty years old. I should never have lived this long."

"You know, I'll be fifty-one as of midnight tonight."

Kingsley stretched out his legs and crossed them at the ankles. "You're a priest. Priests are born in their fifties. You were fifty-one when you were seventeen," he said. "I have a two-year-old daughter. A man with a toddler should be thirty, not fifty."

"I'm recalling your thirtieth birthday party," Søren said. He sat down on the ottoman directly across from him, and lifted Kingsley's feet off the floor and put them on his lap. "And I'm using the word 'party' loosely. Orgy would be a more accurate term. And not a pleasant sort of Bacchanal either. People ended up in the hospital. Many of them."

"It wasn't that bad."

Søren stared at him, not speaking.

"Fine, it was that bad," Kingsley said. He hadn't ended up in the hospital, although he probably should have gone. He'd drunk so much that night and smoked so much pot that he'd vomited until blood came up along with everything else he'd ingested. Søren hadn't spoken to him for two weeks after. Kingsley had broken his promise to take better care of himself.

"Would you really go back to being thirty again if you could?" Søren asked.

"I thought about that," Kingsley said. This was a hard conversation, but resting his legs on Søren's thighs was making it a little easier. "And the only reason I would is for Nico. Except I wouldn't, since I know how much he loved his other father. As much as it kills me, I couldn't in good conscience take those years he had with his father away from him."

"Spoken like a true father. You pass Solomon's test." Søren pinched his thigh. "I thought you'd be happy to be here with me."

"I am. That's the problem. I'm suffering from a parental guilt complex. I'm thousands of miles from both my children. I shouldn't be this happy."

"You're allowed to enjoy your time without them."

"I know I'm allowed. Juliette even encourages it. I thought having children would be it, though—that I would need nothing, that I would want for nothing ever again," Kingsley said. "I hate that I still need things they can't give me."

"It's the parent's job to give children everything *they* need. It's not the child's job to give the parents everything they need."

"I need you," Kingsley said.

"And me you have. So stop complaining."

"I think it's my liver," Kingsley said, poking on the side of his stomach.

"That's not your liver. That's your appendix."

"No wonder I'm having liver trouble then. It's in the wrong place."

Søren rolled his eyes to the heavens. "God save me from the French and their obsession with their livers," he said.

Then, to Kingsley: "Come on. You need to walk in the woods. It'll be good for your liver."

"Or you could beat me and fuck me."

"How will that improve your liver?"

"It won't. But it might improve my mood."

Søren dumped Kingsley's legs off his lap and onto the floor, and quickly found himself being hauled out of the chair and onto his feet.

"Out. Now." Søren pointed at the door.

"Going. Going." Kingsley returned to the bedroom and pulled his new black winter coat and gloves out of the suitcase. He found Søren already standing by the door wrapping his scarf around his neck. "Ready. You?"

Without warning, Søren shoved him against the hallway wall and kissed him. A rough kiss, the sort that leaves the lips slightly swollen and the recipient panting. Oh, and there it was, the teeth. Kingsley loved the teeth, that vicious nip Søren always gave his bottom lip when in the right mood.

Søren ended the kiss but didn't pull away. He put his mouth at Kingsley's ear. "I need you, too."

"Now?" Kingsley asked.

Søren kissed him on his neck at the point his jawline met his throat. "Always."

Then Søren pulled back while Kingsley struggled to catch his breath.

"Liver feeling better?" Søren asked.

"It's very hard and throbbing a little."

"I'd see a doctor about that if I were you."

"I'd rather see a priest about it."

"You are seeing a priest about it." Søren gripped him by the hair and dragged him out the front door and onto the porch. "And he prescribes a long walk in the forest."

"But baby, it's cold outside," Kingsley said.

Søren glared at him, a glare like the fire of a thousand suns.

"It's a song," Kingsley said hastily. "I wasn't calling you 'Baby.' I would never do that."

"No, you wouldn't."

"I'm going to walk now."

"Yes, you are."

Kingsley walked, Søren at his side but just ahead by a nose, leading, as always. Søren carried the kerosene lantern in his hand, the wick turned down low. It gave enough to keep their feet from tripping over roots but not enough to dispel the bleak winter's gloom. The trees loomed over them, branches thick enough to block the sky from view. What light did penetrate the tree cover cast eerie shadows all around them. Kingsley had been joking about the lions and tigers and bears, but the possibility of seeing a wolf or some other dangerous animal existed.

"Aren't there wolves in Maine?" Kingsley sighed. "I should have brought my gun."

"I think we'll survive without it," Søren said. "Although...remind me, which of us can outrun the other?"

"That isn't funny."

"I thought it was very funny."

"You would," Kingsley said. "You can outrun me."

"Don't worry. I doubt we'll see any wolves. There aren't many—or any—of them in the state as far as I know. Now coyotes on the other hand..."

"This is your sadism at work, isn't it?" Kingsley demanded. "You bring me to the middle of nowhere and force me to stay in a cabin without electricity and you drag me into the woods and expose me to wolves and coyotes for your entertainment and amusement."

"You told me you used to hunt KBG agents in forests denser and far more dangerous than this one."

"First, I was in my twenties when I did that. Second, I was nearly killed doing it. Third, I had a sniper rifle on me the entire time."

Søren shook his head in mock disgust. "You really have lost your sense of adventure."

"I have," Kingsley said, not joking this time. "I'm not happy about it either."

"Tell me what's wrong," Søren said.

Kingsley stopped and leaned back against the trunk of a tall cedar tree. He dug his hands deep into his coat pockets and shrugged. "I don't know. Nothing I can put my finger on. Earlier today Griffin implied that I've changed since we had Céleste."

"You have changed. For the better, I might add."

"J'espère," Kingsley said. *I hope.* "Since Céleste—and Nico, too, though not as much since he's already grown—I feel obligated to behave myself. I don't want Céleste growing up without a father. I don't want her growing up ashamed of her father. I think...perhaps, ah, I'm just feeling my age. If I'm going to get my prostate fondled, I want it to be in bed, not in the doctor's office."

"Seduce your doctor," Søren said.

"There's an idea."

"Tell me," Søren said, serious once more. "What do you think would help you feel better?"

"I wish for one night I could feel seventeen again. Too much to ask?"

"Maybe," Søren said. "Maybe not."

"I was wild when I was seventeen. Wild like an animal is wild, you know. Not crazy. Just...free. Having a child tames you. It *should* tame you. I know that. But there's a

part of me that chaffs at the bit, as they say. I've been domesticated."

"You have two lovers, one of which is a Catholic priest
who had you forcibly relocated to a cabin in a forest in
Maine. You have a huge fortune, most of it earned in border-
line illegal ways. You're bisexual, extremely kinky, and
you've slept with about a thousand people in your life.
There are people in this world who still dream of killing you
and people in this world still terrified you might show up
any moment and kill them. And you run a private sex club
in New Orleans. You and the dictionary clearly have very
different definitions of 'domesticated.'"

Kingsley laughed softly as he peeled himself off the tree.
"You may have a point."

They walked on deeper into the dark wood. Two hours
passed, which meant it would take them another two hours
to get back to the cabin.

"I hope you know where you're going," Kingsley said.

"I've been marking a trail. Also..." He pulled something
from his pocket and showed it to Kingsley.

"Compass," Kingsley said. "Good thinking."

"Christmas gift from Eleanor. She thought I might need
it out here."

"She helped you plan this little escapade?"

"She did."

"Her idea, I assume?"

"My idea. But I did needed her assistance, which she
was happy to give."

"Why?"

"Why what?" Søren asked.

"Why was she happy to help you spend your birthday
alone with me?"

"I told her how much I needed some time alone with you. She understands this."

"Why me and not her?"

"Because when I want you, only you will do."

"And she wasn't jealous that I get you alone on your birthday?"

"Eleanor's never been the jealous type."

"And here I am, jealous that she isn't jealous."

"The only difference between my love for her and my love for you is that she's secure in it, and you aren't."

"Can you blame me?" Kingsley asked, pausing to face him. "Can you?"

Søren met his eyes and Kingsley admired him for that. It took courage to look someone in the face after being asked a question that brutal.

"No," Søren said. "I can't blame you."

Kingsley nodded, and then turned and started walking again.

"In fact," Søren said, "that's part of the reason I wanted to be alone with you for a few days. There's something I want to tell you. Something I've held onto for too long. A... confession of sorts."

"What is it?" Kingsley asked. He would have stopped, but Søren clearly wanted to keep walking.

"You remember when I went to Syria for those few months, what was it, six years ago?"

"Of course I remember. I've never checked the news so often in my life. I was terrified every day you wouldn't come back."

"You were right to be terrified."

"You must have been terrified, too," Kingsley said. "When you came back, you were like a different man. No, not different really. You were like you used to be, like you were in high school sometimes. You know, before..."

"I know."

"You were closed off. Usually you're a locked door, but Elle and I, we could usually find a way to pick that lock. After you came back, though, you were an impregnable fortress. And you were cruel like you were in high school. Cruel for the sake of cruelty. What happened over there?"

"Nothing," Søren said.

"Nothing?"

"Nothing. Nothing bad anyway. The work was hard but meaningful. I enjoyed the company of the other priests, of the Syrian children and teenagers we worked with. But I wasn't threatened, wasn't injured. No one tried to hurt me or harm me. I didn't see anyone killed before my eyes. It wasn't what happened over there that changed me. It was something that happened when I came back."

They had walked to a break in the tree line. Before them stood a snowy hill and atop the hill a solitary tree. And there was the moon and there were the stars. They looked so bright and so close it was if they'd bent low, as eager to hear Søren's confession as Kingsley.

"Something did happen in Syria. I made a decision," Søren said. "I wanted to be with Eleanor again."

"I knew that."

"And you."

Kingsley's eyes flashed open wide. "And me?"

Søren nodded. He put his foot up on a flat rock and turned his gaze to the sky, giving Kingsley his profile.

"I missed you," Søren said. "And I...I *ached* for you. And not your friendship. I had that. I ached for you physically. I wanted you in bed again, on your knees again. I wanted to be inside you again. I wanted to own you again. I realized the reason I was so angry at Eleanor when I found out you'd taught her to top was jealousy, plain and simple. If you were going to be beaten, it should have been me doing the beating, not her. And I planned to tell you all that as soon as I came back."

Kingsley covered his mouth with one hand. He had never...no, never dreamed of such a thing. He couldn't speak. He could only wait for Søren to go on.

"I flew back and Claire, she met me at the airport. We went back to her house where she'd been keeping the Ducati for me in storage. I changed clothes and kissed her goodbye and rode straight to the townhouse, looking for you. But you weren't home."

"Where was I?"

Kingsley realized as soon as he said it how stupid that question was. It didn't matter where he was. He should have been there.

"Out with Juliette. Someone told me you were at the theater and would be out late. So I went to see Eleanor. I would tell her how wrong I'd been, trying to stop her from being who she needed to be. I would tell her that I wanted her—and you—back, without conditions of any sort. I wouldn't make her quit working for you. I wouldn't ask you to give up anything for me, especially not Juliette since I knew you two were planning to have children together when she was ready. If I could only have you one night a month I would take it. I would take one night a year. I felt mad that night, like I would lose my mind if I couldn't see you both, tell you both. I couldn't wait for it to all be settled. That's why I didn't wait for you to come back from the theater. I couldn't have sat still if someone had chained me to the floor. I'd never needed you both more than I needed you that night. It happens to me sometimes. Something comes on me that's more animal than human. I wish there was a word for it. The only word that comes close is 'bloodlust.' I'd felt it that night in the woods, the first time with you."

"When you chased me and ran me down."

"I wasn't chasing you, Kingsley. I was hunting you."

Kingsley shivered at the darkness in Søren's tone.

"Ah," Kingsley said. "There are wolves in Maine after all."

Søren almost smiled. Kingsley could see the hint of it in his eyes.

"What happened?" Kingsley asked. "You went to see her."

"If you asked me who I trust in the world more than anyone, I would have said you. All those letters you sent me in Syria. But not one of them mentioned that Nora had fallen in love with a college freshman named Wesley."

And at once, Kingsley understood.

"He was there," Kingsley said. "Wesley was there when you went to see her."

"She was helping him move his things into her house. And I don't know if I had ever seen her looking so happy in her life. She looked like a woman in love. Because she *was* a woman in love. All those letters you'd sent me, and you hadn't told me about him. I stood there in the shadow of the tree in her front yard, hiding like a common thief, watching the woman I loved being carried across the threshold of her home, giddy as a virgin bride on her wedding night. My heartache in that moment was as great as my anger was volcanic. In an instant, I turned on you both. Her for replacing me with a younger model. You for not warning me what I was coming home to."

Søren finally met Kingsley's eyes. "And that is my confession."

Kingsley swallowed. He didn't speak. Couldn't.

"I should have told you sooner, I realize that," Søren said.

Kingsley turned his back on Søren, and strode away from him into the clearing. "Do you have any idea what you've just told me?" Kingsley demanded.

"Tell me," Søren said.

"You just told me that six years ago I won a billion dollars in the lottery and you cashed in the ticket and kept the money for yourself."

"You flatter me."

"You have no right to decide what your love is worth to me. None. That is for me to say and only me."

"You're right, of course. I apologize."

"Stop." Kingsley raised his hand. "The more furious I am with you, the more rational you pretend you are. I'd rather you punched me in the gut."

"It seems I already have."

"She fucks up, and I pay the price. Again."

"She didn't, as you say, fuck up. She fell in love. But you knew about him and didn't tell me. Are you going to deny you knew about him and deliberately concealed that from me?"

"I won't deny it. It wasn't my secret to tell. It was hers."

"Of all the times to take the high road."

"You think I'm lying?"

"I'm certain you had ulterior motives."

"Such as?"

"Such as hurting me?" Søren said. "Do you deny that part of you wanted to hurt me and you knew this would do it?"

"Are you asking me to forgive you or demanding I apologize?"

"I don't blame you for wanting to hurt me. I only told you because, were the situation reversed, I would—"

"But the situation isn't reversed, is it? It never is. You always hold every card. Every last fucking card while the rest of us stand around with nothing in our hands but our hearts."

"You accused me a thousand times of picking her over you," Søren said. "You chose her over me that time. And now I know how much it hurts. I am sorry, Kingsley."

"So am I," he said. "As always."

Kingsley turned and strode into the woods.

"Where are you going?" Søren called out after him.

"Anywhere you aren't."

FOUR

THE HAWK AND THE HARE

KINGSLEY WALKED AWAY, shocked by the enormity of his own anger. He shook with it, breathed steam like a dragon, almost wanted a wolf to attack him so he could kill it with his bare hands.

He headed west, in the direction of the cabin, his fury guiding his feet. He didn't know for certain what he'd do when he got there. Probably get his phone and find the path to the road and take it on foot until someone picked him up and drove him to the nearest town. Of course Søren would bring him to the middle of nowhere to tell him this secret. Had they been home in New Orleans, Kingsley could have simply gotten into his car and driven away.

If he couldn't drive, he would walk. If he couldn't walk, he'd crawl. Whatever it took to get away. He'd walk until he couldn't walk anymore. He'd walk to Portland if he had to. Fuck it, he'd walk all the way to New York.

He'd walk...

"Ah, *merde.*" Kingsley stopped walking.

He was lost.

"Fuck. Fuck. Fuck."

He was lost.

Again.

He wasn't scared. Not like he'd been that night long ago. He knew how to survive a night in the woods now. He had warm enough clothes on him to live out here if he had to. All he had to do was find a clearing and see where the moon was in the night sky, and he could get his bearings enough to find west. He could have used the compass on his phone, except he'd left it in his other coat pocket. Didn't need it since he was with Søren, and it was almost dead.

Except he would have liked to have it now.

And his gun—he could always use his gun.

Kingsley looked up through a break in the trees at the sky and did something he wouldn't have thought himself capable of doing ten minutes earlier.

He laughed.

Ah, well, this is what he got for wishing to feel seventeen again.

"God, you have a sick sense of humor," Kingsley said.

Then he heard a twig snap.

"Case in point," Kingsley said to God. Then he turned around. "You again?"

"Did you think I would let you wander off into the forest?" Søren asked, stepping out of the woods.

"That was the idea."

"Should I leave?" Søren asked. "You can take my compass. I know the way back without it. I'll even lend you the lantern."

To prove he meant it, Søren set the lantern on the snow between them and placed the compass on top.

"That way," Søren said, pointing. "Road. Take it northwest and you'll make it to a small town call St. Mary's in three miles. Take it southeast, and you'll be back at the cabin in thirty minutes."

Then he turned around and started to walk away.

"Stop," Kingsley said.

Søren stopped, but didn't turn.

"This isn't Simon Says," Kingsley said. "You can turn around without me telling you."

"I've never taken orders from you before," Søren said, turning to face him. "It was a novel experience."

"Go fuck yourself," Kingsley said. "How's that for an order?"

"A logistical nightmare, fucking oneself. But I've always relished a challenge."

"You wanted me back."

"Yes."

"You wanted me back six years ago."

"Yes."

"You wanted me back six years ago and you didn't tell me because I didn't tell you about Wesley moving in with Nora."

"That sums it up nicely."

"You're an asshole."

"I've never denied that," Søren said.

"You know, I might not have taken you back," Kingsley said. "You skipped off to Syria to play Father Flanagan and my life went on just fine without you. I had Juliette. I had Nora. I had the clubs. Did you really expect me to jump back in bed with you the second you returned?"

"Yes."

Kingsley laughed. He didn't want to laugh, but he had to. But only because it was true. "You're right," he said. "I would have. But I would have hated myself after."

Søren said nothing.

Kingsley sighed, exhaling steam along with his anger. "Are you as heartless as you seem to be sometimes?" he asked.

"If I were heartless, I wouldn't have been as devastated as I was to see Wesley moving in with Eleanor. I wouldn't have been furious to think you two had purposefully kept such a secret from me. Especially since I asked you... No. I *begged* you to let me know how she was while I was gone. We stood together at the bottom of the stairs at your house and you promised me you would."

"I did," Kingsley said.

"But you didn't keep your promise."

"No," Kingsley said. "And I was wrong to break it. But you made certain to punish me, didn't you?"

"Yes," Søren said. "Though I punished myself as well. I could have had you back, but through my own fault I lost you again. From where I stand, my loss was far greater than yours. You lost me. I lost you. And you're worth much more than a billion dollars to me."

Kingsley swallowed hard. He didn't realize until Søren had said all that how much he'd needed to hear it.

He inhaled deeply and caught a scent in his nose. The scent of winter.

"I love that smell," Kingsley said.

Søren closed his eyes and inhaled.

"Snow," Søren said. "Clean snow. Someone's fireplace in the distance, probably ours. Pine needles. Moonlight. Starlight."

"You," Kingsley said. "Smells just like you. Even when we're making love and the room is hot as a sauna and I can't tell your sweat from mine...your skin smells just like this."

Kingsley inhaled again. "I love the scent of winter," he

said. "I love the scent of winter enough to suffer the cold for it."

Søren exhaled heavily and steam rose like smoke from his lips and up, up into the sky. "Kingsley..."

Kingsley waited for him to continue, but it seemed to be all Søren could say.

"It's not normal for a man to smell like snow," Kingsley went on. Might as well, if they were being honest tonight. "I think sometimes you're not quite human. Like you said, the night in the forest, our first time together, you weren't chasing me like children chase each other, or lovers who play at running from each other only to run back. You were hunting me. Hunting me like a wolf. I never hated my dogs when they nipped at me. You keep Rottweilers as pets and you'll get teeth marks in you from time to time. It's simply in their nature and I loved them for that little bit of wild wolf in their blood. And you. Whatever you are. Why would I think I could fall in love with a wolf and never get bitten?"

Kingsley paused, smiled. "That being said," he continued, "I do love it when you bite me."

"Even when I break the skin?"

"Especially then," Kingsley said. "Answer this question, though. When you returned from Syria, you came to see me first, you said. Not her. Why? Was it because I was closer?"

"I didn't fly into New York. I flew into Bradley. Claire has a house in Old Saybrook and I was planning on staying there with her a few days. Bradley, as you know, is in Connecticut. I was closer to Eleanor's house than yours by an hour's drive."

"Then why did you come to me first?"

"Because she knew I loved her. You didn't. And I felt I would die if I couldn't tell you as soon as possible."

"Have you told her any of this?"

"No."

"Will you?"

"Eventually."

"She'll forgive you in a heartbeat," Kingsley said. "For-give you without question, won't she?"

"I have no doubt that's true," Søren said.

"She's self-aware. A gift. She knows the pain she's caused others. She's quick to forgive because she wants to be forgiven."

"Something about that in the Bible," Søren said. "If I had my collar on, I'd tell you the exact verse, but I'm off-duty tonight."

Kingsley smiled. "But when you tell her...will you tell her you came to me first?"

"I will if you ask me to. If you need her to know that, I will tell her."

"It will hurt her."

"Yes, it undoubtedly will," Søren said. "And I've already hurt her deeply this year. But that's what we do, the three of us. Hurt each other."

"Don't tell her. Let her think you came to her first. I know you love me. I don't need you to hurt her to prove that to me. I love her, too."

"Can you forgive me?" Søren asked. "You don't have to tonight. But it would mean a great deal to me if you'd consider forgiving me eventually."

"I forgive you. Of course I do." Kingsley paused to inhale another deep beautiful breath of pure winter air. "I thought of telling you so you would know what you were coming home to. But I was afraid that if you knew about him, that he was moving in with her, you might not come back to us at all. You thought I didn't tell you out of vengeance. The fact is, I didn't tell you out of cowardice."

"She had every right to love him and live with Wesley. You had every right not to tell me about him. And while I had every right to be hurt, I didn't have the right to take my pain out on you and her like I did."

"Would you have come back if you'd known about him?"

"Yes. For you."

"Ah, now you tell me."

Søren grinned. "Let me make it up to you," he said. "Name it."

"All I want is for you to take me back to the cabin and beat me and fuck me within an inch of my life."

"The French use the metric system," Søren said.

"A millimeter then," Kingsley said.

"That can be arranged," Søren said softly, and then kissed him within a millimeter of his life. "This way."

Kingsley followed him southwest through the woods until they reached a narrow country road. On one side stood forest. On the other, a snow-covered field edged with white-tipped shrubs and outlined by a barbwire fence.

They made quick progress on the road. They could go much faster when they didn't have to watch every step.

"Can I ask a follow-up question?" Kingsley said. Søren nodded. "Why tell me now? Did you just forget to tell me you were in love with me six years ago? Were you having a blond moment?"

Søren smiled but didn't laugh. "Too many secrets, I suppose," he said. "They're weighing heavily on me. And Eleanor, too. We had to clear the air recently of a few secrets we'd been keeping from each other. It was harrowing to say the least, but we both felt better once we'd done it."

"You said you'd hurt her already this year? What happened?"

"I kept one secret too many from her. She found something in my Bible I'd never shown her, nor had I planned to show her. Habit, I suppose. All three of us have to keep secrets in our work. I don't know anything about any of Eleanor's clients anymore. Or your work at your new club."

"That's for your own good. Plausible deniability."

"Unfortunately we three have gotten so good at keeping secrets, we keep them from each other even when we don't have to. Even when we shouldn't." Søren stopped and faced the woods. "We have as many secrets from each other as there are trees in that forest. No wonder we all keep getting lost."

"Who's getting lost, Søren?" Kingsley asked. He knew that look on Søren's face. He wore it when his mind and his heart were elsewhere, across the ocean, where his son lived. Kingsley knew that look because he'd worn it himself every day since learning about Nico.

"Fionn," Søren said at last.

"Fionn? I don't think he has any secrets."

"He *is* the secret. That's the trouble."

"You're a priest. He has to be a secret."

"Does he?"

"I don't know," Kingsley said. "You tell me. What are you thinking of?"

"I'm considering telling my superiors about Fionn," Søren said.

Kingsley's eyes went wide with shock. This was unexpected news.

"Won't there be consequences?" Kingsley asked. What he wanted to ask was, *Are you out of your fucking mind?*

"Undoubtedly. Jesuits aren't supposed to go around fathering children. Then again, they aren't supposed to do a lot of things I do. Best case scenario, I'll be asked to take a long leave of absence. Worst case—excommunication. But that's highly unlikely. Whatever happens, it won't be pleasant."

"Why do you think they need to know?" Kingsley asked.

"Not them. Fionn."

"Fionn needs to know?"

"Last week, I was at your house," Søren said. "And Céleste needed help tying her shoes. She came to you and stuck her feet in your face."

"She does that. Often."

"I watched you tie her shoes and it was such a simple thing. The child who needed help running to her father. Her father helping her without giving it a second thought. It's how it should be, isn't it? Since then, I can't stop thinking, *What if Fionn needs my help someday?* When he's ten or eleven or fifteen or sixteen... What if he wants to talk to me but is afraid to because he believes he's my dirty little secret? I need him to know he can come to me. I need him to know he's not something that has to stay hidden.

"You and Eleanor chose to be with me knowing I was a priest. Eleanor knew we could never marry and have children. You knew that I'd have to introduce you as my brother-in-law if you wanted to be part of my life. But Fionn had no choice in this. And someday he may need help, the sort of help only I can give him."

Kingsley sighed. For a long moment, the only sound was their boots crunching across the snow.

"You know," Kingsley said. "Nico and I are exactly the same height. Same belt size. Same shoe size. Same size hands. Nora even says we—"

"I hope this isn't going where I think it is."

Kingsley laughed. "She says we *stand* the same way," he

said. "What I'm saying is he takes after me. It must scare you to think Fionn might take after you in ways you'd prefer he didn't."

"I pray about it every day," Søren said. "I pray for him."

"Does God ever answer?"

"Not in words. Only in joy. There were four times in my life I felt utterly certain God was real and He was pointing His finger into my life, telling me what path to take. The day I met you. The day I joined the Jesuits. The day I met Eleanor. The night I fathered Fionn. All four of those moments fill me with the deepest peace and the most incredible joy when I think of them. Fionn especially, since I know what joy he's given Grace and Zachary."

"And the joy he's given me and Nora," Kingsley said.

"And me," Søren said.

Kingsley smiled, and felt a glowing warmth inside him. "It's good to hear you talk about him. You don't very often."

"We've been in a magnificent snowy forest for over three hours and you haven't once said it's beautiful."

Kingsley shrugged. "What can I say? What words would do it justice?"

Søren nodded. "My point exactly."

"There's really a chance you'll be kicked out of the order when you tell them about Fionn?" Kingsley asked.

"Grace is married. It was adultery."

"She had her husband's permission to be with someone else."

"Even the most liberal people have trouble under-standing the concept of the marital free pass. You're asking a lot of the Jesuits."

"She was a woman desperate to have a baby. I know how she felt. It was nothing more than sperm donation."

"We had sex, Kingsley."

"So it was sperm donation the old-fashioned way. We'd all been through hell that week. Any angel would have fallen."

"I appreciate your defense of my indefensible behavior. But the simple fact is, I knew the rules, I broke them, and now I must accept the consequences."

"Do you want me to try to talk you out of telling them?" Kingsley asked.

"Only if you think I'm doing the wrong thing. If I were expelled from the order or excommunicated, Fionn might blame himself the way children always blame themselves for the sins of their parents. I would never want that. And I would never want anyone in the Church telling Fionn he was conceived in sin. I knew a priest in Rome who left the clergy to marry, and both his wife and his children were treated very cruelly."

Søren took a breath, and Kingsley saw his eyes were clouded with concern.

"He's a child," Søren continued. "He should never be the center of a scandal. This is why I'm so torn. You're a father. What's your advice?"

His advice? Søren was asking his advice? It was an awesome responsibility, advising Søren about something with such potentially life-altering consequences. Kingsley was inclined to demur. He considered Søren's calling to the Church something between him and God alone.

But tonight he would speak. Kingsley had held Fionn and wept with the joy Søren had spoken of so movingly, the deep joy nothing and no one could touch. So he knew the answer to this question. He knew it as if God were whispering it in his ear and all Kingsley had to do was open his mouth and God's good true counsel would come out.

"You should tell them about Fionn," Kingsley said. "Tell

them you have a son and tell them with pride. Whatever happens, we'll take care of you and Fionn. I've only held him once, but I already love him like my own child. So you tell your superiors about your son, and then tell them to fuck off if they brand him a sin. What do they know about bringing children into the world anyway? What could they possibly know about that kind of love?"

Kingsley found himself suddenly shaking, and not from the cold. After a pause, he continued:

"I thought I knew. I was wrong, though. I thought I knew how much fathers loved their children. Then I had Céleste and Nora found Nico. I thought when you loved your child, you'd tear out your own heart to save their life if you had to, if that was the only way. I didn't know until I held my baby girl in my arms, five minutes old, that I'd tear out my own heart so she could play soccer with it in the backyard. I didn't know until that moment I laid eyes on Nico that I'd kill anyone who harmed a hair on his head. I'll tell your Jesuit superiors myself if you want me to. I'll tell them you're a better priest because you have a son. You brought a child into the world and that makes you more like God, not less, because God fathered a child with a girl who was married to another man, and those priests have been worshipping that girl's scandal of a son for the last two thousand years. And if that child wasn't a sin, no child ever could be. Especially not yours. Never yours. Never Fionn. You've never held him, but I have. That boy is perfect. Absolutely... But of course he's perfect—he's your son."

Søren stared at him for a moment before taking off his gloves and shoving them in his pockets. Then he placed his hands on Kingsley's face and brushed the tears off his cheeks. Søren had shed a few tears of his own.

"I'll tell them," Søren said. "I'll tell them every word you said."

"Good," Kingsley said. He took a shuddering breath and rested his forehead on Søren's shoulder. "Good."

Kingsley was still shaking and didn't know why. "Sorry."

"Don't be," Søren said. He caressed Kingsley's hair and kissed his temple. This wasn't one of Søren's three kisses—it was a fourth type. A kiss of comfort, a kiss of blessing.

"Fatherhood does this to you," Kingsley said. "Makes you a little crazy. I miss my children."

"I miss my son, too. And I haven't even met him yet."

"I can't wait until you do. When Nora introduces you to him, make sure I'm there. Please."

"Of course you'll be there. I want you there."

Kingsley breathed again, a deep breath. Finally, he pulled himself together and was able to step away from Søren, clear-eyed, calm.

"You think our girls are out there wondering what we're doing?" Kingsley asked.

"I'm sure it's crossed their minds," Søren said, drawing his gloves on again.

"When we tell them what we did on this trip, let's skip over the part where we stood in the forest crying like babies while talking about our children."

"It's not a very commanding portrait of dominant manhood, is it?"

"Slightly humiliating," Kingsley said. "Walk. Please. I need a very tall glass of red wine, and I need it twenty minutes ago."

They walked on for a few minutes in silence. Companionable silence. The silence of lovers who'd just done something even more intimate than making love and now needed a few quiet minutes to put their armor back in place.

They rounded a bend in the road. In a blur of movement, something shot out from one of the shrubs that lined the lane.

"What the hell?" Kingsley said.

Søren grabbed him by the arm, halting him mid-step.

"Snowshoe hare," Søren said, pointing ahead at a furry blur. "We must have flushed it from the bushes. See it?"

The little rabbit-like creature with the white fur sped across the wide bend in the road, leaving tiny V-shaped tracks behind him.

"Not us," Kingsley said. "Her."

As soon as the hare was in the open, a bird shot out from seemingly nowhere, bursting from the woods in a flurry of feathers and muscle and flight. The hare darted left, then right, and Kingsley watched it, not knowing who to root for in this deadly battle—the hawk or the hare.

The hare made a break for the shrubs along the field and the hawk followed, disappearing into a thick copse of aspens.

"Reminds me of something," Kingsley said.

"What?"

"Our first night together."

Søren looked at him through narrowed eyes. It was not a friendly look.

"I didn't say which one of us was the hare," Kingsley said.

Søren shook his head and started to walk on, leaving the mortal combat behind them. But when he stepped forward again, the hare shot out from under the bushes, breaking for the safety of the forest again. The hawk didn't follow.

"That's a surprise," Søren said.

"My money was on the hawk, too." Carefully, so as not to startle it, Kingsley crept toward the bush where the hawk had followed the hare.

"Kingsley?"

"I want to see it."

"That was a goshawk and a hungry one at that if she's hunting at night. We do not pet the hungry ill-tempered goshawks in the forest."

Kingsley ignored him. "Something's not right," he said. He saw movement within the bush. "She's not flying away."

"Hawks don't roost in bushes," Søren said, following him to the bush. "Not when there's an entire forest of trees twenty feet away."

The bush shook and quivered again. Kingsley knelt on the snow and peered through the branches. He could hear fluttering sounds, and a cry that sounded to him like distress.

"Lantern," Kingsley said. Søren handed it to him. Kingsley held it up and by the light saw the bird struggling. "I think she's injured. We need to get her out."

Søren stripped off his coat and Kingsley took it from him, using it to pry apart the branches so he could grip the hawk with his gloved hands. It took a few tries and a lot of swearing before Kingsley managed to get a firm grip on the bird, her wings folded close to her sides, under his hands. Kingsley finally immobilized the hawk so Søren could attempt to free her leg from whatever had it trapped.

"I see the problem," Søren said. "Got it. Pull her out but don't let her go. Careful."

Kingsley lifted the bird from the bush. Though she screamed out in terror and fury, she didn't seem to be injured.

"What is it?" he asked as held the hawk tight to his

chest. Søren used his own scarf to hood the frightened bird. Once the hawk's eyes were covered, she went still.

"Jesses," Søren said. "Leather straps used to train birds."

Kingsley and Søren were kneeling face to face in the snow now, the hawk between them and the lantern below them.

"This is someone's pet hawk?" Kingsley asked.

"It was once," Søren said, ripping off both his gloves and dropping them on the ground. He held two leather straps in his bare hand. "This is old leather, rotted. This hawk flew away from its owner a long time ago. One of the jesses was snagged on a loose strand of barbed wire. That's why she couldn't fly away."

"Can you take them off?"

"The leather's too stiff. If you have a knife I can try to cut them off," Søren said.

"Swiss Army knife in my left coat pocket."

Søren dug through Kingsley's pocket. He pulled out the knife and selected a blade. As soon as Søren touched the hawk's talons, it screamed again, indignant at being manhandled.

"Hold still, darling," Kingsley whispered to the hawk. "We're only to trying to help you."

"I'll be quick as I can," Søren said. "But I don't want to hurt her."

"I've got her. Just hurry. If she gets away, she's gone for good."

Kingsley watched in the lantern light as Søren did his best to hold the hawk's leg still as he sliced through the rotting leather straps.

"One down," Søren said. "This is insane, you know."

Kingsley grinned. "What? You hadn't planned on saving a bird's life tonight?"

"This is not a bird. A canary is a bird. A swallow is a bird. This is a full-grown goshawk. We're saving a serial killer."

"But such a lovely serial killer, aren't you?" How could Kingsley have left her trapped in that bush, fighting for freedom until she succumbed to exhaustion and starvation? "Who did you belong to, sweetheart?"

"Someone who didn't know what he was doing with something so dangerous and wild," Søren said. "A fool, obviously. Probably a young one."

"Ah, don't be too hard on him. Who wouldn't want to tame something this beautiful?"

Søren met his eyes and Kingsley winked.

The second jess fell to the snowy ground.

"Get back," Kingsley said. "She's big enough to carry us both off."

Søren stepped to the side as Kingsley came to his feet.

"Take the scarf off her eyes," Kingsley said. His heart was beating faster than it had since the night Céleste was born. The adrenaline coursed through him so madly he imagined he could fly away too if he wanted. Søren lifted the scarf off the bird's face.

"*Adieu,* you beautiful monster," Kingsley said, tossing the hawk up into the air. "God, please let her fly. Please let her fly..."

It was his second prayer of the night.

She flew. She opened her wild wings and beat them hard against the cold air. She stumbled once before finding her stride, but then she was off, flying free, and far, far away from them.

He looked at Søren, and Søren looked at him.

Then they laughed.

"We just caught a goshawk," Kingsley said. "That doesn't happen very often."

"That doesn't happen ever."

"You think it was an angel in the form of a hawk and it was testing us?" Kingsley asked. "Isn't there something like that in the Bible?"

"No."

"It should be in the Bible." Kingsley took a shuddering breath. "That was incredible, wasn't it?"

"I'll certainly never forget it," Søren said. "Are you ready to go on or would you like to see if there's a black bear or a coyote nearby we can play with, too?"

"Let's go back," Kingsley said, grinning broadly. But before they started, he returned to the scene of the rescue and found the jesses still lying on the snow.

"Are you keeping them?" Søren asked.

"Proof," Kingsley said. "No one will believe us otherwise."

"Why tell anyone? It can be our story alone. No one else needs to know."

"What happened to keeping fewer secrets?"

"This isn't a secret," Søren said. "It's simply a moment and it was ours alone."

Kingsley could ask for no better Christmas gift than that, a memory only the two of them would ever share.

But still...Kingsley pocketed the jesses. He saw Søren's curious expression as he watched him do it. Kingsley would have explained why he wanted to keep them, except he didn't know, only that they spoke to his soul for reasons best left unexamined. Luckily Søren didn't ask, and twenty minutes later, they arrived back at the cabin.

Inside, Søren turned up the wick on the kerosene lantern so

they had enough light to divest themselves of their winter gear. They kicked off snow-packed boots, tossed scarves over hooks, beat snow off their coats, and brushed snow from their hair.

"It's twenty degrees out," Kingsley said. "Why am I drenched in sweat?"

"A long walk in the woods causes the liver to release its toxins."

"You're mocking me."

"You make it too easy. Go. Shower."

"We have running water here?"

"Yes."

"Hot water?"

"The magic of propane."

"Clean water?"

Søren glared at him.

"Shower. Yes, sir." Kingsley turned on his head and headed to the bathroom.

"Stop," Søren said. Kingsley spun back around. "You'll need this."

Søren handed him the lantern.

Kingsley sighed. "Next time I fall in love with a priest, I'm going to make sure he's a normal priest."

"No such thing," Søren said.

Kingsley sighed.

"I was afraid of that."

THE SCENT OF WINTER

THE BATHROOM DID HAVE RUNNING water, thank God. And the water was scalding hot—even better. Kingsley always liked taking a hot shower before playing with Søren when possible. He could take more when his muscles were relaxed from heat and steam. He dried off, wrapped the towel around his waist, and went in search of wine.

Søren already had it waiting for him on the bedside table.

With glass in hand, Kingsley found Søren sitting on the floor in front of the fireplace. He seemed to be performing some kind of surgery with an X-Acto knife on a black elk-hide flogger.

"Do I want to know?" Kingsley asked.

"Shoo." Søren waved his hand. "I'll meet you in bed."

Kingsley obeyed, but only after taking three extra seconds to try to discern what the hell Søren was doing.

"Kingsley..."

"Going, sir."

He went to the bedroom and lit the bedside lamps again, along with the bank of candles and wood stove.

Soon, the room was aglow with both soft heat and warm light. He finished his wine and felt much better now. Warm inside and out. He tossed his towel aside, pulled down the covers, and laid on the bed naked. He meant to think about kink and sex and all his favorite subjects of reverie but all he could think about was that hawk. The floor creaked and Kingsley opened his eyes. Søren stood in the doorway of the bedroom, gazing at him. Søren had taken off his sweater and wore only a white t-shirt and jeans.

"How did you know that was a goshawk?" Kingsley asked.

"My father," Søren said. He sat on the bed next to Kingsley's hip. Kingsley rolled over to lay on his side facing him. "Falconry and hawking are traditionally old English sports. For centuries the sport was the purview of only the aristocracy. The summer I was eight or nine, I was allowed home for a few weeks over the summer. When I came home I discovered my father had decided he would join the ranks of the great austringers."

Kingsley shivered with pleasure as Søren ran his hand over Kingsley's naked side. "Austringer?"

"Falconers fly falcons. Austringers fly hawks. Hawks are harder to train, therefore the glory is greater when you do. So said my narcissist father." Søren gave a sad smile as he pushed Kingsley's wet hair off his forehead. If Kingsley had been a cat, he would have purred. "I was treated to days and days of lectures about the glory of 'Merry Olde England' and the beauty of goshawks and how only the greatest men could subdue such magnificent wild beasts. He'd ordered the bird and she arrived... I was enamored of her at first sight. My father would never let me touch her though, even hooded."

"Who buys an animal to keep as a pet, and then doesn't let his son touch it?"

"It was a beautiful bird. I imagined myself walking along a field with that lovely thing on my fist. Lonely children have fantasies like that. But my father's attempt to join the ranks of Merry Old England's greatest huntsmen ended badly. During a training session, the hawk gripped his bare arm with a talon and drew blood. My father snapped her neck."

Kingsley touched Søren's hand, a better way to show he was sorry than to say such inadequate words.

"I should have learned my lesson then," Søren said, as he stroked Kingsley's naked hip. That lock of blond hair had fallen over Søren's eyes again and Kingsley could scarcely breathe, much less speak. "To train a hawk you must be infinitely patient. They respond only to gifts of food. They can't be punished into loving you. And if you treat a hawk with any cruelty whatsoever, the moment you let her off the leash, she'll fly away, never to come home again—and possibly die, if her jesses get caught on something. Training a hawk requires patience and love, qualities my father lacked in abundance."

Søren was silent for a long time, too long. Kingsley feared he'd lost him. It was easy to do when Søren went wandering down the dark paths of his childhood.

"Where are you?" Kingsley said. "What are you thinking?"

"I was thinking..."

"What?" Kingsley asked. "Tell me."

"I was thinking...I would've liked to have shown Fionn that hawk." Søren closed his eyes. "But I would have let...I would have let my son touch her."

Kingsley almost wished he hadn't asked. The sheer

heartache in Søren's eyes, in his voice, hurt more than any knife to his heart would have.

"Proof, then," Kingsley said after he managed to swallow the lump in his throat.

"Of what?"

"That sons don't always take after their fathers."

It must have been the right thing to say because as soon as Kingsley said it, Søren ran his hand up his back, gripped him by the hair and pulled. Kingsley exhaled the breath he'd been holding as Søren dragged him onto his back by his hair.

"God, I love when you do that," Kingsley said. Søren held tight to Kingsley's hair, forcing him to bare his throat, a throat Søren kissed and kissed and kissed...

He tried to put his arms around Søren's shoulders, but Søren had other ideas. He pinned Kingsley by his wrists to the bed.

"I love when you do that, too," Kingsley said.

"Is this commentary going to continue all night?" Søren asked.

"Only if you keep doing all the things I love."

"I could gag you." Søren said, straddling Kingsley's stomach. "But then I couldn't hear you whimper."

"I don't whimper. I'm a grown man."

"Is that so?" Søren nipped Kingsley's earlobe. Kingsley made a sound that may or may not have been a whimper, and Søren laughed a low, sensual laugh.

"That wasn't a whimper," Kingsley said.

"It was."

"Was not."

Søren bit his earlobe again, much harder this time.

Kingsley panted, "I admit...that one might have been a whimper."

Søren rose up and sat on Kingsley's lower stomach. This was something very erotic and delightful when Juliette did it. When a six-foot-four, two hundred pound sadist did it, it was mild agony.

"Why aren't you naked?" Kingsley asked.

Søren pulled his shirt off and threw it on the floor.

"Better," Kingsley said. He ached to touch Søren's broad, taut chest and shoulders, but he was still pinned to the bed.

It seemed Søren read Kingsley's desire in his eyes. Søren pulled Kingsley's left arm to his chest and pressed the hand flat over his heart.

"Don't move," Søren ordered. "I'm going to do something to you that you'll hate."

He reached into his pocket and pulled something out. A long strip of leather, one of the tails from the flogger that Søren had cut off with his knife.

"Søren."

Søren met Kingsley's eyes. "I know you hate collars," Søren said. "This is not a collar."

Kingsley swallowed. His heart pounded. No other lover had ever gotten to him the way Søren could. There was a reason theirs could never be an everyday love affair. Kingsley wouldn't survive it. Kink was one thing. Having his soul flayed open was another.

He'd hoped Søren would break him tonight. Instead, Søren seemed intent on breaking him open.

Though he found it humiliating, Kingsley nodded his consent. Humiliating it was, yes, but arousing, deeply. For him and for Søren.

"Hawks can't be tamed," Søren said very softly like he was telling a secret. "Did you know that? They can be trained, but never tamed."

Søren wrapped the leather strip around Kingsley's wrist and slipped the dovetailed end through a slit cut in the center and tied it off. Søren met his eyes again and Kingsley slowly offered him his right wrist. And after, Søren slid off Kingsley's stomach and tied leather strips around his ankles as well, knotting them securely. Of course, this wasn't enough for Søren. He had to put a snap hook through one of the ankle jesses and run a leash from it to the bedpost.

"Now you can't fly from me," Søren said.

"I did once, didn't I?"

Søren met his eyes. "That was my fault."

"I won't fly away again."

"No. I wouldn't let you." Søren's eyes were dark and hooded by his thick dark lashes. He ran his hands up Kingsley's chest and down his arms, pausing to tug on the jesses on his wrists. "You hate them, don't you?"

"With every fiber of my being."

"Good."

Inflicting pain aroused Søren, but so did inflicting humiliation. Kingsley could see he was aroused. His pupils were round as dimes and his breathing unsteady, labored. His hands grasped and gripped and left bruises with every touch.

"Fuck me," Kingsley said.

"I haven't even beaten you yet."

"Fuck me first. Beat me after."

"If you beg for it, I'd consider the request," Søren said. "But the beating will be twice as severe if I have to wait..."

"Beg for it? I'd pay for it. I'd give you every cent I had for it. I'd let you wipe your shoes on my heart for it. I'd give you wine glasses full of my blood for it. I'd even sell my soul for it if I still had it to sell."

"What did you do with your soul?" Søren asked.

"Don't you remember? I gave it to you one night in the forest."

"You broke my cross. I took your soul in repayment."

"Keep it," Kingsley said. "It's worth nothing to me unless you own it."

Søren bent down and kissed him as Kingsley continued begging. He begged in English. He begged in French. He begged in Spanish and Russian. He begged in whimpers and sighs and he begged with his heart and with his hands as he opened Søren's pants and stroked him. Søren was hard and ready, though he'd never admit he wanted it as much as Kingsley did. He didn't have to admit it. Kingsley knew.

No sadist Kingsley had ever been with struck harder and faster than Søren. Even hawks could learn from him. Halfway between one "please" and another, Søren seized Kingsley by the arms and threw him onto his stomach. Few people on earth would likely find the sensation of a knee pressing into one's lower back erotic, but Kingsley was one of those happy few. Happier still when Søren dug his fingers into Kingsley's hair, holding him fast down on the bed. Why Søren held him so hard was beyond Kingsley. It wasn't as if there was anywhere else in the world he would have rather been at that moment.

Søren moved down Kingsley's body and nudged his thighs apart with his knees. Kingsley moaned as he always did when Søren took possession of him. As usual, Søren laughed his mocking laugh.

"Whore," Søren said, and Kingsley smiled.

"You made me this way," Kingsley said.

"Hardly. You were born a whore. All I did was find your price."

Kingsley laughed, but the laugh died in a heartbeat when Søren pressed two very wet fingers inside him. The violation was so delicious that Kingsley turned his face into the pillow to stifle his own sigh of bliss. He'd debased himself enough already tonight.

"Do you like it?" Søren asked.

"Yes."

"Does it hurt?"

"Yes."

"It's all the same to you, isn't it?" Søren asked, his tone taunting. He slid off the bed and finished undressing. "Why is that, I wonder?"

"Just lucky, I guess," Kingsley said, watching him.

"Or you're a whore for me?"

"This isn't fair. She gets the cute pet name 'Little One' but I'm 'Whore'?"

"You want me to start calling you '*Little* One'?"

Kingsley thought about that. "No, bad idea," he said. "Terrible idea. Forgot I said anything. 'Whore' is perfect."

Søren slid back on top of him. Slowly but not too slowly, Søren entered him fully. And then, because Kingsley had apparently been a very good boy this year, Søren kissed his back from shoulder to shoulder and neck to the bottom rib. "I love when you do that, too..."

"Stop talking," Søren said, "or I will cut your tongue out, put a metal hook through it, and hang it on the Christmas tree as our one and only ornament."

Kingsley stopped talking.

He couldn't have spoken if he'd wanted to. Søren thrust into him and Kingsley was rendered speechless. The only sounds he could make were inarticulate cries of pain and pleasure, the combination of the two far more potent than they ever could be apart. Søren filled and filled him utterly, completely, to the breaking point.

Yet Kingsley didn't break.

Søren bit down hard on the back of Kingsley's neck like lions did when mating. But it wasn't enough to hold him with his teeth, and Søren had Kingsley by the wrists again. He was spread out and staked, split open and pinned down. Søren gave with long deep rough thrusts and Kingsley took and he took and he took, happy to be used by this man he loved, happier still to be loved by this man who used him.

What he would remember most fondly from this little trip away from the world, Kingsley didn't know, but if he had to guess he would say it would like be the vision of Søren's hand clamped over his wrist and the black leather jess against the white sheets. Kingsley's cock throbbed, desperate to be touched, but he was content to wait. He needed Søren to come in him more than Kingsley needed to come for him. Søren was close. Kingsley could tell from the sound of Søren's ragged breathing. The grip on Kingsley's wrists grew even tighter and he whimpered in pain, forgetting momentarily that grown men do not whimper.

Søren's thrusts grew even harder, somehow even deeper and Kingsley could do nothing but dig his fingers into the bed to brace himself. The teeth at the nape of his neck broke the skin and Kingsley flinched and cried out as Søren poured into him, filling him and sealing them together. Kingsley grunted unhappily when Søren pulled out, but quickly found himself being turned over onto his back again, with Søren kissing his way down Kingsley's sweating chest and stomach. Søren took him in his mouth and the sudden shock of wet heat on his cock was too much to bear. Kingsley orgasmed as powerfully as he had that night in the woods when Søren had deigned to pleasure him. He came so hard his back arched, lifting his shoulders off the bed. He almost took flight. It felt like he could have. He could have but he didn't, he wouldn't. Something kept him grounded and that something wasn't the leash on his ankle but the love that bound him to Søren tighter than any collar, cord, or fetter.

When it was all over, Søren brought him a tin cup full of water so cold it set Kingsley's teeth on edge. Søren dragged him to a sitting position and held the cup while Kingsley drank. When he finished, Kingsley collapsed back onto the bloody pillow. The blood was his of course. A few drops spilling from the bite mark on his back. Søren lay on his back and Kingsley rested his head on Søren's stomach, which was always his favorite place to sleep. Especially if Søren's hand was wrapped up in his hair just as it was right then.

They were silent for a long time, doing nothing but breathing together. Kingsley closed his eyes and inhaled the scent of winter on Søren's stomach. It smelled not just of the cold of winter and the bitterness of winter and the purity of winter, but the wildness of winter, too. It was an untamed season as dangerous as it was beautiful.

"I was right," Kingsley said.

"About what?"

"When I said I would still love you when I was fifty." Kingsley lifted his head and met Søren's eyes. "Thank you for bringing me here, for telling me the truth."

"Thank you for forgiving me."

Kingsley nodded and laid his head down again.

"Is it after midnight?" Kingsley asked.

"It is."

"Happy birthday."

"It is indeed."

"What would you like for your birthday?" Kingsley asked.

"One big French whore," Søren said. "Preferably male. Ideally a masochist of the extreme variety."

"In a pear tree?"

"Optional."

"Good news," Kingsley said. "I happen to have a masochistic French whore on me. And he's all yours."

Søren sighed contentedly. "What to do with him..."

"Keep him," Kingsley said. "Keep him and never lose him."

"I don't have to. He's quite good at losing himself."

"Yes," Kingsley said, wincing. "Sorry about that."

"I swear on all that is holy, if you ever get lost in the woods again..."

"You'll kill me?"

Søren dug his hands deep into Kingsley's hair, holding it so tight he whimpered.

"No," Søren said. "I'll find you."

BONUS SHORT STORY:
BLOOD & SNOW

AN UNEXPECTED VISITOR

Author's Note: This story takes place at the same time as December Wine.

ROME, ITALY

MAGDALENA WAS in the middle of a beating when someone knocked timorously on the door.

"Magda?" Delphina whispered, then knocked again.

What part of *Never interrupt me when I'm with a client, or you will be murdered in your bed with a pickaxe* did people not understand?

Resolved to ignore the interruption, she lifted the whip again, wincing at a flash of pain in her right shoulder. Getting older was hell.

"Magda, I'm sorry. We have a guest."

A guest. Well then. Perhaps Delphina had a good reason for interrupting her. They often had very important guests here at what was once the *Abbazia di san Girolamo nel deserto*, the Abbey of Saint Jerome of the Wilderness, a Benedictine monastery. Princes. Kings. Business magnates. Vice presidents of the United States. *Vice* being the operative word.

"Who is he?" Magdalena turned and called through the door. Behind her, hanging on a hook and bleeding from his back, was a member of a European royal dynasty.

"Ah...I don't know."

Magdalena rolled her eyes. She repeated the madam's lament. "Why are good whores so hard to find?"

She opened the door and there stood Delphina dressed in pigtails and a pinafore—only a pinafore—along with Mary Jane shoes and bobby socks.

"Talk," she said.

"There's a man at the door. He didn't say his name. You should go see him."

"Why?"

"He's worth looking at. Everyone should see him."

"Is he important?"

"I wanted to bow to him."

"You're a submissive prostitute," Magdalena said. "You want to bow to every man. It's your job."

"For him I would bow for free."

"Did you bow to him for free?"

"Maybe I curtsied. A little."

Magdalena sighed. She hired her girls for their sadism and/or masochism, not for their brains.

"Where is he?"

"In your salon. He said he would wait."

Magdalena touched her forehead, eyes closed, and breathed through her nose. "Then why are you bothering me?"

"I wouldn't let this man wait."

Usually Magdalena wouldn't have bothered with a guest arriving during a session, but she felt the tiredness in her bones tonight. A few minutes rest would do her good.

"Do I have blood on me?" She was wearing her favorite dress, a long-sleeved ankle-length wrap dress in winter white. Flattering to her silver hair, which was in a braided crown.

"Not much," Delphina said.

"I'll see to our guest. You, stay with the boy." Magdalena inclined her head to the aforementioned royal who had begun to softly moan. "Keep him from dying. Otherwise, don't touch him." She turned and called to the man, "I'll be back soon, puppy. Or perhaps not. I may leave you there all night. Comfortable?"

He moaned in agony.

"He's fine," Magdalena said, and waved her hand, dismissing the moan and the blood. She glanced over her shoulder again. The moaning had gotten a little louder. "If he does die, you know what to do."

She hadn't lowered her voice when she said that. Psychological torture was part of the package service offered here at St. Magdalena's, as she'd rechristened the monastery.

Magdalena left them and strode down the hall, descending the wide and curving stone staircase to the main floor. The salon was her best reception room, where the most important guests were entertained. And, apparently, also strange men who showed up uninvited two days after Christmas at nearly midnight.

She entered the salon, a grand room of stone floors, fur rugs, brightly-colored medieval tapestries depicting the court of King Arthur hanging on the walls. She expected her visitor to be warming himself by the grand mosaic tile fireplace, which they always kept lit in winter. But no one stood there, though it was a bitterly cold and snow blown winter's night. Instead, she found her visitor standing at the tall dark window, his back to her. But even with his back to her, she recognized him. No mistaking the height, the regal bearing, the broad shoulders, and the hair...that blond hair with nary a single strand out of place.

Magdalena laughed. "Hello, Bambi. I should have known it was you."

AN UNEXPECTED ANNOUNCEMENT

HE TURNED AROUND and Magdalena smiled at her old friend. Had Delphina said there was a handsome and intimidating priest at her door, she would have known it was Marcus immediately. But he wasn't dressed in his clerical garb tonight. He wore a sleek dark gray suit. Either he'd left the priesthood or he was traveling incognito. Both possibilities intrigued her but not nearly as much as the question of why he'd come to her out of the blue so soon after Christmas.

"Hello, Magda," he said, not quite smiling but certainly not frowning, either. In the years between visits, she always forgot just how handsome a man he was. Until he showed up on her doorstep again—and here he was, winter personified. Exquisite face, but always wearing a cold expression. Pale skin, hair like the morning sun coldly glistening on snow, and eyes like the January sky, a granite gray to chill you to the bone.

"Come with me," she said. "I need you."

He walked toward her and she waved him into the hallway. Bless him, she did have him well-trained.

"I have one of Queen Sofía's grandsons or great-nephews or something like that hanging from a hook in my dungeon," she said. "Or was it Princess Grace? Doesn't matter. My bursitis is acting up. I need your arms."

"You could consider retiring," he said.

"You could consider shoving your lovely head up your lovely arse."

She'd learned her English in England, where she'd spent time as a teenager as the property of a wealthy Tory who'd picked her up from a pimp. It had given her great pleasure, years later when she was a rich and free woman, to give her pimp's name to one of her dear friends in the Cosa Nostra. Since she was fluent, she spoke English whenever possible. It made it much harder for her girls to eavesdrop on her conversations.

"Not to state the obvious, but you aren't getting any younger," he said, removing his suit jacket in one smooth motion and tossing it onto a red brocade armchair they passed. She'd been in her forties when they'd met—thirty years ago, now. Terrible math. Like her, Marcus was a sadist, which was why he'd oh so casually alluded to her advanced age.

"And *you* aren't getting any better-mannered. Good. I hate when people change for the better." She quickly changed the subject. "So, how do you like my new establishment?"

"A converted Benedictine monastery. Really, Magda?" He sounded equal parts amused and disgusted as he unbuttoned his shirt cuffs and rolled up his sleeves. She appreciated a sadist who whipped first, asked questions later.

"I tried to buy an old decommissioned Jesuit house but they wouldn't sell to me. I like this place better, though. More rooms. Older. The stone walls keep the sounds of the screams in better. I was so tired of getting arrested in Rome. The countryside suits me much better."

The door to her dungeon was solid oak, carved, 500-years-old at least. He pushed it open and little Delphina, who'd been poking the young royal in the ribs with the business end of a 14-inch dildo, gasped in surprise, dropped the phallus, and scampered out of the room.

"Can't follow instructions to save her life," Magdalena said with a sigh. She went to stand in front of her princeling, who kept his eyes trained on the floor as she'd taught him. "I brought a friend, puppy. He's going to whip you while I supervise. Weep if you understand."

He understood.

She waved toward the whip wall. Marcus picked up two or three, hefted and tested them before settling on a black bull-hide whip.

"At your pleasure," she said, standing with her arms crossed over her ample chest and watching from a safe distance as Marcus lashed the princeling across his lovely young back.

"You aren't even going to ask why I'm here?" He lashed the boy again.

"You aren't here to wish me a happy Christmas?"

He looked at her. "Happy Christmas," he said, then lashed the boy again.

"It was a very happy Christmas. My lover James bought me a new yacht. You'll have to come out to the Riviera this summer with us. Did you have a good Christmas?"

"I did. In fact, it was the best I've ever had."

Another lash.

"Someone got a good present. Let me guess. Did my Bambi get a new motorcycle?"

"One Ducati is more than enough for me."

Her princeling was close to coming now. Poor soul was so addicted to pain he could hardly orgasm without being beaten into a pulp first. Sweet boy. Very handsome. Good body. Only twenty-four. She might make him her own personal pet.

If he survived.

"New shamefully-underage girl to use and abuse?" she asked.

Marcus gave the boy another vicious lash.

"Eleanor is thirty-five," he said.

"New obsidian scalpel set?"

He struck the little prince again, turned to her and met her eyes.

"It seems I have a son."

THREE

HOSPITALITY & HOSTILITY

UNFORTUNATELY, Magdalena didn't have a chance to ask her Bambi what in heaven and hell's name he was talking about. Her princeling chose that inopportune moment to come. He came hard, came loudly, and then passed out, as was his wont to do. She sent for Delphina to show their guest to his room, while she cleaned up the princeling and put him to bed with a little kiss on his forehead and a "Good puppy."

She strode the stone halls to the guest wing, which once housed novice monks and now would be the temporary home of a veteran priest. Without knocking, she opened the door to the room and found Marcus sitting in the blue velvet armchair in front of the fireplace. It came as no surprise to find a cat perched on his lap.

"Who's this one?" he asked, glancing up as she came into the room and stood by the fire. One downside of owning a converted monastery was that monks wore heavy wool robes for a reason—drafty hallways. She burned up in the rooms and froze in the hallways.

"Lucrezia," she said, nodding toward the sleek black

and orange cat on his thigh. "I'm convinced all cats are descended from the Borgias, this one especially. I've never had a better mouser. Funny, she usually avoids our male guests, but I can't say I'm surprised she's taking a liking to you. You do attract dangerous females, don't you?"

"Why is that, do you think?"

"Dangerous ladies like dangerous men. They can talk shop."

He smiled, stroking Lucrezia under her chin. The cat twisted her head this way and that to give him better access to every inch of her head.

"I apologize for turning up unannounced," he said. "Thank you for the room."

Politeness. Very suspicious.

Magdalena decided to play along.

"You're welcome," she said. "Although the Benedictines are long gone, I try to keep up their practice of hospitality."

"Yes, well, Delphina offered to let me give her a pelvic exam if I so desired."

"We have our own definition of hospitality here."

"I've noticed." He smiled contentedly, still stroking the cat.

"Why are you here, Bambi?"

He glanced at her, returned his attention to Lucrezia's chin. "Would you believe me if I said I wasn't sure why?"

"Yes," she said. "But you must have a theory or two. When you were in seminary, you practically lived here. But once you moved to the States, you only ever come to see me when things are falling apart. What was it the last time? Oh yes, your Little One ran off and left you after you proposed marriage, you beautiful fool."

"Seven years ago."

"That was the worst I've ever seen you, and I've seen you at your worst."

He nodded. "Only fair," he said, "that you see me at my best every now and then."

"You're happy."

"An understatement. The understatement of the century." He dropped his hand to the arm of the chair. The cat lightly leapt off his thigh and sauntered to the rug in front of the fireplace, turned two circles and laid down into a ball.

"If he's hers because you talked her into it, I may put a sword through your guts. Then again, if he's not hers, I may do it anyway."

"He's not Eleanor's. I wouldn't do that to her."

"But you would betray her with another woman."

"It wasn't a betrayal. Eleanor would tell you that herself. She sent Grace to me."

"Grace. That's her name?"

"Yes. She was instrumental in saving my life and Eleanor's during a very difficult ordeal."

"A feat that is usually rewarded with flowers, or perhaps a medal of valor, not a child."

He leaned back and gave her the most arrogant smile she'd ever seen a man wear.

"She didn't want a medal."

Magdalena raised her hand, shook her finger at him. "I forget you're a man sometimes. Then you remind me."

"That didn't sound like a compliment."

"It wasn't."

"Do you even want to know his name?"

"No."

"Fionn," he said. "After Fionn Mac Cumhaill."

"The Irish mythical hero."

"The blond Irish mythical hero. Grace is half-Irish."

"Do you have a picture?"

"Of Grace or Fionn?"

"Fionn."

"Not yet. I only found out about him two days ago. Although, I confess...I had hoped. Not hoped...that's too strong of a word. Wished. Wished and didn't let myself believe it would come true."

"Yet it did."

"It did. You don't seem happy for me."

"I'm not."

He surprised her by looking momentarily wounded. She wasn't used to seeing such a human expression on his face. She wasn't moved by it, not a bit.

"You are still a priest, are you not?"

"I am."

"Your son will either grow up as a scandal or without a father, and I'm supposed to congratulate you?"

"He is a child, not a scandal. And he has a father. Grace is happily married."

"Better and better. Now it's adultery."

"I didn't realize you'd gotten so moralistic in your old age."

"One of us has to be, you smug bastard."

He glared at her.

She gave her best nonchalant wave of her hand. "You had a rough day and you fucked a married woman to make yourself feel better. She got pregnant, had the baby, and now you want me to pat you on your head and call you a good boy? If you insist."

She walked over to him, held out her hand as if to pat him on the head. Before she could, he grasped her by the wrist and held it, firmly. Not firmly enough to hurt her, but firmly enough.

"Good boy," she said.

"I truly don't know why I come to you for anything," he said. "Except that you're so incredibly sadistic you make me feel almost vanilla in comparison."

She laughed softly. He released her wrist. Now free to do what she wanted with her hand, she brought it to his face and stroked his cheek. He still had the smooth skin of a much younger man, but his eyes were ancient. They'd always been ancient, as if he'd lived a thousand lives before and carried what he'd seen in all those lives into every incarnation. He wouldn't have liked that theory of hers. Catholics didn't believe in reincarnation.

"It's not fair. How do you stay so handsome? Must be a deal with the devil. It certainly isn't, as they say, clean living and a clear conscience."

"Are you finished insulting me yet?"

"No." She sighed wistfully. "Why didn't I seduce you when I had the chance?"

"Because you never had the chance." He smiled. Too cruel. It was times like this she really wished she had taken him to bed. Ah, perhaps in their next lives.

"It's good to know I still despise you," she said. "I thought I was getting soft in my old age."

"Shall I go?" he asked.

"Not until you tell me why you've come."

"I told you, I don't know. I thought, perhaps, I wanted to tell you my good news. There aren't many people I can tell. But I should have known better than to think you'd care."

"Yes, you should have. Which is why I don't think that's why you came."

"Then you tell me, Magda. Why did I come here?"

"The same reason you always come to me. Pain. Either

to give it or because you're in it. And you've already given it and you're still here...so what's left?"

"I'm not in pain. I've never felt better in my life."

"Then why, pray tell," she said, tapping him under the chin, "do you look so scared?"

His eyes widened and he glanced away once at the fire —she saw the reflection of it dancing in his eyes—then back up at her.

"Because I'm terrified."

Good. Good, she thought. Now they were getting somewhere.

"Come with me. I want to show you something."

FOUR
TERROR & JOY

SHE LED him down one flight of stone steps and through two echoing corridors, one short, one long, until they arrived at a set of heavy double doors, carved wood and iron. She pushed one open and revealed to him...

"Beautiful chapel," he said.

She didn't disagree. The chapel was original to the monastery—16th century and still looked it, though it had been through restorations and repairs many times. The walls were stone and the ceiling vaulted with small arched Norman windows. A humble chapel, small and ancient, but made lovely by the candles burning on the altar and at the windows.

"I could have turned it into a fabulous dungeon. I thought about it, even spoke to our architect about it...but I didn't. I wanted to keep it this way." She turned and looked at him. "For you."

He glanced at her, his eyes wide at first, then narrowed in suspicion.

"Don't look at me like that," she said. "You know I love you. And you always—"

"Hurt the one you love. Yes, yes, I know this."

She pulled on the heavy door behind her, but Marcus waved her off and shut it for her. Ah, to be young again. She would kill to be that age again—specifically, she would kill him.

They went to the front pew, nearest the bank of burning candles, and sat side by side. She had made one change to the chapel, adding cushions to the pews. Very lush ones. Her ancient backside needed it.

"I love to come sit in here at night," she said. "I don't pray. But it comforts me to think I own my very own Catholic chapel. The Church didn't want me but when the time came, they wanted my money."

"I would have thought you'd taken a sledgehammer to it, after what the Church did to you."

"Ah, I'm above petty revenge."

"No, you aren't."

"True. But I'm too old for hefting sledgehammers. And I wanted you to see it."

He rose from the pew. She watched him walk around the altar, run his hands over it. She saw his fear but couldn't say for certain what the source of it was. They were so much alike, she and him, both sadists, both damaged, and yet both had their own strict, strange moral codes they lived by. If she had to guess, take a stab in the dark, she would say he was afraid he would be forced to leave the priesthood because of his son.

Or, since he was a sadist and the son of a sadist, perhaps he was terrified his son would take too much after him in that regard.

"I have to wonder how many masses have been cele-brated here over the centuries by how many priests. Who were they? What did they hope for, dream of?" His voice was far away, as if speaking to himself.

"Fear?"

He met her eyes over the altar, over the candles. "Yes."

"Are you afraid they'll make you leave the priesthood?"

"No. They might if they find out, but I'm not afraid of that."

"Are you afraid you'll never have a relationship with your son?"

"I don't know if I should, honestly. I haven't even decided yet if I want to. It feels almost enough to know he exists. He has a mother. He has a father. He doesn't need me. My part is done."

She rose and walked to the altar, stood on the opposite side of it, a dozen dripping white candles burning between them. "Then what is it, Bambi? Tell me."

He lifted his hand and ran it over the flames of the candles, letting the fire lick his palm.

"You knew Eleanor and I would be together," he said, "years before I met her. And after she left me and I came here, you told me she would come back to me, eventually, and she did."

He'd always scoffed at her claims she could divine the future from reading palms and tea leaves. How terrified must he be to admit that he might possibly believe, even a little, that she did have the ability to see what was coming?

He ran his palm over the candle flames again, then turned it, held it out, offered it to her. "Can you answer this question—is she going to leave me again?"

FIVE
AN UNEXPECTED QUESTION

THE CANDLE FLAMES danced from the force of her sigh.

"You do everything in your power to make me think you're as cold on the inside as you are on the outside," she said, "and then you say something like that, and I find myself not wanting to gut you in your sleep with my claymore after all, just to see if there's anything warm and alive in you."

"I'll keep my door locked tonight anyway."

She returned to the pew, sat down heavily. He came and sat at her side again.

"I remember," she said, hating those two words. So much of her life was behind her now, so little of it ahead. "When Caterina found out her grandmother was dying, back in Lisbon."

"Stop," he said, but she didn't stop.

"I always kept the girls scared to death of me. Only way to run a house like mine and keep order. She was too afraid to ask me for the money to go and see her grandmother. She asked you instead, a baby Jesuit under a vow a poverty. It's the way you speak, you know. English, Italian, Spanish, it doesn't matter. No matter the language, you speak with the accents of the rich and powerful. That's how she knew you came from money. I'll never forget overhearing you on my telephone, begging your father to wire the money to you. 'Yes, sir,' you said a thousand times if you said it once. 'Yes, sir, I know, sir. I am worthless, sir. Yes, sir, I know I don't deserve anything from you.' *Yes, sir. Yes, sir. Yes, sir...* Over and over he made you dance for him, made you tell him everything he wanted to hear."

"He thought I'd gotten her pregnant and needed money to pay her off or get her an abortion," he said. "He wanted to believe that. I was happy to let him."

"You'd think I would have enjoyed it, hearing you debase yourself to another man for money, but I couldn't bear it. It was like...like watching Michelangelo licking shit off the pope's feet for a few coins to buy drawing paper. It offended me, the way you were letting him treat you. And nothing offends me." She'd gone to Marcus and put her finger on the receiver, ending the call. Then she'd slapped him. The only time she'd ever slapped him, though the temptation, on many occasions, had been mighty. He'd looked at her, confused, hurt, embarrassed. How rarely—was that the only time?—she'd ever seen him embarrassed.

I'll give her the money, Magdalena had said to him. *I'll give her every coin I have, but don't you dare ask that evil man for anything ever again.* Then she'd grabbed him, holding him like a mother whose child was nearly struck by a car. She held him, then let him go with the instruction *We'll never speak of this again.* And they hadn't. Until now.

"She said her grandmother was the only person in her life who loved her," he said. "Her grandmother kept a room just for her so she knew she could always come home. My mother did the same for me."

"And I did the same for you," she said and raised her hand, indicating the chapel, the room she could have turned into the most magnificent dungeon in all the land, but had kept as a chapel for him, for her Bambi.

"When my mother died, Eleanor was the first person I called. Even though she'd left me. I called her and she came right to me. She even went with me to Denmark, to my mother's home, to the funeral."

"Playing wife."

"She played it too well. Sometimes I forgot we weren't married. My nieces latched onto her and wouldn't let her go the entire time we were there. She helped Gitte put on her pajamas, talked to her, read her bedtime stories, went for long walks with Laila, had heart-to-hearts with her. And at night, she slept with me, stayed with me, took care of me. It was the week my mother died, and it's one of my most cherished memories of Eleanor. What does that say about me? About her?"

"It says that if the Catholic Church ever allowed priests to marry, and your Eleanor said yes, you'd marry her that day."

"That hour," he said. "That minute, if we could say the vows quickly enough."

"Even if she did marry you, you know she doesn't want children. But I suppose you found a way around that..."

"Ever since I heard the news, I find myself bouncing back and forth between joy and terror. Joy that I have a son. Terror that I'll lose Eleanor over him."

"You should have thought about that before you fucked a married woman."

"You make it sound so sordid." He shook his head. "It

wasn't like that. She had permission to be with me, not only from her husband—who'd been with Eleanor and told his wife she could have her fun, too—but Eleanor as well. This was not..."

"You know I don't care. I only torment you because I enjoy it, not because I believe a word I say. How many married men have I taken to bed? Most of them? A good ninety percent."

"I come to you for help and you mock me."

"It's what I do." She smiled at him so he would know she didn't hate him, not completely, anyway. "Joy and terror —they're twins, you know. Joy is born first. Then terror a few minutes after. Joy arrives when you recognize what you have. Terror comes on its heels, terror that you'll lose the thing that gave you all that joy."

He looked her in the eyes. "If she leaves me, I don't know how I'll survive it."

"By coming and moaning to me, as usual. So let's hope she doesn't leave you. I'd rather not have a lovelorn priest moping around the house. Bad for business."

"Then it would behoove you to help me, wouldn't it?"

Laughing, she turned toward him, put her elbow on the back of the bench and rested her head on her hand. "You don't really believe I can see the future, do you?"

"No, but you're a woman, a dominant. You love *and* hate me, just like Eleanor. I think you understand her on a level I can't. And perhaps me, as well."

Even if Magdalena were to admit she had no sooth-saying gifts—not that she ever would—it didn't take a psychic to see that her Bambi, though a sadist and a domi-nant himself, was drawn to dominant women. He'd hung around her house every chance he had when he was in seminary in Rome. Oh, he claimed he only wished to learn from her but that didn't explain the long quiet evenings they'd spent together talking of anything but sadism. Only a matter a time before he fell in love with a dominant woman.

"She *should* leave you," Magdalena said. "I don't think you can fathom how much you've complicated her life. Isn't it enough she has to share your heart with Kingsley? Now she has to share you with your son?"

"Wives have always shared the hearts of their husbands with their children. And husbands have shared the hearts of their wives with their children. This is nothing new."

"She's not your wife. She's the mistress of a Jesuit priest. She's been your dirty little secret since she was fifteen years old. She can't even walk down the street with you without being terrified she'll ruin your life. That woman has given you her entire adult life, and when you're in public you have to pretend you only know her from church. A slap in the face to any woman with pride. The bad sort of slap in the face."

"It intrigues me how you always take Eleanor's side, though you've known me thirty years and never met her once."

"I *have* met you. That's why I take her side. And I'll always take the side of a dominant woman."

"Let's say I agree with you, that she should leave me. Eleanor never does what she should—so she'll stay."

"I didn't say that either."

He bent forward, elbows on knees, hands pressed together, fingertips at his lips. He looked like he was praying. She put her hand on his back, gently and with affection.

"Was it revenge? Sleeping with this woman? Having a child with her?"

He made a sound, almost a laugh. "Revenge? For what?"

"You know perfectly well. You're a Catholic priest. She had an abortion. You can't look me in the eye and tell me that didn't bother you at all."

"You really think so little of me? That I would have a child with another woman in order to punish Eleanor?"

"Yes, I think that little of you."

Now he did laugh, a real laugh. He sat up again, shook his head.

"You can laugh all you want," she said, "but don't pretend that it didn't hurt."

He took a long breath. "It hurt. It did. That she didn't discuss it with me first. I know why she did. She didn't want to make me complicit in the decision. But still...yes, of course it hurt."

"You would have talked her out of it. Wouldn't you?"

"I don't know what I would have done or said. I didn't get a chance."

"So it did bother you."

"It was her decision. And it wasn't even mine."

"No, but *she* was yours. Wasn't she? And yet she made the choice to not have a child, entirely without you. And then a few years later *you* made a choice to *have* a child, entirely without her."

"My son is not an act of revenge against Eleanor. Perhaps you would do something like that, but not me. Not to her. And if you think that about my son, that he is the product of something as vile as petty revenge against Eleanor, then this is the last conversation we should ever have. You can think as little of me as you like, but you will not say a word against him."

He stood and started for the chapel door.

"Søren," she said. His name, his real name, felt so strange in her mouth, awkward. *Suurrn.* Saying it *did* get his attention. He stopped at the door, but didn't turn around.

"Your Kingsley told me your name years ago," she said. "You've never given me permission to call you Søren, so Bambi it is." Bambi, short for Bambino. He'd been a little baby Jesuit when they'd first met.

"You may call me Søren."

"Thank you, Bambi."

He returned to her.

"You're a manipulative bastard," she said to him. "You know I never want you to leave. It's the only threat that works on me."

"It wasn't a threat. I really was going to leave."

"Of course you were."

She held out her hand and—reluctantly—he put his into hers.

"I'll look and see what I can see," she said, squeezing his fingertips. "But we do it my way. And my way requires blood money."

He smiled down at her. "I couldn't bring my scalpels on the plane with me."

She slipped her hand into the left pocket of her dress and pulled out a small knife in a leather case.

"Then we'll use mine."

SIX

BLOOD & SNOW

"ALTAR?" she said.

"I would prefer we didn't."

"Sometimes, you're such a...such a *priest*. If you insist. The window, please. I am taking a candle from the altar, whether you like it or not."

"I can accept that."

The monastery was so old that every window had a window bench under it. In the long, dark centuries before electricity, the monks would sit in those benches by day to read or mend their robes in the only bright light they could find. Now she sat there to read the palm of a priest by the light of the winter moon.

She brought over one candle and set it on the bench, sat by it and gestured for him to sit across from her.

"I'll need snow," she said. "Blood and snow. Warm blood for your heart. Ice cold snow for your soul."

As she ran the blade of her small, sharp, wicked little scalpel through the flame of the candle to sterilize it, he opened the iron latch on the window. The wind was still that night, so the cold air merely sauntered into the chapel instead of blasting in. The snow was fresh, thick and heavy on the window sill. He scooped up a handful, brought it inside, and closed the window.

"Hold the snow in your right hand until it melts," she said. "Give me your left."

He gave her his left hand. With the tip of the scalpel, she cut a diagonal line into his palm.

"This is the secret of my happiness," she said. "I learned how to change my fate. You don't have to live with the lines fate draws for us. We can cut our own lines if we're willing to take up the knife and put the blade to ourselves."

Blood welled up in the inch-long cut. A thin cut, it would heal by the time he returned home to his Eleanor. She smiled to herself when she saw his pupils begin to dilate. They took over his eyes until his gray irises became nothing but silver frames encircling ebony stones.

She ran her thumb over the blood on his palm, spreading it over the lines of his life.

"Bring your hands together in prayer," she said. "Palms flat."

He did as ordered.

"Open them."

He opened his hands and held them palms up. The snow had melted and mingled with the blood, tinting the insides of his hands pink.

She put on a good show of tracing the lines in his palms, reading the drying blood. It was a pretense, a game, really. She'd cut him because she wanted to cut him, because it pleased her to cut him.

"No," Magdalena said softly, "she won't leave you. Although she probably should."

"You're certain?"

"I would bet what little of my life is left on it." She

pointed. "There. The line of love, it's unbroken to the end."
She traced the line from one side of his palm to the other.
"She will not leave you, even when future events tempt her.
She will love that little boy as foolishly as she loves you.
Because he is part of you and you are part of him."

Marcus leaned forward, pressed his forehead to hers.
She let him, then lifted her chin to kiss his temple.

Ah, like old times again, when she'd break him apart,
only to put him back together afterwards, a little stronger
than before. She ran her fingers through his golden hair,
gold and silver now.

"Relieved?"

"Profoundly."

"I wouldn't be if I were you."

He looked up at her.

"You might be above petty revenge, but she isn't."

"Oh God, what is she doing now?"

Magdalena grinned. Had she seen something in his
hand, in his fate? A dark, handsome, *very* young man with
thick, waving hair and kissable lips pressed to the arch of
Eleanor's foot? Had she seen it in his palm, or was she
simply imagining what she herself would do in Eleanor's
position? It didn't matter, really. What was coming was
coming, sure as winter comes after autumn, sure as night
comes after day.

"You'll see. If it's any comfort at all, when she gets her
revenge on you...you will deserve it."

ABOUT THE AUTHOR

Tiffany Reisz is the *USA Today* bestselling author of the Romance Writers of America RITA®-winning Original Sinners series from Harlequin's Mira Books.

Her erotic fantasy *The Red*—self-published under the banner 8th Circle Press—was named an NPR Best Book of the Year and a Goodreads Best Romance of the Month. It also received a coveted starred review from *Library Journal*.

Tiffany lives in Kentucky with her husband, author Andrew Shaffer, and two cats. The cats are not writers.

Subscribe to the Tiffany Reisz e-mail newsletter and receive a free copy of Something Nice, *an Original Sinners ebook novella:*

www.tiffanyreisz.com/mailing-list

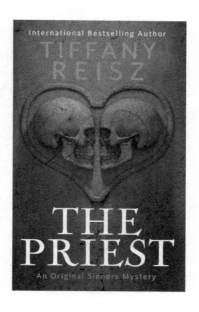

The Original Sinners series begins a new chapter in April 2020 with *The Priest,* the long-awaited sequel to *The Queen*.

"Tiffany Reisz's The Original Sinners series is painful, prideful, brilliant, beautiful, hopeful, and heart-breaking. And that's just the first hundred pages." — *New York Times* bestselling author Courtney Milan

eBook, Paperback, and Audio | 8thCirclePress.com

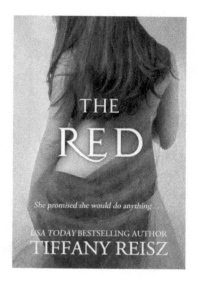

Mona Lisa St. James made a deathbed promise that she would do anything to save her mother's art gallery.

Just as she realizes she has no choice but to sell it, a mysterious man comes in after closing time and makes her an offer: He will save The Red...but only if she agrees to submit to him for the period of one year.

"Deliciously deviant... Akin to Anne Rice's 'Beauty' series." — *Library Journal* (Starred Review)

eBook, Paperback, and Audio | 8thCirclePress.com

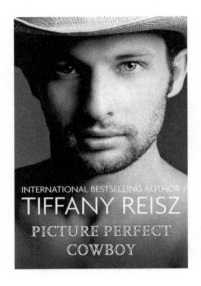

Jason "Still" Waters' life looks perfect from the outside—money, fame, and the words "World Champion Bull-Rider" after his name. But Jason has a secret, one he never planned on telling anybody...until he meets Simone. She's the kinky girl of his dreams...and his conservative family's worst nightmare.

***Picture Perfect Cowboy* is a standalone erotic romance from Tiffany Reisz, set in her bestselling Original Sinners series.**

eBook, Paperback, and Audio | 8thCirclePress.com

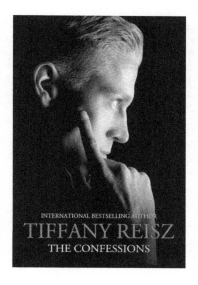

Father Stuart Ballard has been Marcus Stearns' confessor since the young Jesuit was only eighteen years old. He thought he'd heard every sin the boy had to confess until Marcus uttered those three fateful words: "I met Eleanor."

So begins "The Confession of Marcus Stearns," a moving coda to the RITA® Award-winning Original Sinners series.

"This is the reward for the tempestuous journey of all those who have read the series..."
— Heroes & Heartbreakers

eBook, Paperback, and Audio | 8thCirclePress.com

CPSIA information can be obtained
at www.ICGtesting.com
Printed in the USA
BVHW030234191119
564183BV00001B/49/P

9 781949 769128